She's on Top

She's on Top

SUSAN LYONS

APHRODISIA

KENSINGTON PUBLISHING CORP.
http://www.kensingtonbooks.com

KENSINGTON BOOKS are published by

Kensington Publishing Corp.
850 Third Avenue
New York, NY 10022

ISBN-13: 978-0-7582-1703-5
ISBN-10: 0-7582-1703-X

First Trade Paperback Printing: April 2008

10 9 8 7 6 5 4 3 2 1

Printed in the United States of America

Acknowledgments

Thanks as always to my brilliant critique group, Betty Allan, Michelle Hancock and Nazima Ali for their wisdom, patience, inspiration and fun company.

For research assistance, I'd like to thank Doug Arnold, Christine Carter, Brenda Fedoruk and Domenica Guadagni. Kate Austin, thanks for telling me about, and loaning me, the Yo-Yo Ma DVD.

This is a work of fiction so on occasion I've played free and loose with the facts. All errors are either intentional or my own darned fault, so please don't blame my critiquers or research assistants!

Last but not least, thanks to my editor, Hilary Sares.

I invite my readers to visit my website at www.susan lyons.ca, e-mail me at susan@susanlyons.ca or write c/o PO Box 73523, Downtown RPO, Vancouver, BC, Canada V6E 4L9.

1

"Excuse me?" Rina Goldberg carefully put her teacup on the coffee table. Her heart was racing. A moment ago she and Al had been discussing the Spanish film they'd seen tonight and now he'd . . .

No, she couldn't have heard right. She stared at Al, who was calmly sipping his own Earl Grey at the other end of her couch. "What did you say?"

His gray eyes narrowed slightly. "I said, I think we should get married." Then he hurriedly put down his cup. "Sorry, I forgot." He fumbled in the pocket of his navy Dockers. "I got you a ring."

A ring. A marriage proposal. Rina could only gape at the man. Was this for real?

He handed her a tiny jeweler's box and, heart pounding and hands shaking, she flipped it open to see a medium-sized diamond solitaire sparkling up at her. Oh my God.

"You like it, don't you?" he asked. "The store said it's one of their most popular designs."

A generic engagement ring.

"Rina? Say something." He ran a hand through his short auburn hair, pulling it away from his forehead and revealing his receding hairline.

Shit. A man—a very nice man who she'd been dating for two months—had just proposed and all she could think about was his male pattern baldness?

This wasn't how it was supposed to happen.

This wasn't the way she'd always imagined it.

Damn. Since she'd been a little girl, she'd dreamed of the day Mr. Right would propose. He'd go down on bended knee, declare his undying love, slip a gorgeous ring on her finger. She'd cry, "Yes!" and fling herself into his arms, knowing they were destined for a happily-ever-after.

Crap, this just wasn't fair!

Al wasn't doing it right. Or, maybe, *Al* wasn't right. Wasn't her heart supposed to be leaping with delight, rather than hammering wildly as if she was on the verge of a panic attack?

"Rina?" He was starting to look annoyed.

She put the ring box on the coffee table and dragged both hands through her black Medusa locks, tugging her hair away from her face. "This is so sudden. I don't know what to say."

"Jesus." His usually even voice held a note of disgust. "You're *supposed* to say yes and put on the ring, then we'll kiss and go to bed. And tomorrow we'll talk about the wedding."

The kissing and sex had definitely been in her plans. That had become their Saturday-night pattern. An early dinner at a nice restaurant, a mutually-agreed-upon movie, conversation over a cup of Earl Grey. Then bed, where there'd be one very nice orgasm for each of them.

She'd been looking forward to that orgasm. But now it looked like she'd only get it if she said "yes." And that word just didn't feel like coming out.

In fact, she seemed to have been struck dumb. What she really wanted to do was climb into bed by herself, pull a pillow over her head and moan.

She wrapped her fringed scarf more securely, hugging it across her chest with crossed arms. Then she forced words out, voice soft and gentle. "I didn't expect this." She met his frustrated gaze with her own troubled one. "We were taking things slowly. One date a week, then two, then . . ." God, she wasn't even comfortable saying the word *sex* to this man. "You know, being intimate."

"And all of it's been good, hasn't it?" he demanded.

She nodded slowly. "Yes, it has. But I thought we'd . . ." The truth was, she hadn't thought ahead. Things had been drifting along so comfortably. She'd been happy to have a regular guy in her life. Steady sex.

Her arms still hugged her body and now he tugged them away, clasping her hands in his. His touch should have felt warm and loving, but instead it made her feel trapped.

"Look, I'm thirty-two," he said. "You're turning twenty-seven in November. Why waste time? When something's right, it's right."

Yes, but were she and Al *right*? If they were, wouldn't her heart have leaped for joy when he proposed? Or was that a silly girlish dream? Kids reacted with emotion; adults had to be rational. Her girlfriends were always teasing her that she was such a romantic. They thought it was cute, but she guessed it wasn't very mature. Romantic dreams only came true in movies and novels, not real life.

Except, her friends seemed to have found amazingly wonderful men . . .

Was Al an amazingly wonderful man? He was nice, great even, but somehow the adjectives *amazing* and *wonderful* had never sprung to her mind.

Did he actually love her? He hadn't said so, not tonight and not in the weeks they'd been dating. She could ask—but then he might ask her back, and she wasn't sure how she'd answer. She was fond of him and that fondness had been growing but—

His grip tightened, cutting off her train of thought. "Rina, focus! It would be silly to wait any longer. We're compatible, we have a good time together, we're not getting any younger. It's not that complicated."

But it was. At least for her. And because it was, she couldn't give him an answer now. Nor could she decide this alone. She needed her best friends' advice.

Now that she'd made a decision, of sorts, she felt a surge of relief and her heartbeat steadied. She tugged her hands free. "Al, I'm flattered and honored. You're a fine man and I care about you. But I need time to think. After all, you've had time." Time to go to a store and select a ring that dozens of other women were wearing.

He sucked in a long breath and let it out slowly, audibly. "You're right. I guess this did come as a surprise. Think it over, and you'll see it's the right thing. Now, shall we go to bed?"

Damn. Much as she'd been looking forward to that orgasm, she couldn't imagine having sex with Al tonight. Gently she said, "I don't think that's a good idea right now."

"Perhaps you're right," he said grudgingly, then got to his feet. "I'll head home then."

She stood too, then picked up the jeweler's box. The diamond sparkled up at her before she closed the box and handed it to Al.

It really was a lovely ring; she could see why it was so popular. And in a way it was kind of sweet how he'd chosen it, figuring he'd have the best chance of pleasing her by picking a favorite design.

It was so typically Al. He was a steady, practical, considerate man. The kind of guy who'd make a perfect husband and father.

Perfect, if only there'd been a dash of romance and a spark of passion between them, she thought as he gave her a quick, dry good-night kiss at her door.

Lips, soft yet insistent, pressed against hers, urging her to open for him.

Rina sighed against them, then his tongue was stroking her lips, sweeping into her mouth. She answered him, hunger flooding her body as their kisses grew more demanding and passionate.

His mouth left hers and she moaned at the loss.

But then she felt his fingers tracing the lines of her face, her neck. Down to mold her breasts, caress them, gently squeeze her nipples.

She moaned again, as each touch sent echoes of sensation coursing to her pussy.

The room was dark; she couldn't see him. Yet she knew who he was.

His fingers drifted down her stomach and now he created magic no other man ever could. The soft curve of her belly was the keyboard, and he the pianist. Playing a melody that was a private, very sensual message between them.

And then his fingers played lower, across her mons and down to her inner thighs. She spread her legs eagerly, craving his touch.

Those quick, deft fingertips darted across her vulva, and she could no longer tell whether he was playing a tune or simply playing *her*. His mouth was there too, licking, sucking, blowing soft air across her hot, damp flesh. Her aching flesh.

Her body was so full of amazing sensations, all centered around his touch. She was an instrument and he a master musician, playing her to perfection.

She heard a sound, a keening sound, and realized it came from her own throat. Need, hunger, the peaking of desire as it built higher and higher. The sexy melody was reaching a crescendo.

His fingers played faster, driving her wild, driving her to breaking point.

Rina climaxed with an earthy cry of satisfaction.

And woke up.

Damn! Why had she been dreaming of *him*?

On Monday evening, Rina parked her car and checked her reflection in the rearview mirror. As usual, her hair was a mass of unruly black curls, not comb friendly. Her olive-toned skin looked pale; her summer tan was fading, and a couple of nights of near sleeplessness had taken their toll. She scrubbed her fingers across her cheeks to bring up some color, then hauled herself out of her old silver Honda. An autumn nip to the air made her pull her fringed burgundy pashmina close around her shoulders, over her black top and calf-length skirt.

As she climbed the steps leading to Kalypso Ouzeria, a Greek restaurant above Vancouver's busy Robson Street, her heart quickened with anticipation. For two days, all through the toss-and-turn nights and the clarinet squeals and piano poundings of her students, she'd been puzzling over her dilemma. And the bottom line she'd reached was, *I'll wait for Monday. It's Awesome Foursome night.*

If anyone in the world could help her figure out what to do, it was her three best friends.

At the top of the stairs, the theme song from *Zorba the Greek* greeted her. She glanced around the restaurant—past dark wood tables, Greek paintings and hangings, trailing plants—up to the seating area by the windows. And there they were, Suzanne and Ann and Jenny.

She rushed over. As the others looked up, she burst out with her news. "Al proposed!"

"Oh my God!" Suzanne Brennan leaped up to hug her. "The first of us to get engaged."

"Rina, that's amazing." Ann Montgomery sprang up and joined in.

"Let's see the rock," Jenny Yuen said, flinging herself into the group hug.

A waitress appeared, with middle-aged laugh lines and a big smile. "Champagne? Did I overhear there's cause to celebrate?"

Rina took a step back. "No champagne! Definitely not." She glanced around at the three familiar faces and one unfamiliar one. "I haven't accepted. I have to think it over."

"If you have to think—" the waitress started, then broke off. "Oops, sorry. Just wave me over when you're ready to order."

Rina realized that other diners and staff were staring at her and her friends. She flushed. "This is embarrassing. Let's sit down." She sank into a chair and slowly the others did the same, puzzled expressions on their faces.

Ann handed her a glass of red wine. "Are you all right?"

Rina nodded. Except, she wasn't, not really. In her dream, she'd have been thrilled to bits to tell the entire world she was engaged and to have everyone fuss over her. But now, nothing felt right. She took a sip of her wine and gazed around at three concerned faces.

Jenny leaned forward, shampoo-commercial black hair falling sleekly on either side of her face. "Rina, what's wrong? I thought everything was going great with Al."

Rina nodded again, more vigorously, and her dangly earrings tinkled like miniature wind chimes. "It has been. But I wasn't expecting a proposal."

Ann touched her hand. Her hazel eyes were full of concern. "You like him, but he's moving too fast?"

"He says, if something's right, then do it. Why wait?"

"To make sure." Suzanne leaned on her forearms, wavy

blond hair falling over her shoulders, green eyes flashing. "Like with me and Jaxon."

Suzanne was a vet student in Vancouver, and her lawyer boyfriend lived in San Francisco. Far enough apart that they only got to see each other every two or three weeks, for a weekend.

"Suzie Q's right." Jenny leaned forward too. "Every relationship is complicated; there are always so many issues. You need to see if you can work stuff out. If your feelings for each other grow." She winked. "If the sex gets better and better or fizzles out." She gestured with one graceful hand—going up, curving over a hump, then zooming down with a "whee-oooo-oops."

"Issues," Rina said thoughtfully. Suzanne and Jaxon had issues of geography, though thank heavens no one was making a big deal of the fact she was Caucasian and he was African-American.

The race issues were Jenny and Scott's. Her Chinese-Canadian family hated her dating a white firefighter, and his German-Canadian farming family was no keener about a white-collar journalist of Asian descent.

And then there was Ann and Adonis. Until a few weeks ago, Ann had been a workaholic lawyer. Now she and her new guy, a laid-back massage therapist, were trying to find a lifestyle that worked for both of them.

Hmm. Rina'd been envious of the girls, having hot sex with amazing men, but the truth was, they also had serious complications to deal with. "You know, Al and I don't have any issues. We're compatible. We've never argued about anything."

In fact, the only subject they'd disagreed on was whether they were ready to get engaged.

Ann ran a hand through her tawny hair. "Remember when I was stewing about Adonis and David? You told me to close my eyes and figure out what I really felt about each of them. Have you done that about Al?"

"I've been doing nothing else since Saturday night." Well, except for having that crazy dream, which had absolutely nothing to do with Al's proposal.

"Really?" Ann asked, affection in her eyes. "Or have you been thinking and dithering, rather than feeling?"

Jenny, who was drinking at that moment, gave a splutter of laughter that almost spewed wine across the table.

Rina had to smile, both at Ann's comment and Jen's reaction. "Okay, you caught me. I've either been dithering or telling myself not to think about it, to wait until tonight." She glanced around, still worried but also hopeful. "I get so confused when I'm on my own. I knew you'd help me sort it out."

Their waitress drifted by and Jenny said, "Let's order calamari, hummus and pita to get us going."

They all nodded agreement and the waitress topped up their wine glasses.

Then Suzanne said, "Okay, Rina, do it. Close your eyes and concentrate on your feelings. What does your heart say about Al?"

"Breathe deeply," Ann put in. "It can help take you beyond all the surface buzz, down to a deeper level."

Rina hid a smile. Adonis sure was having an impact on Ann. She took a long, slow drink of wine, then put her glass down. She took a breath, tried to make it go deep. Good God, she played the clarinet; if anyone knew about breathing properly, it was her.

Gradually the outside world receded. She was only dimly aware of Greek bouzouki music and the buzz of conversation elsewhere in the restaurant.

What did she feel for Al? A dentist with a successful practice, he worked reasonable hours and kept a good balance in his life. He was such a nice man. Supportive of her career. He'd come to the operatic society's last performance.

No, wait, she was supposed to be feeling, not thinking.

Softly she said, "I always thought, when a man was *The One*, I'd know. Maybe that was a foolish romantic notion. Al's great, but my heart isn't jumping up and down for joy. When I see him, I feel a nice warm feeling, but ..." She opened her eyes. "You all feel more than that, don't you? With your guys?"

"Sparks," Jenny said, and Suzanne and Ann nodded.

Rina sighed and reached up both hands to pull the thick curls away from her face. "I thought once we'd been lovers for a while, I'd start feeling that kind of chemistry."

"You said the sex was good," Suzanne said gently.

"*Good* isn't good enough," Jenny said.

"Unless it gets better by leaps and bounds each time you're together," Ann added. "But you're not saying that."

"Maybe it's me," Rina said. "I mean, it takes two for there to be sparks. Passion." Like she'd felt in last night's dream.

"Passion," Ann repeated. "Remember what you asked me, about Adonis and David? Whether I could imagine having romantic love, a grand passion, with either?"

Rina bit her lip. "I can't imagine having that with Al. But maybe it's not my destiny."

"Of course it is," Jenny said. "You're not even twenty-seven. Destiny didn't hit Ann until she was an old lady of twenty-eight." She winked at Ann, the oldest of the Foursome. "If Al doesn't feel like *The One,* then wait, Rina. Your destiny will come along when the time's right."

"My *bashert*," Rina murmured. "Aunt Rivka says Uncle David is her *bashert*. It's Yiddish for destiny, and we also use it to mean that special person who's just for us."

"Rina?" Ann said. "You're a romantic, and that's great." She hesitated. "But is it possible you're expecting too much? Maybe no man could ever live up to your romantic vision.

What if Al really is your *bashert,* but you're not letting yourself recognize that?"

"That's what I'm worried about. I don't know how to tell." Rina scowled just as the waitress arrived with the appetizers. "Sorry, I wasn't frowning at you."

"No worries." The waitress winked as she put the plates down. "But take it from me, men can give you wrinkles."

When she'd gone, Jenny squeezed lemon on the calamari and they each speared a ring. Rina, perennially trying to lose weight, was still pulling the batter off her first one when the others eagerly dived in for more.

She put down her fork. "So, how do I know if Al's the right man? How do the three of you know?"

"My tough little heart turns to mush," Jen said with a rueful grin. "Something I'd never believed was physically possible, but that's what Scott does to me." Her grin widened. "And you all thought I was going to talk about sex. So, not to let you down, I'll also say the sex is off the scale, and it's not just technique, it's the emotional connection."

Ann and Suzanne were nodding so hard they looked like bobble-head dolls.

"No mushy heart," Rina said sadly. "And the sex is warm and affectionate, but not—"

"Really, really intimate," Suzanne said.

"Where you can't tell where one of you leaves off and the other begins," Ann said. "It's like you've merged totally together, body and soul."

"Wow!" Distracted from her worries, Rina stared at her, wide eyed. "You really do belong with Adonis."

"Yeah, I know." Ann gave a smug smile, then her face sobered. "But let's get back to you and Al." A frown line—the one that hadn't appeared nearly so often since she hooked up with Adonis—grooved her forehead. "You say he's really nice, you're so compatible, you have no issues. Rina, does he stimulate and challenge you? Make you examine what you believe and wonder if you're right? The way Adonis did with me, about my obsession with work?"

Rina frowned too. "N-no." She tried a smile. "But maybe I'm perfect already. Well, except for being fat, but you know, I've actually started doing yoga."

"You're not fat!" Jen screeched, as Suzanne said, "Yoga? I don't believe it," and Ann came in with, "I hate to say it, but no one's perfect."

"What?" They all stared at each other, then began to laugh.

"Yoga?" Suzanne repeated. "You hate yoga. We *all* hate yoga. It's a Foursome Rule."

Yoga was how they'd met. A couple of years ago they'd each signed up for a class, bitched about it in the change room afterward and ended up going out for coffee. An immediate bond had formed, and they'd been having dinner every Monday night since then.

"What I really hated about it," Rina confessed, "was exercising in public. I feel so heavy and self-conscious." When Jenny opened her mouth, Rina held up a hand. "Shut up, Jen. I know you're going to say I'm not fat, I'm statuesque—"

"Stacked," Jen interrupted. "Voluptuous, lush." She went back to scooping a pile of hummus onto a slice of pita. Jenny, at five foot nothing, a hundred pounds on her heaviest day, could outeat all three of them and never gain an ounce.

"Whatever." Rina waved a hand, dismissing the polite lies. No way, in a society where size 6 was considered big, would her abundant curves ever be acceptable. "You're all sweet, but I have eyes in my head and I know what kind of women are considered attractive. If I lived in the days of Marilyn Monroe and Sophia Loren, I might be okay, but today curves equal fat."

"Rina, you're not—" Ann started

Rina cut her off. "You're sweet, but I invoke the Agree to Disagree Rule."

Ann sighed loudly. "All right. But we're not being sweet. Well, Suze might be, but Jen and I don't have it in us to be sweet."

"Thanks, bitch," Jen said cheerfully. "And yeah, Rina, Annie's right."

"*Anyhow,*" Rina said, "if I could get back to my *point?*"

They all nodded, and she said, "I decided to give yoga another try. At home, with a DVD, and only my cat Sabine to laugh at me. I'm kind of getting into it." She raised her arm and pulled back the loose sleeve of her gauzy black top. "And even developing some muscle tone." Then she frowned. "Not losing any weight, though."

"Muscle weighs more than fat," Suzanne said.

"Oh, great," Rina groaned. "Now you tell me." She forked up some hummus, foregoing the pita bread.

"Let's get back to Al," Ann said. "Rina, what was your first thought when he asked you to marry him?"

"Uh, shock, I guess." She told them how he'd proposed.

"Jesus, men can be dunces," Jen said with disgust.

"He said you *should* get married?" Ann frowned. "That's more of an order than a proposal. Is that how it came across to you?"

"Kind of. Then when I said it was awfully soon, he got pushy. That's *not* the way to win me over."

"And it's an indicator of what your marriage might be like," Ann said firmly.

"I agree," Suzanne said. "Damn, Rina, that's too bad."

"Better to find out now, before you invest more time in the loser," Jen said.

A loser? Al? No, she didn't believe that. He'd always been so considerate, until Saturday. "Damn, I'm exaggerating this. I shouldn't have said he was pushy. Maybe he was just hurt. If he'd really thought we were heading toward marriage, and I so obviously didn't see it coming . . . No wonder he reacted strangely."

"True," Ann said. "We shouldn't write him off so quickly. You need to talk to him again."

Rina nodded. Of course, he'd be wanting a "yes, I'd love to marry you," and she wasn't ready to give it.

"Suze?" Jenny asked, and Rina looked up to see Suzanne toying with her wineglass.

"Hmm?" she said. "Sorry. I was thinking. Rina, there's something I've been wondering."

"Yes?"

"About men. Special men. Remember a few months ago, when we were all talking about the best sex we'd ever had?"

"Giancarlo." The thought of him sent a rush of adrenaline— the same kind of buzz as just before a performance, or in a sexy dream—rushing through her body.

"The piano man," Jenny said. "Whose magic fingers made you come three times in a row, on top of a grand piano at Banff music school."

"Wow, you have a good memory," Rina said.

Jen gave a mischievous grin. "When it comes to great sex stories."

"Anyhow," Suzanne said, "when I tracked Jaxon down on the Internet, you were thinking about doing the same with Giancarlo."

Rina took a breath, then admitted her guilty secret. "I did."

"Way to go, girl!" Jenny said. "And?"

"I traced him through the alumni office at the Banff School of Fine Arts. He didn't turn out the way I expected." She sighed. "He was such a great pianist. Just a skinny, nothing-special-to-look-at Italian kid, but he had charisma as well as talent. We talked about our dreams and I honestly thought he'd achieve his and make it big on the concert circuit. You know, as a guest performer."

"He was that good?" Suzanne asked.

"I thought so." Rina shook her head. "But he sold out. Went over to the dark side."

"The dark side?" Jen wiggled her eyebrows. "Sounds kinky."

"He's a music video director. Yuck. Should've known, with the last name Mancini, he'd go crass and commercial."

The other three glanced at each other. "Huh?" Jenny said.

"As in Henry Mancini?" Rina said.

Three more blank looks. Rina sighed. "He wrote the *Pink Panther* theme? 'Moon River' from *Breakfast at Tiffany's*?"

"I love the *Pink Panther*," Jenny said. Predictably, because she was addicted to pink.

"And 'Moon River' is lovely," Suzanne said. "Very romantic. I'm surprised it doesn't appeal to you, Rina."

"It's a *catchy tune*." Rina said the last two words with distaste. "Mancini wrote catchy tunes."

"You say that like it's a sin," Ann said. "What's wrong with catchy, popular songs?"

"They're beneath the talents of a classical musician."

"Music snob," Jenny taunted.

Rina smiled. "That's not an insult, you know." She turned to Ann, who was spearing the last piece of calamari. "What do you think of lawyers who work in shopping centers and turn out conveyance after conveyance, or will after will? Like, maybe it's beneath their talents?"

Ann grimaced. "I see your point. Yeah, I'm a law snob. I like the high-end, intellectual stuff."

"Anyhow, speaking of music," Rina said, "I so don't need distractions right now. I have another audition for the VSO on Friday."

"That crazy Vancouver Symphony Orchestra," Ann said. "Why can't they make up their minds?"

"Last go-round, they opened the auditions only to Canadian citizens. I know I played well, and I'm sure others did too, but for whatever reason they weren't satisfied. So they went inter-national, and they've finally scheduled the auditions."

"Poor Rina," Suzanne said. "That must be so frustrating. I know how badly you want to play principal clarinet for them."

"Yeah. It's my dream." Another dream, but this one might actually be achievable. Though the fact that they hadn't chosen her in the last set of auditions was definitely ego damaging.

Their waitress came up to ask, "Want another bottle of wine? Something more to eat?"

"Yes, and yes," Jenny said. "How about dolmades, and an order of that yummy roasted lamb to split?" She glanced around.

Suzanne and Ann nodded, and Rina joined in. She loved food though she tried to stick to protein and veggies.

When the waitress had gone, Rina brushed her audition angst aside and thought again of her one-time lover. "When I Googled Giancarlo, I found out he's been directing videos all over the world. A few months ago he was in Vancouver. Then New York, Paris, Vegas. Now he's actually back here again."

"He's in Vancouver?" Jen said. "Hey, that's fate. You have to see him."

Rina shrugged. "We'd have nothing in common. He lives this fast-paced, commercial life. He's not the same person I used to like. And he wouldn't like me either. I love my life, my little house and garden, my music students, my job with the operatic society, but the whole thing would bore him to tears." She laughed. "Truth is, we'd bore each other to tears. I am *so* not interested in those God-awful videos."

"Maybe he still has magic fingers," Jenny teased.

"I doubt it." Only in her dreams.

Her expression must have given her away, because Jen said, "Okay, spill. What's up?"

"I dream of him sometimes," Rina said softly. "Like, last night."

"Last night, the night after Al proposed?" Jenny demanded.

"Yeah, *that* last night."

"Your subconscious is definitely telling you something," Ann said. "What would it hurt to get in touch with him and find out if the two of you still have that magical something?"

"I agree," Suzanne said. "I got together with the special guy from my past, and look how it turned out."

"I don't think Giancarlo and I are going to fall madly in love," Rina said dryly.

"Ah"—Jenny lowered her voice to sound witchy and mysterious—"but who are you to mess around with destiny? He's here, you're here, maybe he's your—what was that word?"

"*Bashert*," Rina said softly. Then she shook her head. "Of course he's not."

"But you said he was the best, right?" Jenny probed. "The best sex you'd ever had?"

Rina nodded. "The first sex, and the best."

"Wow." Ann looked impressed. "That's saying a lot. What made him the best? Those fingers?"

"Partly. And the way we connected, on all levels."

"You *so* have to see him," Suzanne said firmly.

"I don't know." Rina sat back as their waitress came with a fresh bottle of Greek red wine and filled all their glasses. Then she said briskly, "Enough about me. I know what I need to do. Talk to Al again, see how it goes, concentrate on my feelings. So, what's happening with everyone else? Ann, sounds like you and Adonis are doing great."

Ann, who had classic features and a totally classy presence, grinned like a teenager who was crushing over the boy of her dreams. "Yes. He's teaching me more about tantric sex, and on Sunday we went kayaking again and I'm actually getting it. Then we did dinner with his family, and I swear, they're addictive. If I didn't l-like Adonis for himself, I'd want him for his family."

"She almost said the L word," Jenny pointed out.

"It's too soon," Ann protested, but her cheeks were pink. She broke off as their waitress brought the stuffed vine leaves and roasted lamb, and they all helped themselves. Then she lifted her head. "I keep thinking, if I hadn't met Adonis, I might have actually ended up with David." She wrinkled her nose. "Think of the life I'd have had. I'd have missed so much."

"How's your mom doing with all this?" Rina asked. Ann's mother had raised Ann alone and taught her that career achievement was the only important thing in life. Women's lib taken to a bizarre extreme, as far as Rina was concerned.

Ann's lips twisted in a half smile, half grimace. "She's disappointed. She keeps trying to persuade me to see the error of my ways. It's rough, because I've always been so oriented to wanting her approval."

"Stick to your guns," Jenny said firmly. "Or, in this case, your guy."

Rina, whose own mom—now deceased—had been pretty damned controlling, nodded in agreement.

"Oh, I intend to," Ann said. "My life's so much happier, and healthier, since I met Adonis. More exercise and sleep, regular meals—"

"Regular sex," Jen broke in with a wink, and Suzanne added, "And massage on demand. I could sure go for that."

Rina forked up some of the Greek salad that came with the lamb. "All the same, I bet your mom's worried about you. She loved and trusted a man, and he betrayed her. Now she's probably afraid the same thing will happen to you."

Moms were protective. Rina knew that. Her own mom had wanted so much for her. Too much. To be slim, popular, a great musician, a good Jew. They'd rubbed each other the wrong way a lot of the time, and Rina had been more of a daddy's girl. But now that both her parents were gone and Rina was older, she could see how much they'd both loved her and wanted the best for her. Her mom, like Ann's, had just been more aggressive about it.

Ann's face had softened. "Thanks, Rina. It would be so nice if she'd accept—well, at least try to understand—what I'm doing."

And that would be especially tough, because Ann's mom was in Toronto and lived for her work. Phone calls with her daughter were rare, visits even more so. "I'm sure she will," Rina said hopefully. "Maybe not right away, but in the long run. It might help if she met Adonis."

"Speaking of which," Jenny said, "it's getting so *old,* no one having met anyone else's man. I mean, when I think of Suze's Jaxon, all I see is Denzel Washington. And Ann, my picture of Adonis is a Greek god statue who's much better endowed."

"Much, much better." Ann's eyes twinkled.

"And we've all seen Scott, a whole lot of Scott," Rina teased, "when he did that sexy dance number at the firefighter calendar competition, but we've never met him."

Suzanne turned to Rina. "And then there's Al. Maybe."

Rina groaned. "Perhaps I am expecting too much. No real live man could measure up to my romantic dreams. So he got a little pushy; he was upset. And yeah, we don't have sparks, but maybe that's because we're so compatible. Compatible's a *good* thing."

"You need to see Giancarlo," Ann said quietly. "You'll never be sure if Al's right for you until you resolve the past."

"I don't think I have the guts."

Jen groaned and Ann waved a hand to hush her, then said briskly, "What's the worst-case scenario? One, he doesn't remember you. Two, he remembers but doesn't want to see you. Three, he sees you and, as you suggested, the two of you bore each other to tears. The important thing is, you'll be able to get him out of your mind. *And* your dreams."

"And focus on whether Al's *The One*," Suzanne agreed.

"On the other hand," Jen grinned wickedly, "you might have another triple-O."

Driving home to her bungalow in North Van, Rina thought back to how she'd left things with Al on Saturday night. After they'd kissed, she'd said she'd give him a call. He'd asked, "When?" and she'd answered, "I'm not sure."

Had he actually muttered, "Let me know when you come to your senses"? She didn't trust her memory. At that point, she'd been too distraught.

And tonight she'd hoped that somehow, magically, the girls would help her reach a "yes or no" decision.

Well, at least they'd helped her figure out a starting point. Talk to Al again. And maybe a second one: contact Giancarlo. Could she?

She drove up the lane beside her house and parked in the old-fashioned one-car garage. Outside, the garden smelled of autumn. Leaves were turning color and starting to fall. It was probably time to dig up bulbs or prune shrubs. She'd have to ask Mrs. Zabriski, the neighborhood's garden expert, once the VSO audition was over.

Rina gave a sigh of relief as she walked up the back steps and into the welcoming embrace of her cozy home. She was so happy to have a permanent home of her own that she'd bought, decorated and loved.

"Mmrp?" Sabine prowled into the kitchen and Rina squatted down to say hello. Three years ago she'd adopted the short-haired calico as a kitten from an animal rescue society.

Rina sank her short-nailed musician's fingers into the soft white fur of the cat's breast. Scratching and stroking, she worked her way up to Sabine's chin and ears. The cat arched into her hands, purring happily.

"The girls say I need to contact Giancarlo," Rina said.

Sabine tilted her head, slitting her lovely green-gold eyes.

"The idea scares the shit out of me," Rina confessed. "But I think they're right." She did need to resolve her past before she could decide about the future.

Though she'd dated a few guys, Giancarlo had been the only one she'd ever had strong feelings for. That summer she was seventeen, they'd felt like soul mates. The skinny small-town Italian boy, the fat Jewish girl who called no place home. What they'd had in common was big noses, big dreams and amazing sex. They'd both had the sense to realize it was a summer thing, though. When they'd talked about keeping in touch, they'd agreed it was pointless.

And she'd never regretted that. Not seriously. But it was time to stop fixating on that summer *thing* and get on with her life.

She straightened, then lifted Sabine into her arms and headed toward the music room. It occupied what had originally been the dining room of her one-bedroom house, and was the room where she practiced and taught. It housed her piano, five clarinets, desk and computer.

When Rina put the cat down, Sabine leaped onto the desk chair, then to the top of the desk, as if to supervise.

Rina sat down in front of her computer. "Giancarlo probably didn't fixate on me. In fact, chances are he doesn't remember me."

"Mmrrr?" Sabine responded, in a tone that sounded amazingly like, "You really think so?"

Rina chuckled softly. "Yeah. I mean, we were kids, it was so long ago. He's in this whole music video thing, with gorgeous, svelte performers. Famous ones, up-and-coming ones. He's successful enough that even if he's still a skinny guy with a big nose, I bet he's had more sex in a month than I've had in the whole time since I last saw him."

No response from Sabine. The cat had gone to sleep.

"See, I even bore *you*, and you love me."

Okay, time to stop stressing and procrastinating and get it over with. Rina typed in the e-mail address she'd found on Giancarlo's website, then paused at the subject line.

Blast from the past

she finally typed. Then she tabbed to the message box.

I came across your name the other day, Giancarlo. It brought back memories of Banff, when we were both naïve young music students. Don't know if you remember me, but I was the pianist who also played clarinet, who . . .

She paused. What on earth did she intend to say? Who you had sex with all summer? Nope, not good. Either he remembered or he didn't. She backspaced over the last few words, leaving it at,

Don't know if you remember me.

Then she added,

Anyhow, if you do and feel like catching up, I live in Vancouver and maybe we could get together. I see from your website you're in town for a few days.

She stared at the screen. Jenny would say, be more assertive. But that was Jen. Rina was the passive type. Set it up to give the guy the opportunity and see if he took it.

In other words, leave it in the hands of fate.

2

Giancarlo Mancini yawned as he unlocked the door of his room at the Opus Hotel. His bleary eyes barely noticed the blue walls and stylish, starkly modern décor. All he cared about was crashing on the king-size bed.

They'd done location shoots all day and into the evening, then followed up with a private party. He squinted at the clock by the bed. Three in the morning. Late, even for a night owl like him.

What time were they starting today? Fuck, he couldn't remember his own shooting schedule. Better check, and set the alarm.

He turned on the notebook computer that served as his portable office. While he was waiting for it to boot up, he went to take a piss, wash his face and brush his teeth. He pulled off his shirt, noting that it stunk of smoke.

Yeah, the club they'd gone to was supposed to be smoke free, but his group had had their own room and their own special rules—i.e., no rules. Coke, primo BC marijuana, ecstasy, not to mention cigarettes, cigars and booze. Something to suit every taste. His own choice had been grappa, the Italian wine-based liquor his grandfather had introduced him to when he was a teen.

Yawning again, he went back to the computer to call up the shooting schedule. Yeah, right, he'd planned a short day in the studio. So the talent and crew could recover from the partying.

For him, the party scene he'd once thrived on was getting old. Still, it had been the first day on this project, and he was trying to build everyone into a team that could loosen up and have fun together. Videos took creativity, and creativity required trust and a sense of play. That was his philosophy as a director.

Hard work, a party, a slack-off day, then back to the hard work. As everyone worked through hangovers today, he'd strongly recommend an early-to-bed night.

His own plan was to look for a good Italian restaurant. He could sure handle a great lasagne. Something basic, not all fancied up. The kind of food his mamma used to cook.

The staff at his hotel would have a recommendation. They bent over backward to assist their guests.

Maybe he'd ask that pretty redheaded lighting assistant—what was her name? Tabbi?—to come along. She'd be up for dinner, a little action. Anything to get in good with the director.

He yawned so widely his jaw cracked and his eyes teared up. Nah. The meaningless sex had gotten old, just like the parties. He'd rather eat alone, really relax, get a good night's sleep. That had its appeal too.

While he had the computer open, he figured he'd better check e-mail.

He skimmed subject lines, then paused and went back to one. "Blast from the past?" Well, damn. Rina Goldberg.

Banff. His first trip outside Italy. His family had scrimped and saved to send him to the summer music school a Canadian relative had recommended. And there he'd found himself in a village not so different from the one he'd left, tucked under mountains as spectacular as the Italian Alps. With a bunch of other eager young musicians with big aspirations.

A homesick kid, he'd laid eyes on Rina Goldberg and immediately felt better. Her coloring made her look Italian. And she was warm and generous, willing to befriend an out-of-his-depth foreign kid.

Sexy too. Man, she'd been sexy. A ripe body, huge brown eyes, masses of curly black hair. His dick pulsed, just remembering how she'd looked. What the hell had she seen in a scrawny runt like him?

He'd have been intimidated, except he'd quickly learned Rina was shy, naïve, as inexperienced as he. They'd both been virgins. And they'd learned about sex together.

Giancarlo ran a hand over his fly, cupping his growing erection. Hell, yeah, he remembered Rina Goldberg. He'd had more than one thought of her over the years. Missed her responsive, generous sexuality. Missed, too, the easy natural connection between them, the way they could talk about anything under the sun.

Did he want to get together with her?

He began to smile, not feeling so exhausted anymore. Lasagne at an Italian restaurant, gazing across the table into those melting brown eyes. She had hung on his every word. Lots of people did that now, but she'd done it before he became successful.

Was she still as sexy? Probably even more so, with maturity and experience.

Would there still be chemistry between them? He sure as hell could imagine himself and Rina rumpling the sheets of this huge bed. That sex wouldn't be meaningless, it'd be damned fantastic.

He unzipped his pants and slipped them off, along with his underwear. His swollen penis begged for attention and he curled his hand around it.

Hell, he was getting way ahead of himself. A girl like her, some guy had probably snapped her up. She'd be married with a couple kids by now, have the life she'd dreamed of. He should take her at her word. All she'd suggested was a little catching up.

Yeah, sure. He might be tired but he wasn't dead, and a guy couldn't help but hope.

Memories of sex with Rina filled his mind as he slid between the sheets. God, had her breasts really been as full and lovely as he remembered? Who cared? His throbbing erection wasn't concerned with accuracy, just with stimulation.

He pumped firmly, envisioning lush breasts, curvy hips, petal-soft skin. Thick, dark curls between her thighs. Pouty labia, swollen and wet, telling him she was hungry for him.

Moistening his hand with saliva, he returned it to his engorged dick and imagined sliding inside her. The way she took him in, welcomed him, moved around him as they both drove toward satisfaction.

The high, keening noise she made when she was close to coming. The way her climax pulsed and shuddered around him. The way his own ripped through his body.

Giancarlo let out a wrenching groan as he came.

There was nothing like a morning routine. Over the past couple of months it had become Rina's habit to rise before seven and go for a three-mile walk with her elderly neighbor, Levi Fischman. Breakfast, after the walk, was Earl Grey tea and low-fat yogurt, which she consumed while checking e-mail and her appointment book, planning her day.

Today, she plunked her strawberry yogurt down beside the computer and checked her watch. Only eight. No chance Giancarlo would have checked e-mail and responded yet, but—

"Oh my God." Hurriedly she clicked open his message and scanned it.

"Oh my God," she breathed. She turned to her cat, who was gazing out the window. "He wants to see me!"

Sabine turned to her, sat down neatly with her tail wrapped around her body and began grooming herself.

"Tonight? Oh no, he wants to see me tonight. I don't have anything to wear." Nor could she shed twenty pounds in one day. "What was I thinking? This was crazy. Stupid. I don't really want to see him."

The cat tilted her head and said, "Mmrp?"

Rina sighed. "Yeah, okay, I do. I want to, but I don't want to be me. I want to be a skinnier, prettier version of me."

Sabine studied her for a long moment, then stood slowly, stretched and sauntered over. She leaped into Rina's lap and began to purr.

"Okay, you love me just the way I am." Rina stroked the soft fur and immediately felt calmer. "You're right. It's not like I *want* the man to be attracted. The whole point is for us to *not* be attracted to each other, so I can stop dreaming about him and move on."

All the same, that didn't mean she had to wear her dowdiest clothes. Mind busily inventorying the contents of her closet, Rina quickly typed,

Sounds great! Tonight at 7 is good. Where?

Then she headed for the shower where she shampooed and conditioned her hair, shaved her legs and armpits, then trimmed her bush, where the curls grew as exuberantly as on her head. Not, of course, that Giancarlo was going to be getting any peeks at her private parts, but anything that made her feel a tad more feminine would be a confidence booster tonight.

After toweling her hair, she spritzed on a healthy dose of leave-on almond oil conditioner in an attempt to subdue the frizz. Then she examined her face in the mirror and plucked a few stray eyebrow hairs. Could a woman *get* any hairier?

Though she couldn't complain about her long, full eyelashes. And her eyes were her best feature. As for her nose— what could she say? It was Jewish, and she was damned if she'd have it fixed. Lips weren't bad. Full, naturally rosy.

Knowing she'd be teaching until six, she decided to make her clothes-for-dinner decisions now and get everything laid out.

Her wardrobe, much of which she sewed herself, consisted mainly of clothes designed to cover up the body that her girlfriends called voluptuous and her Aunt Rivka called *zaftig*. A body that was, in fact, just like Rivka's. Rina's mom had been svelte, her dad had been fit and muscular, yet she'd managed to get the same *zaftig* genes as her mom's sister.

Rina'd been dieting since she was nine, when her mother first started worrying that her puppy fat wasn't disappearing. "You don't want to end up looking like your aunt," her mom had said. But sure enough, that's exactly what had happened.

Now she studied the dark skirts and pants in her closet. Actually, since she'd been walking and doing yoga, her legs weren't so bad. Maybe she'd go with a knee-length skirt rather than a longer one. Black, of course. With black pumps that were higher heeled than she normally wore and gave her calves some nice definition.

She added a loose, gauzy black blouse and her favorite scarf, a huge, fringed, silk one with gigantic red poppies embroidered on it. Of course she had dangly earrings to match, with satiny jet beads and glittery red ones.

What a contrast she'd be to the performers Giancarlo was used to working with, who bared nine-tenths of their bodies in tiny skirts, tube tops, bustiers or even skimpier clothing.

She sure hoped that at least he was still kind of funny looking, or she'd be completely intimidated and regret she'd ever e-mailed him.

* * *

The hotel had made a reservation for Giancarlo at a restaurant they recommended—Don Francesco's on Burrard Street. Where, apparently, the Italian owner had studied opera and could, on a special occasion, be persuaded to sing.

It was less than a mile from the Opus Hotel. Freshly showered and shaved, dressed in black pants and a slim-fitting black V-neck sweater made of a cashmere/silk blend, Giancarlo decided to walk. Along the way, he absorbed sights, sounds and smells, storing away each impression for possible use in a video. Vancouver was funky and unpretentious, he thought. A real mix of people: all ages, races, economic levels and sexual orientations.

When he walked into the restaurant, the aromas of Italy greeted him. He sniffed appreciatively, savoring the scents of garlic, rosemary, roasting chicken and lamb.

He gave his name and a waiter in a white shirt and black pants led him to a white-clothed corner table by the window. The restaurant had an elegant simplicity, with creamy yellow walls, gilt-framed paintings of Italian scenes and a wall of dark shelving holding wine bottles. The music, soft enough so as not to interfere with conversation, was classical guitar. His hotel had done well by him.

He'd barely sat down when a man in a suit came over. Perhaps sixty, his face had smile lines and his close-cropped black hair was silvered. "*Buona sera, Signor Mancini. Benvenuto a mio ristorante.*" He smiled broadly and held out a hand. "*Sono il padrone, Francesco Alongi.*" In Italian, he went on to say that the Opus Hotel, when making the reservation, had made special note of the fact that they were countrymen.

"*Buona sera.*" Giancarlo continued on in Italian, exchanging pleasantries, happy for the rare opportunity to speak his native language.

Francesco asked him if this was an evening with a special lady, and he answered, "*Spero de sì.*" I hope so. That led to a consultation about the appropriate beverage. Always the optimist, Giancarlo placed an order, which Francesco passed along to a waiter.

As he and Francesco chatted, Giancarlo kept an eye on the door.

He recognized her the moment she stepped into the restaurant. She hadn't changed, except to grow more beautiful. When he let out an approving sigh, Francesco turned to look, and both men spoke at the same time. "*Bellissima.*"

Now that, Giancarlo thought, his dick pulsing with appreciation, was what a woman was supposed to look like. Curves that, as he well remembered, were soft and utterly genuine, not the product of a plastic surgeon. A lush body covered in a way that was modest yet seductive. Beautifully shaped legs and graceful neck, the glimpse of a forearm as she reached up to brush hair back from her face. A temptress's hair—an abundance of undisciplined curls that whispered of sensual pleasures.

One day, if he found the right performer, he'd do a video that played on this seductive subtlety. Not the usual in-your-face sexuality so many young—and not so young, if you counted Madonna and Cher—entertainers flaunted.

"She doesn't recognize you," Francesco murmured.

Giancarlo realized he'd been staring at Rina for several minutes and she hadn't moved. She'd been gazing around the room, eyes wide. Fiddling with her fringed shawl, searching for a familiar face and not finding it.

He snapped his fingers. "I forgot how much I've changed since she knew me."

He rose to his feet and hurried toward her. "Rina." He caught her hands in his, feeling an immediate surge of warmth, connection. Arousal. He squeezed her hands lightly. No rings. Yes, he could let himself hope.

She stood gaping, then her cheeks flushed and she blurted

out, "Giancarlo? Oh my God, I can't believe it's you." She glanced down, up again, shook her head. Then she stared at his face. "Okay, your eyes. I recognize your eyes. And your hair. That long curly hair." Finally she smiled and her own brown eyes began to twinkle. "Your father still hasn't gotten you to cut it?"

He remembered telling her that his father hated his hair, and said he was lucky he was a musician because no other occupation would allow a man to look like a girl. "He's given up." It was the only thing his family had stopped nagging him about, no doubt because they now considered his hair the least of his sins.

"I'm glad. I like it." Then she flushed brighter. "Not that, I mean, my opinion isn't—" She broke off. "Sorry, I sound like an idiot. But you caught me off-guard. I expected—" Again she broke off, then finished lamely, "Something different."

"The same scrawny kid?"

She nodded. Then, apparently just becoming aware that he still held her hands, she tugged them free. "You must have grown six inches."

"Five. And over forty pounds."

"None of it fat," she muttered, sounding almost annoyed.

What was up with that? Did she like chubby men?

"And you're the same," he said. "Only more mature. More beautiful."

"Mature, maybe," she said wryly. "Hardly beautiful."

"Of course you are." Why couldn't women just accept a compliment? Or did Rina hear so many, they were like water off a duck's back? "Come, let's sit down and talk."

Again he captured a hand, to lead her to their table. Touching Rina brought a sense of peace, as well as sexual awareness. Oh yes, she was the same. Back then, he'd thought how unusual that he could feel both comfortable and yet wildly excited. Now, after nine years with other women, he knew the feeling wasn't just unusual, it was unique. To this one special woman.

"Is this our table?" Rina gazed at him quizzically.

He realized he was standing beside the table, gaping at her while his brain processed his revelation.

"Giancarlo?"

The way she said his name—accent perfect, the way he'd taught her all those years ago—warmed his heart. "You're not married, are you?" he asked suddenly, needing to know she was available.

She frowned. "Married? No."

"Engaged?"

Her cheeks flooded with color. "No, but why are you asking?"

Was she playing coy, or did she truly not feel the connection between them? Trying to sound casual, he said, "Just curious. Sorry, there's so much to catch up on. Come, sit."

Francesco was there to pull back a chair for Rina. "*Signorina*, welcome to Don Francesco's. I hope you enjoy your evening." He gave her a smile that oozed Italian charm.

"Thank you. I'm sure I will." She gave the other man a smile of her own.

Giancarlo caught himself scowling. Shit, was he actually jealous? He'd liked the other Italian man when it was just the two of them chatting, but now he wished he'd go away.

"Are you ready for a drink?" Francesco asked Rina, as Giancarlo took his own seat, unassisted.

"Why, yes, that would be nice." She glanced across at Giancarlo. "Wine?"

"I already ordered. I hope you approve."

Francesco turned, waved an arm, and a waiter hurried up with an ice bucket and a draped bottle. Francesco shooed him away and extracted the bottle himself.

"Champagne?" Rina's huge brown eyes went even wider. "Giancarlo, really?"

"Do you like champagne?"

"Yes, of course. I love it." She squinted at the Veuve Clicquot label, then beamed at him. "Especially when it's the real thing. This looks so much nicer than the cheap bubbly we drink at music events." Then she frowned slightly. "Are you sure? It must be terribly expensive."

He liked that she neither took the champagne for granted nor protested too much. "How often do old friends rediscover each other?"

While they'd been talking, Francesco had peeled the foil off the top of the bottle and undone the metal twister. Now he eased the cork free on a dignified puff of air and poured gently into two delicate flutes. "*Salute,*" he said, then finally withdrew and left them alone.

Giancarlo lifted his glass and waited for her to do the same. "To old friends," he said, "and new beginnings."

Her hand froze, her lips parted. Then she touched her glass to his. "It's good to see you again."

Damn. She hadn't accepted his toast.

He took a deep breath. *Un bambino viziato.* A spoiled child, his mother called him to this day. Too impatient, too obsessed with getting his own way.

Ever since he'd read Rina's e-mail last night, he'd had trouble concentrating on anything but memories. Her lush breasts tumbling free of her bra, overflowing his greedy hands. Her soft, utterly feminine skin under his fingertips as his fingers—used to piano keys—learned a whole other style of touch. The hungry whimpers as her excitement built and the rich cry of satisfaction that accompanied her climax.

Even more than the sex, that feeling of rightness, just being with her. Seeing her smile, hearing her laugh, watching as she picked up her clarinet and got lost in a world of her own. Man, he hoped she'd stuck with her gut feeling and gone with the clarinet rather than the piano. Yes, she was a brilliant pianist, but her face didn't take on that same look of rapture as when she played a clarinet. There was so much to learn about her, and yet . . .

He'd wondered how he'd feel, being with her again. And now he knew. The same, and even stronger because now he had the experience and wisdom to appreciate who she was and what they could have together.

But still, he cautioned himself, they'd barely spoken. He was leaping to crazy conclusions, based on the sight of her, the touch of her hand. Now it was time to get to know each other all over again.

"It's good to see you, too." He watched as she sipped from her glass. "Do you like it?"

"It's wonderful." She favored him with a brilliant smile.

He took a sip too, and bubbles exploded on his tongue. How many glasses of champagne had he drunk in the last few years? But this tasted different, fresher and richer, because of the woman who sat across from him.

He wanted to reach for her hand. Damn, he wanted to take her hand, drag her out of there and make love to her all night long.

His dick, already throbbing with arousal, went hard. Oh yeah, he wanted to savor every inch of this woman with his fingers, his eyes, his lips, his tongue. Then he wanted to plunge inside her and claim her as his own.

"Giancarlo?" That little frown was back, creasing her forehead. "Are you all right? You look kind of . . . intense?" She raised a hand and fussed with that silky scarf.

He was making her nervous. And probably not in a good way.

"*Pazienza*," he muttered under his breath. Patience came

hard for him, but he could do it if the prize was worthwhile. "Are you hungry? Shall we order an appetizer?"

She grabbed the menu and studied it, as if relieved to escape his gaze.

He glanced at his own. Lots of classic dishes and a few more exotic ones featuring fresh game. But there, that was what he craved. Lasagne. Satisfied, he turned back to the antipasto selection. "Shall we get a couple of appetizers and share?"

"I can't possibly eat an appetizer and a main course."

"Don't tell me you're one of those women who exist on salad," he teased. "I work with them all the time—anorexics, bulimics, constant dieters. Man, it's a pain to eat with them. Food's made to be savored, not picked at."

She cocked an eyebrow. "I could point out that salad's food too. And I'm sure you don't want fat women in your videos. Right?"

Ruefully he grinned. "Yeah, okay, you got me. Societal standards dictate skinny, except for breasts, of course. And I know that's tough to achieve, for a lot of women. But hey, we're not making a video together, we're friends having dinner. Tell me you're eating more than salad."

She sighed and he guessed he wasn't completely forgiven for being insensitive. "I was looking at the grilled salmon," she said. "How about you?"

"Lasagne," he said promptly. "Not glamorous, but I'm sick of fancy food."

Her lips curved up. "Craving some of your mamma's home cooking?"

He laughed. "I told you about my family, didn't I? Yes, I've eaten in many of the fine restaurants of the world, but there's something about Mamma's lasagne and spaghetti bolognese that can't be topped." He tapped his menu against the table. "If I order an appetizer, can I persuade you to at least taste it?"

Her lips curved. "I can usually be tempted."

Those words, coming out of that sexy mouth, made his dick surge hungrily. He adjusted his napkin to hide the bulge in his lap. "Then, how about the paté? Or the oysters? Do you like oysters?"

She shook her head. "I may not be a practicing Jew, but I still avoid certain foods like oysters. And paté's too rich for me. Try again."

"That's right, I'd forgotten you were Jewish."

"Goldberg?" She raised her eyebrows.

"Yeah, right." He laughed. "Okay, let's see. How about *funghi?*"

"That's mushrooms, right?" She studied her menu. "Sautéed with garlic, lemon and basil. Mmm, that sounds good."

"*Funghi* it is." And how wonderful that she didn't steer away from garlic, another habit that was endemic among the women he worked with.

The moment Rina put the closed menu down, Francesco was there, easing up behind her. He rested a hand on her chair, almost touching her shoulder. "*Bella,* the wine is to your liking? And you are ready to order dinner?"

Rina tilted her head to smile up at him. "The champagne's wonderful. And yes, we're ready to order."

Fuck. Why was she giving her smile to Francesco? And wasn't the guy the owner of the place? Why was he playing waiter?

Was he hustling Rina?

Francesco glanced over at him with a knowing smile then, behind Rina's back, tapped his left thumb against his wedding band.

Giancarlo let out a long breath. The guy was only being Italian, showing his appreciation for a beautiful woman. Giancarlo's beautiful woman. And giving him special service, because he was a fellow Italian. Francesco's behavior was a compliment.

Damn, he wasn't used to being jealous.

He gave Francesco a rueful, apologetic smile, then gestured to Rina to go ahead.

She ordered salmon and asked what it came with. When Francesco answered, "Rice and a selection of vegetables," she said, "Could you leave off the rice and give me extra vegetables, please?"

"Anything for you."

Giancarlo rolled his eyes. Then he said, "If you don't like rice, why not get potatoes or pasta?" He slanted a grin at Francesco. "After all, you can have *anything* you want."

She gave a composed smile. "Thanks, but I prefer vegetables."

Giancarlo placed his own order, and then he and Rina were alone again. He watched her sip champagne, enjoying the sparkles in her eyes and in the wine, enhanced by the candlelight. "You're lovely, Rina."

Her jaw tightened. "Giancarlo, it's kind of cute when Francesco does the flattery thing. It's part of his shtick, you know? But I'd rather you didn't do it."

"It's genetic with Italian men, to appreciate female beauty."

She raised her eyebrows. "Gimme a break."

"I don't think so," he said softly. "I'm afraid you're going to have to get used to it." He heard her breath catch and held her gaze across the table.

She softened. Something inside her—the something that had been keeping her guard up—let go. He saw it happen when her eyes began to glow. With warmth, attraction, passion. Yes! He wasn't alone in his feelings.

He was about to reach for her hand when she blinked and the glow was gone. She sat back in her chair and folded her arms under her breasts, which plumped their abundance even more. That semisheer top was tantalizing. Was that a black lace bra he could glimpse underneath, or just his lustful imagination?

His hands ached to cup those full breasts. He wanted to bury his face in them, suckle her nipples, hear her cry out. Rina's breasts, as well as being the epitome of femininity, were sensitive, he recalled. Her entire body was responsive. She was as well crafted and tuned as the finest of musical instruments and, for the first time in ages, his fingers itched to play.

So did his dick. If he didn't stop thinking about making love with her, he was going to embarrass himself.

She shook her hair back from her face. "What do you want from tonight?"

He almost groaned. If he told her the truth, would she run? *Pazienza,* he cautioned himself. "What you said in your e-mail. To see you, catch up."

"That's not how you're acting. You keep, uh, kind of . . . Oh damn, never mind."

What had she been going to say? Flirting? "What do you want, *cara?*" he asked.

She made another of those little catch-breath sounds and glanced away. "I w-want—" Her voice broke and she cleared her throat. "I thought we'd talk about what we've done since we last saw each other."

He noted she'd said, "I thought," and not told him what she *wanted.* "And reminisce about that summer at Banff?" he asked. If they did, she'd have to remember how great they'd been together. He might have been an inexperienced kid, but there was one thing he was confident of: he'd satisfied his girl.

Rina tugged on the end of her scarf and the whole thing began to slip, but she caught it and wrapped it tighter around her neck. "That was a fun summer. I'd been looking forward to it all year."

Okay, he'd accept her diversion. For now. "Me too. Though I was terrified." He grinned at the thought of the boy he'd been. "I was in such a hurry to get away from my small village,

Domodossola, and big extended family. But the moment I got to Banff I was homesick."

"You were lucky to have a home to be homesick about."

"Your father was with the army—no, air force—wasn't he? I remember you saying you moved a lot."

She nodded. "I've lived on Forces bases all over the place. God, I've had enough travel to last me a lifetime. Dad was training fighter pilots in Cold Lake, Alberta, the year I went to Banff."

"And now you're in Vancouver. What brought you here, and do you plan to stay?"

"I am *so* staying." She said it with total conviction. "Along with all the places we lived, we also did a lot of tourist-type travel. Vancouver stuck in my mind. The ocean, the mountains. Cosmopolitan, yet beautiful and not overdeveloped."

"I can see that. Just from the few days I've been here."

She nodded happily, accepting his compliment of the city she so clearly loved. "A decent symphony orchestra too. Anyhow, when my parents died—"

"Oh, Rina, I didn't know." He'd reached over to cup her hand in both of his before he even thought. "I'm sorry. When did it happen?"

She didn't pull away, and he savored the feel of her warm hand between his as she said, "Right after Banff. They were both killed instantly when a truck crashed into their car."

"That's terrible. And you were so young. Seventeen? And an only child."

She nodded. "My Aunt Rivka—Mom's sister—and Uncle Daniel took me in. They lived in Toronto, which is where Mom grew up. I'd just started grade twelve in Cold Lake, so finished in Toronto. Anyhow, what with life insurance and my inheritance, I had enough money to pursue my musical education and buy a house. So I went—" She broke off and slid her hand free from his as a waiter approached with a plate of sautéed mushrooms, mostly portobello.

When the waiter went to put the plate in front of him, Giancarlo said, "In the middle, please, so we can share." Then he urged Rina, "Taste," and picked up his own fork.

The mushrooms were firm, not overcooked. The garlic, lemon and basil made an effective combination. "Good," he said. "Yes?"

"Excellent."

She put down her fork but he said, "No, we're sharing. Remember?" When she'd speared another mushroom, he said, "Go on, tell me what happened after high school. And, did you choose the clarinet in the end?"

She chuckled. "Yeah, your advice was good. I had an amazing teacher in Toronto. And then . . ." She paused, then finished quietly, "I went to Juilliard." He saw the glow of pride in her eyes.

"Juilliard," he said reverently. "You did make it to Juilliard." She'd wanted it so badly. They both had, back then.

She nodded, her lips curving as if a smile was fighting to get out. "My Toronto teacher had a connection there—one of the instructors—and I could afford to go to New York and take a couple of lessons with him. Then, not to boast, but I aced the audition. Piano and clarinet." Now she let herself smile widely. "You remember that it was one of my dreams to go there?"

"Of course. Rina, that's wonderful. Sad, though, that it was your parents' death that got you to Toronto, and the instructor with connections."

Softly she said, "Yes, though I know they'd have been so happy I got in."

He reflected a moment. "The house was one of your dreams too, wasn't it? You said you wanted to find a cozy home in a lovely place, and no one could ever again force you to move." After a sip of champagne, he went on. "Juilliard, the house, first chair in a major orchestra, and a husband and kids." He put his glass down. "You said you're not married. No kids?"

She was about to answer when Francesco dropped by to top up their champagne and ask if they were enjoying the mushrooms. Giancarlo told him even his mamma couldn't better them.

Rina sat back, enjoying the banter between Giancarlo and the restaurant owner, who was treating the two of them like celebrities. No doubt the star treatment had far more to do with Giancarlo's status in the entertainment world, not to mention the fact he was Italian, than to her own charms.

She sipped champagne. Like sunshine distilled into a glass. She'd recognized the label, knew this was the real stuff, but had no idea how much it must cost.

Was she in the middle of a fantasy? Another crazy dream?

The man across from her was easily the most handsome she'd ever met. Had she had the slightest clue he'd have morphed from gawky kid to *GQ* cover model, she'd never have had the nerve to e-mail him. But, despite his transformation, she could still see the old Giancarlo in the curve of his lip, the sparkle in his eyes, those lovely long-fingered hands, his enthusiasm for food and wine. And his apparent interest in her.

The man had focused on her as if she was the most fascinating woman in the world. Ten minutes ago, three extraordinarily striking young women had walked by on their way to a neighboring table and he'd never even glanced up. His gaze had been intent on her face.

And when he'd held her hand . . . it felt like they were alone in the world.

Maybe she should stop drinking. She was so confused.

For minutes at a time she'd forget the years that had passed and feel like it was the old Rina and Giancarlo, the fat girl and the skinny boy, taking up where they'd left off.

Then she'd refocus and really see him. See how those mischievous curls now framed a strikingly masculine face, see the breadth of his shoulders and the great musculature revealed by that sexy V-neck sweater. Note the silky quality of that sweater, not to mention the flashing ring on his finger that could only be a diamond. This man was very different from the boy she'd known.

This man could have pretty much any woman he wanted. And probably had.

And yet here he was, being charming and apparently sincere with her. Plain old Rina Goldberg. The fat girl with the big shnoz.

Her fork had been sneaking toward the mushrooms and she hurriedly pulled it back. Sure they were vegetables, but she knew damned well they'd been sautéed in butter and olive oil.

"Eat, eat," Giancarlo urged, and she realized Francesco had departed while she'd been musing.

"You sound like my aunt."

He laughed. "And like my mamma. Now, on the subject of mothers, you have no children?"

She shook her head. Kids were still one of her dreams, but he didn't need to know that.

"And the music? You're still playing, of course?"

"I'm principal clarinet with the operatic society. I hope to make it to first chair with the symphony orchestra." Should she mention the audition?

Before she could decide, he was saying, "Of course you will. You were very talented even then, before Juilliard." He raised his glass to her. "And what else with your music? Where else do you play? And I imagine you teach?"

"Yes." She smiled. He knew how tough it was for a musician to make a living. "I play for the CBC Orchestra, and I'm part of a quintet that does a fair number of gigs. I teach clarinet and piano—classical—to adults and kids, and love it." Not all her students had talent, but she felt such joy at helping others develop an appreciation for music.

For her, music was such a huge thing. Spiritual, uplifting. Her mother had stressed the Jewish creed of *tikkum olam*, repairing the world. Though Rina wasn't a practicing Jew, she felt that filling other lives with music was her way of practicing *tikkum olam*.

"And where, after the Vancouver Symphony Orchestra? On to New York? Chicago? Philadelphia?"

Damn, he had to ask that. He'd unerringly named the three top symphonies in North America. Slowly she said, "My home's here."

"Truly? Forever? I mean, yes, I understand you want stability after all the moving, but you'd cut off your career because of a house, a city?"

He was right. The VSO wasn't a top, or even second-rank, orchestra. Maybe she did have the talent to play in one of the best. But she'd have to move again. Leave Vancouver . . .

"It's not just a house," she said softly, "it's my home. For now, that matters a lot. Once I make it to the VSO, I'll see if I'm happy there. For the rest of my musical career."

He squinted at her. "The opportunity to play with the best in the world versus a home?" She could tell from his expression that he didn't get it. All the same he nodded slowly and said, "I can see how, for you, that'd be a tough decision."

For her. Not for him. It seemed pretty clear he'd always put career ahead of home. And yet, this music video thing of his was so different from the career he'd once dreamed of.

She tilted her head. "How about you, Giancarlo? You were going to be a concert pianist. You wanted Juilliard, too, then to perform all over the world."

Was it the restaurant lighting or did a shadow cloud his eyes for a moment? He waved a hand dismissively. "A child's dream.

Even more, it was my parents' dream. The truth is, I didn't have the talent."

"You did! You were brilliant."

He shot her an amused look. "Ah, and you were qualified to judge, at all of seventeen?"

Maybe he was right. She'd seen him through the admiring, biased eyes of a friend and lover. "Well, I thought you were brilliant." How sad for him to lose his dream because of lack of talent. "I'm sorry it didn't work out for you."

"No, no. It was partly, too, that I didn't want to work that hard. You, now, I remember how hard you practiced. But me, I was always ready to desert the piano and go play."

Or play—that is, have sex—*on* the piano. She tried not to blush.

"Do you play at all now?" she asked.

His mouth tightened. "There's no time."

"But you enjoy what you're doing? Directing music videos?" She tried to keep her tone neutral and not sound like she was criticizing him for having turned commercial.

"I love it." His face lit. "It's creative, exciting, challenging, fun. On a good day, it feels more like a party than a real job."

Yes, she did remember his irresponsible, carefree side. She shook her head affectionately. "You haven't changed." Then she quickly added, "Well, of course you have, especially physically, but that boy is still inside."

"Of course he is. And he's very happy to be sitting here with you, Rina."

Giancarlo's voice had always been appealing, and now it had deepened to a resonance that sent shivers of awareness through her. Especially when he was saying nice things and gazing at her with soulful chocolate eyes.

3

Rina straightened her spine and pulled the scarf tighter around her neck. No doubt he'd patented this routine, and used it to get into the panties—no, make that thongs—of countless stars and star wannabes.

But why would he be wasting it on her? No matter how close and sexy their relationship once might have been, no way could she still be his type.

"Rina? What's wrong? You're scowling at me."

Although she hated confrontation, she'd long ago learned—partly by watching her mom with her dad—that things left unsaid could fester dangerously. "I asked you earlier what you wanted from tonight, and you said to catch up, which is great. But you . . . God, I'm hopelessly naïve, but I'm not used to men like you. The way you look at me, the inflection in your voice . . . Oh, this is crazy." How pitiful, to read a come-on into an old friend's attempts to be nice. Why on earth should she think he—

"I want far more than just to catch up."

Wait a minute. Had she thought those words or had he actually said them? "Giancarlo?"

His gaze darkened, heated, and he leaned toward her, that thin sweater stretching across firm pecs and revealing bronzed skin and a few curls of black hair. Under it, he was naked. She imagined warm skin over firm muscle, enough hair to tangle her fingers in—all new since she'd known him. One thing wouldn't have changed though: the milk chocolate nipples that had hardened so readily under her exploring fingers.

She sucked in a breath, feeling her own nipples tighten.

Again Giancarlo captured her hand. His touch robbed her of any hope of thinking straight. His fingers were long and graceful, yet firm and masterful as he stroked her hand then gripped it in his. Her skin grew warm and tingly, heat darted through her veins, her breath quickened. Between her legs, her sex throbbed and tightened.

"I don't want to rush you, *mia carissima*, but the moment I saw you tonight, I felt the same as all those years ago." His hand squeezed hers, his gaze was intense and—oh my God—passionate.

No, what was she thinking? Things like this never happened to Rina Goldberg. The man was just horny and looking for an easy lay. She jerked her hand free. "Giancarlo, you may think you're flattering me, but what I'd appreciate most is honesty."

His mouth fell open, then he shook his head vigorously, all those shoulder-length dark curls tumbling wildly. "No," he said, a little too loudly. Then, more softly, "I'm telling the truth. Why don't you believe me?" He leaned forward, his gaze hooking her and not letting go. "Tell me you looked at me and felt nothing."

"I—" Even before she'd recognized him, when he'd been a stranger across the room, she'd felt attracted. Then, when she'd looked into those familiar eyes . . . Yes, she'd felt, for a moment, like everything was the same as it used to be. Before she came to her senses and took another look at the handsome, successful man he'd turned into. "All right, maybe I felt like I'd gone back in time. But we can't just . . . pick up where we left off."

That couldn't be what he was suggesting. And yet, her needy body tingled with hope.

He reached out and with his index finger stroked the back of her hand, from the tip of her middle finger down to her wrist and up again, barely skimming the surface yet creating havoc with her senses. Oh yes, he still had that magic touch.

"Why not?" he asked. Now he danced all five fingers across her skin and she knew what he was doing. The piano man was playing music.

Could she recognize it?

Of course. It was "Für Elise." When she'd been seventeen she thought the piece was hopelessly romantic, this music Beethoven had supposedly composed for the woman he hoped to marry.

Rina remembered all the other pieces Giancarlo had played for her, and the parts of her body he'd played them on. Running scales up and down her back, pounding chords with both hands on her buttocks, tinkling delicate melodies across her breasts.

And, between her legs, composing songs just for her, to make her body sing for him.

A wave of lust poured through her and she gave a wrenching shudder. Her scarf slid off her shoulders but she made no effort to retrieve it.

She did make a grab at her scattered thoughts. "Why would you want to pick up where we left off? In your work, you must be surrounded by beautiful women."

He shook his head. "I'm surrounded by girls who are trying desperately to create an image, an illusion, that appeals to their target audience." He shrugged. "Not the company I would choose to share—" He broke off as a waiter lifted the champagne bottle from the ice bucket, then finished, with a smile at the waiter—"a peaceful meal in a fine Italian restaurant."

What had Giancarlo been going to say? From that gleam in his eye, she'd guessed he was thinking about a long, sweaty, passionate night in bed.

The waiter poured the last of the champagne into both their glasses. "Another bottle?"

"No," Rina quickly protested.

"We need something to drink with our dinner," Giancarlo said. "How about a glass of white wine, to go with your salmon?" When she nodded he asked the waiter what was available by the glass. Rina chose a pinot grigio and Giancarlo picked a chianti classico to go with his lasagne.

When the waiter went to get their wine, Giancarlo raised his champagne glass to Rina. "No, I can think of no woman I'd rather share an Italian meal with, or a glass of champagne. Or any of the things that, if a man is very lucky, may come after."

Rina knew her cheeks were rosy from his suggestion, and her own arousal. So was her chest, now bare of the draped scarf. She really must have had too much wine, because damned if the man didn't come across as genuine. Helplessly she raised her glass to click it gently against his. "To sharing," she murmured.

Quickly she added, "Dinner, I mean. And talk. That's it, for now. We don't even know each other anymore. Okay, maybe there's an attraction—"

His knowing smile made her falter. Yes, there was no question she craved the man, and it seemed as if, by some miracle, he was attracted too.

"But," she went on firmly, "that's not enough. We're probably not even compatible anymore."

Another meaningful grin made her flush. "Damn it, I meant

as *people*," she said. "Not as l-lovers. I'm not going to bed with someone I barely know."

Besides, Al had proposed to her and she hadn't given him her answer.

Although . . . didn't she know the answer?

The girls had told her she had to see her old lover before she'd be sure how she felt about marrying Al. And now she knew.

Sparks. Yes, they flew through her body whenever Giancarlo touched her, when his gaze even lit on her. Passion? Yes, if erect nipples and the burning ache between her thighs were any indication. Romance? What could possibly be more romantic than the most handsome man in the world toasting her, Rina Goldberg, with French champagne?

If she didn't seize this opportunity, she might never have the chance again.

And yet, she'd never been the kind of woman who could date, much less sleep with, two men at the same time.

"Damn," she muttered.

"Sorry?"

She shook her head. "Nothing." Just the end of a caring friendship that quite possibly might have turned into a companionable, even loving marriage. But no, she wasn't willing to settle. She wanted those damned sparks. Wanted the kind of passionate romance her girlfriends had found.

Even if only for one night.

Even if it was only a fantasy, an illusion, a creation of a charmer who was here today but might be gone tomorrow.

She was a fool. Al was a good man, a forever kind of man. They could have worked out that issue about him getting pushy when he didn't get his way. How could she hurt him, cast him away for a crazy, enchanted fling with a man like Giancarlo?

Because, for her, there were no other men like Giancarlo. When she'd been a girl, she'd loved her time with him but hadn't realized how truly amazing it was. Hadn't known theirs would remain the standard against which she measured other relationships. A standard that had yet to be topped.

This was too confusing. She'd always believed in the romantic idea of *The One*. That for each woman there was one special man. She was almost twenty-seven and Giancarlo was the only man who'd ever felt special to her—and it had happened twice now.

Still, she reminded herself firmly, he wasn't *The One* for the long term. She didn't want a crassly commercial jet-setter any more than he'd want her. But if he was offering her romance, passion and fantastic sex for even just a night . . .

Was she utterly insane to consider it?

"Rina, what's wrong?"

Inside her head, she bid a quiet good-bye to Al. She'd make it official tomorrow, but for her they were broken up as of this moment.

Raising both hands, she dragged her hair back from the sides of her face. "This wasn't what I expected when I came tonight."

"What did you expect, *cara?*" he asked gently.

Clenching her hair, she thought about his question. She hadn't expected him to be so handsome. Or to come on to her. Nor had she anticipated finding him so impossible to resist.

She released her hair and it sprang free. "A high school reunion," she said wryly. "Where people who used to be best friends no longer have anything in common. Where the chat is superficial and forced and there's just no . . ." She shrugged. "No connection anymore."

"And here we most definitely have a connection." There wasn't an ounce of uncertainty in his heated gaze, the conviction in his voice.

"Yes," she admitted softly.

A smile of delight split his face. "I'm so glad you feel it too. Now, stop fighting it and just enjoy. Yes?"

"I'll try. We'll talk, eat dinner, see where things go."

Even as she spoke to Giancarlo, a part of her was still worrying about Al. How could she have led the poor guy on—to the point he'd propose—then reject him?

But she hadn't meant to lead him on. Every step of the way, she'd been honest. She'd never told him she loved him. Maybe he'd assumed it, because she slept with him.

Not a mistake Giancarlo would ever make. If—big if—she did go to bed with him.

"You're still worried about something," he said softly. "Something more than tonight."

She nodded. "There's something I need to do. Something unpleasant, and sad. It's going to be very hard."

"I'm sorry. Can I help in any way?"

The more she looked at him, the more she saw the boy he'd been. The engaging tilt to his head, the way unruly curls tumbled over his forehead.

She smiled across at him. "I have to do this on my own. But thank you."

"Can you do this thing tonight?"

"No. Tomorrow." Al was a dentist; he worked all day. She'd arrange to meet him in the evening, to break the news. Hopefully not to break his heart. Or to get into another argument.

"Then put it aside and don't worry about it until then. Here we are, with good food growing cold, enough champagne in our glasses for a toast, so much yet to talk about. Let it go, Rina."

He'd always been like that. Quick to shove problems aside, take the easy route. But tonight, he was right. She'd enjoy tonight and tomorrow face the consequences.

"You're right." She shook back her hair, as if that one head toss could free her of all troubling thoughts. "What's the toast?"

He raised his glass. "To us, being together."

She lifted hers and clicked it gently to his. "To us, being together." The warm intensity of his smile brought another flush to her cheeks and chest.

She drained her champagne just as the waiter arrived with their glasses of wine and their dinners. Then she took a forkful of salmon, swirling it in tomato, lemon, olive oil sauce. "Delicious. How's your lasagne?"

Giancarlo had been tasting too, and let out a sigh of contentment. "Fancier than Mamma's, but very good. Here, have a taste." He extended his fork, which held a sizable mouthful of pasta, meat and cheese.

Had to be a hundred calories in a bite. But man, did it look and smell good. She leaned forward and closed her lips around the food. She closed her eyes too, the better to savor the taste as she drew the lasagne into her mouth. "Mmm." Heaven.

When she opened her eyes, she found him staring at her, his face taut with . . . was that excitement? Sexual excitement?

An unusual sense of female power filled her. Before she could talk herself out of it, she leaned forward so that her loose top slipped off one shoulder, revealing a lacy black bra strap and more than a hint of cleavage. His gaze moved down, lingered, and his eyes glittered with heat.

"More, please," she murmured, trying to sound seductive.

He exhaled with a quick rush of air. When he scooped up another bite of lasagne and held out his fork, his hand was actually shaking.

Even a woman of her limited experience could tell he was seriously aroused.

And so was she. If she'd had Jenny's nerve, she'd have grabbed his hand and said, "Let's go find a bed." Instead, she leaned forward and parted her lips to slide the lasagne off his fork.

"You have a sexy mouth," he said, voice rough at the edges. "It makes a man imagine all sorts of things."

"What do you imagine?" she dared to ask.

His eyes widened, and he gave a quick bark of laughter. "I can't tell you; I'm too turned on as it is."

"What do you want to do about that?"

"Want?" His smile flashed wickedly. "To tell the absolute truth, I want you to slide under the table, unzip my pants, and . . . well, you can figure out the rest."

"Giancarlo!" God, she'd loved having him in her mouth, and loved the way he responded. The memory made her squirm with desire.

"I'd never ask you to do anything embarrassing. Besides, I'm trying to learn *pazienza*." At her curious look, he explained, "Patience. All good things are worth waiting for, yes?"

"They are. We've waited a long time for . . . this." Nine whole years, and now that she'd felt his fingers on her hand, she craved the whole-body experience.

"Do you know what I'd been thinking just before I got your e-mail?" he asked.

She shook her head.

"That my life's been crazy and I wanted to slow down, enjoy a quiet evening, a nice lasagne. And then I read your message and thought, yes, this is what I want. To do these things, with this woman."

He'd really thought that? And yet, obviously, he'd chosen her company over that of whatever females were working on his current video. "Well, that's what we're doing," she said, trying to regain control, "so let's continue. The food is wonderful."

"I'm so glad you enjoy it. We should eat before it gets cold."

And we'll talk about . . . what would you like? Anything other than sex. You must help me be patient."

His wink made her smile. She considered various topics of conversation. If he got onto his career in music video, the romantic mood would be spoiled. After all, what was she thinking, contemplating sex with a man who'd chosen a career she couldn't respect?

No, enough. For tonight she wanted to preserve her rosy-colored romantic glasses. "If we're to take up where we left off, then we need to go back. Let's relive that summer, share the memories we've carried with us." She slanted him a grin. "And I promise, I won't mention sex unless you do."

He smiled. "You are a tease, *bella*. Very well then, do you want to know my very first thought when I arrived in Banff? It was that I'd circled halfway around the world, only to end up back home, in a small village in the mountains. Except with people who were far richer and spoke English."

"Your English wasn't so great," she remembered. "It's sure improved, even though you've kept a touch of the accent."

"I was so eager to learn." His dark eyes sparkled as he added, "And you were such a great teacher."

She flushed, thinking, as she knew he'd intended, of all the things they'd learned together. Mostly about their sexuality.

They continued to talk casually, exchanging reminiscences, as they ate their main courses. Both had chosen meals they could eat with one hand, and it wasn't long until their free hands were linked across the table. A connection, a bond, a hint of more to come.

When their waiter cleared the empty plates and wine glasses, he asked, "Something more to drink?"

"Coffee," Rina said. She'd had more to drink than usual, not to mention being intoxicated by Giancarlo's charm. And she had to drive home.

Or did she? Would this evening really lead into bed? Either his or hers?

"I'll have coffee as well," Giancarlo said. "Rina, dessert?"

"We have an excellent tiramisu," the waiter said.

"I'm full," she said. If there really was a possibility she and Giancarlo were going to have sex tonight, she didn't want a bulging stomach.

The waiter brought two cups of coffee, along with two liqueur glasses filled with something clear. "Sambuca," he explained. "Compliments of Francesco. Please, enjoy."

"Would you tell him *molte grazie?*" Giancarlo said.

Then, when the waiter had gone, he said, "Rina, will you excuse me a moment?"

"Of course." She needed a trip to the ladies' room anyway.

She collected her purse and made her way to the back of the restaurant, past a wall of photographs taken at one of Francesco's earlier restaurants. Down a hallway she found a nicely lit bathroom in shades of pumpkin and stared at herself in the mirror. Flushed cheeks, wild hair, blouse slipping off one shoulder. She looked like a gypsy. Or a witch.

Did Giancarlo actually find this picture appealing?

Well, there was nothing much she could do to improve on it. No point trying to get a comb through those tangled curls. She splashed cold water on her cheeks, brushed her teeth, put on some lip gloss and made her way back to the table.

Giancarlo rose to his feet and held her chair.

Once she'd sat down, she slid her Sambuca across the table to him. She wanted to know what might come next, and this was a subtle way of asking his intentions. "I can't drink this. I'm driving."

"Ah yes, you drove here. From North Vancouver, you said in your e-mail." He slid the glass back. "I think you've had too much wine already to be driving."

"It's a very long taxi ride to where I live." And he'd been drinking too, so he could hardly suggest he'd drive her.

"I think—" He broke off as Francesco again appeared at the table.

This time, though, rather than speaking to them, the man broke into song. Opera. Rina recognized it immediately. "Nessun Dorma" from *Turandot*. Where the prince sings to Turandot, hoping to win her love.

Giancarlo captured her left hand in both of his and winked, making her realize this was his doing.

Rina didn't know where to look—at the one Italian who was serenading her or the other who was gazing passionately across the table at her. She glanced around the restaurant, realizing all conversation had died and everyone else was watching Francesco. And her and Giancarlo, the favored couple.

She shoved embarrassment away and gave herself up to the moment, absorbing the powerful voice and beautiful words, the warm clasp of Giancarlo's hands. Savoring each sensation and filing it away so she'd never forget. A gift, from Giancarlo to her.

When the song was finished, there was a moment of hush, then Francesco bowed and everyone in the restaurant burst into applause.

"Thank you," Rina told him, her words swallowed up in the clapping. Then, as the applause died down, she dug into her tiny stock of Italian. "*Grazie*."

"*Prego, bella*," Francesco responded. "It's my pleasure." He strutted away, shoulders back and chest out, to be complimented by other diners as he crossed the restaurant.

Rina said to Giancarlo, "How did you arrange that?"

He shrugged. "They told me at the hotel, when they recommended this restaurant, that Francesco had studied opera and still sang on occasion. I thought you—we—might enjoy it. Something special, to mark our first night together."

She had to laugh. "As if champagne wasn't enough?" And his company, and the way he looked at her with wholly masculine appreciation?

"A man should treat his woman well."

His woman. Maybe she was, at least for tonight. Already her relationship with Al felt as if it had happened long ago.

Rina raised the glass of Sambuca to her lips and tasted, savoring the licorice flavor. "If I can't drive home anyhow, I might as well enjoy this." She took another sip and said, feeling bold, "I seem to have a problem. I'm marooned downtown with no easy means of transportation."

"My hotel is less than a mile away." He raised her hand to his mouth and kissed the back of it, his lips soft and tantalizing, raising goose bumps. "It has a very large bed, an extra bathrobe and everything you could possibly want in the way of toiletries."

"You had me back at large bed," she admitted softly, finally acknowledging to both of them that this was what she wanted. One night with this man who was both the old and the new Giancarlo. She'd take this one night, then see what happened next.

"I'm afraid I'm not very good at this," she said. "It's new to me. Agreeing to, uh, spend the night after a first date."

"I'm glad. But we're hardly strangers, Rina. Remember what we said? Picking up where we left off? Don't be nervous, it's just me, the scrawny homesick kid who speaks broken English."

She laughed. "That is *so* not the case. And yet, it is. It seems natural to relax with you. To let down my guard and be myself."

"Why should you need to keep up a guard?"

"I guess I don't trust my judgment. It takes me a while to get to know people, to decide if I can trust them." Moving around all the time as she'd done as a child, one option had been to leap into instant friendships, with all the risks that entailed. She'd done that a couple of times and learned she'd rather have no friends than choose unwisely.

He nodded, eyes narrowing thoughtfully. "Yes. To know whether they like you for who you are or only want something from you."

She studied him. "I suppose in your work you get a lot of that."

"Oh yes. Some see me as a star-maker. At the very least, I can make them look attractive. Or ugly."

If only he could make her look beautiful. On the other hand, the gleam in his eyes said that was how he saw her. How very strange. Teasingly she said, "And you're so sure I don't want to be on your next video?"

He laughed. "I'm positive."

Because she was too heavy, not pretty enough? Hurt, she said, "Oh, and why's that?" Yes, make him say it, admit he'd just been flattering her to get her into bed.

He gripped her hand firmly. "Because you're the genuine thing, Rina. There's no artifice in you. I may not have seen you in nine years, but that much I know."

"Oh," she said weakly. It seemed Giancarlo, too, was being sincere.

"Drink up," he said. "I'm afraid my *pazienza* is wearing extremely thin. I can't wait to have you in my arms."

She wanted that too. So much. But she was nervous as well. When he held her, he'd discover how very much of her there was. But once she got Giancarlo into that big bed with the lights off, she'd make him forget her extra pounds.

One thing she was confident about was that she was a good lover. She'd learned a lot, all those years ago with Giancarlo, and she knew she'd pleased the few men she'd been with since. Her insecurity about her attractiveness made her try harder, and she knew many ways to make a man happy in bed.

The thought of pleasuring Giancarlo—and being pleasured in return—almost made her whimper with need. "My patience is wearing thin, too." Lifting her Sambuca glass, she drained the last few drops.

Giancarlo beckoned their waiter and said, "The bill, please. And can you call us a cab?"

"There are taxis across the street at the Sutton Place Hotel. If you wave, one will come over."

When they were ready to leave, Rina draped her scarf around her shoulders again and bent down to find her purse. Before she could rise, Giancarlo hurried to assist her. He stood behind her for a moment, not touching, but she could tell he was only inches away. His body generated a heat that made her back tingle. He rested his hands lightly on her shoulders for an instant, then he released her. "Come, *cara*, it's time to be alone."

Francesco came to wish them a pleasant evening—with a "*Ciao, bella.* I hope you return soon," for Rina—but thankfully didn't linger.

Rina's whole body felt flushed, needy, impatient. She was glad when the door of the restaurant closed behind them and they were standing alone on the sidewalk.

The air was cool against her heated skin and she gave an involuntary shiver. She pointed across the street. "That's the Sutton Place." Sure enough, there were three cabs waiting outside.

"First, we need to do this." Giancarlo turned her to face him.

He took a step closer—now he was so much taller than she—and she rose to meet him as he leaned down.

His arms swept around her and pulled her to him, firm and close, then his lips were on hers. And again, there was the comfort of familiarity combined with a heady rush of excitement.

Softly he nibbled the corner of her mouth. She did the same back, slanting her lips against his, teasing and nipping and savoring his firm, soft skin. Her eyes drifted shut. Her heart pounded and began to race as she wrapped her arms around him, snuggled closer into his embrace and felt the unmistakable ridge of his erection against her belly.

A hard, impatient cock, yet soft, patient, gentle lips. Another tantalizing combination.

The man was pure seduction.

Heat sizzled and throbbed through her, centering in a hot pulse of need in her sex.

He lifted his arms from her back to fist his hands in her hair and adjust the angle of her head. The tip of his tongue teased the crease between her lips. She sighed with desire, opening to him. He slipped inside, his tongue meeting hers in a slow greeting that quickly turned heated.

She wanted to savor his mouth too, so chased his tongue back and followed it. Mmm, he was so hot and wet, his taste purely Italian, a combination of licorice and coffee with an undertone of red wine.

So much sensation. The textures of lips and tongue, the inside of his mouth, the occasional gentle nip. That Italian taste, and the scent of something herbal like verbena from his shampoo or cologne. Under her hands, the silky fabric of his thin sweater and beneath it, the tensile strength of taut back muscles. And always, at the firm center of everything, the bold press of his cock.

She wriggled her pelvis, rubbing against him.

He groaned and thrust against her.

Damn, if they weren't on a main street, if she were a small girl like Jenny, he could lift her up, give her the contact her body craved, drive her to satisfaction. It wouldn't take much. She was so aroused and ready.

Funny thing was, at this moment, with this big and strong new version of Giancarlo, she felt almost petite. Well, not petite but . . . not huge either.

Feminine, for sure. Purely feminine.

Meltingly, bonelessly feminine.

Achingly, hungrily feminine.

She summoned the willpower to pull her mouth free of his and step back—but only because she honestly couldn't wait much longer. "Giancarlo, I need you. Now."

"Jesus." He glanced around and ran a hand through his hair. Those long, beautiful fingers were shaking. "I forgot where we were." His breathing was ragged. "Rina, you make me forget everything but you."

"Me too." She glanced around. It wasn't eleven yet, and Burrard Street was busy. How many cars had driven by, perhaps even honked? How many pedestrians on their way home from dinner or movies had walked past and either smiled or scowled at them?

"We'll get a taxi." He glanced down. "Should've worn pants with pleats."

She looked too. Oh yes, his hard-on was unmistakable. God, she wanted to touch it. Unzip his pants, take out his penis, wrap her lips around him. She barely suppressed a whimper.

But damn, why should she play innocent with Giancarlo? Once upon a time, they'd explored every single inch of each other's bodies, done everything sexual they could imagine.

So she looked up at him and, feeling amazingly liberated and deliciously bold, said, "I want to taste you. Every inch of that luscious cock. I want to suck you. Make you beg me to stop because you have to be inside me."

"Jesus, *cara*." He took a deep breath then let it out slowly. "You're wicked. You know what you're doing to me." Then his eyes began to twinkle. "But I don't agree. You'll be the first to beg."

She chuckled, "I don't think so. I give a very . . ." she paused deliberately, ". . . very . . . excellent . . . blow job."

"Woman, you could make me come just hearing those words from your sexy mouth."

"Well, that would be a waste," she said huskily. "When you come, I want it to be inside me."

"We're getting a taxi *now*." He raised a hand, waved in the direction of the taxis across the street and for good measure let out a piercing whistle.

"Thought you'd never get around to it." She tossed back her hair as the first cab in the rank moved forward.

And yet, she was nervous. He'd cast a magic spell around her, one that made her feel free and easy, powerful and womanly. But when she glanced at her reflection in the window behind them, what she saw was the same old Rina.

Could the new Giancarlo truly be attracted to the old Rina?

4

Rina and Giancarlo slid into the back seat of the cab.

"Opus Hotel, please," he said to the driver.

Seeking reassurance, Rina moved over to snuggle against him. He slid away, lifting a few locks of hair and whispering in her ear, "Oh no you don't, you temptress."

Okay, that was promising.

The taxi ride was only a few minutes, then they were pulling up in front of the trendy Opus.

The lobby had cream marble floors, cinnamon walls and retro furniture in primary colors. Not to her taste, but classy. Giancarlo, in his stylish sweater and pants, fit the place. She, on the other hand, looked more like a gypsy tarot-card reader come to harass the guests.

It didn't matter, because she was with him.

With him. The urgency of his grip confirmed they were soon going to be together in the most intimate way possible. The idea made her shiver with nerves and need.

Alone in the elevator, he pulled her to him. He didn't kiss

her, just rested his hands on her shoulders and gazed into her face. "This is my lucky day. Together again."

"After nine years of—" She broke off, because the word she'd been going to say was *waiting*. Damn, was that true? Now she knew why she'd judged every other man lacking. Subconsciously she'd been comparing them to him.

Waiting for him to come back to her.

Well, shit, that wasn't a good thing. And he certainly didn't need to know. Quickly she said, "Nine years of not even being in touch."

He reached out, isolated one curl of her hair and twisted it around his finger. "Why did we make that agreement? We were crazy about each other. It was silly to let that go." He released the curl and it bounced free.

"We each had separate lives to get on with—on opposite sides of the world." Besides, her parents had died. There'd been so much emotion, so many changes in her life. The next few years had been crazy.

"It's true, it would have been hard to maintain a relationship."

And here they were again, in the same situation. After tonight, would she spend more years of her life comparing? Waiting for him to reappear?

No, because he wasn't the kind of man she wanted. For one magical night, yes, but not for life.

"I suppose you're right." He nodded. "Besides, I was a boy. I wasn't ready for you."

What did he mean by that? Before she could ask, the elevator pinged. He hurried through the doors, tugging her behind him down the empty hall.

He slipped his key card into a slot, and then they were inside his room. Giancarlo didn't reach for the light switch. Nor did she. They fell into each other's arms with near desperation.

Hungry, demanding kisses, so many she could hardly breathe.

Or was it just one incredibly long one? She pressed shamelessly against him, seeking every inch of his erection. In the dark, feeling the strength of his body and unable to see the familiar eyes and hair, she could have been embracing a stranger. And yet there was something familiar in the way his hands caressed her back.

Finally he wrenched his mouth away. "Too long. It's been too long."

Since they'd seen each other? Had sex with each other? Or did he mean the evening had been too long, the buildup to this moment? "Yes," she said against his lips, "it's all been too long."

"*Cara,* you're sure? You really want this? Here, let me turn on the light so I can see your eyes." His hand left her back and she knew he was reaching for the switch.

She didn't mind him seeing her eyes, but there was a whole lot more that she had no intention of revealing. Quickly she captured his hand, threaded her fingers through his. "No. No light. And yes, I'm positive I want this. Now, where's the bed?"

The drapes were drawn tightly and she couldn't see a thing.

He chuckled. "How can I find it if you won't let me turn the lights on? I want to see you. Every lovely inch of you."

She winced. What he'd see was every extra pound. Thank God this hotel had thick, expensive window treatments.

But tonight she was supposed to be sexy, not pitifully insecure, so she tried for a sultry purr. "And I prefer the dark. It's mysterious, exciting."

"But—"

"But what?" She cut him off. "This, perhaps?" Unerringly she found the waist of his beltless pants and undid the button. The zipper. "Mmm, there's something in here. I wonder what it is?" At last she could cup her hand over the hard-on that stretched his underwear. Her uncertainties fled, replaced by confidence and a surge of lust.

"It's dark," she said, "so I can't really tell. I'll have to figure it out by . . . feel." She breathed the last word seductively.

Her hand slid under his underwear—some kind of silky feeling jersey fabric—and then . . . Oh yum. A hot, pulsing shaft filled her hand. Filled it.

And her hand, a pianist's hand that could easily span an octave, wasn't small. Her vaginal muscles clenched. God, he was going to feel good inside her.

He gasped, tensed for a moment, then began to breathe again. Fast.

"Oh my." She licked her lips, letting him hear her do it. Then she ran her hand up and down his shaft, plunging deep inside his clothing to explore his balls, then slowly back up to the head of his penis. Her pussy was aching and crying with need, but she didn't give in. She had to make Giancarlo forget any desire for light.

She circled the velvety head of his cock with a finger and captured a drop of pre-come. "Mmm, very interesting," she purred, "but I'm still not sure what I have here. Touch isn't enough, I think I'll have to . . . taste." She raised her finger to her lips and sucked, exaggerating the noise. "Salty. Hmm, what could that be?"

Then she slid off her shoes and dropped to her knees on the carpeted floor. After tugging his pants and boxer-briefs down farther, she took him in her mouth.

"Oh, sweet Jesus," he said, hands tangling in her hair.

Sweet cock, Rina thought, tightening her thighs against the relentless ache of arousal. He was silky soft at the crown, salty, a little musky from hours of arousal. She ran her tongue down him, tracing the bulging vein to its root, moving on to tease his balls. Then she licked back up, slowly, and finally slid her lips over the head of his penis and began to suck.

And with each suck, her sex pulsed in response.

Giancarlo tugged gently on her hair. When she didn't stop,

he pulled more urgently. "Rina, I surrender. You're right, I'm the one begging." She raised her head and he let out a sigh of relief, then gave a teasing chuckle. "Stop, or you'll regret it."

She touched her tongue to the head of his cock to remind him who was in control. "And if I do stop? What's my reward?"

Hopefully, amazing sex with the lights off, so she could ditch her insecurities and continue being a bold, sexy woman.

"Anything you want." He reached for her shoulders, drew her up. "I'll explore all your secret places with my tongue. I'll play any song you want, anywhere on your body, at whatever tempo you request. And when you're ready, our bodies will sing a duet until, together, we reach that glorious final climax."

Good God. He'd melted every bone in her body until she felt like a puddle of lust.

She swallowed hard. "Th-that sounds good." Another swallow as she fought to regain her composure. "And what will you do for an encore?"

He let out a laugh that no doubt could be heard in the neighboring rooms. "Oh, Rina, you always did keep me in my place."

Had she? "All I know right now is, our place is together. You did say there's a bed in this room?"

"And we'll find it, even in the dark." He reached down to pull off his loafers and socks, then she heard him kick out of his pants. And his briefs?

Rina reached out to check, and encountered a hot, rigid penis.

She clasped it while he thrust both hands under the hem of his sweater and yanked it over his head. Too bad there wasn't some way of lighting his body but not hers. Still, she was skilled with her fingers and tongue, adept at using them to gather information.

Already she'd learned a lot about his cock.

"Now it's your turn," he said.

"Oh." Never her favorite moment. She was a woman who far preferred donning clothes to taking them off.

He led her across the room, the carpet soft under her bare feet. She'd thought of wearing pantyhose but now was glad she hadn't. They were so awkward to struggle out of. Following as he tugged her along, she wondered nervously if he'd undress her or leave her to do it herself.

Giancarlo felt like a blind man in this pitch-black room, stumbling his way in the direction of the bed. "Ouch." He stubbed his toe against the bed frame, lost his balance and began to fall. Laughing, he pulled Rina down with him, onto the bed.

"Oh," she squeaked, then a lush armful of female curves landed on top of him.

What more could a man ask for? Except that those curves be naked.

If he could see, it would be a hell of a lot easier, but he had to admit this game of hers was sensual. It gave him a good excuse to explore her body shamelessly as he searched for the waistband of her skirt. God, but her skin was soft.

Not too soft, not plump, but definitely not stretched tight across her bones. He wasn't into models or athletes; he liked a real woman. This one in particular. He slid the button through the hole and unzipped the skirt.

She rolled off him, and the bed shifted as she moved around. He reached over, to verify she was taking off her skirt. His hand encountered more soft skin so he explored further, identified a curvy thigh. He stroked upward, tempted to head straight for her center but not wanting to rush her. Mind you, she'd gone right for his dick. And he'd damned well loved it.

Using just the tips of his fingers, he caressed her thigh in circles, each circle nudging its way inward, toward the juncture of her thighs. And as he went, her flesh grew warmer and more moist, her breathing quickened.

His index finger teased the damp edge of the crotch of her panties.

Her voice came out of the darkness, sounding breathy. "I like your sense of direction. If you're hunting for something, you're definitely getting warm."

"So are you." He stroked the moist strip of silk between her legs, feeling the shape of her vulva underneath, plump and firm. She writhed under his touch, and the silk grew drenched. God, she was so beautifully responsive.

He wanted to slip a couple of fingers under her panties and ease inside her. But before he got to that, he had a serious craving to free her breasts and rediscover them.

He eased away, and she said, "Damn, where are you going?"

"In search of another treasure. There's something I've been wanting to do ever since I saw you." He slid up the bed beside her, one hand tracing the outer line of her leg, her hip.

"I know what *I* want you to do, and you're going in the wrong direction."

"*Cara*, I'll be back. I promise. Here, sit up for a minute."

"Okay, but I'm going to remember that promise."

As she rose to sit, he hunted for the hem of her blouse, then lifted it over her head. He glided both hands gently up her torso, feeling the strength of her rib cage, then coming across more silky fabric.

A black bra.

He couldn't see it, but he knew, just as he knew her panties matched. If he closed his eyes he could call up an image of her pale olive skin, those full curves barely confined by black silk. One day he'd see that vision for real, preferably in the bright sunlight of midday, but for now his imagination was enough.

A Sophia Loren body, he thought as he stroked her breasts

through silk, and every inch of her was genuine. A real woman, not one who looked like a prepubescent child or an artificial Barbie doll.

The young Sophia Loren had become his idea of a sex goddess when he was all of twelve—thanks to a poster in his uncle's tool shop of her in an old movie called *Yesterday, Today and Tomorrow.*

Then, when he was seventeen, he'd met Rina Goldberg and discovered his universe was large enough to contain two goddesses.

Rina's nipples were hard. She had rosy-brown areolas, he remembered, shading to a deeper pink where the nipples budded.

And speaking of hard, his dick, pressing against her hip, was feeling damned frustrated. Rina was a sensual overload to his system. It was just as well he couldn't see her, or he'd likely explode before he got any further.

She thrust her breasts into his hands as he fondled them, letting him know she enjoyed his touch. But now he couldn't wait; he needed her flesh in his hands. "Unhook your bra," he said.

When she reached behind herself, his hands were ready, greedy to be filled to overflowing with the soft weight of her breasts. There was nothing, absolutely nothing, to compare to the feel of a woman's full, natural breasts. "My God, you're amazing." He buried his face in her cleavage, inhaling a rich scent that was both flowery and spicy, with a hint of something exotic. It reminded him of . . .

"You smell like roses," he murmured, dropping tiny kisses along her cleavage. In fact, her scent reminded him of the peach-colored rosebush by his Nonna—Grandmother—Alba's door. In midsummer, when the blooms were at their peak, he'd always buried his face in those blossoms and inhaled, wanting to take that scent into his lungs and hold on to it, all through the long, cold winter. Now he breathed in Rina's scent, so he could remember it too.

He cupped one breast in both hands, massaging it lightly, caressing and teasing it so her nipple drew up even tighter. Then, having prepared it to perfection, he dipped his head and touched the tip of his tongue to the tight bud.

Her body tensed.

Gently he sucked her nipple into his mouth and played with it, touching his teeth to it, rolling it between his lips, sucking it as if it were her clit.

She shuddered and gave a whimper of pleasure. "Oh yes, Giancarlo, that feels so good." She reached for his dick again, circling it with hungry fingers.

He groaned. "No, don't. You can't. I'm so close."

"I am too."

Her hands released his dick and instead gripped his head, one hand on either side. As she pulled him away from her body, her nipple popped free of his mouth. "I don't want to wait," she said.

"Ah, Rina, but I want to do so many things with you."

"Yes, but later. Right now I need you so badly it hurts." She paused, then made a breathy little sound. "Giancarlo, come inside me. Now."

His self-control vanished.

He wanted to strip off her panties and bury himself inside her. But first, a condom. Damn, they were all the way across the room, in the bathroom.

"I have to get protection," he muttered, finding the edge of the bed and heaving himself off. Now, where the hell was the bathroom? Both hands in front of him, he made his way across the floor in the general direction of the bathroom door, bumped into the wall, eased left and there he was.

Surely he could turn a light on in here. And so he did, then grabbed his toiletry kit and pulled out a small box of condoms. His gaze was caught by his reflection in the bathroom mirror.

God, he looked like a madman, curly hair every which way, cheeks flushed, a raging boner reaching hungrily into the air. Yeah, there was something to be said for Rina's idea of darkness.

He clicked off the bathroom light and stepped through the door. "Say something so I can find you."

A sexy feminine giggle came from across the room. "I'm naked."

That raging boner twitched, urging him forward. "Keep talking. I'm coming."

"Hopefully not quite yet."

That was another special thing about Rina. Her sense of humor. And the wisdom to know that sex was best when it was fun as well as passionate.

"Oh fuck." He'd stubbed the same toe and again lost his balance. "I did it again. Watch out," he warned as he crashed to the bed.

She rolled out of the way, then back toward him. "Poor baby." Her deft musician's hands began to explore, finding his shoulder, tracing down an arm. "Did you hurt yourself?"

"Stubbed my toe."

"Mmm, I'll have to kiss it better." She was touching his ribs now, then heading down his hip. She paused midway down his thigh. "You're sure it's your toe that hurts?"

He answered promptly. "Nowhere near as much as my dick does."

"Isn't it called triage, where you treat the most urgent problem first?"

God knew. He only cared that her soft warm lips were wrapping around him.

Was this heaven or hell? He fought his body's reaction to her touch, which was to surge toward climax.

Then he *had* to pull her away. "Lie back, *cara.*"

As she did, he sheathed himself. Then he oriented himself by touch until his fingers were drifting across her stomach, finding a thick nest of curls, under it a cushiony soft mound, then slick, swollen lips. He stroked the petals of her labia, relearning every intimate detail, enjoying every sigh and moan.

Oh yes, he remembered making love with this woman. How he'd use his fingers or mouth to make her come, then he'd thrust inside her and they'd move together, fast, slow, whatever rhythm one of them picked, until she was ready. Then they'd both climax at the same time.

Back then, he'd thought it must be normal to come together. Now he knew how rare it was.

Would it still happen?

When her hips began to twist, he danced his fingers around her clit, faster and faster, then caught it gently between thumb and index finger and squeezed.

"Oh God, yes!" She let out an exultant cry and her body shook in orgasm.

He raised himself above her and, in one swift movement, plunged into her. And, as he did, he lowered his head to kiss her.

Her body clung to him, inside and out. Lips to lips, arms circling his back, legs around his thighs, vaginal walls hugging his penis.

"*Sono in paradiso,*" he murmured.

"What?"

"This is so good. I'm in paradise."

Slowly he began to move and she responded, their bodies finding a sexy harmony, their kisses keeping the rhythm. But God, he couldn't maintain this slow pace; his body was making its demands clear.

As he pumped harder and faster, her hands reached down to grab his butt, urging him on. Her body rose to meet his with each stroke and his balls tightened, everything in his body centering on that one overpowering need.

To merge with Rina.

She tore her mouth away from his and made a high, keening sound that he recognized. She was close again. He let himself go wild, driving hard into her as she ground herself against him. And then they both cried out in release, a duet of joy and intimate connection.

It was a few minutes before he could catch his breath. "Oh yeah," he said with complete satisfaction. "That's how it's supposed to be."

"Mmm," she purred against his neck.

Her body was so welcoming, so pillowy soft. He wanted to collapse into her as if she were a down comforter and drift off to sleep in her arms. Instead, Giancarlo forced himself up to deal with the condom.

"Can I turn the light on now?" he asked as he stumbled in the dark.

"No." Her answer came quickly. Then she gave a little laugh that sounded more nervous than carefree. "I like it this way. I feel less inhibited."

As he found his way back onto the bed beside her, he said, "I don't remember you being inhibited." He reached out, exploring in the dark. When he realized she'd climbed under the covers and was lying on her side facing him, he slid between the sheets too and took a similar position. He stretched out a hand and began tracing down the side of her body.

"N-no. But I think that's the only time in my life."

He paused in stroking the womanly curve of her hip. "Really?"

"Mmm." Her hand found his shoulder, cupped and squeezed it, then her fingers spread and slid down, learning the shape of his upper arm.

He took some pride in knowing he wasn't that same scrawny

kid. Not only had he filled out, but he exercised as often as he could. His job was demanding; he needed to stay in good shape.

"Not to be a complete egotist," he said, "but did I have anything to do with that lack of inhibition?"

She chuckled softly. "I guess."

"Well, you're with me again. Lose the inhibitions, Rina."

He felt curls brush his cheek as she shook her head. "You're different now. We're different."

"I don't think so."

Her hand slid down to his forearm. "You were a boy, and now you're a man. A man who's traveled all over the world, met famous people, beautiful women."

"You'd traveled a lot before I met you, and met all sorts of people."

"Which helped me feel more self-confident. You were a brilliant musician and had charisma, but you were also a scrawny small-town boy, no more sexually experienced than I."

"Okay, but now we're both adults and—Wait a minute. You're not saying you haven't had other lovers since me?" That couldn't be possible, not for a lovely, passionate woman like her.

"I've had a few lovers. Some good sex. But the men were just, you know, normal guys."

"Christ, Rina, I'm a normal guy." Except, he wasn't. Not like his brothers, who were content to stay in Domodossola. To marry local girls, raise families. Have what most people would consider *normal* jobs.

No, he'd never wanted that. First he'd dreamed about being a concert pianist, then he'd shifted to the music video world. He'd wanted life in the fast lane, in the glitzy world of entertainment. Success, kudos.

"Not by any definition of normal *I* know," she said, a note of dry humor in her voice.

"So, what are you saying? You can't feel intimidated by me?" Didn't the woman realize he'd drop to the ground at her feet and worship her?

"Sometimes," she said softly. "And it's easier to pretend it's the old us when the lights are off."

"I don't want to be the old us. I want you to feel comfortable with who I am now."

She sighed. "Wishing doesn't make things happen. Please don't force me into something I'm not ready for."

Ready. Okay, that was a word that allowed for hope. She would learn to trust him. He smiled to himself in the dark. Usually women fell all over themselves to be with him, and he got to set the terms. Yes, he'd been spoiled and had become used to it. But there was one thing he knew. He could charm the birds down from the trees. Everyone said so. Rina would succumb.

"If I can't see you, I need to feel you," he told her. "Come closer, *cara*."

She curled into him, head nestled into his neck, a leg over his thighs.

He turned his own head to breathe in the scent of her hair—not rose this time, more like almond—and felt the vitality of those springy curls against his skin. His own hair was long, plentiful and curly, but Rina's was a whole different thing. It was like each strand jumped with energy. "Your hair's amazing."

She snorted a laugh against his neck. "Amazing's one word. Uncontrollable's another. I can never do anything with it." Another chuckle. "When I was a teenager, I called it my Jewfro."

"I remember that. But I like it. It's got a life of its own. A mischievous spirit."

"Mischievous? I'd say downright disobedient."

"Obedience is highly overrated. Following the rules never got anyone anywhere."

"Hmm. Don't tell my music students that."

So Rina's love of music still involved structure and discipline. He wondered if she ever just let loose and played. Explored, heard melodies in her head and translated them into notes. Not that he'd done that himself for more than a year.

Thank God they both let loose in bed.

Speaking of which . . .

His body was recovering from that wonderful orgasm. A part of him wanted to give in to the sense of peace and relaxation Rina's presence brought and doze off. But then again, he could start all over—and this time, do it properly. Slowly. Relearn every inch of her body in the darkness, and pleasure her with his fingers, his tongue.

His dick twitched, registering its vote.

"You're quiet," he said. "Falling asleep?"

"No, just marveling at how incredible this is. You and me, like this." She gave a contented sound, like a cat's purr. "Truth is, I'm a night owl. I only need a few hours sleep."

"I'm the same. There's too much to do to waste hours sleeping."

"What things do you do, Giancarlo, in the middle of the night?"

"Work, sometimes, depending on how a project's going. Brainstorm or party with the talent and the crew. Start envisioning the next project. Watch other directors' videos and think how I'd have done them better."

She laughed. "No small ego, eh?"

He shrugged, not too apologetically. "Okay," he conceded, "maybe not always better, but differently. According to my own vision of the music, the lyrics, the personalities. The message. Each director has their own interpretation and we probably all secretly think ours is the best. Don't you feel the same way when you're playing music?"

"Okay, I confess." She paused a moment, then said, "Sounds like even when you're not working, you're working."

"Guess so, even if it's only subconsciously. Can't turn the brain off; it's always absorbing images and ideas. I do lots of stuff like explore the cities I'm in, go to movies and the theatre, watch TV. Every impression is something that may become useful."

"So serious," she teased.

"God, no." He laughed. "It's all play. Even the longest, most tedious day in the studio, with performers who are idiots and a crew that's technologically impaired." He squeezed her shoulder. "Be warned, Wendy."

"Wendy?" She stiffened. "Who's Wendy?"

"I have a feeling you are. And I'm Peter Pan, and I'm giving you fair warning, I never intend to grow up."

"Well," she said slowly, "I guess that's really none of my business."

It might become her business, though, if things between them continued so well. And if that's what he had in mind, stressing his own immaturity wasn't the best way to go about persuading her.

"How about you?" he asked. "What do you do in the middle of the night?"

"Play for my own pleasure. Sew. Read. Watch old movies. Do yoga."

Not all that different from him, a lot of nights. "Not a party girl?" he asked.

Her hair tickled as she shook her head. "No, but I like to socialize. Dinners with friends or neighbors, or going out with the other musicians after a rehearsal or performance. You know what it's like, where you can't just go home and unwind, you need that transition time?"

"Yeah. You're wired, you need to process, debrief with your colleagues."

"It's the same with what you do?"

"Sometimes. Depends where we're at in the shooting schedule, and how the day went." He spoke offhandedly because his mind was following a track of its own. Rina had an active social life, she was beautiful and warm and generous, talented and intelligent. She had a fun sense of humor and she was terrific in bed. "How come no man's snatched you up by now?"

Her body tensed again. Damn, had he said the wrong thing?

In a low voice, she said, "One or two relationships have headed toward being serious, then . . . things just haven't been good enough, I guess."

Good, but not good enough? Yeah, she was picky about guys. Well, she could afford to be. But right now, he was the lucky one whose bed she shared. Maybe it was time he shut up and let his body do the talking.

He eased his arm out from under her.

"Giancarlo? What are you doing?"

"You're the one who wants the lights off. You'll just have to guess." He shifted in the bed and leaned close, breathing in her scent of sun-warmed rose, a hint of almond, musky sex.

His lips made contact with her shoulder, and she started. "Hmm," he murmured, "I wonder what I've found." He trailed his tongue over her, nipped lightly, sucked soft flesh into his mouth. Underneath the softness, he felt bone. "This one's easy. Collarbone. And that means . . ." He nibbled his way along it until he came to the delicate hollow at the base of her throat. "Mmm, what a sweet spot."

Her pulse speeded up against his lips.

His own pulse was hammering and his dick was throbbing. He pressed it against her thigh, needing that deliciously frustrating pressure. "God, you make me hard."

"I like you hard." She nudged his erection with her leg, increasing the tension.

He kissed his way up her neck, moving her springy hair

aside as he did. "You have shy ears, always hiding under all that hair." He freed one and licked the soft skin behind it. "Virgin skin, never before touched by man."

She gave a soft giggle and he said, "Let me have my illusions."

"It's probably true. Who ever kisses behind ears?"

Good point. He didn't. He wasn't a bad lover, but usually he focused on the obvious spots. But this was Rina, and he wanted to know every inch of her. In the dark. Then one day, when they made love in bright sunlight, he could discover her all over again.

If there was one thing he was positive of, it was that he'd never be satisfied having just one night with this woman. He hoped she felt—or could be persuaded to feel—the same way.

He nibbled the rim of her ear, then explored into the center as she shivered and let out a sigh. "I kiss the backs of ears, the rims, the inside shell," he whispered, letting his breath tickle the skin his kisses had moistened.

From her ear he moved to her face, kissing her forehead and hairline, finding soft baby hairs. "Because everywhere I kiss tastes and feels so nice." He dropped little kisses on her cheeks, tickled her nose with his eyelashes, then swallowed her giggle with another kiss.

A kiss that turned long and slow and sensual. God, but she could kiss.

Rina put her whole self into whatever she did, be it playing the clarinet, tasting lasagne or kissing her man.

It was a trait they had in common, the tendency to lose themselves totally in the moment.

And right now, he was perfectly happy to lose himself in her body, and in bringing her pleasure.

5

Giancarlo eased free from the kiss and leaned across her to lavish attention on her other ear. His chest brushed hers, hairy pecs against soft curves, and he loved the way she thrust up to press against him.

"Want something?" he teased.

"Your hands, your mouth on my breasts." With a sparkle of humor she said, "If it wouldn't be too much hardship."

"Your breasts are my idea of paradise." He slid down to play with them. Gently he caressed the unbelievably soft skin surrounding her areola as his mouth teased her nipple into a hard bud.

She sighed with pleasure. Lifting a hand she threaded her fingers through his hair, held his head against her. "You're a breast man?"

"Breasts, hips, a sweet ass. Curvy legs, gentle eyes, sexy lips."

"In other words, you like women," she said dryly.

"I like you, Rina Goldberg."

"That's a very good thing." Her teasing tone had softened. "Because I like you too."

Like. When he said the word, he meant he was strongly, maybe even deeply, attracted to her. Did she mean it the same way? Hoping so, he moved down to kiss his way across the soft skin that covered her ribs, then puffed air into her navel and followed it with his tongue.

Her hips twisted in a silent request that he move lower, then she sighed. "I should be doing something. Not just lying here, enjoying."

"Enjoy, Rina. Feeling you respond gives me so much pleasure."

"You're unselfish," she murmured.

Was he? It didn't feel that way. "Today I've been given a wonderful gift. Having you in my arms. This is the best way I know to celebrate that gift." He blew another puff of air into her navel. "Sensually." Then he circled the soft hollow with the tip of his tongue. "Erotically."

She shivered. "I like the way you celebrate."

His hands moved outward to find her hips, so strong and curvy. His nonna would say she'd been built for childbearing. Seemed to him she'd been designed for a man's enjoyment. He began to play the notes from "Für Elise" again, rippling his fingers over the flare of a hip.

"You play that piece so well," she murmured.

"It's because I have such a fine instrument."

With a lighter touch, he moved across the gentle curve of her belly. "So soft, so womanly." Then into her springy pubic hair. Thank God she didn't wax away those womanly curls. He leaned down to press moist kisses along her bikini line.

She moaned, pelvis twisting against him. "God, Giancarlo, you know exactly how to touch me. Even better than when we were kids."

He'd been a virgin. It was only the magic between them that

had let him please her at all. Now he had experience to add to the magic. He slipped his mouth between her legs, where her labia were hot and full, slick with her juices. Delicately, he licked her. A cat lapping cream.

"Oh yes," she whimpered. "More."

She was close to coming, he realized, so he firmed his tongue, stroked harder, then sucked gently on her clit.

"God, yes," she cried as the spasms of climax shuddered through her.

Gently he eased two fingers inside her and her body gripped them. After a moment her muscles relaxed and he slid another finger in. A fresh gush of moisture greeted it, giving him plenty of lubrication as he thrust his fingers in and out, mimicking sex. "Beautiful lover," he murmured against her clit, knowing that, even if she couldn't hear the words, she'd feel his lips, his breath.

Her hips writhed, telling him her arousal was peaking again.

His dick ached with the need to come, but he held back. One more, just for her, to tell her how wonderful she was.

He curved his fingers inside her, found her G-spot and stroked, and at the same time he teased her clit with his tongue. He heard that keening sound, then he felt her body come apart around him.

She came generously, extravagantly, no holding back. Making him want her even more.

When the tremors eased, he slipped away from her and found a condom. She was still gasping for breath, her breasts heaving, when he spread his body over hers and kissed her.

He wished he could see her face, yet memory supplied the image.

Her mouth met his. Then she spread her legs wider and reached between them. Gripping him, she murmured, none too coherently, "So big. Hard. Want you."

"God, yes."

So much for patience. His had run out. He rolled, taking her with him, then said, "Sit up. I want you on top."

She shifted position until she sat astride his pelvis. Then she raised her body and he reached between them, grabbed his dick and found her entrance, soaking wet for him.

With one quick thrust he entered her and they both moaned. "So good," he told her, stopping to enjoy all the sensations.

He stroked her thighs, wishing the lights were on so he could see her above him. And yet, he could. Full breasts with rosy tips, black hair a wild, sexy tangle, cheeks flushed from sex. Funny how memory and imagination filled in the blanks.

"Okay, I'm on top," she said, speaking more coherently than a few minutes ago. "Any other requests?"

He considered for a moment, then decided that anything she did would be just fine with him. Flinging out his arms dramatically even though she couldn't see him, he said, "Use me however you will. My body's at your disposal."

She sucked in a breath. "Now there's an appealing thought. Mmm, let me see, how shall I dispose of you?" Slowly she raised her body, only an inch or two, baring the base of his shaft to the air. Then, equally slowly, she lowered herself.

"Killing me with sex would be good," he gasped. Very, very slowly, the way she was doing. Drawing out the actions, pausing in between. Talking, shifting their focus away from the drive toward orgasm, yet tantalizing him with innuendo.

His fingers went back to her thighs and drifted up the inside. "I dare you to try."

She lifted and lowered again. "I have a friend who's a lawyer. I'm sure she'd find a way to get me off."

Her phrasing made him laugh. "Ah, Rina, it's me who's supposed to be getting you off."

She laughed too. "And so far you've succeeded very nicely."

Again she raised and lowered herself, then again. A little

pause at the top, another at the bottom. Each time picking up the pace a bit. Her pussy gripped him with a velvety touch that stimulated every inch of him as she slid back and forth. Stimulated, tantalized, increased his arousal to the point he wanted to thrust hard, fast, over and over.

But then he'd come and this bliss would be over. Instead, he let her control the action.

He'd never been one to give over control in any area of his life, but when it came to sex he trusted Rina.

She leaned forward, changing the angle, and gripped his shoulders to brace her body. He reached up, found her breasts and cupped them in both hands. Gently, so he could feel them sway as her body rose and fell on his.

The muscles inside her began a rhythmic contract-and-release that matched the slip-slide of her flesh on his. Neither of them spoke now. The only sound was the rasp of his breathing, her whimpers and the soft sucking, slapping sounds their bodies made when they came together.

The air was rich with the scent of summer roses and sultry sex, and Rina's nipples were tightly furled buds under his fingertips.

He couldn't take it any longer; he had to thrust. As her body lowered, he rose to meet her, driving his dick deeper into her welcoming heat.

She bucked and cried, "Oh yes!" Then she picked up her pace, matching his, both of them driving, slamming together, harder and faster.

Rina straightened her torso again, so he had to let go of her breasts. Then her hand was reaching back, cradling his balls as they drew tight. "Jesus," he gasped, knowing he'd come any second now.

But that was okay because she was making that sound of hers and her body began to shudder. Giancarlo let himself go, let the pure bliss of the moment carry him away. The orgasm ripped through him. He let out a yell as he buried himself to the hilt in her lush, lovely body.

Rina woke in the dark, disoriented.

Sensations came slowly. First, the awareness of her own body. Heavy, satiated, pleasantly achy. Sticky between the thighs. In the air, the smell of sex. And beside her . . .

Oh God, she'd done it. Really done it. All of it. Decided to break up with Al and had sex with Giancarlo.

She froze. Was she crazy? What did this mean?

The sex had been out of this world, but now what?

Was this a one-nighter or the beginning of something? But how could it be *something* when he'd only be in town for a short time? When they were opposites in so many ways?

Reality crashed in on her. She was still the same Rina Goldberg, not some skinny, glitzy entertainment-biz babe. If she stayed here, dawn would come and . . .

And Giancarlo would see her. Naked. Every inch and every pound.

Besides, what about her neighbor, Levi Fischman? He'd be expecting her to knock on his door at seven for their morning walk.

She shouldn't be here, naked in a luxury hotel with a music video director. She belonged at home with her cat.

Rina inched her way cautiously to the edge of the bed, then held her breath. Giancarlo hadn't stirred and his breathing was slow and regular. Not a snore, just a contented, restful sound.

She slipped out of bed and dared to slide the curtain back a couple of inches so she could find her clothes, which lay scattered about the room. When she'd gathered everything, she crept into the bathroom, closed the door and turned on the light.

"Oh God," she moaned as she stared at her reflection. How

could she walk out of the hotel looking like a crazed gypsy? Not to mention smelling like an orgy.

She moistened a washcloth and cleaned herself up a bit, then hurried into her clothes. Running damp fingers through her hair, she tried to tame it into some semblance of order.

Straightening her shoulders, she wrapped her fringed scarf securely around herself then turned off the bathroom light and opened the door. Holding her shoes in one hand, she tiptoed across the carpet to the door, where she turned and gazed longingly at the bed.

Would she ever see Giancarlo again?

Would he be upset she'd left this way, or relieved not to have to deal with a morning after?

Stifling a sigh, she opened the heavy door and stepped into the corridor. Her pumps felt tight, the heels too high for easy walking, and her legs were so limp they could barely hold her up. Still, it wasn't like she had an alternative. The marble of the Opus's lobby floor would feel wonderful to her bare feet, but she suspected the night staff wouldn't be impressed.

She glanced at her watch as she rode down in the elevator. Three o'clock. She'd probably caught a couple of hours sleep and could get another couple at home. Normally she didn't need more than four or five anyhow.

The elevator dinged and she lifted her chin and sauntered brazenly out. A slim young man in the hotel's black uniform stepped from behind the desk. "Is your car valet parked, miss?" he asked.

"No, I'll need a taxi, thanks."

"There's one outside now."

As he escorted her toward the front door, she thought that maybe it wasn't such an unusual thing for guests to depart the hotel in the wee small hours. After all, the Opus did cater to the entertainment industry, and showbiz folks probably kept weird schedules.

The staff person and the taxi driver both leaped to open the cab door for her, and she slid into the back seat with a murmured "Thanks" to both. Then she told the driver, "Don Francesco's restaurant on Burrard."

"But it will be closed." A dark face topped with a turban turned to her, brown eyes concerned.

"I know. But I parked my car there."

"Ah, yes, I see." The man turned back and pulled away from the curb. The streets were almost deserted and he made an illegal U-turn—flashing a white grin over his shoulder—then drove swiftly up Davie. She directed him to her car and paid him.

She noticed that he waited until she was safely in her Honda and had turned on the engine and lights before he drove away.

As she headed toward the Lions Gate Bridge, Rina thought it was a lucky thing traffic was so sparse. Her brain wasn't inclined to concentrate on driving.

This had been a romantic, amazing, incredibly sexy night. On the other hand, what the hell did she think she was doing?

"I need a Foursome lunch," she finally said, and immediately felt better. Every once in a while, one of the girls called an emergency lunch to discuss a matter of dire importance.

"It's my turn." Over the summer, first Suzanne, then Jenny, then Ann had done it, and all over the same issue. Men.

She zipped across the Lions Gate and along the familiar route home, and soon was letting herself in her back door. Sabine didn't come to greet her and, when Rina located her in her basket in the music room, the cat merely deigned to open one eye, then close it decisively again.

"Fine, shun me," Rina told her. "You'll miss hearing a good story."

Yawning, she headed for bed. She should shower but preferred to savor the feel of Giancarlo on her skin for another few hours, so instead stripped off her clothes and tumbled between the sheets, where she promptly fell asleep.

She woke to her alarm. Right. Time to put on sweats, bundle her hair into a baseball cap and go walking with seventy-something Levi Fischman, a neighbor she'd grown close to over the years. In fact, sometimes she'd swear he was channeling Aunt Rivka, all the way from Toronto.

They'd instituted the morning exercise routine three months ago after Levi returned home after heart bypass surgery. She'd had him over for tea, and he'd said his doctor told him to start walking.

"I like gardening," he'd said, "but I got no use for walking. Waste of time. Boring. Lonely. What's the point?"

"Your health." She poured more tea into their bone china cups. "Stop kvetching and be glad you're alive."

He lifted his cup to his lips and peeped slyly over the top. "You don't get enough exercise either."

Yeah, because she'd always hated exercise and thought it a waste of time. But how could she say that? She'd undermine his doctor's efforts to improve his health. So she'd forced a smile and said, "You're right. Let's walk together."

And they had been, religiously every weekday morning at seven o'clock. They'd started with a mile of sauntering and were now up to three miles at a decent pace. She was surprised to find herself enjoying it. This form of exercise wasn't so bad and, while she hadn't lost any weight, her body was firming up.

This morning she kept falling behind. It wasn't that she was tired, but her thoughts drifted to last night with Giancarlo.

"You're dragging your butt, girlie," Levi said. "Whassa matter? Spend the night out on the town?"

"Something like that." She tossed him a grin. "A lovely dinner at an Italian restaurant, with champagne and an operatic serenade."

His face crinkled into a hundred wrinkles as he smiled. "Good for you. You got that Al towing the line."

Oh damn. She shouldn't have said anything, not until she broke up with Al. She ducked her head. "It wasn't Al. I won't be seeing him anymore."

Levi stopped and pulled her to a stop too. They were both the same height, five-foot-eight, so he could really get in her face. "That man hurt you, Rina? I'll go and, and . . ." He spluttered as he hunted for the right words.

"Defend my honor?"

"Bust his balls."

She chuckled. "You're a tiger, but leave his balls alone. He didn't do anything. It's me." And telling Al she was breaking up was going to be plenty bad enough of a ballbuster.

"You met someone else? This champagne singer guy?"

"He wasn't the one who sang," she said absently. "Come on, we're supposed to be walking." She started off, taking the route that led gently uphill past houses of increasing grandeur.

He scrambled to catch up. "So, you got *two* more men? A champagne one and a singer? Way to go, girlie."

"The singer isn't mine. Well, the champagne guy isn't either. He's just . . ." A one-night stand? "An old friend."

"Sounds like he treats you right. Treats you the way you deserve."

Did she deserve champagne and compliments? Stunning sex? "He did treat me well," she admitted. "But he's in entertainment so it's probably normal for him."

"Hey, big spender," Levi sang off-key, "spend a little time with me."

She chuckled again. "Ouch. As a musician, I have to say your voice hurts my ears."

"Dontcha always say, it's the love of music that counts?"

"I'm not sure that qualifies as music," she teased. "Now

come on, we're behind schedule." And she'd just as soon avoid more questions about Giancarlo.

They pushed the pace, each breaking a sweat, giving an occasional wave and a "Good morning" to neighbors out walking their dogs or collecting the morning paper. Both avid gardeners—taking instruction from Mrs. Zabriski, the neighborhood authority—they studied the yards as they strode by and commented on anything that had changed since yesterday morning.

North Van was green. Lots of evergreens and deciduous trees and lush expanses of lawn, thanks to the plentiful rainfall. Most residents had the money to pay for landscaping, and the gardens had lovely touches of color. Although, at this time of year, the flowering trees and bushes were mostly over, and the maples were turning gold and red.

A couple of blocks from home, they slowed for a cooldown. "Always feel like a horse when we do this," Levi said. "Just when I want to rush home and stick my nose in the feed bag, someone's making me go slow."

"Your doctor said it was a good idea to start out and finish off more slowly."

"Doctors, schmoctors, what do they know?"

"Enough to keep your ticker ticking." She bumped her arm against his. "For which I'm grateful."

"So, this champagne guy," he said. "He Jewish?"

She sighed. Too much to hope he'd have forgotten. "No. He's Italian, so I'd guess Catholic."

"Ouch. Your mama'd roll over in her grave."

"Come on, we're not even dating."

"So what's not *dating* about champagne and fancy food?"

"One dinner with an old friend. I'm not even sure he'll get in touch again. He's only in town for work; I'm sure he's busy."

"You back in the dark ages, girlie? These days, can't women call men? They still s'posed to sit home by the phone, waiting?"

"Yeah, I'm back in the dark ages. It's not in my makeup to call a guy."

"A man should be so lucky as to have Rina Goldberg phone him. Why, if I was twenty years younger . . ."

"Make it forty and I might've taken you up on that," she teased, but she put an arm around him and gave him a hug. "Okay, I have to go in and get ready. I have a lesson at nine."

In the kitchen, Sabine greeted her warmly, twining around her ankles.

"So now you're friendly." Rina glanced at the empty food bowl. "Yeah, that'd explain it. Okay, I'll give you breakfast but I don't have time to stay and talk."

After attending to Sabine, Rina grabbed an apple cinnamon yogurt and hurried to the music room to e-mail her friends about lunch. When she opened her e-mail program she found a message from Giancarlo, sent at six.

Rina, why did you leave? It would have been wonderful to wake up with you. Last night was fantastic and I can't wait to see you again. I have a long day, we'll be shooting late. Are you busy tonight? Thank heavens we're both night owls. Can we get together around ten? A late dinner at my hotel, perhaps? Whatever you want— I just want to be with you.

I'm going to hit the hotel gym, since you aren't here to give me anything better to do. E-mail me back, or if you don't get this message until later, call me on my cell.

He gave his cell number, then ended with:

Hugs and kisses, and other good stuff.
Giancarlo.

"Oh my." She stared at the screen, yogurt spoon sticking out of her mouth.

Well, that answered one question. He didn't want it to be just a one-nighter. And he assumed she felt the same.

"So, how *do* I feel?" she asked, staring at Sabine, who unhelpfully just stared back.

Rina spooned up another bite of yogurt and ate it slowly. "Of course I want to see him, but I'm not sure it's a good idea."

"Mmrp?"

"For all sorts of reasons." Then she glanced at her watch. "Damn, I don't have time for this."

Giancarlo didn't know she'd picked up his e-mail. She could wait until this afternoon and call his cell. After she got the girls' advice.

There was another thing she needed advice on. How to tell Al she was turning down his proposal.

"*Oy veh,* what a day it's shaping up to be!"

She hurried to get ready for her nine o'clock lesson, dressing in her usual comfortable outfit of long skirt and loose top, brightened with sparkly chandelier-style earrings.

Tara was a pre-med student who said she had to keep up with the piano or she'd become a science nerd. Because of the girl's financial circumstances, Rina gave her a fee discount.

At five past nine, Tara rushed in, her long carrot-colored hair caught up in a haphazard ponytail. "Sorry, sorry. I fell asleep studying last night and didn't set my alarm."

"It's okay. Relax and get settled."

Tara flashed her a quick grin. "I'd kill for a cup of strong black coffee. I didn't have time to stop at Starbucks on my way."

"Coming up."

In the kitchen, Rina prepared coffee—her favorite blend, from Umbria. Italian, like Giancarlo. The sound of scales drifted from the music room, starting slow then getting faster. Tara'd been playing since she was eight and was very good for an amateur. Right now she was on a Schubert kick. She began to play the piece they'd been working on, "Piano Sonata in B Flat." Played a little too fast.

Oops. Rina winced as Tara made a mistake and said, "Crap." She poured coffee into mugs and went back to the music room. "Slow down, you're rushing it."

"Sorry. Rushing's the story of my life these days."

"And you're playing the piano so you'll remember to slow down and savor the good things in life. Right?"

Tara laughed and raised a hand to straighten her wire-rim glasses. "Would you put that on a Post-It note and stick it on my music?"

Her student had meant it as a joke but Rina went to her desk, found a pad of bright pink Post-Its and wrote, in big block letters, "SLOW DOWN! FEEL THE MUSIC." She slapped the note down over the title of the sonata. "Don't take that off."

"Yes ma'am." Tara giggled, took a cautious sip of hot coffee. "Let me try this again. *Slow-ly.*" She drew the last word out.

"Go for it."

Rina settled in the chair beside the piano and, as Tara began to play, Sabine hopped into her lap and curled up in a purring ball. The cat loved music and was completely indiscriminate. She'd purr approval to the worst fumblings of a rank beginner as well as to playing like Tara's that really merited appreciation.

Rina took a sip of her coffee. Italy. It had great coffee, great food. Great opera. At least one fantastic lover . . .

Damn, her thoughts were drifting. Guiltily she refocused on the music only to find Tara was finishing the piece. "You played that well. I don't know if it helped *you* relax, but it sure helped me."

"Great. Let me do another."

Tara had just started working on the next sonata a couple of weeks earlier, and her fingering wasn't as sure. Rina stopped her a few times to offer suggestions, and once took the bench herself to demonstrate.

"You make it seem so easy," Tara said. "And piano's not even your main instrument."

"I've spent a lot of time at it." And the truth was, Rina was a natural musician. She'd been born with that talent—thanks to genes on her mom's side of the family. Her parents had recognized it early and encouraged it.

Her mom had wanted everything for her. To be good in school, popular and a brilliant musician. She couldn't see how hard it was to have a social life what with all the moving, the hours of practice and the reputation of being a musical wunderkind. Not to mention being Jewish when no one else was and having a big nose, frizzy hair and an unfashionably plump, curvy bod.

Tara ran through the sonata again, getting into the emotion of the music now that she was more confident of playing the right notes. When she finished, she swung around, face glowing. "I love this!"

Rina grinned back. "I know."

"I feel recharged, and ready to face the day." Tara reached into her backpack and found her wallet. As she handed over a twenty, she said, "You're so good about my fees. I promise, promise, promise, when I'm a rich doctor I'll pay you back."

"Just keep playing. That's my best reward."

After Tara had gone, Rina checked messages and found all the girls had confirmed lunch at twelve. Jenny recommended a place she and Scott had gone to, called Hell's Kitchen, on Fourth Avenue. Rina noted the address.

As she walked past the piano, she shook her head. "Oh, Tara." The girl's "Sonata in B Flat" music still sat there, with the "slow down" note attached.

Okay, time to get in some practice. She'd been given a list of the repertoire from which the audition would draw, and now pulled out her music.

After practice, she packed her B flat and A clarinets into their double case to go for a lesson. Not all performers at her level took lessons, but from time to time she valued getting another perspective on her work. Once or twice a year she flew to San Francisco to work with the principal there, a woman she greatly admired. And occasionally she took a lesson in Vancouver from Thomas Field, a British Columbian who'd played first clarinet with the London Symphony Orchestra but had to retire because of arthritis.

She was on her way to get a sweater when the doorbell rang.

Sabine, who was nervous with strangers, skittered across the hall and disappeared into the bedroom.

"Oh my God, are you sure you have the right house?" Rina said when she opened the front door to a delivery boy holding a vase with two or three dozen peach-colored roses.

"Goldberg?"

"Yes, that's me." Carefully she took the heavy vase, and the scent of the flowers made her bury her nose in the velvet blooms. "But who on earth . . . ?"

"Someone who thinks a lot of you." He gave her a grin. "There's a note. Enjoy."

"Thanks."

Dazed, she moved inside and went to put the vase on top of the piano. She extracted the note, which read,

> *Bella, this is the closest I can come to your beauty and*
> *your lovely scent. But they pale in comparison.*
>   *Giancarlo.*

The handwriting was bold and black, and she guessed he'd actually gone to the florist shop, picked out the flowers, looked up her address and written the note rather than arranging it all over the phone.

"Well, just . . . holy shit."

No one had ever done anything like this before. She wasn't the kind of woman who prompted romantic, extravagant gestures. Oh my, but this felt good.

She glanced at her watch and pulled herself from her dreamy reverie. "Damn, I'm going to be late."

She grabbed up her clarinet case and music and rushed out to her car, realizing when she got there that she'd forgotten a sweater. Absent-minded and in a rush, just like Tara. Oh well, she could live without it.

Thanks to some pretty serious speeding, she arrived on time, though a little frazzled.

One thing she loved about playing the clarinet was that the moment she got into the music, she lost herself. Whatever was going on in her own life, it didn't matter. Everything gave way to the power of the music.

Today, as she ran through the pieces she'd practiced, the music worked its usual magic. When she finished, Thomas, a distinguished man with deep-set black eyes and silver hair, clapped. "Brava, Rina."

"Any suggestions?"

He shrugged. "It's a matter of personal interpretation, as you know. Here, see what you think of this." He took up his own B flat and began to play one of the pieces, but a little differently.

She listened carefully. The man was an amazing musician. Such a pity his arthritis had robbed him of the ability to play for more than half an hour at a time. "I see the difference."

She picked up her own instrument and gave it a try, then played the movement the way she'd played it before. "I honestly don't know. I like them both."

"Record them, then play back and listen. Each tells a slightly different story. Your ear will know which one is yours."

"Thanks. I'll do that. Any other advice?" It was her last lesson before the audition.

He laughed. "Only what you already know. Practice, practice until your body knows the music by heart. Then forget about the audition committee and let the music fill you. That's what works best for you, Rina. Relax, let go, enjoy." He gave her a big smile. "After all, isn't that why we play? For love of the music?"

"It is."

As she drove away, she thought of Giancarlo and the difference between them as musicians. She loved music. Even if she'd never been able to make a living playing, music would still have been a part of her life, as with Tara. But Giancarlo had abandoned the piano, which to her meant he'd never really loved music.

Sad. He was missing so much.

Ann had e-mailed that her car was in for an oil change today, so Rina'd arranged to pick her up on her way through town. She pulled the Honda into a loading zone on Georgia and listened to CBC FM as she waited. After a couple of minutes, her friend burst from the glass door of one of the office towers and hurried toward her.

Ann slid into the passenger seat. "Sorry I'm late. Had to get off the phone with a client."

"I just got here." Rina smiled at her. "You look nice."

"Same old clothes."

It's true, Ann wore her usual tailored suit, plain blouse and conservative pumps, but a coral-colored scarf brightened the outfit and matched her earrings. More important, she looked rested, healthy and happy. "The new Ann, though," Rina said.

Ann grinned. "I'll give you that." Then her smile faded. "What's up? Are you okay?"

"I'm fine." Rina pulled out of the loading zone. "Just confused. Now, what's the best route to take to get to Kitsilano?"

She followed Ann's instructions and soon they were parking on the street, half a block away from Hell's Kitchen.

Inside, the room was dark. Jenny stood out, though, in a bright pink sweater. She was chatting with a waitress about—as Rina found out when she and Ann arrived at the table—the selection of pizzas.

Ann took the seat beside Jen, and Rina sat on the other side of the table. "Jenny, you know I don't eat pizza." It was one of the foods on her forbidden list because of the calories in the crust.

"Hi to you too, and I'm dying to know why you called this lunch. And," Jen grinned, "they have salads too. Great sounding salads."

"Okay, you're forgiven."

The waitress took their orders for soft drinks, then went away.

Ann studied the menu. "I should have salad too. It's healthier."

"God." Jen grabbed her head between both hands. "Now there's two of you. And here I thought Adonis was a *good* influence."

Ann's lips twitched. "Maybe I'll have pizza and just not tell him. Pizza with lots of meat on it. When he cooks, it's mostly vegetarian."

"Thank God Scott eats meat," Jenny said fervently, then waved as Suzanne hurried over.

Suze, golden hair in a thick braid today, slid into the chair beside Rina. "You okay?"

"Mostly yes." She thought about sex with Giancarlo, the roses, his desire to see her again. "But I have too much to process by myself. I need help. Let's order, and I'll tell you all about it."

6

They studied the fancy menu, debated, then Jenny, Ann and Suzanne decided to split a pizza with pesto, smoked chicken, sundried tomatoes, roasted almonds and asiago. Rina chose a spinach salad with julienne peppers, pancetta bacon, sautéed wild mushrooms, crispy onions and feta in sundried tomato vinaigrette.

When they'd placed their orders, Jenny said to Rina, "Okay, girl, spill it."

Rina toyed with one of her dangly earrings. "It. Well I guess *it* is Giancarlo."

"You contacted him?" Ann asked. "Have you heard back?"

"You have, haven't you?" Suzanne said. "And now you're debating what to do."

"I'm way ahead of you," Rina said. "I met him for dinner last night."

"Oh wow!" Jenny said, as Ann asked, "How did it go?" and Suzanne said, "What was he like?"

Rina took a deep breath. "It was the most romantic evening I've ever spent in my life."

"Oh. My. God." Jenny said the words slowly. "And you're Little Miss Romance. This sounds serious."

"It's not *serious*," Rina said promptly, "but it was a lot of fun. I even started to get used to his hokey flattery."

"What do you mean?" Ann asked.

"He kept giving me compliments, effusive ones. I think it's an Italian male thing. Insincere and over the top."

"Well, he is in the entertainment biz," Jenny commented. "Guess it goes with the turf."

"Are you sure he wasn't being sincere?" Suzanne asked.

"Oh puh-lease." Rina rolled her eyes.

"So, it was one of those things where one minute the guy's flattering you," Jen asked, "and the next moment he's gaping at some long-legged blonde." She shot a teasing wink at Suzanne, a long-legged blonde.

"N-no," Rina said. "Giancarlo barely took his eyes off me all night. And his eyes . . ." She gave a shiver of sexual awareness as she remembered. "He looked intense, passionate, like he was seriously into me."

"And you felt sparks, right?" Suzanne asked.

Rina nodded.

"Hah!" Jenny pumped a fist into the air. "I knew you were a sparks girl at heart. You just needed the right guy."

"But he's not. He's this jet-setting music video director and I'm an at-home girl. He'll be here only another few days and then God knows where he'll be. Somewhere else, with someone else."

The other three glanced at each other, then Ann said, "Okay, that does sound like a problem, if you were thinking long term. Are you?"

"Of course not," Rina said promptly. "We're way too different from each other."

Jenny tapped a long pink fingernail on the table, drawing

their attention. "Hello? Sparks? You can't ignore sparks. You have to find out where they lead."

"I already know." Rina wasn't sure whether to moan or laugh. "Into bed. For amazing sex."

"You had sex with him?" Jenny squealed. "Already? Last night? On a first date?"

"Okay, now the whole restaurant knows I'm easy," Rina grumbled, but she couldn't help grinning. It was fun to be the outrageous one for a change, rather than her normal conservative self.

"Rina?" Suzanne frowned over the rim of her glass of Diet Coke. "What about Al?"

Well, so much for her moment of exhilaration. Rina sighed. "I can't marry Al."

"Wow, big decision," Jenny said. "How did he take it?"

Rina gulped. "Uh, I haven't had a chance to talk to him. I decided last night and broke up with him in my head."

"In your head?" Suzanne was frowning.

"Look, I didn't know until I was with Giancarlo. You girls told me that seeing him would help me resolve my feelings about Al, and it did. I knew." She glanced around. Jen was grinning, Ann nodded, and Suzanne's face still wore a frown.

"Yeah, I know, I acted pretty sleazy."

"It's not like you," Suzanne said softly.

"No. All I can say is, the thing with Giancarlo felt so damned *special*. It was one of those opportunities that might only come along once, and I really, really wanted it."

"You're sure you're breaking up with Al?" Ann asked. "Even if things don't work out long term with Giancarlo?"

"Positive. But I wanted your advice first." She shook her head. "I really do feel crappy about it. I didn't mean to hurt him, to lead him on."

"Lead him on? Gimme a break," Jen said.

"You wouldn't do that," Ann said. "You were honest with him, right? He was the one who pushed for something you weren't ready for."

"Yes, but I did sleep with him."

"And everyone knows that means you have to get married," Jenny said with an eye roll.

"She's right," Ann said. "No one thinks that way. You were taking it slow, seeing where the relationship might go. And now you know it's not going anywhere because you don't have strong enough feelings for him. Right?"

Rina nodded. "Exactly."

They broke off as their waitress brought their lunches. Rina forked a bit of crispy onion from the top of her salad. It was so good she barely felt envious as the others pulled gooey slices of pizza free from the big circle.

"So what do I tell him?" she asked. "I don't want to hurt him any more than I have to."

"What are you thinking of saying?" Suzanne asked.

"I guess . . . that I really like him, I've enjoyed getting to know him, and I'm flattered by his proposal. But I don't feel—" She broke off and glanced at Ann. "You said it well. I don't have strong enough feelings for him."

Ann nodded. "Okay. And if he's pushy like he was on the weekend, he'll counter with, 'Those feelings will develop in time'."

Rina suppressed a smile. Ann, the lawyer. "They won't," she said firmly. "I mean, we might have an affectionate relationship, but I want more." She frowned, thinking that those words sounded familiar. "Oh God, this is what you went through with David, isn't it? He seemed like the man you'd been waiting for, but you weren't in love with him."

"Yeah," Ann said. "And sometimes it takes a while to figure that out."

"How is he, by the way?" Suzanne asked.

"Bearing up admirably." Ann gave a wry grin. "He's already flirting with one of the young paralegals. I told him I thought he needed time on his own to figure out what he wants, and he should be wary of rebound relationships. Obviously he didn't listen."

"Thinking with his dick," Jenny said.

"Or his male ego," Ann responded. "I hurt his pride, therefore he's got to prove he can get a younger, prettier woman." She turned to Rina, who'd been enjoying her salad while the others talked. "How do you think Al will respond? Will he be shattered? Mad?"

"God, I hope neither one." She glanced around at the others, who were munching pizza. "Do I say I hope we can stay friends?"

"Depends on his personality," Jenny said. "Some guys take it as a sign you haven't really said no. They keep thinking there's hope."

"Guess I'll have to play it by ear."

The other three nodded, and for a couple of minutes they all ate in silence.

Then Jenny said, "Okay, Rina, you good with the Al stuff?"

"As good as I can be until I get it over with. Why?"

"Because I want to hear about sex with Giancarlo. Are his fingers just as talented as when you first knew him?" Jenny rippled her pizza-stained fingers like she was playing the piano.

This was a change of subject Rina was delighted to follow. She grinned. "Fingers? Oh yeah. Not to mention his other natural assets. The man's definitely talented."

"How many O's?" Jenny probed.

"Jesus, Jen, you have absolutely no boundaries, do you?"

Jenny shook her head vigorously, sending her pink flamingo earrings dancing. "Nope."

Rina couldn't hold back another grin. "Well, since you insist. Let me add them up." She raised her left hand and counted on her fingers. "Okay, the first time there was mouth, then cock. The second time . . ." She stopped talking—not being quite so bold about sharing intimate details as her friends were—and kept tapping fingers until she finished with her thumb.

"Five?" Ann said loudly. She dropped her voice. "He gave you five, on your first night together?"

"I *like* that man," Jenny said.

"We're good together," Rina admitted. "And it's the other stuff too. The way he plays music across my skin, kisses me everywhere. He does have a magic touch."

"So, what next?" Suzanne asked. "Once you break up with Al, you're seeing Giancarlo again?"

"He asked if he could see me tonight, but I haven't answered yet. And this morning he sent these incredible roses. Peach colored. Three dozen, in a gigantic vase."

"Wow. *I'll* see him if you don't want to," Ann joked.

"He's seriously hot for you," Jenny chimed in. "You have to see him again. How can you resist roses and orgasms? And don't forget sparks."

"But you're a romantic, Rina," Suzanne said, a note of caution in her voice. "If there's really no way the two of you could end up together, is it smart to keep seeing him? What if you fall for him? He sounds like a man it'd be easy to fall for."

Rina shook her head. "Sure, the romantic gestures are . . . amazing, and so is the sex, but that stuff is superficial. For me, there has to be substance. Shared values. I want a man who's a nester, not a high flyer. And one who respects music, for God's sake."

"Didn't you have those things with Al?" Ann asked softly.

"Yeah." She sighed. "But I wanted the romance and passionate sex too."

"Put the two guys together and split them down the middle just right, you'll get your perfect man," Jenny said.

"True," Rina agreed, laughing. "But since that's not going to happen, what do I do?"

"If you're so sure you won't lose your heart to him, why not get together?" Ann said. "Seems to me, you learn things from each relationship. With Al, you learned you really wanted that spark. Seeing Giancarlo again confirmed it. There'll be some other lesson to be learned if you spend more time together."

"Yeah, like how to exceed any normal woman's orgasm quotient," Jenny quipped. "A lesson you gotta promise to share with us."

Suzanne put down her slice of pizza. "Rina, do you *want* to see him again?"

"Yes. Mostly."

"But you have hesitations?"

"I had one perfect evening. Another wonderful memory to add to the Banff ones. If he sees me again, things will change. Maybe he won't find me attractive. Maybe we'll get in a fight over all the things we disagree about."

"You can *maybe* yourself to death," Jenny said.

"If any of those things happen," Ann put in, "then *maybe* that's where you learn the lesson."

"Besides, nothing can touch the perfect memories," Suzanne said. "Remember, that's what you all told me when I decided to look for Jaxon, after we'd had that one magical afternoon on Crete."

But it had worked out for Suzanne. With her and Jaxon, the magic was still strong.

Right. And if it fizzled between Rina and Giancarlo, then she'd have a great memory but wouldn't romanticize him. She'd be free to get on with her life. To find that man who was part Al and part Giancarlo.

"You're right," she said. "I'll tell him yes. Now, the next question is, do I want to do what he suggested? Go to his hotel for a late dinner? Last night he was in control of everything—the location, food, champagne, the 'Nessun Dorma', the—"

"Whoa!" Jenny held up her hands in a stop gesture. "What the hell's a 'Nessun Dorma' and what's this about champagne?"

"Yes, Rina," Ann said, "you've clearly left out a few important details."

"You're sure you have time to listen to it all?" Rina teased, knowing they were dying to.

Three heads nodded insistently.

So she told them, and their eyes grew wide and wider. She ended up with, "So, last night Giancarlo made all the decisions."

"Decisions like buying Veuve Clicquot champagne and having a love song sung to you?" Suzanne said. "I like his kind of decisions."

"Yeah, but I understand Rina's point," Ann said. "A relationship has to be equal. Giancarlo may have lots of money and do romantic stuff, but he shouldn't dominate Rina."

"Tell me how buying a girl champagne fits into the category of dominating?" Jenny asked.

"It's more like overwhelming," Rina said. "He's so... much, I feel almost intimidated. And if we're at his hotel, he'll be in charge again."

"So ask him to your place," Jenny said. "It's not like you live with five thousand Chinese relatives."

Rina's lips twitched. Jenny's parents, sister, grandmother and aunt hardly equaled five thousand. Still, it was true that live-at-home Jen sure couldn't take a man home to bed, or even home for dinner, without it becoming a huge family issue.

"I think that's a good idea," Ann said. "Last night he showed you who he was. Wealthy, extravagant, hobnobbing with a man who owns a restaurant and sings opera, staying at that ritzy hotel. Tonight, show him who you are."

"You are so not selling me on the idea," Rina said. "He'd be bored to tears."

"Why?" Ann's eyes flashed. "You're not boring. Your house, your interests, are equally valid and interesting as his. Different, but—"

"And you already know the two of you are different," Suzanne broke in. "If he's bored going to your lovely house and having a snack by the fire with some of your music playing, then that's not such a bad thing to know."

"A fire," Rina murmured. "I haven't had a fire yet this fall, but the weather's getting cool enough. I love fires."

"See if he does," Jenny said. "And find out if your cat likes him. Animals are good judges of character, right, Suzie?"

Vet student Suzanne grinned. "Absolutely. Yes, Rina, take him home and introduce him to Sabine."

Giancarlo in her house. The cozy home she'd created. The home that welcomed her girlfriends, fellow musicians and neighbors. "When I think about the man I ate dinner with last night . . . Him, in my house?" She shook her head. "I can't make that picture work."

"Well, that definitely tells you something," Ann said, her tone sad.

"You're judging him," Jenny said sternly. "Like I did with Scott. Saw a hottie firefighter and figured he'd be a blue collar dimwit. Turned out the guy's bright and deep, and he's taught me way more than I've ever taught him."

"She's right," Ann said, perking up. "Absolutely right. Don't judge by your first impression. Give the man a chance."

Rina chewed the last bite of salad as she reflected. Then she said, "Ann, would you mind getting a cab back to the office?"

"Of course not," Ann said, just as Jenny said, "I'll give you a ride."

"What're you going to do?" Suzanne asked Rina.

"Go to Granville Island and pick up some snacks at the market. Cold meats, cheeses, marinated vegetables, salads. Ten's too late for a real meal; besides I'm not much of a cook. But we can snack and drink wine." She smiled at Ann. "By the fire, like you said. So keep your fingers crossed the weather doesn't warm up."

"Don't forget to pick up some bread, crackers, stuff like that," Jenny said. "Remember, normal people do eat carbs."

Later in the afternoon, Rina was back home, groceries stowed away in the kitchen. She had a couple of after-school lessons with kids, but today a double set of nerves made it impossible to concentrate.

Tonight, she'd see how Giancarlo reacted to the home she'd created. And before that, Al would be dropping by after work.

When she'd told Al, "I need to talk to you," he'd responded with, "That sounds ominous." Unable to deny it, she'd just said, "Uh, er, I'll see you later."

Oh yeah, she so had to get this over with!

By six, her second student had left. Rina sat in the chair she used for clarinet practice, holding her instrument but staring out the window rather than playing. When Al's car parked at the curb she went to the door, scrubbing cold, sweaty hands across her skirt.

It had become a habit to kiss him when they met, but tonight neither of them stepped forward. Everything about him was familiar, from the auburn hair and gray eyes to the golf shirt and Dockers he typically wore to work at his dental practice. Yet he seemed more like an acquaintance she hadn't seen in a while than a man she'd had sex with last week.

He walked past her into the house and she closed the door. Still in the hallway, he faced her, shoulders back, hands in his pockets, a frown creasing his face. "I'm guessing this isn't good news."

SHE'S ON TOP / 111

She let out her breath in a long sigh. "I'm sorry but I can't marry you."

His eyes narrowed. "Can't?" His voice was rough. "Just say it, say what you mean. You don't want to marry me."

Slowly she nodded. "I like you, I really do, but not in the right way. I'm so sorry."

"Damn, Rina." He pulled his hands from his pockets, took a step closer and gripped her shoulders. "You're throwing something good away. Why? I don't understand what went wrong." He sounded hurt, confused, pissed off.

"Nothing went wrong, but . . ." Her shoulders lifted then lowered against the weight of his hands. "I wasn't sure where we were heading and I liked that things were moving slowly."

He studied her through narrowed eyes, then grudgingly said, "I rushed you. We can go back to dating. You'll soon see I'm right." He sighed. "Okay, I'm sorry if I tried to push you into something before you were ready."

He wasn't listening. She'd never be ready to marry him.

She bit her lip. "When you, uh, pushed, I had to really think about our relationship. About how I feel about you." She gazed into his eyes. The anger had drained and they looked more tired and sad by the second. "I like you a lot, Al. But I don't see my feelings growing into love."

"Shit," he said softly. He let go of her shoulders, closed his eyes for a long minute, then opened them and sighed. "You're not giving me any hope?"

She shook her head. "I'm sorry." Damn, she really did care for him. She wanted to reach out and hug him, find some way to ease his pain, but that might give him the wrong idea.

"So, it's just over?" he said disbelievingly.

"Y-yes." She thought about suggesting they remain friends but remembered Jenny's warning. Maybe after some time had passed.

"Well, shit. One moment I'm hoping, planning for a life with you and the next . . . I'm alone again."

"You're a great guy." If he could get over making assumptions and being pushy. "You have so much to offer. You'll meet someone else."

"I'm thirty-two, and you're the only woman I've thought I could love."

Thought he *could* love. The words were a relief. Thank God he hadn't been head over heels. "Someone will come along when the time's right."

"Stop with the platitudes." His voice was level, drained rather than bitter.

"I'm sorry."

"I'm going now." His gray eyes searched her face, perhaps hoping she'd stop him.

"Okay," she said softly, fighting back tears. Tears of loss, and of sympathy for Al.

He turned, walked to the door and opened it. Then he paused, his back to her. When she didn't say anything else, he stepped outside and closed the door quietly behind him.

Rina resisted the urge to walk to the window and watch a good man, a man who'd cared enough about her to propose marriage, walk out of her life.

Now that he was gone, she could let the tears come.

She knew what Aunt Rivka would say. "Are you *meshugeneh, bubeleh*?" Are you crazy, child?

No, she wasn't. Even if right now she felt miserable.

Scuffling slowly into the music room, she picked up Sabine and buried damp eyes against her fur. "What was crazy," she told the cat, "was inviting Giancarlo over."

The cat's only response was to purr contentedly.

This was who Rina really was. A clarinetist and music teacher. A homebody who lived with her cat, whose closest male friend was a Jewish neighbor old enough to be her grandfather. She wasn't the kind of woman who drank champagne and was serenaded in restaurants, while the sexiest man in the world seduced her with his eyes and danced piano bagatelles and rondos across her skin.

"Well, just screw it." Rina lifted her head, put Sabine down and brushed the tears away. "I have to practice for my audition. After all, music's way more important than men."

The cat slitted her eyes and gave a questioning, "Mrrp?"

Rina ignored her and picked up her clarinet. She concentrated on the piece Thomas Field had commented on, running through his suggested variation several times until it came smoothly. Then she recorded both versions, taping from a high-quality microphone into her computer.

After, she listened intently to the recording. The variations were subtle. Both were good, but which worked best? The phone interrupted and she hurried to answer it.

"Giancarlo!" Her first reaction was a rush of pleasure. Then she glanced at her watch. He was more than two hours early; this couldn't be good. She stifled a disappointed sigh. "Don't say it, I can guess. You have to work late and you're canceling tonight."

"No, *cara*, just the opposite. We got almost every shot in a first take. I figure, you're my lucky charm."

Suddenly everything in the world felt bubbly and bright. She laughed with pleasure. "Idiot, I wasn't even there."

"Ah yes, you were. Every minute. In my head, on my skin; I swear I could even smell roses." His tone was intense. Sensual.

A shiver of sexual awareness brushed her own skin and her voice trembled when she said, "I know I can smell roses, because the lovely ones you sent are on top of the piano." She walked over to brush a petal with gentle fingertips, bury her nose in an unfurling bloom.

"*Cara*, does it work for you if I come over earlier than we'd planned? I can't wait to see you."

"I want to see you too." And yet, she hadn't even decided which version of the music to play, and the audition was so close. Damn it, her career had to be more important than a couple of extra hours with a passing-through-town lover. "But I really have to practice awhile longer," she said reluctantly. "On Friday I have an audition for principal clarinet at the VSO."

"You'll play brilliantly. But yes, of course you want to practice." He sighed. "Ah well, it was a nice thought. And to be honest, I have work too, on a treatment."

"Treatment?"

"It's a summary, a proposal, for a music video. The concept, theme, kind of shots that'll be used. Basically, how the director intends to treat the song and the performer."

"Have you been hired to do this video, or is the treatment kind of like an audition?"

"It's sort of an audition piece. The way it usually works, the music commissioner at the performer's label asks a few directors to submit treatments. Then the label—with input from the performer—decides who they'll hire to direct."

"I didn't realize it worked that way." Not that she'd even put a moment's thought to it.

Now she had a crazy idea. "What stage are you at? Writing up the treatment?"

"No, I'm still developing the concept. I have a couple of DVDs to watch and I need to spend more time with the lyrics, then I'll play around with ideas for a while."

Her lips curved. "Want to play around here?"

"Play around?" A note of mischief entered his voice. "With you, yes. But you said you had to practice."

"Maybe you could work here? Bring the DVDs and watch them? You can work with lyrics anywhere, right? And—" She stopped herself. No, she wasn't going to beg for his company. He'd decide whether he'd rather work in his hotel room or share her bungalow. To her, there was something appealing about the idea of each of them in a different room, engaged in their current project.

"Let's see," he said slowly. "I could bring my computer, my notes. There's a file of photographs I've—"

"If it's too much trouble . . ."

"No, not at all," he said quickly. "Let me gather my things and I'll be there soon."

"Great."

When they'd hung up, Rina hurried into the bathroom to take a quick shower and rub lotion into her skin. That lotion was the reason she smelled like roses, but she'd never tell Giancarlo. In fact, she hid the bottle under the sink. A woman was entitled to a secret or two.

Then she opened her closet and sighed. Her skirts and blouses were comfortable but boring, even when she brightened them with a colorful scarf. She slid hangers along the rail until she came to the silk lounging pajamas she wore when she wanted to feel luxurious.

Man-tailored and loose, they were absolutely respectable, even partially disguising her substantial curves. The silk was heavy and satiny, not skimpy, but she loved the way it glowed, and the feel of it against her skin. The color was a rich garnet.

From her lingerie drawer she took a fancy black bra and matching panties. Not that the man was going to get a look at her in her undies—she'd be clicking the light switch before that happened. But the lace would show at the neckline. And later, if the evening went well and she and Giancarlo ended up in the dark together, they'd both enjoy the feel of the slinky silk and delicate lace.

Now for the right accessories. She was an earring girl and tonight chose dangly ones with ornate gold curlicues and red crystals.

She went back to the music room. How long would it take him to get here? When they'd arranged the evening earlier, by e-mail, he'd said he'd use one of the vans they'd rented for transporting people and equipment. She'd e-mailed driving instructions.

"Giancarlo, here in our house," she said to Sabine, who lay in her favorite spot on the chair. "Am I crazy? Me playing in here, him sitting in the living room working? Us snacking by the fire? That seems way too domestic for a man like him."

Sabine stretched, yawned widely, then curled up again.

Rina dragged her focus back to her music. Again she clicked her mouse to Play and listened critically. Darn it. Both versions sounded good, and she had no idea which the audition committee would prefer. Her cat was no help, giving equal purr-weight to each.

The doorbell cut through the music and Rina clicked Stop. Sabine did her disappearing-cat act as Rina hurried to the door. This time her palms weren't cold and sweaty, but her heart was thudding as loudly as a metronome. She took a deep breath, then opened the door to Giancarlo.

The porch light bathed him in a golden glow. She'd had two men on her front stoop, just hours apart. Al was a nice-looking man, but Giancarlo was in a whole different category. His damp black curls gleamed, his features were strong and masculine. So was his body, tonight in a black T-shirt that clung to his muscles and jeans that hugged his lean hips. Her gaze drifted down his fly, lingered on the bulge of his package.

Already, he was growing hard. For her.

Her mouth was dry and her sex began to throb with need.

He stepped toward her, caught her in his arms, bent to kiss her. His chocolate eyes glowed with an intense, hungry heat.

His embrace was tight and his kiss went straight to fiery, his tongue delving between her lips, plunging into her mouth, mating with her own tongue. His passion flamed hers instantaneously. Her pussy responded as if he'd plunged his cock between her thighs, and she kissed him back eagerly. Against her stomach, his erection grew, and she pressed shamelessly against it.

Then he eased away a few inches and gazed intently at her face, almost as if he was checking every detail to see if he'd remembered it correctly. "I missed you."

"I missed you too." Now that he was here, now her fingers were stroking the soft cotton of his shirt and feeling the tensile strength of the muscles beneath it, she wondered how she'd survived waiting all day to see him.

He sighed, smiled, then bent to kiss her again. This time more slowly, gently, savoring her mouth like a delicacy.

The quick flame of desire mellowed, turned to a flow that pervaded her whole body. Her hips twisted gently as she rubbed against his erection.

He broke the kiss but didn't release her. "Thanks for letting me come early."

Come early? Her body urged her to suggest they retire to the bedroom and both come earlier than planned. But if they did, they'd probably never get out of bed again. She groaned. "I wish I didn't have to practice."

"It's okay." He released her and stepped back. "Last night I waited over four hours to make love to you. I can handle an hour or two." He stepped out to the porch to pick up an assortment of cases and bags, then entered the house again and focused on her. He gave a low wolf whistle. "You look beautiful, Rina."

Damn, she wished he wouldn't say stuff like that.

Knowing she was blushing, she reached past him to close the door. As she turned to lead the way into the living room, she hoped the pajama pants disguised the size and sway of her booty. "Oh come on, I'm almost wearing men's clothes."

"There's nothing so sexy as a woman in men's clothing. Hmm. You give me ideas."

Over her shoulder, she shot him what she hoped was a confident grin. "Sexy ideas?"

Damn. His eyes were narrowed in concentration rather than sparkling with desire.

He grinned quickly and the desire was back. "Those, definitely. But also ideas I might use in videos. So many female performers think it's sexy to bare their bodies. But what's sexy about leaving nothing to the imagination?"

"I don't know. I'm not a guy."

"Thank God for that." His voice, coming from behind her, was heartfelt.

As they stepped into the living room, she paused to see his reaction. He glanced around, smiling a little, nodding. She looked around too, wondering what he thought of the soft couch, the intricate wooden cabinet she'd fallen in love with at a secondhand store. The books and books and books, the paintings of country gardens. The few pieces of glass in the window that, when the sun shone through, glowed in jewel colors.

He walked over to the window and gently picked up a carafe in ruby glass. "Is this Venetian crystal?"

"I don't know. I fell in love with the colors."

His hand caressed the curve of the carafe, then he put it down and turned to her. "This room is you. Warm, interesting, welcoming."

"Thank you." What could a man who traveled the world as he did, stayed in hotels like the Opus, find to admire in her assortment of garage sale and secondhand store collectibles? Still, even if he was only being polite, she appreciated what he'd said. "Here, take the chair; it's really comfortable." She indicated her favorite reading chair, with the tilting back and footrest.

He sank into it, staring up at her. "Okay, to get back to what's sexy. What about with men? Do you find it sexier when a man strips down to a Speedo?"

She gave a mock shudder. "Only Olympic swimmers look good in Speedos." Although, actually, Giancarlo might. She pondered his question. "I know what you're saying. This past summer I went to a firefighter calendar competition with three girlfriends."

"Now that sounds interesting."

"Most of the guys stripped down to their underwear. But they weren't the sexiest ones. Understated worked better. Scott was the best. He stripped off his turnout gear and wore tuxedo pants, a tux vest and a bow tie. As he danced, he peeled off the vest but left the pants on, and it was so seductive, the way they shaped his body as he moved."

Giancarlo's eyebrows rose. "So you know this Scott guy?"

Wow, was that jealousy in his voice?

"Not yet, but I'm looking forward to meeting him." She was testing, and his scowl confirmed the jealousy. Stifling a smug smile, she clarified. "My friend Jenny picked him up that night, and they're now a serious item."

"And do you wish *you'd* picked him up first?"

As if she could! Her, compared to gorgeous Jenny?

But on the other hand, Jenny'd confessed how nervous she'd been, a petite Asian woman barging through a cluster of tall, stacked blondes, intent on her mission to seduce Scott.

Maybe no woman was confident of her own attractiveness.

"Rina?" Giancarlo's scowl had deepened.

What had he asked? Oh, right. "No, of course I don't. He's not my type."

Her *type* was sprawled in her chair like he belonged there, long jean-clad legs stretched in front of him. Tan loafers showing the scuffs of wear, worn with no socks. No socks and no jacket despite the cool autumn night. One of those men who didn't notice the cold.

Her gaze drifted down to caress the hard-on pressing against his fly. How could she resist unzipping him, climbing into his lap and caressing him with more than just her gaze?

"You have to practice," he reminded her, eyes glinting as if he read her thoughts.

She nodded reluctantly. "Right. Can I get you a glass of wine? Or tea or coffee? Fruit juice?"

"Red wine, please." He nodded toward one of the bags he'd brought, with the Opus Hotel logo. "I brought a bottle of white and one of red. Wasn't sure which you'd prefer."

"Thanks. I like both, but I'm going to hold off until I finish practicing." She picked up the bag and took it into the kitchen. The white was from Tuscany, called Vernaccia di San Gimignano. She put it in the fridge then examined the red. It, too was Italian, the label reading Montepulciano d'Abruzzo.

She poured a glass, then held it up and sniffed carefully. Yeah, it smelled like red wine. She snickered to herself. Okay, so she wasn't a connoisseur.

When she took Giancarlo the wine, he'd already pulled a notebook computer from a shoulder-strapped carrying case. She handed him the glass. "Pronounce this wine for me."

He did, then she asked him to say the name of the white one.

"They sound like poetry when you say them."

"Italian, the language of romance." He winked. "Now, *bella,* you go and practice, so we can be together."

She sank down on the coffee table. "Before I practice, I have to decide *what* to practice."

"Sorry? Didn't they give you a list?"

"Yes, but I'm trying to decide between a couple of interpretations of one of them." She explained about her lesson with Thomas, and finished with, "I recorded both and have been listening to them so many times I'm not hearing anything anymore."

He nodded. "I know what that's like. I listen to songs dozens of times, analyzing each beat of music. Sometimes I stop hearing. That means I need to put it away for a while. But you don't have time, so why not try a fresh pair of ears?"

"Really?" Rina gazed at him doubtfully. He'd shunned classical music for commercialism. She didn't want to insult him, but would his opinion be helpful?

"Why not?"

He was her lover. Of course she wouldn't be rude. "If you have the time, that would be great. Come into the music room."

When he followed her in, he walked to the piano and leaned over to smell the roses. Then he glanced at Tara's music, with the Post-It note on it. "Slow down, feel the music?"

"It's a student's." Rina chuckled. "She was in such a hurry to get to university, she forgot her music and her slow-down note."

"Perhaps she should have it tattooed on her hand," he said lightly. "Where she can't forget it."

She grinned. Tara just might do it. "I'll suggest that."

His gaze kept returning to the music, the piano keys.

"Sit down and play," Rina invited.

His head jerked away from the piano. "No. No thanks." He sat on one end of the bench, facing away from the instrument and toward her. "Let's hear what you've got."

She felt a moment of nervousness as her finger rested on the mouse button. He hadn't heard her in years. What would he think of her playing? She cleared her throat. "All right, the first one is—"

"No." He held up a hand. "Don't tell me. Let me listen."

One push with her finger and music filled the room. Giancarlo smiled, then closed his eyes. Rina, too antsy to sit down, stood watching.

As the piece played on, one version then the next, his expression was both peaceful and intent. He didn't say a word until the music ended. And then, just one. "Again."

This time she did sit, and saw that Sabine was creeping into the room. Music always called to her. The cat darted a couple of wary glances at Giancarlo, then hopped onto Rina's lap and began to purr.

Giancarlo smiled but said nothing until both versions had played through. Then he opened his eyes. "An interesting accompaniment, the purring cat."

"Her name's Sabine." And she'd stopped purring the moment she heard Giancarlo's voice. She was still curled up, but her body had tensed.

"For Sabine Meyer?"

Sabine Meyer was a clarinetist from Germany. Rina nodded. "I love how she plays."

"And I love how you play. You've come a long way."

"Thanks." She ducked her head, filled with relief and pleasure even as she reminded herself that the opinion of a music video guy shouldn't count for much.

He leaned forward, slowly extending his hand toward her cat.

Sabine sniffed it, eyes slitted and whiskers twitching, then tilted her head.

Giancarlo accepted the invitation and began to scratch under her chin and behind her ears. Sabine started purring again.

"You should be flattered," Rina said, remembering what Jen and Suzanne had said about animals being good judges of character. Then, "What do you think about the two versions?"

"The first is the way you've been practicing it, yes?"

"How did you know?"

He shrugged, then glanced over his shoulder at the Post-It note. "You felt it more. The second was played as competently, but you haven't played it enough times to make it part of yourself. You play best when the music flows through you."

How perceptive of him. "Thomas, my teacher, says my body needs to know the music by heart, and then I should relax and let it fill me."

"Yes, exactly."

"So you think I should stick with the first one."

He shook his head, hand still gently scratching Sabine. "I think your teacher's right. The second will work better for you in the end. It'll have a, mmm, how to say this? A joyousness the other lacks. Spend another few hours on it, feeling it and taking it into yourself, then tape the second piece again and compare. You'll hear it."

She didn't mind putting in the time—she'd do it anyway—but she wanted to practice the right thing. Could she trust Giancarlo's judgment?

He sounded so certain. Joyousness, he'd said.

When a musician interpreted a piece of music, she felt it and told a story with it. For Rina, music was joy, so it made sense to tell a joyous story.

"All right, I'll do it. Thank you." She smiled. "I suppose I should start. And I should let you work on your treatment. If you brought DVDs, do you want to use my TV?"

He gave Sabine a final stroke then stood. "Thanks, but no. I'll use my laptop and the headphones."

Of course. Her practice would duel with whatever he was listening to. Too bad their taste in music wasn't as compatible as their taste in sex.

7

Giancarlo went back to the comfy chair in the living room and took out a DVD, but he didn't start it up or put on his headphones. Instead, he sipped wine and listened as Rina began to work on the movement they'd discussed.

He leaned back in the chair, smiled, let the music wash over him. She had the whole package. Natural talent, an instinctive understanding of music and the discipline to achieve her goals. He'd had his share of the first two, but discipline had never been his forte.

Oh well, he'd have hated a concert pianist's life. Yes, the applause would have suited him fine, and the travel. But he didn't like doing what Rina was absorbed in. Playing the same piece over and over. For her, she seemed to work her way deeper and deeper into the music, making it more her own. For him, he got increasingly bored and the music became stale.

The life of a music video director could be frustrating as hell, but it was never boring. Each song, each performer was different. Each crew, producer, director of photography. Each locale.

Weather, moods, love affairs and breakups, people on drugs. He coped with those things on a daily basis.

He opened a file folder and flipped slowly through a couple dozen photos of Karina Bright, a relative unknown. Yes, he wanted to direct the video for her upcoming release, "Crashdown." The girl fascinated him, and so did her music. This could be her breakthrough to the big time, and he wanted to be the guy who put her there. Not because he had any romantic interest in her, but because she deserved it.

He'd better get working on ideas for the treatment. He put the open computer on his lap, secured the headphones over his ears and decided to listen to her song a few more times before looking at the DVD she'd told him about.

Before starting the song, he paused a moment to think how pleasant this was, being in Rina's comfortable house with her just a room away, rather than working in a sterile hotel room.

Then he did what he did best, a combination of concentration and drifting. Not working hard to focus his thoughts but letting ideas pop into his head. One leading to the next, sometimes in a flow, sometimes an explosion.

It could have been an hour, maybe two, when he surfaced to find Rina bending down beside him, peering at the computer screen. Apparently unaware that her pajama top gaped open, revealing an inch of black lace and a cleavage so impressive it sent blood rushing straight to his dick. God, but the woman was stacked.

One of her dark curls tickled his cheek and he captured it, took off the headphones and tugged her in for a kiss. If the computer hadn't been on his lap, he'd have pulled her all the way down and explored the full curves under those tantalizing tailored pajamas. It took only a couple seconds around her abundant femininity for his body to respond.

God, he could fuck her right here and now. His body clamored for it, but he resisted. This woman deserved better.

Consideration, a gentle touch. Foreplay, lots of it, until she grew as hungry as he was.

Perhaps his expression revealed his thoughts because Rina pulled away with a knowing grin.

"You finished?" he asked. "How did it go?"

"I'm feeling good about it. But I've played long enough. My body's tired; I'm tensing up." Her gaze flicked back to the screen. "Is that figure skating?" she asked, sounding as if she couldn't believe her own eyes.

He turned the screen so she could see more easily and unplugged the headphones from the computer. Music flowed into the room.

"The cello?" she said. "And that's Bach, isn't it?"

He nodded. "Played by Yo-Yo Ma. As you'll see in a minute."

Sure enough, the image went from two skaters dressed in conservative dark clothing, skating in the simplest of sets, to Ma, playing his cello on a traffic island with vehicles and pedestrians streaming around him.

"What on earth?" Rina sank onto the arm of the chair to see better.

Giancarlo took the opportunity to put his hand on her thigh. Mmm, those pajamas were silky and the skin underneath them was firm and warm. "The music is Bach's 'Cello Suite #6: Six Gestures'. The skaters are Jayne Torvill and Christopher Dean, Olympic gold medalists from the 1980s, interpreting Ma's rendition of the music."

She stared, apparently fascinated, and he glanced back at the screen. Yo-Yo Ma had the same kind of expression on his face as Rina got when she played. Serene, happy. Like this is what he'd been born to do.

The scene shifted back to the two skaters, who also looked totally involved in the music, the movement, each other. Yes, there was nothing like doing something you truly loved. It was how he felt when he was directing a video.

How he felt now, sitting quietly with Rina.

Well now, wasn't that interesting? His mamma had always chided him about his womanizing, said it was childish and foolish. She'd said that one day he'd meet that one special woman—*una donna speciale*; yes, that was her exact phrase—and then he'd grow up and become a man.

Could Rina be that woman?

She was mesmerized by the video, completely unaware of what he was thinking. Maybe even of his presence. Well, there was only so much of *that* his ego could take. He squeezed her thigh. "That's enough for now. If you're finished practice, I'll call it quits on work too."

"This is work?" She slid off the arm of the chair as he began to shut the computer down. "What does this have to do with music videos?"

"Pour yourself a glass of wine and I'll tell you."

"I have snacks, too. I'm starving. How about you?"

"I am too, now you mention it." Hungry for her ripe body, but also for her company. And for food, and more wine. There was something both secure and tantalizing about knowing he could relax for a while with Rina, and at the end of the evening there'd be as much hot sex as he could handle. "I'm glad you're a night owl like me," he told her, thinking how compatible they were.

She led him into her kitchen where she took a bunch of little packages and containers from the fridge. He poured wine for both of them, and the cat came running when Rina began spreading cold meat and cheese, deli salads, olives and marinated vegetables on a big platter.

"A picnic," he said with delight.

Rina put a few shrimp in the cat's bowl. "And that's it for you, Sabine. The rest is ours."

She extracted a loaf of crusty Italian bread from a brown

paper bag and handed it to him, along with a serrated knife. As he began to slice, she said, "I thought we'd light the fire. If it's too warm, I'll open a window. But I haven't had a fire yet this fall."

"A real fire? Wood, not gas or electricity?"

"Yes. I know I should convert, to be kind to the environment, but there's something romantic about a genuine fire."

Romantic. So this was her typical way of entertaining a date. A picnic by the fire.

Jealousy surged, as it had earlier when she'd mentioned the firefighter. But hell, of course she'd dated, had lovers. And so had he. More than he could count. But that was the past.

Only the present mattered.

"Do you want butter for the bread?" she asked.

"Got any olive oil and balsamic vinegar?"

She opened a cupboard. "I should have thought of that. It's the Italian way, right? Swirl them together and dip the bread?"

"Right." When she handed him the two bottles, he stared at the olive oil in disbelief. Lite? Damn, he had to buy her some of the real stuff: extra virgin, aromatic and tasty, the same rich green-gold as her cat's eyes. Working with what he had, he poured a few spoonfuls from each bottle into a saucer. Then he took a slice of bread and stuck the corner in, making sure to get both vinegar and oil. He held it to her mouth.

"Oh, I—"

He slipped the corner between her full, sexy lips, and after a moment she bit down. When she'd chewed and swallowed, she said, "Mmm, that's good."

He refrained from saying how much better it would be with proper olive oil. Instead, he swirled the bread again and ate the rest of the slice himself. "Want me to get the fire started?"

"You know how?"

"Just because I work in entertainment, don't assume I don't

have any practical skills," he joked. Now it was a point of pride to do at least as good a job as any other man she'd entertained in front of a *romantic* fire.

In the living room, he found a wood chest with all the essentials. It had been a long time since he'd built a fire, but he'd done it often as a kid and remembered the tricks. Some crumpled twists of newspaper on the bottom, alternating layers of kindling, then small pieces of wood. He shoved the damper open.

Rina came into the room carrying a tray, which she put on the coffee table. Her cat followed, tail high, gaze hopeful, but Rina banished her to the kitchen and shut the door.

Then she came to join him at the hearth, and he tried to look confident as he lit a match and touched it to the paper at several points.

The paper blazed, the kindling sparked and flared. As it burned, the pieces of wood began to catch. He watched with satisfaction and pride, then laid a couple of larger chunks of wood on top and rose to his feet.

"You're a pro," she said. "It's beautiful."

It was. Fresh and raw, the flames leaped exuberantly in shades of orange and gold, and the summer-dried wood crackled under their bite. A hint of musky woodsmoke drifted into the room. He put his arm around Rina's shoulders and she put hers around his waist, leaning into him.

Why was it that being with this woman made him think of coming home?

He wasn't a home-oriented man. When he was young, he'd been in a rush to leave Domodossola. To escape the village life, the parental pressure to be a classical pianist. To explore the world, make his mark in his own way. When his parents saved up to send him for piano lessons in Rome and Venice, he'd seen tantalizing glimpses of an exciting world he couldn't resist.

Yet as a youth he'd had a homey side too. He'd spent a lot of time in his mamma's kitchen, and sitting by the fire while his Nonna Alba crocheted and his grandfather told stories.

In the past years, caught up in the excitement of work and success, his homey side had gotten lost. He rarely made it back to the village. His grandparents were both alive but getting on in years. He'd miss them terribly when they were gone, yet now he barely saw them.

He was the only gypsy in his family. The others were all into home and hearth, the way Rina was. And here he was now, standing at her hearth.

"What are you thinking?" Rina asked softly.

"Of home," he said wryly.

"You mean home, as in Italy? Not wherever you're living these days?"

"Yes, Domodossola, the village I grew up in. I have a tiny flat in New York but I'm hardly ever there and I don't miss it."

"Do you get back to Domodossola often?"

He shook his head. "I don't need the guilt trips."

"Guilt trips? For what?"

"Abandoning my God-given talent as a pianist," he said, hearing the bitterness in his voice. "Letting my family fund my musical education, then betraying them. And yes," he added quickly, "I've paid them back many times over, but money's not the point. They won't even try to understand what I do and why I do it."

"Hmm."

He shut his eyes briefly. Yeah, Rina'd take their side. No doubt she thought he'd sold out too.

The two of them weren't as compatible as he'd wanted to think.

"Then there's the fact that my younger sister and brother are married," he went on, "and starting families. I'm the oldest, so everyone's after me to settle down."

"Settle down?" She chuckled. "That doesn't sound like

you." She shook her head, so her hair tickled his neck. "Could two people get any more different than the two of us?" There was a note of humor in her voice.

But damn, he didn't want to think they were *all* that different. "We're compatible in many ways. Like this one." He pulled her into him for a quick, hard kiss that heated his blood more than the fire had. Then he moved toward the coffee table. "But first, let's enjoy the food and wine."

Rina stayed though, staring into the fire. "I know what you mean about family," she said, not turning to look at him. "My mom was always hassling me. I wasn't a good enough Jew. I didn't practice the piano hard enough—though she'd raise hell if I practiced on Shabbos. I needed to make more friends—even though, as Jews we were the chosen people and there were rarely any other Jews around. And of course I had to watch—"

She broke off abruptly, then said, more softly, "Guilt trip after guilt trip, and believe me, a Jewish mama can really lay them on. But in the end, family's family. When they're gone, you're left with their voices in your head, and all the issues that never got resolved." Her shoulders lifted then fell again. "And the regrets."

Before he could reply, or really even digest what she'd said, she turned briskly and walked over to turn out the light. With only the dancing fire for illumination, she selected a CD.

He listened to the first bars and smiled. "Ella. You like jazz?"

She nodded. "It's complex, challenging."

And appealed to music snobs, he thought wryly. Oh well, he liked it too and was very happy to listen to Ella Fitzgerald.

They both sank back and just listened to the music for a few moments, as the fire crackled and danced in the background. Yes, it was romantic. Erotic, even. He wanted to make slow, intense love to her in front of the fire. For a moment he wondered how many other lovers she'd done that with, then he banished the thought.

Rina sat up and gestured to the platter of food and the basket of sliced bread. "Dig in, Giancarlo."

Food first. They would satisfy one hunger. And perhaps he could use that hunger, that satisfaction, to fuel another hunger in her.

She selected a shrimp. "I'm still curious about Yo-Yo Ma and the skaters. What on earth were you watching?"

All right, so she wasn't in a romantic mood right now. He'd have to ease into this slowly. In the meantime, he began to load a plate, taking a taste or two of everything she'd laid out. "It's a short film, one of six commissioned by Ma to interpret his performances of Bach's cello suites."

He spread tomato antipasto on a slice of bread and added a couple of shrimp. "I'm not sure what the other films are, but this is the only one with figure skaters." Half the miniature sandwich went into his mouth and he moaned with enjoyment.

Rina took a slice of Swiss cheese, put provolone on it and topped with antipasto. "And what does it have to do with music video? It seems pretty far removed." Not bothering with bread, she took a bite into the layered snack.

The satisfaction on her face was purely sensual and sent a surge of lust through his body. He cleared his throat, tried to focus on the conversation. "Not so far removed. Think about it. What's music video but music, words and images?"

She licked her fingers, her tongue quick, catlike, sexy. "You're looking at the film because you want to do something similar?"

"God forbid. I don't want to do anything that's similar to anyone's else's work. No, I'm studying it as a source of ideas for a treatment." He held the second half of his shrimp–antipasto sandwich out to her but she shook her head so he ate it himself. "Do you know the British singer, Karina Bright?"

"No," she said, "but that doesn't mean much. I'm not into popular music."

He swirled bread in olive oil and vinegar, paired it up with provolone and strips of red pepper and took a bite. "She's young and hasn't had much exposure. But she's got a killer song, talent and great presentation. Her label's looking for the right vehicle to break her through to the top."

She smiled. "You want to be the one. I can hear the excitement in your voice. But where does figure skating come in?" She picked up a shrimp and sucked it into her mouth.

Giancarlo couldn't figure out whether it was more fun watching her eat or hearing her express interest in his work. "I talked to Karina to get a sense of her personality, interests, the image she wants to present. She's a fascinating girl. English, with a mother from India. Wealthy family, upper crust accent, classical music training, exotic looks. Yet she can get down and dirty with the best of them. No matter how outrageous she is, there's an undertone of class that most female performers lack. Her voice, her features, her bearing. And her classical music training shows in her work too."

"Sounds interesting, but where does the skating come in?"

"She skated as a kid and loves ice dance. Says it's poetry on ice, an interpretation of music using two bodies. They interact with each other, the ice, the audience and the music. It requires great skill and training, like music does, but in the end it comes down to emotion, performance, the ability to tell a story and move the audience."

Rina smiled in understanding. "She sees parallels to her work as a musician."

He nodded. "She told me she loves this DVD. I can see why. The elegant skating. Ma with that classical cello and his pure joy in performing the music. It all comes together powerfully, in some way I haven't quite figured out yet. When I do,

I'll use the concept in the video, because it'll work for Karina too."

He glanced at Rina. "Hey, you're not eating. And the food's great." He'd been snacking steadily as they'd talked but she'd stopped. Was he boring her?

He dipped bread in vinegar and olive oil, added provolone and shrimp, and held it out to her.

She picked off the shrimp and cheese and popped them in her mouth. "That was fascinating, what you said." Then she forked up a mouthful of Greek salad and studied him as she ate. No, she didn't look bored, but what was she thinking?

She glanced away, toward the fire. "It needs more wood." When she started to get up, he stopped her.

"I'll do it." He had a proprietary interest in that fire.

After he'd poked it into shape and added a log, he sat beside her again. "More wine?" He held up the bottle. When she nodded, he added another couple of inches to both their glasses.

"You have beautiful hands," she said. "Pianist's hands." She held up her own. "More so than mine."

She was right. Although she could easily stretch more than an octave, she didn't have his finger spread. He studied her hands with their short unpainted nails, unadorned by rings. They looked feminine yet strong and capable. Capable of anything she set out to do, including bring him intense pleasure with their touch. His groin tightened at the thought.

"Maybe not a pianist's hands," he said. "But then, you weren't born to play the piano. Your true instrument's the clarinet." And equally, a man's body.

He held out another shrimp and she took it, her lips lingering sensually against his finger and thumb. Teasing him, he thought. As much as he was, in feeding her.

"And you?" She cocked her head. "What were you born to do? Not play the piano?"

He shook his head. Not the piano. Something more creative. Had he found it yet? But then, gazing at her in the firelight, he knew at least one answer. "To make love to a beautiful woman. Like you."

To his surprise, she frowned.

"You're scowling. Did I say something wrong?"

She sighed. "Look, we already have a sexual vibe between us. You don't have to woo me into bed." Her cheeks were flushed but she held her chin up proudly, almost defiantly.

He didn't *have* to woo her? "Ah, but the wooing is half the fun." Just thinking of all the ways he'd like to woo Rina—from food and fires to seductive touches—quickened his blood.

She stared at him for a long moment, like she was trying to figure him out. Didn't she realize, he wasn't very complicated? He wanted her, plain and simple.

He wiggled his eyebrows, and her face softened. She shook her head and chuckled. "You're incorrigible."

Relieved that she'd gotten over whatever was bothering her, he said, "I hope so. I don't think I'd take well to being cor-ridged, whatever that is. Sounds too close to rules and restrictions."

"I'll try not to corridge you too hard," she teased back, "if you'll stop calling me a beautiful woman."

"Hmm." What on earth was her objection to being called what she was? He sat back and studied her. Then he glanced down, to where her shapely bare feet rested on the carpet, the nails prettily painted a rich, deep red. "May I say you have beautiful feet?" he asked, testing.

One foot crawled on top of the other, as if she was embarrassed. "They're too big."

"They're not. You're a tall woman. You'd look silly with tiny feet. Your feet are strong and well shaped, and I love that burgundy nail polish."

"Claret. But you're close." She wiggled her toes and stared at them. Then, slowly, she said, "Fine, you can call my feet beautiful."

And so he would. With his gaze fixed on them rather than her face, he said, "All right then, beautiful feet, would you enjoy a massage?"

She chuckled again, then danced her feet up and down. "That's their way of saying yes."

All right, now she was letting him woo her. He wasted no time in bending to lift both feet into his lap. Rina shifted position on the couch so her back was against one of the cushioned arms.

He held one foot in both hands, stroking her skin first, then digging his fingers gently in. He'd never massaged a woman's feet before, but he was rapidly developing a taste for it. Especially when she let out soft moans of pleasure. And when the foot he wasn't massaging found its way to his groin and began to play with his package. His dick had never been caressed by toes before either, but it responded immediately.

A groan escaped him. "That feels so damn good."

"I can tell." Her cheeks were flushed again, her curly hair black and tousled against the pajama top that matched her toenails. She looked even more lovely by firelight. He wanted to say so, but decided not to run the risk of annoying her again. What guy could ever figure out what a woman was thinking?

He massaged her other foot, then tugged the loose pajama legs up and stroked his hand over her shins, then her calves. "Mmm, very fine calves too. Womanly, curvy." She tensed under his touch and he glanced up.

That sexy tousled look had changed to one of worried concentration as she studied the legs he'd revealed.

"Some muscle definition," he said, "but not too much. Feminine. Beautiful. Yes?"

"I guess I don't hate my calves," she said almost grudgingly.

What was with her? "Rina, how could a woman's calves be nicer than yours?"

"Smaller," she muttered.

"Maybe if the woman was smaller. For you, these are perfect. Beautiful. Trust me on this." He pressed one of her feet against his erection.

Her lips twitched. "Well, maybe."

But now she let herself relax as he stroked her, and he enjoyed the glide of his finger pads over her silky smooth skin. She'd shaved and applied satiny lotion recently. For him.

It made him feel special. Appreciated.

Now both her feet were in his lap, one resting atop his dick, keeping it warm. And hard.

He slid the pajama legs up farther, over the top of her knees. "Aren't knees the strangest things? Not what a person first thinks of as a thing of beauty, but I have to say, these are exceptional knees."

"Okay, that's far enough." She slid her legs away from him, swinging around until she was again seated on the couch.

Far enough? Last night they'd made love and now she wouldn't let him caress her legs?

He moved closer. "You won't let me unwrap the rest of this fine parcel?" Puzzled and hoping to persuade her, he ran his fingers down the neckline of her pajama top to slide under the lace at the top of her bra, caress her soft skin.

She caught her breath. "Yes, but not here, not like this."

"Uh . . ." He glanced around. A flickering fire, lovely music, a comfy couch. What more did she want? "Then where?"

Her shoulders straightened. "In the bedroom, with the lights off."

"The lights off? Again?" Baffled, he shook his head. "What's up with that?" Last night, her game of sex in the dark had been tantalizing, but tonight he wanted to see her.

She raised her hands and buried her face in them. Then she said something he didn't catch, because she was muttering into her palms.

Gently he eased her hands away. "I didn't hear you."

"It's my rule," she said softly, staring at the fire rather than meeting his gaze. "If you want to make love with me, it has to be in the dark."

"But why? We'll miss so much."

She drew in a noisy breath. "That's the general idea." The words almost snapped out, like she was pissed at him.

"I'm not getting this."

When she didn't answer, he reached out cautiously, captured a curly lock of hair and tugged it gently. "Look at me, *cara*. Tell me what's wrong."

Her shoulders rose and fell a couple of times, then she turned to him. "Fine. I'm embarrassed about my body. I don't want you looking at it."

Nothing she could have said would have stunned him more. "But you have a lovely body."

"Yeah, and I'm a beautiful woman," she said sarcastically. "Stop saying that. I know I'm too plump."

"You're not." Good God, was that her problem? Yes, it fit. Her rule about having the lights off, her reluctance to eat bread, pasta, rice. The figure-concealing way she dressed. Well, damn. "You're perfect as you are."

She stared at him defiantly. "Oh, sure. Tell that to all the models and actresses who're on the covers of magazines."

"Most of them are too thin."

"Haven't you heard, a woman can never be too thin or too rich?"

"That's a stupid saying." He shook his head vigorously. "You can't believe that."

"It's what's staring at me every time I see a magazine rack, turn on the TV or go to a movie."

He had to admit she was right. "But that doesn't mean—"

Rina cut him off. "You don't know what it was like, growing up as a chubby girl with a model-thin mom who kept pointing to glamour magazines and telling me to watch my weight, because that's what I should look like."

"She was wrong." He reached for her hand and she let him take it.

"She did it because she loved me. She knew how much appearance matters. Especially for a woman."

But Rina was beautiful. Not anorexic; no fake parts. A womanly woman. Damn her mother for hurting her, for making her doubt her own beauty.

Yes, he had to admit Rina's kind of beauty wasn't the most fashionable one. All the same there were lots—maybe the majority—of men who, like him, preferred womanly curves to adolescent leanness.

By now he was coming to realize that complimenting her wouldn't make her believe he was sincere. And yet . . . "Okay, that's how you grew up, and it had to be rough. But at Banff you didn't have this crazy lights-off rule."

She bit her lip. "No, but . . . I'm afraid this is going to sound insulting, but I don't know how else to say it."

"Go ahead." He squeezed her hand encouragingly.

"You were as skinny as I was fat. You had charisma, but when it came to looks you were, uh . . ."

He grinned ruefully. "Not tall, dark and handsome?"

"Well, dark." She scrunched her face up. "Sorry, but you were kind of homely."

He chuckled. "Yeah, I know. I couldn't believe a girl like you was interested in me. I figured you were out of my league."

Her dark brows drew together. "You did? I thought we were the two losers in the group, when it came to looks, so I felt comfortable with you."

"Just comfortable?" he teased, daring to caress her cheek, tuck unruly hair behind her ear, toy with the rim of that soft ear.

She shivered. "And sexy. Confident. By the end of the summer, I was almost feeling like a normal, attractive girl. But then—"

"What happened?" he prompted.

She ducked her head. "The boy I dated in grade twelve told me I needed to lose weight. He dumped me when I couldn't. Then, at Juilliard, there was a Jewish guy I was good friends with. I was attracted to him and thought it was mutual. One night I had too much to drink and I came on to him." Her voice went so low he could barely hear. "He was embarrassed. He said, he thought I'd realized I wasn't his type. That, when it came to dating, he was into slim, sexy girls."

Giancarlo wanted to rip that asshole's tongue out of his stupid throat. "You're sexy, Rina."

He could only see her profile, but the corner of her mouth moved in what he thought was an acknowledgment. "Yeah, I can be sexy. But only when I'm not inhibited about my body. That's why I have the lights-off rule. In the dark, I can be a different woman."

He didn't want a different woman.

Except, maybe he did. He wanted a Rina who believed in her own beauty the way he did.

A Rina who would not only let herself eat whatever she wanted, but relish it.

She'd said that, at the end of their Banff summer, she was becoming confident. If he'd helped her get there once, he could do it again.

Giancarlo usually believed in avoiding personal problems whenever possible. That was one of the big reasons he stayed away from his family.

But Rina was important to him. Every minute he spent with her, she became more important. He was seriously starting to wonder if she was his *donna speciale.*

Damn, she had to get over this stupid self-image issue.

Giancarlo opened his mouth to argue every point she'd made. Then, abruptly, he closed it again and instead reached for their wine glasses. Rina's feelings ran deep. They'd been there since she was a little girl. Except for a few weeks with him, everything her mother had instilled in her had been reinforced by her experiences and the way she interpreted them.

Like, when he told her she was beautiful, she thought it was a sleazy line.

No, talk wasn't the way to persuade Rina.

As he handed her her wine glass, he said, "Okay, I'll obey your rule. As long as you want me to." Already he was hatching a plan that would eventually result in her tossing her own stupid rule out the window. A bright, uncurtained window.

Pazienza. Ah yes, this woman was going to teach him patience.

And he was looking forward to every moment of his lesson. And hers. Because in the end, their relationship was going to be worth it.

As Giancarlo studied his wine glass, Rina wondered what had brought that secretive smile to his lips. Did he think she was crazy? Neurotic?

Okay, so maybe she was a little neurotic. But once she got him in her dark bedroom, she'd make both of them forget about her neuroses.

"Do you want anything else to eat?" she asked. "Or are you ready to move on to dessert?" She purred the last words, so he'd know she meant sex.

"Dessert?" His eyes lit with a speculative gleam. "What's for dessert? Something that comes with whipped cream?"

She barely restrained herself from rolling her eyes. Yeah, that's what she got for believing she could be seductive. He was more interested in whipped cream than sex. "Sorry, I don't keep much dessert food in the house. I have apples."

"Eve's fruit of seduction? Hmm, we'll see." He had risen and was picking up the platter.

She followed him into the kitchen, gave the three leftover shrimp to Sabine then began to package things up.

Meanwhile, Giancarlo conducted a search of her fridge and cupboards. When he ended up with empty hands, she said, "Sorry. Nothing sweet in the house."

His lips curved and his eyes gleamed. "Not true. I know exactly what I want for dessert." He rested his hands lightly on her shoulders and leaned down to kiss her gently, lips framing hers. Nibbling, but not seeking to part them.

Even that softest of touches was arousing. Her nipples hardened and she moved closer, circling his waist with her arms, pressing the front of her body against his. Finding that, as she snuggled against him, he was growing firm against her belly.

Thank God her embarrassing confession about her body image issue hadn't dimmed his attraction to her.

He groaned softly and his hands moved from her shoulders down her back to her waist, then lower, cupping her bottom and urging her even closer. His tongue slipped into her mouth but just as she was going to touch it with hers, it retreated. Then he thrust it in again, and this time she was ready, meeting it with her own.

He slid back, out, then forward again. Before he could withdraw she captured him, teeth holding him gently, her mouth sucking as if his tongue were a miniature penis.

She sucked, tongued him, released but only for the briefest second, then applied suction again.

His hips moved, thrusting his erection against her. Her sex

responded, throbbing, burning, growing damp. If she were another woman, she'd beg him to hoist her up on the kitchen table, strip off her pajama bottoms and take her, then and there.

If she were a woman who didn't have wobbly thighs and a plus-size booty. No, she needed to be confident, sexy Rina, and there was only one way to achieve that. She released his tongue, broke free of his mouth. "Let's go to bed."

"Dessert in bed." His voice was rough. "What a treat."

She led him down the hall and into the bedroom, where she closed the door. For now the bedside light stayed on so he could get his bearings.

"I feel like I should count how many steps it is to the door," he said, "before you turn off that light. Can we have candles?"

She shook her head. "Music, though." Her choice this time was classical guitar, ripply and sensual.

"I like your brass bed." His hand stroked the metal frame.

"I got it for a steal because it had been painted over. I worked for ages stripping off the paint, polishing the brass, but I love it."

"Good things are worth a little effort," he agreed, turning from the bed to her.

As she clicked off the lamp, he moved up behind her. He put his arms around her, rocking his aroused body against her back. "You feel so good in those pajamas. Silk over curves."

More confident already, she said, "Want them on or off?"

He slid his hands under the loose top and found the drawstring waist of the pants. "I think . . ." His hands moved; he must have undone the bow she'd tied, because now, as he stepped back, the silk slipped down her legs to pool at her feet. "Off would be even better."

She stepped out of the pajama bottoms and kicked them aside. His hands found her waist. Slowly she moved a step or two with him holding on, then leaned over, reaching out with both hands until she'd found the edge of the bed. "Let's lie down," she said.

"No, don't move. Stay just like that."

Bent over, butt sticking up in the air?

Yes, apparently that's what he meant because his hands were caressing the soft skin at her waist, then curving out over her abundant hips and behind. Stroking the lace-trimmed silky underwear she'd worn for this very purpose, for how it would feel to both of them when he touched her.

"*Cara,* these curves are designed to give a man ideas."

And the way he was touching her was giving her ideas too. Her pussy was hot and damp, her breathing quicker with every soft caress. Maybe she wasn't so ready to leap into bed after all. Not if he kept doing this.

Two fingers traced down the crease between her buttocks, outside the panties, and found their way between her legs.

"Oh yes!" she moaned as he touched the hot, wet silk, stroking gently and tantalizing the hungry flesh beneath.

Then he was gone and she began to straighten. "Giancarlo?"

"Don't move."

She heard the sound of a zipper. Ah, that's what he was doing. Anticipation built as she heard the sound of clothing rustle. Her body shivered, wondering where he'd touch next. How he'd touch her. Oh yes, there was a lot to be said for the dark.

His hands found her waist again and he moved up behind her, not quite touching yet close enough that she could feel his heat. She was at his mercy in this position, needing her hands for balance, not able to touch much less see him. What would he do next?

One hand moved down and his fingers followed the same path as before, down her butt to the damp crotch of her panties, where he stroked, rubbed his palm against her, stroked again.

She pressed against his hand, body craving his touch, arousal flaming.

With his other hand, he urged her thighs farther apart and

she spread her feet more widely. This brought her body lower, thrust her bottom out even farther. And then he stepped that final inch or two toward her and brought the front of his body into contact with the back of hers.

"Oh God." Naked—he was utterly naked. And gloriously hard. She wondered what he looked like. But, even if the lights had been on, he was behind her where she couldn't see him.

His erection slid between her legs, taking the place of his fingers, and she moaned. "You have the sexiest cock."

"You have the sexiest everything." One of his arms hooked around her waist from the front, holding her steady as he slid back and forth between her thighs, against the wet silk of her panties.

She couldn't do anything but try to keep her balance and give herself up to the sensations he was creating. Powerless, in the dark, her back to her lover. Everything was up to him.

The thought was exciting, almost as thrilling as the friction of hot male flesh against wet silk against her sensitive sex. In fact, if he changed the angle a little, she might even climax.

Shifting her weight, she leaned down so her left forearm rested on the bed, supporting her. She lay her head on it, hips tilting forward, her butt thrust even higher.

Now Giancarlo's penis rubbed against her silk-covered clit with each forward thrust.

And she had a hand free. She reached down and pressed loosely against his cock, letting him slide against her palm without stilling his thrusts.

His free hand came down too, and when his cock drew back, he gently rubbed her aching bud. First the firm press of his penis, then the gentle fingerings, then the head of his cock returning again. It was as if Giancarlo had choreographed a sexual dance, designed entirely for her pleasure.

"That feels so good," she managed to gasp, then all she could do was pant and whimper as tension built within her body.

"Let go, *cara,*" he murmured, leaning forward to trail damp kisses across her back.

The seductive command, that bit of unexpected sensation, and Rina's body clutched, spasmed, and she let out a cry of pure pleasure.

Giancarlo thrust a couple more times, prolonging her climax. Then he stopped moving and just held her from behind, both arms warm about her waist as she recovered.

Her legs felt so limp, she might have fallen to the carpet if he hadn't been there.

Her hand still rested on his penis and now she curled her fingers. "Such a generous lover," she purred. "Taking care of my pleasure first. Now it's your turn."

8

"I won't object," Giancarlo said.

"What would you like?" Did he want sex now, taking her from behind? Or maybe for her to go down on him?

"To kiss you," he murmured. "It's been so long since we kissed."

Pleased, she smiled in the dark. "And whose fault is that?"

"Yours, for having such a seductive behind."

She sucked in a breath, then reassured herself the bedroom really was pitch black. Teasingly, she said, "As if you could see it with the lights off."

"I could see it in my mind's eye."

Where, with any luck, it had appeared half its real size.

He began to straighten. His cock slid free of her hand and, using her body to brace himself, he eased away. Then he steadied her as she stood up and turned to him. "Wow," she said, "that was wonderful."

"The beginning of dessert." He somehow found her head in the dark, his hands weaving through her hair on either side, pulling her face toward him so he could nibble her lips.

"Beginning?" she asked through his kisses.

"Dessert, like any good meal, should have three courses. That was the appetizer. How was it?"

She licked his top lip, then his bottom one. "Very appetizing."

"It definitely made me want more." He brought his body up against hers. His erection was rigid and hot.

A few minutes ago she'd thought she was satiated, but she couldn't resist that wonderfully male press against her stomach. "I think it's time for the main course." She nipped his bottom lip. "Shall I tell you what's on the menu tonight?"

"How about I ask the chef to surprise me? I think I can trust her to give me something I'll enjoy."

"And I think she's up for the challenge." She guided him gently toward the bed. "Sit on the edge."

All set to get down on her knees in front of him, she had an inspiration and found her way to her dresser. Her fingers explored the old-fashioned wooden mirror and found the carved curlicue frame. She hooked up the pearl necklace that always hung there, though she seldom wore it.

She'd read about this trick in a magazine but never had the nerve to try it out.

"What are you cooking up over there?" Giancarlo asked.

"Just getting a surprise ingredient."

Used to moving around her bedroom in the dark, she easily found the bed and then her lover. She nudged his legs apart and kneeled between them, then reached up with one hand, found his head and guided him down for another kiss.

A kiss that started with gentle teasing but quickly escalated. She read his passion and hunger in that kiss.

Using both hands, she twined the pearls in strands around his cock.

"My God, what are you doing?"

"How's it feel?" She ran her fingers over the concentric strands, rolling them, making the pearls shift and rub against his skin.

"Unbelievable. What is that, a cock ring?"

Rina giggled. "Prim and proper pearls."

"They sure as hell don't feel prim and proper. Man, that's the weirdest sensation I've ever felt."

"But good?"

"Damn good. Almost as good as your mouth."

"Then how about this?" She lowered her head and settled her lips over the engorged head of his cock. Exploring with the tip of her tongue, she found a drop of pre-come and licked it up. Oh yes, he was liking this.

She took him deeper into her mouth, sucking gently while she continued to rub the pearls against the base of his shaft.

"God, that's wonderful." After a few moments, he fisted his hands in her hair and tugged gently. "But you have to stop."

She lifted her mouth. "You can come."

"I want to be inside you."

"Next time."

And there'd better be a next time, because she was getting more aroused by the second.

She licked the head of his cock, then down the shaft, and slid the pearls up and down. Then she took him into her mouth and he groaned as she did to his cock what she'd earlier done to his tongue. Suck and release, tease him with her tongue, let him feel the tiniest pressure from her teeth. Teeth, pearls, tongue, the suction from the roof of her mouth.

Her pussy clenched as she imagined him inside her. She caressed his balls, felt them draw up, knew he was going to climax.

Then he was coming with a ragged groan of pleasure, semen spurting into her mouth. She swallowed, then again.

After, she held his cock in her mouth until it began to wilt. She could feel the weight of his hands resting on the top of her head.

The man was drained. And she was all turned on and anxious to do something about it.

The Foursome always said, a woman should be able to ask for what she wants.

"Giancarlo?"

"*Bellissima,* that was incredible."

"I liked it too. It turned me on again. Hint, hint."

He gave a wicked chuckle. "Well, I said I wanted to be inside you, but you wouldn't let me."

"And now you're going to make me suffer because I gave you a fantastic blow job instead?"

"When you put it that way—"

He began to rise, tugging her up with him. "Your turn to sit on the bed."

"Sit?"

He eased her down. "Sit, then lie back."

When she'd done it, he slid her panties off her legs, then spread her knees and buried his face against the warm softness of her inner thigh. He kissed, licked, teased his way inch by inch toward her center. Her hips began to twist impatiently.

He ran his tongue along the slick folds of her labia, then hardened it and thrust inside her.

She gasped. "Oh, that's good."

"And how about this?"

His tongue came back into her, but what else was he doing? "Oh my God, the pearls."

He must have gathered them into a double strand, and he was sliding them between her legs while he thrust his tongue inside her entrance.

The pearls that had wrapped around his cock were now driving her pussy crazy. The sensation really was incredible, all those little beads dancing over her most sensitive skin, flirting past her clit.

She writhed and thrashed on the bed as he licked his way up to her nub. Lips, tongue, pearls. The stimulation was so much, so good, it drove her over the brink. Her lower body lifted off the bed and she let out a shriek as she climaxed.

She didn't actually pass out, but it was a few minutes before she came back to earth. Giancarlo was still on the floor, resting his cheek against her stomach.

"Come lie down, where I can hold you," she said. Feeling as limp as an overcooked strand of spaghetti, she shoved herself up the bed and found her way under the covers.

After some stumbling around, he climbed in beside her, putting an arm around her and urging her head down on his shoulder.

Contentedly she curled into his body, one arm across his chest. Two orgasms, the promise of intercourse to come. But more than that, a sexy, considerate lover, an old friend, lying beside her. It was a perfect night.

Giancarlo listened to the lilting guitar music, the only sound in the dark room. When they'd been making love, he hadn't noticed it. Now it seemed the perfect accompaniment to his sense of overwhelming satisfaction.

Things felt so right with Rina.

Once he got past her silly insecurity about him seeing her body, everything would be perfect.

"You're a terrific lover," he told her.

"You too," she murmured. "That was a wonderful three-course dessert."

He held in a chuckle. "Actually, the third course is still to come."

Her head lifted, then fell back. "I'm too full to even think about more for a while."

"I know what you mean." They'd both need to regain their

strength for what he had in mind. "Let's talk," he said, eager to know her better. "Tell me more about how you grew up, with this Air Force family." To him, it sounded ideal, compared to spending an entire childhood in one tiny village, with only occasional tantalizing glimpses of Rome, Venice. Still, he knew Rina'd had problems with all the moving around. Not to mention a mother who guilted her out over all sorts of things, including her weight. He suppressed a surge of anger.

"There were good things and bad," she said. "Like any childhood, I guess."

"What was the best?"

"Music teachers," she said promptly. "At a couple of Air Force bases, there were wonderful teachers. Women who could have played professionally but chose instead to marry and follow their husbands."

"Your parents recognized your talent early?" His had, when as little more than a toddler he'd climbed onto the piano bench at a neighbor's and mimicked the tune she'd just played. "Were they musical themselves?"

"No, but my mom's mother was an excellent pianist, so she grew up around music and loved it. She started me on lessons early, and that first teacher saw my potential. I learned the piano, then discovered the clarinet. And I knew music was what I was made to do."

"No question about that." He hugged her closer.

She lay quietly for a few minutes, then said slowly, "The worst thing about my childhood was not having friends. Being Jewish didn't help, nor did being shy, overweight, a music prodigy. I never fit in. And the other hard thing was, my mom was so unhappy."

He stroked her shoulder. "Really? Why?"

"She was like me, a woman who wanted a stable home. She'd been raised in a Jewish community and was a good Jewish girl who married a nice Jewish boy. He was in law school—for Jewish boys back then, the choices were pretty much medicine or law—and she'd begun a fine arts degree. Everything was on track. He'd go into practice with an uncle. They'd have kids, live close to their relatives, be one big happy Jewish family."

"That's a far stretch from the Air Force."

Soft breath sighed against his skin. "Dad had always dreamed of being a pilot. He tried to put it aside, do what his parents and Mom expected. But he hated law school. He wanted to follow his dream."

"Bet the family was pissed off," Giancarlo said, thinking that her father's experience was a lot like his own.

"Yeah, and so was Mom. But she went along, because it was a wife's duty to support her husband."

He could understand following dreams, but her parents' story seemed awfully one-sided. Dropping a kiss on the top of Rina's curly head, he asked, "Didn't she have dreams of her own that he should support?"

"Being close to her family, practicing her faith. She shoved them aside, hoped somehow things would work out. But they didn't. With him, she had no stable home and rarely even got to visit her family. As for her faith . . ." She shrugged.

"You can practice a religion anywhere."

"I suppose. But there weren't many Jews in the Forces. It was often hard to get off the base, and then the closest town might not have a Jewish community, a synagogue. Even the rit-uals she wanted to practice at home were difficult. Dad couldn't even observe Shabbos; he often had to work Friday night and Saturday."

"Shabbos is like Sunday for Christians, right?"

"Yes. To Jews like my mother, it's a gift from God. A day of rest and spiritual enlightenment."

"Do you observe it?"

She shook her head. "Mom tried to raise me as a good

Jewish girl, but there was rarely a Jewish school and I couldn't have a bat mitzvah. Judaism just . . . didn't take. The world around me was so different than what she taught." She sighed. "Like Shabbos. I didn't want to observe a day of spiritual enlightenment, I wanted to practice music or hang out with other girls on the rare occasions I was invited along."

"Yeah, that's like me with Catholicism. My family's into it but I'm definitely lapsed. It never made sense to me."

"I think what makes sense is living a decent life. Trying to make the world a better place, even if only in small ways."

"I guess that's what's at the core of every religion when you strip away the trappings."

"It would be nice to think so. Some days, I'm not so sure."

He squeezed her shoulder and gave her a little shake. "God, woman, we're lying naked in bed together. How did we get talking religious philosophy?"

She was quiet for a moment, then gave a soft chuckle. "I think it's because you were too worn out for more sex."

He jostled her again. "Insulting me's not the way to get me hard."

"Oh yeah? What would you suggest?"

"I think it's time to finish dessert."

"The cherry on top?" she teased.

"I still wish you had whipped cream."

"I can't believe you're still thinking of food."

He grinned in the darkness. The woman didn't have a clue what was on his mind. "I need to excuse myself for a minute." She'd assume he was going to the bathroom, but his destination was actually her kitchen.

When he'd done his quick inventory earlier, he'd seen she was right about not keeping dessert food in her house. Still, there was fruit yogurt—albeit no-fat—in the fridge and liquid honey in a cupboard.

When he returned to the bedroom, he left the door open a

crack, hoping she wouldn't mind. She'd switched the music. This time it was piano. Chopin. "Rina, say something, so I can find you."

"Maybe I fell asleep when you were gone."

"Then I'll just have to enjoy dessert all on my own."

"Sounds lonely. I'd better wake up and save you from that fate."

He'd found the bed by now and felt around in the dark until he located the nightstand. When he put down the items he'd brought, they bumped against the wood.

"What's that?" she asked. "Are you all right?"

"If I said I'd hit my head and was bleeding to death, would you turn on the light?"

"Once I'd wrapped a sheet around myself."

"Hmm. We could have a toga party."

"Would you just come back to bed?"

He slipped between the covers and found her, all warmth, soft curves and silk. "You have too many clothes on."

"Then do something about it."

First, he wove his fingers into her exuberant curls, then leaned over to kiss her. Forehead, nose, lips.

Lips again. Lips some more, then the inside of her mouth.

He kissed her until his dick was hard, then he found the neckline of her pajama top and began to undo the buttons. His fingers encountered the lace of her bra, then brushed the smooth skin across her rib cage and stomach. Her body shifted restlessly at his touch.

When he'd undone the last button, he spread the top open and played her as if she were a keyboard, his fingers moving in time to "Chopin's Ballade No. 1" on the CD. He hadn't played this piece in ages, maybe not even since he was a teenager, but after years of practice his body remembered.

"I love it when you do that," she murmured. "But you're

missing the top octave." She eased herself up and pulled off the pajama top.

The room was a bit lighter than before, thanks to the door he'd left cracked open, but he still couldn't see her. Or could he? Was it only imagination or could he make out her body against the light sheets? Man, would she look lovely in candle-light, with her pale olive skin, sexy black underwear, her dark hair a tousled mass against the pillow.

One day. He could be patient.

He played music on the silky cups of her bra, tapping her budded nipples and feeling them grow even harder. Then he slid open the front clasp and peeled the bra away from her skin. Now her full, lush breasts were free, and all his to cup, caress, worship and tease.

Speaking of which . . .

When he stopped touching her and swung around in the bed, Rina said, "What's wrong?"

"Not a damn thing."

Except that he couldn't see, and it was hard to locate the yo-gurt container in the dark. But he found it and peeled the top off with a soft tearing sound.

"Condom?" she asked.

He had one of those on the bedside table too, but its time had yet to come. He found her body again and eased down be-side her. Dipping a finger into the cup of yogurt, he reached all the way to the bottom and stirred.

Then he smoothed the cool, creamy stuff over her breast.

She jerked. "What are you doing? That's cold, whatever it is."

He leaned down and licked once, along the under curve of her breast. The sweetness of strawberry contrasted with the slight sourness of yogurt. "Delicious." He licked again, and again, working from the outside into the center but avoiding her areola.

"Giancarlo, what is that?"

"Guess." Enjoying the taste of the yogurt and the feel of her skin, he licked closer and closer to her nipple. The quick rise and fall of her chest told him she was liking this too. He found a strawberry in the yogurt container and set it down on her nipple, in a pool of yogurt. Then he sucked it free.

And then he began on her other breast.

Before this, yogurt had been an eat-on-the-run snack, but now he was learning to truly appreciate it. He'd never look at one of those little containers the same way again.

When he'd finished laving yogurt off her other breast, she said, "That felt so good. What on earth is it?"

"Want to find out?"

"Y-yes," she said, a little uncertainly.

He lay down, painted yogurt across his chest and put the container back on the bedside table. "Then come here."

Her hand touched his shoulder, moved down, encountered liquid and stopped. She lifted her fingers to her lips. "Yogurt? You ate yogurt off me?"

"A healthy snack. Have some more."

"You've put yogurt all over yourself?" Her voice quivered with humor and, he thought, excitement.

"Not all over. I figured I'd start you out with something relatively safe."

"Chest? Nipples?"

"Find out for yourself."

She leaned over and tentatively licked his chest. "Yogurt. I don't believe it."

"Whipped cream would have been better. Maybe with some Grand Marnier in it."

Another lick, bolder this time. Then she was lapping him like a hungry cat, each brush of her tongue making him squirm. She toyed with his nipples, using the same suction she'd applied earlier to his tongue and his dick.

"God, you have an amazing mouth," he told her.

"I do like having something to suck on," she purred throatily. "Speaking of which . . ."

His dick surged but he restrained himself from pressing against her. "We're getting to it. Dessert should be savored slowly."

"Is there any yogurt left?"

"Let me look."

While he hated not being able to see her, darkness did allow for surprises. It wasn't the yogurt container he went for this time, but the honey jar. He unscrewed the top. "Spread your legs."

"You're going to . . ."

"Just lie back and relax."

"Relax? You have to be kidding."

"Lie back and enjoy," he corrected himself.

When he found her in the dark, her legs were already spread. He dipped two fingers in the jar, let the excess drip off, then stroked gently between her legs, coating her lightly in honey.

He leaned over to put the jar on the floor and applied himself to the task of licking every smidgeon of syrup from her labia.

He rapidly learned that, while honey might not taste quite as good as Grand Marnier-flavored whipped cream, it did have a benefit. It was so sticky, he had to lick extra diligently to get it off. So diligently that Rina was soon thrashing around and mumbling incoherently. And he hadn't even got to her clit yet.

As nice as strawberry yogurt breasts had been, a honeyed pussy was even better. Hot, swollen flesh, sweet syrup mingling with the salty tang of her sex juices.

He could linger here all night, but Rina's muttering had grown more urgent.

Raising his head, he said, "I didn't catch that."

"Clit! Now!" she moaned desperately.

He'd been working his way along, not rushing the task. Now he went straight for her pleasure spot. He licked around it, then suckled the tight bud until she let out a scream of pleasure and climaxed.

More creamy juice flowed from her, and he licked again, his touch gentle now, until she said, "My turn."

He'd hoped she'd suggest that.

It took him some cautious fumbling around the floor—he didn't want to tip the jar—to locate the honey. Using one finger, he coated his eager erection, then he sucked the extra honey off his finger. "Come and get it."

When her tongue touched his penis, she raised her head immediately. "That's not yogurt, it's honey."

"We finished the yogurt." Besides, he wanted the same sweet torture he'd just inflicted on her.

"I don't eat honey."

"It was in your cupboard."

"I keep it for Mr. Fischman, my neighbor. He takes it in his tea."

"You don't like honey?" Damn, he'd blown it.

"No, I— It's fattening."

He gave a relieved chuckle. "Believe me, we'll work off the extra calories."

"Oh! I hadn't thought of it that way." She sounded pleased.

Giancarlo was pretty damn happy too. Now, any time he wanted her to eat something that wasn't on her normal diet, he'd tell her they'd have to have sex to work it off.

His mind had a vision of Rina as she could be. Glorying in her lush body, enjoying all the sensual pleasures of an Italian feast, making love with him all night long, the room lit by fire and candles.

She lowered her head again and began to lick, at first delicately, then more roughly, in long swipes that made every nerve ending tingle. This was even sexier than the pearls.

Would he be able to survive until she finished, without exploding?

He had to, because he was determined that this time they'd climax together, with him inside her.

"There's a lot of honey," Rina purred. "A lot of calories to work off." Her tongue circled the rim under the head of his dick and he almost came off the bed.

"Maybe we should get started," he managed to gasp out.

"I'm not finished yet." She took tiny, darting licks all over the head of his dick. Fast, tantalizing, each one urging him to let go.

He groaned and reached down to circle thumb and forefinger firmly around the base of his dick, holding back the incipient orgasm.

"I suppose this isn't the time to tell you," Rina said, "that my friend Ann's boyfriend can make love for hours without coming."

"Undersexed," he panted.

"Tantric sexed."

"Jesus. I need to find out his secret."

"That's okay. I prefer loss of control to too much control."

He reached up to grip her shoulders and heaved her off him. "Thank God, because I'm all out of control."

In fact, he could barely manage to find the condom package and rip it open. Her fingers found his, took the condom from him and rolled it on.

Then she was lying back, he was moving with her and, before he knew exactly how it had happened, he was inside her. He let out a groan of relief and pleasure and thrust urgently.

Even as he did, he was aware of her breasts squishing against his chest, their bodies both a little sticky. The scent of strawberries, honey and sex in the air. Her thighs gripping him, his dick lodged deep inside her warm, welcoming body.

"This is so good." He found her mouth, kissed her hungrily.

"Very good."

They'd been moving together for a few seconds before he realized they were making love in time to the piano music. He hadn't intended it, but music did tend to work its way into a person's body and soul.

Just the way Rina Goldberg did.

He had to thrust faster now, his orgasm was so close. He outpaced the piano, setting a new rhythm, and she picked it up immediately, hungrily. They were always so perfectly in synch.

And sure enough, just when his dick was ready to burst, she began to make that keening sound that told him she was close. He let himself go, pulling back and thrusting hard, harder, as her body rose to meet him.

As his orgasm surged through him, he let out a cry that met and mingled with her high-pitched one.

Giancarlo woke to the sound of water running and a pale glow of light seeping around the edge of Rina's thick drapes. Lazily he rose from the brass bed and pulled back a curtain to see what was out there.

The sky was the dull gray of an autumn morning. Nice garden she had, the fall yellows and reds emerging in the dawn.

He found his watch. Just past six-thirty.

Yeah, he should get going. Today would be busy. He hadn't intended to stay the night, but no man in his right mind could have left the cozy sanctuary of Rina's bed. Rina's soft body.

Water sounds told him she was in the shower. Would she mind company?

Yeah, she would. Though maybe if he turned the lights off? Now there was a thought. Showering together in the dark. He'd have to suggest that one to her.

His penis, already engorged with a morning hard-on, twitched hopefully. In the shower, in the bed. Lights off, lights on. His dick didn't give a damn about the finer details.

He was engaged in imagining all the ways he and Rina might make love as their relationship developed, when he heard the shower stop.

A few minutes later, she came into the bedroom.

"Morning, *cara*. Man, do you look good," he said appreciatively.

Her hair was a mass of damp tendrils, her cheeks glowed rosily and her curves were bundled into a white terry cloth robe. She looked fresh and tempting.

Oh yeah, that was a sight he'd happily look at, morning after morning.

She stared at him, eyes wide, gaze scrutinizing every inch of him.

Well, damn. Of course she hadn't seen him naked before—not since they were kids—thanks to that lights-off rule.

And damned if he didn't feel self-conscious. Looks obviously mattered a lot to her. And she'd made such a big deal out of the way he'd changed from the once-homely kid. Was she pleased with the man he'd grown into?

Her hand rose and clutched the neck of her robe, holding the sides together. "Giancarlo. Good m-morning."

Color bathed her chest and cheeks, and her eyes glittered. Yeah, it seemed he met with her approval.

The caress of her heated gaze, the sight of her fresh out of the shower, combined to make his dick rise even more. She watched, apparently fascinated, but didn't take a step closer.

Still looking at his erection, she said, "I have to get going. I'm meeting Mr. Fischman for a morning walk. We do it every weekday."

Do it every weekday? He could think of something he wouldn't mind doing with her, every weekday. And night. And weekend as well.

He cleared his throat. "I need to get to work too." He

glanced down. Yeah, fully erect. What a waste. "Rain check? How about tonight?"

She managed to lift her gaze to his face. "I'd love to but I don't see how I can. I've got lessons today, a couple tonight and I need hours more practice." She sighed. "I probably sound obsessive, and maybe I am. The thing is, they already did the whole audition thing, with Canadians. I made it to the final round, me and the man who plays bass for the VSO. Then they decided they weren't sure they wanted either of us—maybe because we're both from Vancouver."

"Christ. That thing about 'local can never be the best'? So did they open it up to international competitors?"

"Exactly. Meaning that now I have to start all over again, and with the pressure of knowing they didn't choose me the first time." She ran her fingers through her hair. "So I feel insecure, and then Thomas threw that new interpretation at me—" She broke off.

Yeah, he thought ruefully, he needed to get over his habit of expecting women to make themselves available to him. Rina was different, and he wanted to respect her needs and priorities. "*Cara,* you're a wonderful musician. Don't second-guess yourself. Practice, and try to relax and get a good night's sleep."

"That's the plan, if I can manage it. How about Friday night?" she asked, the eagerness in her voice soothing his ego.

"I'm flying out on Friday," he said regretfully. God, just when he'd discovered a woman who might be that one special one, he had to leave town. Sometimes life sucked.

"You're going?" Her voice rose anxiously.

"Not permanently," he hurried to say. "I have a couple meetings scheduled. New York on Saturday, London on Monday. Then I'll be back, doing postproduction work. We can see each other then. Yes?"

"Oh. Sure. Next week." She sounded a little dejected, then

gave a smile that looked forced. "London, as in England? With the singer you were talking about?"

"Yeah. She likes my work; she's lobbying her label to hire me for the video. I told her I'd have some ideas for her and we'd talk them over before I finalized the treatment."

"Sounds like you have the inside track, if she likes you that much."

Was that a jealous note in her voice? Guess that made sense, after the way he'd gone on about Karina Bright's virtues, not to mention her exotic beauty. But Karina, attractive as she might be, was a child compared to Rina.

"It's purely professional," he reassured her.

She nodded but didn't look entirely convinced.

"I'll fly back Tuesday, if everything goes well," he said. "Can we get together Tuesday night? It'll be our one-week anniversary."

A week ago he'd seen her for the first time in nine years, and now he was contemplating . . . What the hell *was* he contemplating? Maybe it was good they'd have a few days apart so he could figure out what he was feeling.

Her expression lightened. "An anniversary? Well, we can't miss that, can we?"

"I'll call when I can." He tried to take her in his arms but she evaded him.

"I'll look forward to that." She glanced down at his dick. "And that. But I can't start anything now; I really have to get ready. Do you want a quick shower?"

"That would be great. Then I can go straight to work."

He hurried through his shower and came out of the bathroom to find his clothes neatly folded on the bed. Once he'd dressed, he went into the kitchen where Rina was feeding her cat.

She gave him a quick but very sound kiss. Every cell of his body tingled with awareness and his poor dick lifted to attention again. He knew that every moment he was away from her, he'd remember the feel and taste of her.

She shoved herself away, flushed, breathing quickly. "Damn, I have to go." She urged him out the back door and locked it behind them. "Wait here and give me a five-minute head start, okay? I don't want Mr. Fischman to see you leave."

Chuckling good-naturedly, he sank down on the top step to wait.

Rina was so busy, and so nervous about her audition, she barely missed Giancarlo Thursday night. Or so she told herself, as she snuggled down into her brass bed, all alone. Still, when she smelled the sultry scent of sex and strawberries, she couldn't resist sliding her hand between her legs and reliving a few of last night's finer moments.

On Friday she had rescheduled her two morning lessons so she could practice. She was to show up for the audition at one, and she intended to be as thoroughly prepared as possible.

So, when she checked e-mail at breakfast and found a message from Ann, calling an emergency lunch, she said, "Oh crap."

It was a Foursome Rule that emergency lunches took precedence over all else. Hadn't she relied on that rule herself, just a few days ago?

Another hour and a half of practice versus letting down one of her closest friends.

Sighing, she typed back

Can do, but only if it's early. 11:30?

What had happened with Ann? Surely she and Adonis hadn't broken up.

9

Ann had suggested Maria's Greek Taverna on Denman.

Rina found street parking, plugged a meter and made sure her clarinets, music stand and music were securely locked in the trunk.

When she went into the restaurant with its wooden furniture, multihued tablecloths and lots of plants and travel scenes, Ann was already there. Her friend sat at a window table, toying with a soft drink. "Are you okay?" Rina touched her shoulder as she took the seat beside her.

"Yes, just a little stressed."

Rina studied her. Recently Ann had been softening her all-business look, but today she was formal in a navy pin-striped suit, tailored white shirt and gold stud earrings. And . . . "Oh-oh. Your frown line's come back. Has something gone wrong with Adonis?"

"No, it's really not that bad. I just need advice. Before tonight."

Rina wanted to ask what was happening tonight, but

Awesome Foursome Rules prevailed. Big news never got spilled until the girls were all there.

"Hey, you two." Jenny, wearing a black jacket and bright pink scarf, flung herself into the seat across from Rina. She studied them both for a moment. "Ann's got her Botox line back and Rina's not wearing earrings. What's going on?"

"I forgot my earrings?" Rina touched her ears. "Damn, I was so nervous about the audition, I—"

"Oh shit!" Ann's hands flew to her cheeks. "Your audition's this afternoon. Rina, I'm so sorry. I got so wrapped up in my own stupid little problems, I forgot."

"It's okay. Now that I know it's not life and death, I'd actually rather hear about your problems than obsess over the audition." She touched her naked ears again. "I just wish I hadn't forgotten my earrings." Dressed in performance black from head to toe, she wanted the bright, fun touch of pretty earrings.

Ann took a navy shoulder bag from the back of her chair and fumbled around in it. She pulled out a small plastic bag. "Will these do? I bought them yesterday at lunch. I was going to wear them today but—Well, I'll get to that when Suzanne arrives."

"She's here," Jenny said, waving through the window.

Rina turned to see Suzanne hurry in the door, and waved too. Then she turned back to Ann, who'd opened the bag and spilled the earrings onto her palm. They were dangly, not quite as elaborate as Rina normally wore, but pretty and feminine with sparkly green beads.

"They're wonderful. You're sure you don't mind? I'll clean them and give them back to you Monday night."

Ann waved a hand. "I hope they bring you luck."

Rina slid the earrings into her ears, shook her head so they brushed her neck and immediately felt more herself. "Now that Suzanne's here, let's order so Ann can tell us what's going on."

They quickly requested an appetizer platter and Greek

salad, and Jenny ordered a glass of red wine. Ann said, "Oh yeah, me too!" and Suzanne said, "I'll have a glass too, please. I'm done with classes for the week."

"You're at home this weekend, *sans* Jaxon?" Jenny asked.

"Yeah. Work, homework, more homework." Suze winked. "And hot-as-hell phone sex." Then she turned to Ann. "Okay, what's up?"

"My mother's flying in tonight."

"Holy shit!" Jenny said, as Suzanne said, "But she *never* visits."

Ann's mother, an intellectual property lawyer of international renown, lived in Toronto. About a year ago, when she'd been attending a conference in Vancouver, she'd seen Ann, but since the Foursome had been together she'd never flown out just for a visit. The woman was a worse workaholic than Ann used to be.

Why would she . . . ? Ah. "She wants to meet Adonis," Rina said.

The waiter put down three glasses of red wine. Ann grabbed one and took a swallow. "Yeah, that's it. I remember you saying Monday that it would help if she met him. Well, I'm not convinced, but I don't have a choice." She groaned. "Mother called last night to say she'd rearranged her weekend plans. I'll pick her up at the airport tonight, she'll stay at my place and she's flying back tomorrow. Adonis says he'll cook dinner for us."

Ann put down her wine glass and buried her face in her hands. "And that's *so* not going to work out. He's a great cook, but he does ethnic stuff, a lot of vegetarian. Hardly haute cuisine."

"Your mom's into fancy food?" Jenny asked, as a waiter slid the platter of appetizers onto their table.

Ann lifted her head and studied the selection of goodies. "You're right, she's not. She barely notices food. It's only fuel." She flashed a tight smile. "Okay, maybe the food part will be all right. Though she'll think it's crazy that he cooks. A man should be working, achieving, not puttering around in the kitchen."

She groaned again. "Let's face it, Adonis isn't ambitious and Mother is. They're going to hate each other. And that's on top of the fact that Mother believes I've chucked my brilliant career in the toilet and it's all his fault."

"So what?" Jenny said as they all began to help themselves. "Who cares what she thinks?"

"Jen," Rina cautioned.

"No, I mean it." Jenny shot her a quelling look, then turned back to Ann. "You're twenty-eight. It's your career, your guy, your life. You need to do what makes you happy, not what your mother wants. After all, it's not like *she* knows how to be happy." She speared a ring of calamari and dipped it in tzatziki.

Suzanne's lips twitched as she cut into a dolma. "This, from the girl who still lives at home and obeys a curfew so as not to hurt her family."

"Yeah, okay," Jen said. "So do as I say, not as I do."

"No," Suzanne said firmly. "Although Jen's basic point—that it's your life—is right, I think you need to try explaining how you feel. That's only fair to your mom. And to you, and Adonis."

Ann glanced at Rina, who was picking the batter off a ring of calamari. "Anything to add?"

"You and Jenny really do have a lot in common. The parent thing. Figuring out your own identity, separate from your parents and their expectations."

Ann began to nod as Rina went on. "Suzanne's had it easy because she and her parents agree on almost everything. And I haven't had to deal with the parent issue in years, because they both died."

She glanced down at the naked ring of calamari on her plate and could hear her mom's lecturing voice in her head. Funny how, since she'd met the girls, Rina had managed to get past the Jewish taboo against eating squid, but she still avoided carbs. "Well, okay," she admitted, "sometimes I have trouble moving past my mom's beliefs. But I'm trying. If she were here I'd either be lying to her, fighting with her, or trying to make her understand my point of view. But she's not, so it's all up to me."

Defiantly she took another piece of calamari, this one battered, and brought it to her lips. "Ann, your mom's still around, though. And she's always put so much pressure on you to do things her way."

"To be a clone of herself," Ann said dryly. "And yes, I see the parallel to Jenny's parents."

"Who want a good Chinese daughter," Jenny agreed. "And instead are stuck with a pain-in-the-ass journalist with a white beefcake boyfriend."

Rina munched the calamari. Wow, it really did taste better this way. "But you both went along for a long time, in your own ways. Until now. Jen, you told your family you were dating Scott, and everyone's had to deal." She turned to Ann. "And now you've done the same thing. You figured out you don't want to be a mom-clone and you told her."

"You make me sound like the strong one," Ann said hesitantly. "Like, for once I'm the one who's made a decision and she's the one who has to cope."

"Exactly." Defiantly Rina took another battered ring of calamari. Even if Giancarlo wasn't around, she could work off the calories with yoga. Besides, she needed energy for her audition.

"Hmm." Ann's lips twitched. "No wonder Mother's so pissed off."

They all chuckled. Rina especially loudly, thinking of how her own mom would react at seeing her inhale the battered squid. Yeah, there came a time in a girl's life when she needed to grow up.

Rina turned to Ann. "But I do agree with Suzanne. I think

you should try to explain how you feel. See if you can make her understand."

"You're right." Ann glanced around the table. "And thanks, everyone." She stuck her fork into a ring of calamari. "Now, what's up with everyone else?"

Rina's mind immediately turned to the audition and her stomach flip-flopped.

"Rina?" Ann said. "Have you been in touch with Giancarlo?"

Eagerly she latched onto a less angsty subject. "In touch? Oh yeah. Very much in touch." She nodded toward Suzanne. "And before you ask, yes, I broke up with Al first."

"How did he take it?"

Rina felt a pang of guilt and regret. "He said I was the only woman he'd ever met that he thought he could love."

"Ouch," Ann said sympathetically. "But on the bright side, it sounds like he hadn't fallen all the way."

"That's how I took it."

"What's wrong with him?" Jenny's blunt voice cut through Rina's guilt.

"How do you mean?"

"He's too old to not have had a fling or two." Jenny stared at her over her wine glass. "Risked his heart, got it bruised. Either that or he's a closet gay or a mommy's boy."

"That's harsh," Suzanne murmured.

Ann tilted her head. "But there's a grain of truth in it. Look at me. I was so damned workaholic I almost never dated. That's not normal behavior."

"Or maybe he's just picky," Jenny said with a wink. "He was waiting for the best. And then Giancarlo came along and scooped you up right from under his nose." She tapped a long, gem-studded pink fingernail on the table. "Speaking of whom, I want to hear about all this touching."

Rina told them about her evening with Giancarlo. "I've never experienced sex like that," she finished.

"Woo-hoo, piano man delivers again," Jenny said, as Suzanne commented, "It sounds wonderful."

"Yogurt and honey, eh?" Ann said, eyes gleaming. "Those ought to be healthy enough for Adonis."

"Giancarlo suggested whipped cream with Grand Marnier," Rina said.

"Ooh, I could so get into that," Jenny said. "Let's see, it could be a fancy dessert fantasy. Scott and I could do strawberry jam, chocolate sauce, whipped cream, liqueurs. Yummy."

"I've never bought whipped cream," Rina said. "Does it come in those spray cans?"

"Yeah," Jenny said, "and spritzing it around would be fun. But honestly, the flavor's better when you buy the real stuff and whip it. And then you can mix in Grand Marnier."

"Guess there's no chance there's a low-cal version?" Rina asked.

Three heads shook vigorously. "It's about being decadent," Suzanne said, eyes gleaming. "It's like good sex. No holding back, no cutting corners. You have to go all out."

Rina's lips curved. "Okay, you picked an analogy that works for me. Decadent whipped cream, then decadent sex to burn off the calories."

After the others left, each hugging her and wishing her luck at the audition, Rina went into the restroom to prepare. She brushed her teeth and pulled her hair back into a knot, the way she always wore it when performing. As she tipped her head from side to side, Ann's earrings danced and caught the light, making her smile.

Lunch with the Foursome had been good for her. She felt relaxed, alive. As Thomas Field had said, her biggest problem was tightening up, concentrating and analyzing. Rushing the notes rather than letting the music flow through her and tell its story.

As she walked to her car, she felt confident. Thomas and

Giancarlo had been right about the new version of the music being better. It was more joyous, and more *her*.

Ten minutes later she breezed into the Orpheum Theatre. Randall Chang, the VSO's personnel manager, greeted her with a harried smile. A short, fine-boned man, he was an energy dynamo as he organized the forty or fifty candidates.

They drew lots to determine the order in which they'd play, and Rina found herself as last in the first group of ten. She told herself that her chances of surviving this first round were high. The audition committee—consisting of seven musicians from the VSO, mainly wind players—simply voted yes or no as to whether each player was capable.

Randall told the first-round players what they'd be expected to play and she went to one of the warm-up rooms, where she tried to tune out every other sound and concentrate on her own playing.

Then, when it was her turn, she took her place behind the screen that separated her from the audition committee and played her heart out.

After that, she looked for a quiet corner where she could hang out until the list of second-round candidates was announced. When all the groups of ten had auditioned, Randall announced the numbers of everyone who would be advancing to the second round. Rina's was called, along with approximately twenty others. It was going to be a long afternoon.

This time she was in the second group. When Randall announced the selections her group would be playing, she smiled because one was the piece she'd worked so hard on recently. The joyous one.

When it was her turn, she took a few calming breaths and thought of how Thomas and all her other teachers over the years had helped her find her own best voice as a musician. Of the good-luck e-mail her Aunt Rivka had sent last night, and Levi Fischman's "You go knock 'em dead, girlie" parting comment this morning. Of her girlfriends' hugs, still warming her skin. Then she remembered Giancarlo's last words. "*Cara,* think of that Post-It note. Slow down and feel the music."

She took up her B flat clarinet, envisioning the shape and emotion of the music. Remembering how it had felt to play it when Giancarlo sat in the next room. And then she raised the instrument to her lips.

When Rina arrived home later that afternoon, she felt drained but thrilled.

She put on a Wynton Marsalis CD, sank into the chair Giancarlo had occupied two nights ago and told Sabine, "I made it. I'm one of three finalists." She, a woman from L.A. and a brand-new graduate of Juilliard who was said to be brilliant.

The cat sat at her feet, studying her intently, then gave a "Mrrp" of approval and leaped into her lap.

"Do I really stand a chance against them?" Rina sank back and closed her eyes. "No, I'm not going to worry about that right now. I just want to relax and pamper myself." Maybe she'd open the bottle of white wine Giancarlo had brought, finish up the Granville Island snacks in the fridge. Take a long bubble bath, read a book.

E-mail Giancarlo too, and thank him for inspiring her.

And that reminded her of all the other people she'd promised to report to. Thomas Field. The Foursome, her friends in the music world, Levi Fischman.

Aunt Rivka first, though. She should telephone her aunt while it was still early in Toronto.

How wonderful to have family and friends who cared.

The phone rang and she laughed. "I wonder which one it is?"

Call display showed an unfamiliar number.

"Rina? *Cara,* how was the audition?"

"Giancarlo! My gosh, I didn't expect . . . Where are you?"

"At the airport waiting for my flight. On a pay phone because my cell's batteries died. But tell me, how did it go?"

She took the portable phone and went to the kitchen. "So well I want to drink a toast to myself. Is it all right if I open that . . ." She took the bottle from the fridge. "Uh, Vernach . . ."

His chuckle was soft and masculine. "Vernaccia di San Gimignano." The words flowed like music off his tongue. "One day I'll teach you to say it properly. Yes, of course open it, and tell me everything. I take it you're a finalist? No big surprise."

"Hang on a second. The corkscrew takes two hands."

The cork came out quickly and she picked the phone up again. "How long do you have? When's your flight?" As she spoke, she pulled down a wineglass.

"Half an hour. Do you have the wine poured?"

"Yes."

"Then let me offer the toast. To Rina, a talented musician and a beaut—sorry—wonderful woman."

Wonderful. He thought she was wonderful. "Okay, that one I'll drink to," she said softly.

But wait, maybe it was just more of his Italian flattery. If she didn't believe his "beautiful," why should she opt into "wonderful?" Oh damn, this was no time to doubt herself.

She lifted the glass and said, "To me. Talented and wonderful me." Then she drank, just a small sip to start. "Oh, wow, that's great." Another sip. "Not bubbly, but there's a little fizz."

"You did final, yes? Tell me everything. From the beginning."

Talking as she went, she walked back to the living room and her comfortable chair. She told him about the unexpected lunch with her girlfriends, even the loan of Ann's earrings, which she fingered as she talked. "I'm never giving these up. I'll have to buy her another pair."

He laughed. "She'll understand."

"I know." Then Rina moved on to the auditions. Each time

she skimmed over something, he asked a question, wanting every detail. She felt so connected, talking to him like this. Even through the background noise of the airport, his voice was sharp with interest, warm with affirmation.

As they spoke, her phone beeped to tell her she had another call, but she let it go unanswered.

"The bass player from the VSO who finaled last time didn't make it today," she told him. "It's me, a twenty-one-year-old Juilliard grad and the principal from L.A."

"No offence to the VSO, but why would someone leave the L.A. Philharmonic to play here?"

"She's hooked up with someone from Vancouver and wants to move here."

"Hmm."

It was a step back, career-wise. That's no doubt what he was thinking. He was right, but Rina believed some things were more important than career. Giancarlo probably didn't.

Here she was, sitting in her favorite chair with her cat, and he was on his way to New York then London, in pursuit of his exciting career.

"We all have our place in the world," she mused. "Where we belong. Whether it's a career, a city, a house, a relationship, a family."

He didn't answer for a moment. Then he said, "You have two, I think. Music, yes? The career, but even more so the music itself."

She smiled. "Yes. Life without music would be . . ." She shrugged. "Inconceivable. And what else?"

"Home. Not just your pretty house, but your community. Friends, neighbors, your cat. Am I right?"

She gave a surprised laugh. He knew her so well. "You are." But where did he belong?

Before she could ask, he said, "Shit, Rina, it's last call for my flight. I have to run."

"Of course."

"Congratulations again. Enjoy the wine, celebrate your success. *Ciao* for now, *bella*."

"*Ciao*," she murmured. She sighed as she clicked off the phone and put it down. How sweet that he'd phoned, yet his call had brought home the differences between the two of them.

Oh, wait, what about the call she'd missed? Had the caller left a message? Yes, the light was flashing.

It was her aunt.

She phoned back, and they gushed and babbled for a good half hour. Rina hung up, grinning from ear to ear.

Now for Levi, and then she'd e-mail all her friends.

Her neighbor answered, "So, Rina, how'd it go?"

When she told him, he said, "Well, I'm *fartoost.*"

He was bewildered? That wasn't very flattering. But he was going on, "Not that I don't know you're good, girlie, but this morning you had me all persuaded you didn't stand a chance."

She laughed. "Yeah, I guess I didn't want to be too hopeful. Didn't want to jinx my chances. Or make myself too nervous to play."

He didn't say anything for a moment. "Yeah, well, you still don't stand a chance. It's flattering they picked you, but you know damned well the other people are better."

"I know what you're trying to do."

"Is it working?"

"I'm already doing it to myself. The Juilliard grad must be amazing to have made the finals. And I know damned well the principal from L.A. outranks me on the world scale."

"Work hard and do your best. Don't worry about the other two."

"You're right." Besides, she had a week to prepare for the final audition.

Suddenly, she didn't want to spend this evening alone. "Are

you doing anything, Levi? I've got an excellent Italian wine and snacks from Granville Island. Want to come over and share?"

"I've got challah and some things from Moishe's Deli."

Challah. Wow, did that bring back memories of her mom. "It's Shabbos," she said softly. "I'm sorry, I forgot."

"No, no. You know I don't keep kosher, girlie. What better way to celebrate Shabbos than with a good friend. You give me a few minutes to clean up and I'll be right over."

Quickly she e-mailed Thomas, saying,

I'm short-listed! One of three.

She named them then went on.

The audition's next Thursday. Thank you so much.

Then she e-mailed her music friends, taking care to sound humble and thrilled rather than gloating. And, finally, the Foursome.

I can hardly believe it but I performed so well I've made the finals!!!! Those !!!! are me, jumping up and down in excitement <g>. I know it's all due to you three, so please take full credit. LOL. No, seriously, the lunch, the chat, the support, Ann's earrings, every little bit helped. I'll tell you all about it on Monday.

Then Rina rushed to get ready for Levi. First, she put Charlie "Bird" Parker on to play, having learned he was an old favorite of her neighbor's. Then she went into the kitchen. The dining room of her one-bedroom bungalow had become the music room, so her only table was the one in the kitchen. She found the pretty tablecloth her aunt had sent her, which she saved for special occasions.

It was so long since she'd practiced the rituals her mother had taught her, and she felt embarrassed she had so little to offer Levi. No Shabbos candles, and besides they should have been lit eighteen minutes before sunset. At least she could manage some deep red tapers in silver candlesticks.

They were burning on the table when he knocked on the back door. She let him in, noting his good pants, white shirt and tie, how neatly he'd combed his few remaining strands of gray hair. He gave her a quick hug, beaming broadly. "Congratulations, Rina. It's a good day."

"Is it ever. Thanks for coming to celebrate with me."

"Thank you for inviting me. This is very nice." He glanced at the table approvingly.

"I don't know how traditional you are . . ." she said nervously as she began to assemble food.

He joined her, pulling goodies out of a couple of bags and releasing the yeasty aroma of fresh-baked challah into the kitchen. "I've been alone too long. I've let many of the traditions slide. But since tonight we're together, why don't we sing some of the prayers?"

"Whatever you'd like." Would she remember them? "Should I turn off the music?"

"No, no. It'll all go together."

And, surprisingly, he was right. As his reedy voice rose, the words came back to her and the two of them chanted the singsong prayers over the background of Bird's jazz. Memories came back too. Some were sweet, of her and her parents celebrating Shabbos in love and harmony. Others were harder, of Friday nights when her father hadn't been able to come home and her mother's anger and hurt had spoiled the mood.

Levi filled a wineglass to the rim and held it in both hands. Rina brushed away memories of the past and focused on the present. She stood beside her friend as he recited Kiddush.

"And now we wash our hands," she said. It was a purification ritual, before breaking bread. Levi blessed the challah, then cut into it, sprinkled a dash of salt on top and handed the slice to Rina. Salt, a preserver. A symbol that this meal wasn't just a passing thing, but an experience that would last forever.

As she knew this dinner would, in her mind. Her neighbor's company, her wonderful news, Giancarlo's phone call, the support of her friends. Yes, Giancarlo was right. She'd found where she belonged.

Could she imagine Giancarlo here?

No, a jet-setter like him wouldn't fit into this quiet, homey world.

Except, when he was over the other night, he'd seemed surprisingly at home . . .

"This is nice." Levi's voice interrupted her musings. "It's good sometimes to remember the traditions."

"It is. Thank you for being here." How lucky she was to have found the life that suited her. And how lucky, too, to have a few sexy nights with Giancarlo to spice things up and create fine memories.

She and Levi raised their wineglasses, wished each other *gut Shabbos*, then dug into the feast on the table. Rina decided it was a rare "to hell with calories" night and let herself enjoy the challah and the potato knishes, then, later, the cheese blintzes he'd brought.

"I've eaten more tonight than I normally do in a week," she said as she sat back finally. "We're going to have to walk extra fast and long next week to make up for it."

"You got yourself a deal. And this weekend, if you want, I'll help you rake your leaves. They're getting ahead of you."

"Did I ever tell you you're the perfect man?"

"No, but my late wife Sophie, God bless her, said it every day." He winked.

She smiled back at him, guessing it wasn't just leaf raking Sophie had enjoyed with this man.

So, where did she find herself a man as fine as Levi Fischman, but forty years younger?

Rina had to hold back a laugh because of course she knew the answer. If she asked Aunt Rivka, it'd be all of five minutes before her aunt had located a *shadchen*—a Jewish match-maker—in Vancouver.

But could a *shadchen* find her a mate as sexy as her Italian lover?

10

As it ended up, Giancarlo's flight sat on the tarmac for two hours as some minor mechanical issue was diagnosed and repaired, which meant he missed his connecting flight from O'Hare. By the time he got to his small apartment in Manhattan it was almost morning.

What he wanted to do was talk to Rina, but she'd be asleep.

It was a pisser, being all the way across three time zones from her. A couple of nights ago they'd slept in each other's arms. Damn it, he'd decided she might well be the one woman for him.

He'd thought it might be good to have time apart, to clarify his feelings, but right now he just felt lonely.

Well, maybe that was his clarification. He'd never missed a woman this way before.

He checked his watch. Okay, his philosophy was to ignore travel weariness and jet lag and live according to the time zone he was in. Which meant, a predawn workout at the fitness facility in his building—one of the reasons he'd chosen this particular complex.

As he pounded along on a treadmill, side by side with a half dozen early risers, his brain gradually caught up with his legs and began to pump.

Today was a planning meeting with the producer of an upcoming project. They'd be discussing—no, arguing over—process and budget. Giancarlo would be negotiating for time, dollars and artistic freedom. Knowing the producer, a sharp-edged woman named Jo Marx, she'd do her best to reign him in to a specific shot list, the bare minimum in resources and an impossible time frame.

It was a game, like any business negotiation in any other industry. He'd go in demanding more than he really needed; Jo would present a budget so low as to be ridiculous. Then, having drawn their lines in the sand, they'd spend hours discussing each item and shifting those lines back and forth until they finally met somewhere in the center.

He'd thought this project through carefully enough that he knew right now which items he'd compromise on and which he'd defend vigorously. He could even give a damn good guess where they'd settle at the end of the day. And so, he was sure, could Jo.

Too bad he couldn't meet her for coffee, say, "As I see it, this is our bottom line," and have her say, "Yes, that fits with my thinking." Then they'd both have the rest of the day free.

He could call Rina. Hell, he could fly back, spend the night with her, fly to London tomorrow from Vancouver rather than New York.

No, it wasn't going to happen. Jo didn't have his wry sense of perspective and took her job far too seriously. Didn't the woman know work should be fun? You could achieve better results if you had a good time along the way.

That's what he aimed for, on each project he directed. As team leader, he did his damndest to get them all to loosen up and let go with their energy and creativity rather than taking themselves so seriously.

No point trying that approach on Jo, though. The woman was a shark.

The treadmill beeped to let him know he was heading into the slowdown phase. He finished off his five miles, pumped some iron then headed back to his apartment to hit the shower.

Thank God for the cleaning service that came in every two weeks. At least he had a pristine bathroom and fresh towels. As he stepped into the shower and lifted his face to the pulsing needles of spray, he remembered showering at Rina's. His utilitarian bathroom was the opposite of hers. She had plush rose-colored towels, a shower curtain that was a garden of summer flowers, enough lotions and bath stuff to stock a small store.

Six different kinds of bubble bath. He'd counted. Even opened a couple to take a whiff.

As he rubbed plain glycerin soap over his body, he imagined Rina in a tub full of scented bubbles. Candlelight.

His hand lingered on his dick, which was growing hard.

Would she bend the lights-off rule for a candlelit bubble bath? Eventually he'd persuade her.

He gave into the growing ache of need in his dick and began to pump up and down.

Rina, lying back in the tub. Her dark curls caught up on top of her head with a few tendrils drifting free. Bubbles decorating her lovely breasts like a string of giant pearls . . .

Pearls. The way they'd felt, wrapped around him, with Rina's wet, warm mouth sucking him. He groaned as he pumped faster.

It was nine that night when Giancarlo and Jo agreed on the final details. She suggested a drink to celebrate, and from the predatory gleam in her eye he suspected the negotiations had turned her on. He refused her politely, claiming a prior engagement.

What he really wanted to do was phone Rina. But it would only be six, Vancouver time. If she was home, she'd want to practice awhile longer, and he didn't want to interrupt.

So he stopped at his favorite neighborhood deli and relaxed with a Reuben, a couple beers and the *New York Times*.

Would eight be too early to call? Damn, he was impatient, he didn't want to wait any longer. He tossed the paper down and headed home.

She answered after a couple of rings, her voice sounding breathy and excited as she said his name.

"*Cara,* I'm so glad you're there." The sound of her voice seemed to fill his entire body, relaxing every tired muscle, every stressed nerve. Oh yeah, this really was the woman for him. "It seems trite to say I'm glad to hear your voice, but it's true."

"Me too." He heard the squeak of a chair, like she was settling back.

"Do you have time to talk? I could call back later."

"No, it's all right. This is good. So, uh, how was your meeting?"

"A waste of time. No, that's not true, it just seems that way sometimes." Not wanting to bore her with details, he summed up with, "Too much talk, not much action."

"And you're such a man of action?" Her tone was soft, teasing.

It roused his dick, which could definitely get into some action with her.

"I like talk too," he said. "I could talk to you for hours. But then *you, carissima,* have interesting things to say." As he spoke, he pulled off his shoes and socks, undid a couple of shirt buttons, sank into a chair.

"I do? I never think of myself as a particularly interesting person."

"Then we disagree." He leaned back, stretched his spine, rested a hand over his fly. "Hey, congratulations again. Feels great, doesn't it, when you know inside yourself you've done well, then it gets acknowledged?"

"It really does. I guess that's the same with you?"

"Yeah. It's great to love what I do, but the bottom line is, I'm creating a product for an audience. Same as you do, when you audition or perform. You want whoever's listening to appreciate what you've done for them."

"Y-yes. Though sometimes it's hard to respect an audience when you know they'd rather listen to movie soundtracks than Bach."

"It takes all kinds. Who's to say Bach's better than Andrew Lloyd Webber? Or the Beatles, or Bono?"

"Oh come on," she answered promptly. "You can't compare them."

Damn. Annoyance flared. She was still a music snob, like his parents.

But then, many of the students at Banff had been that way, and Juilliard had probably only made it worse. He shouldn't be pissed. But he didn't have to agree with her. Struggling to keep his tone light, he said, "Well, *I* can."

"Anyone can put together simple tunes. Where's the talent in that?"

Had she tried? To his mind, it was harder than it appeared from the outside. Especially if the tune was to move people and be memorable. "So, the measure of great music is how complex it is? Rather than how it moves an audience to tears or joy?"

"Hmm." She was quiet for a moment. "I think maybe both, though I put more weight on the composer's talent."

"I guess that's no big surprise. You're a musician." She was what his parents had wanted him to be. "Me, I'm an entertainer. I come down more heavily on the side of emotion. Like, with music videos, some of the most powerful are fairly simple performance videos."

"Performance videos?"

"Yeah, just filming the talent perform. But with expressive performers, great lighting and camera angles, a live performance where the audience energy is high, the impact can be huge."

"If you say so." Her tone told him she wasn't buying it for a moment.

He searched for an example she might relate to, knowing it wouldn't be rock or hip-hop. "Like Yo-Yo Ma playing the cello on that DVD."

"But that's not—" She broke off, and he gave her a moment to think about it. "Okay," she said slowly, "of course that was a video and he was performing. You could see the serenity and joy on his face, the loving way he plays his instrument."

"Pure performance," he affirmed. "To glitz it up would detract from the impact. But intercutting the skaters, as raptly involved in their own interpretation of the music—well, that worked for me."

"For me too," she said slowly. "So, do you mainly make performance videos?"

He glanced across the room at the entertainment unit and piles of videos. "I usually have a pretty high performance component, provided the talent's at all photogenic and expressive. But I use other shots that reflect the theme of the music, the image and personality of the performers. Thing is, there has to be emotion and depth—even if it's just an infinitely expressive face like Ma's—or a viewer won't come back to watch again and again."

Her chair squeaked, telling him she'd shifted position. "I hadn't thought of it that way. It would be like someone coming back to the same symphony or opera performance night after night. Which few people do."

"Uh-huh. And that person's in a different mood each time. If they have problems, they want to be transported away from them. If they're on top of the world, they want that feeling enhanced." He was feeling pretty good himself, now that Rina seemed a bit more open-minded.

"What you do isn't so easy, is it?" she asked quietly.

Yes! It seemed she was developing some appreciation for his work. "Yes and no. Yes, because I love it and I'm a natural, like you are with the clarinet. But it's challenging. Like, the band I was shooting in Vancouver—" Damn, he loved talking like this, but maybe he was boring her to tears. "Sorry, you probably don't want to hear about that."

"I do. Tell me." She sounded like she meant it.

He leaped at the opportunity to share this with her, make her understand why he was so crazy about what he did. "Okay, they're called Tattooed Elf. They're young, new, and while they love their music and songs, they're tense about performing."

He gave a soft laugh. "You know that note you had, about slowing down and feeling the music? These kids, they tighten up in front of an audience. It's like they're facing a firing squad. They still play well, but they look like they're in agony instead of passionate about their music."

She chuckled. "Not quite the image you want on a video. How did you deal with it?"

God, this felt good. He actually had the sense she was on his side. Giancarlo wished he was with her, could touch her, know they'd end up in bed.

His dick gave another throb, but he didn't stroke it. This wasn't the time for sex, but for honest communication. His parents had never respected his work, but it was important to him that Rina come to understand. The two of them didn't need to have the same views on music and musical careers, but if they were to have a happy future, they had to respect each other's.

"There's always a key," he told her. "I just have to find it. When I was talking to the Tattooed Elf kids, working on the treatment, I asked them about Vancouver. They're all from there, and they love the city. Everyone has a favorite place or thing to do. They were arguing good-naturedly over which was best. I told them everything sounded great, from the aquarium to the hot night club. The nude beach to the Grouse Mountain gondolas at night. I said, why don't we incorporate them all in the video? That's what won me the gig. They told their label that I really got who they were."

"Just a bunch of kids having fun in Vancouver?"

"Exactly." Craving a glass of wine, he wandered over to his tiny kitchen. From the wine rack he selected a Barolo. "I set up a series of quickie location shoots. The musicians playing a song at each spot, but fooling around too. After the first few minutes they forgot the camera. Their expressions and body language were great."

"Sounds like fun."

And so was this; having someone to talk to about his work. The sad truth was, his life hadn't allowed time for friends, and sharing was a new and pleasant experience. Especially sharing with Rina, and knowing they were growing closer.

With the phone hooked between his ear and his shoulder, he maneuvered the corkscrew and opened the wine. "Strange thing, it's often when a person forgets the audience that they're at their best."

"Mmm. But it's hard to do that." Her soft voice sounded a little sad.

Something clicked over in his head. "That's how you feel, isn't it? With your thing about wanting the lights off during sex."

"Let's just say, I can relate to your nervous performers."

"I'm good at helping nervous performers relax," he said persuasively, then sipped the wine he'd just poured.

"I'll bear that in mind," she said dryly, making him laugh.

"Okay, change of subject. How was your day?" He walked back to his chair, glass in hand. "Did you practice for hours?"

"Not enough. I had lessons this morning, then the quintet I play in had an early-afternoon wedding reception. After, we grabbed a snack together, but I came home early to practice."

"And I interrupted. You should have told me."

"No, I'm glad you called."

"I've been thinking of you all day. There's one particular image I can't get out of my mind." It made him hard whenever he thought of it.

"What's that?"

"You, with bubble bath and candlelight."

"I love bubble baths."

"No, really? Six different kinds of bath stuff gave me a clue. How about the candles?"

"Sometimes. And wine."

"And a man?" He tried to keep jealousy out of his voice, but he wanted to know.

"No, never. Lights off applies to candles too."

"So, this rule of yours isn't just with me?"

"God, no. Everyone, for years now."

Just how many was "everyone"? Still, he couldn't talk. A few years ago he'd had a different partner each night of the week. The important thing was, it seemed Rina trusted him as much as she trusted any guy.

And she would come to trust him more. He planned to be the man who awakened her to her own true beauty. The one who brought her out of the darkness and into the light.

His heart swelled at the thought. He had to be patient, but he could manage because he had all the time in the world to win her over.

Right now, he had a fine idea for the first step. "Would you do something for me?"

"Depends what it is."

"Pour yourself a glass of wine."

She didn't respond immediately so he said, "You there?"

"I don't drink when I'm practicing. But I've done enough for today. Besides, I'd rather talk to you." Her chair creaked loudly. "Okay, I'm going for wine."

A couple minutes later he heard the fridge door open. "No, you're not getting any more," she said. Then, "Sorry, Giancarlo, I was talking to Sabine."

"Good, because I certainly hope I'm getting more, when I come back to Vancouver next week." Now he did give in to temptation and stroked his dick through his pants.

"I think that could be arranged," she said in a husky, teasing tone that made him grow even harder.

Another few minutes, then she said, "All right, I've poured myself a glass of white wine."

"Do you have any candles?"

"As a matter of fact, there are a couple of half-burned ones on the kitchen table."

Did any woman have a candlelight dinner by herself? "You had"— he cleared his throat—"company?" Damn, did he have competition?

"Levi Fischman, my neighbor, came over for dinner yesterday."

She'd mentioned him before. The man who took honey in his tea, who she walked with regularly in the morning. Giancarlo'd got a whole different impression, one he'd found easy to dismiss. Now, trying to sound casual, he said, "For a candlelight dinner?"

She chuckled. "Not what you're thinking. It's a Jewish thing."

"Okay, would you just put me out of my misery? How old's this Fischman guy?"

"Mid-seventies."

He breathed a sigh of relief. "A Jewish friend. And Friday night's special to Jews, right?"

"Yes, it's the start of Shabbos. Not that I'm usually into the rituals, but Levi thought it would be nice."

"I bet it was." There was something appealing about the picture of Rina with her elderly neighbor, giving their Friday night a special significance.

But right now there was something more pressing on his mind. And under his fly. "You know where you're going with the wine and candles, right?"

"The bath?"

"That's it."

A couple of minutes later she said, "All right, I'm in the bathroom."

"Look around. Am I there?"

"Excuse me?"

"Search every corner, make sure I'm not hiding somewhere."

"What are you talking about?" She sounded puzzled, a little annoyed.

"This is my voice in your ear, but I'm not in the room. I want you to take a bubble bath and we're going to talk, just as if I were there. But I'm not, so you can have candlelight and not feel self-conscious."

"Oh," she said slowly. "A bath with you, but without you."

As a lead-up to one day doing the real thing.

"All right," she said. "But let me run the water and get ready. Call me back in ten minutes."

No problem, it allowed him time to refill his wineglass, strip off his clothes and climb onto his bed. Fleetingly, the thought crossed his mind that he could've shared this bed with any of a dozen women he knew in New York. But he'd rather be alone, with Rina in her bathtub in Vancouver.

Jesus, if he was right about her being his one special woman, he'd never again make love to another woman.

He tested the thought. No panic, no regrets. Only a soul-deep sense of contentment and joy. Yeah, he'd been right about them getting some distance. Every moment apart from Rina confirmed that she was the woman for him.

He glanced at his watch, counting down the few remaining minutes.

Rina sank deeper into the bubbles and checked the call display before answering the phone.

"Hello again, *cara*," he said. "Tell me where you are."

"In a tub full of warm water and lovely bubbles." She reached out a finger, gently detached a bubble and blew on it so it floated into the air.

"In candlelight?"

"Yes." She'd lit both tapers and placed them on the cabinet. "The light glints off the bubbles, making them translucent and shiny, creating rainbows."

"Pretty. And your hair's on top of your head?"

She glanced around nervously and a long curl escaped from the knot she'd tried to secure. "You didn't plant a camera, did you?"

"God, no! Jesus, Rina."

"Sorry."

His voice softened. "It's how I envision you. Hair pinned up, not in some ugly shower cap."

She chuckled. "Okay, you're right. But I should use a shower cap. My hair never stays up."

"Has a mind of its own. It's playful, mischievous, sexy. Like you are."

Wow. He really saw her that way?

"Okay," he said, "tell me the rest. Which of those six bubble baths did you use? What's the scent?"

She sniffed appreciatively. "Rose and patchouli. The closest I could get to those beautiful flowers you sent me."

"Nice. Now, tell me about the bubbles. Are they piled high or barely concealing you?"

"What do you think?"

"Piled high," he said with certainty.

She did it even when she bathed by herself. Looking at her body had always been something she avoided. But, cloaked in bubbles up to her neck, she could truly relax and luxuriate.

"And you're lying back, your head on a bath pillow?"

Obviously he'd noticed the pillow when he'd showered. "Yes."

"Music playing?"

"Softly. Mellow jazz piano. It reminds me of your fingers as they play over my skin."

"Okay, I'm getting the picture."

And it was a one-sided one. She wanted a matching image. "How about you? Where are you and what are you doing?"

"Lying on my bed. Naked. Talking to you."

Now there was a nice picture. Except, she didn't quite buy it. "Uh-huh? And that's *all* you're doing?"

A pause, then, "My hand's on my dick."

She laughed softly. "I hoped it might be." She'd hate to think he was immune to the scene she'd created.

"I can't think of you like that without touching myself. Is that okay? It doesn't put you off?"

"Turns me on." In two ways. First, to think she had that effect on him, and also to imagine him masturbating. His elegant hand on his own thick, pulsing cock. Beneath the bubbles, her nipples tightened, and under the water she squeezed her thighs together against a sweet ache.

Oh yes, she could picture Giancarlo. She was so glad she'd come out of the bathroom when she had Thursday morning. To find him naked. Now she had a visual image to match up with all the impressions she'd gathered by touch, taste and smell as she'd explored his body in the dark.

The image was a little intimidating, though. She almost wished the light had revealed some flaw—couldn't the man at least have love handles?—but the truth was, his body was perfect.

It was so damned unfair.

His voice broke into her thoughts. "The bubbles cover the whole surface of the tub?"

"Yes." Thank God.

"And where's your other hand, the one that's not holding the phone?"

"On the side of the tub, beside my wineglass."

"Have a drink of wine, then put the glass on the floor."

Oh God, he was going to ask her to do something. Something that might spill the wine. Her hand trembled as she raised the glass to her lips, sipped, then put it down safely on the floor.

He was going to make her masturbate.

Not that she hadn't done it herself in the bath. And not that he would actually see. But it seemed so intimate.

Sexy, though. A few minutes ago, she'd got turned on by the thought of him touching his cock. It wasn't so surprising he'd have the same thing in mind.

"Slide your hand under the water, *cara.*" His voice was silky, persuasive. "Over the top of your breast, then down until you're cupping it."

Her chest was rosy from the bath and sexual heat. Gently she pressed her hand against her skin, above the waterline, then slipped it down slowly through the bubbles until it disappeared. She felt her palm brush against her nipple, then move lower to curve around her breast.

"Such soft skin," he said, voice low and mesmerizing. "Feel the warm fullness in your hand. Lift your breast, squeeze it a little, tease your nipple between your thumb and finger. What an amazing thing it is, a woman's breast. Your breast."

She'd never played much with her breasts. When she needed sexual release she went straight to the spots that counted. Besides, her breasts had always embarrassed her. They'd started to grow when she was eleven, which at first was kind of exciting. But they'd kept on going. Boys at school stared, blushed, made stupid jokes. When she was thirteen a girl in her class said, "Those are gross. You look like a cow."

Rina had bought tight sports bras, smaller sizes, to minimize her breasts and stop them from growing. Nothing worked.

At fourteen, she'd realized that every time a boy spoke to her, he looked at her chest, not into her eyes.

Giancarlo had been the first boy who'd seemed to see her as a whole person, not a blob with big boobs, a Jewish nose and frizzy hair. He saw the whole Rina.

When he touched her—then and now—he caressed her entire body. He didn't go straight for her breasts. And when he did, his touch was one of appreciation as much as lust.

She stroked her own breast that way now, felt a thrill of response, then moved her hand over to explore the other one.

"Rina?" His voice was soft in her ear. "How does that feel?"

"Really nice."

"Just nice? You have wonderful breasts. They should feel wonderful."

Under her increasingly confident fingers, they did. "You're right. Wonderful." And not just her breasts. Each caress sent tingles rushing down her body, to center between her thighs.

"Tell me what you feel."

She drew in a breath. He wanted details? Closing her eyes, she concentrated. "Warm, smooth skin. The top of my breast is silky from the bubble bath and my fingers slide over it. I reach the outside of my areola and the texture changes, gets a little pebbly. My nipple's hard now, and when I squeeze it, a sexy, achy feeling of need shoots down to my—" She broke off.

"Say it," he breathed, voice rough.

"Pussy," she whispered. God, she'd never said that word aloud to a man before.

Her sex liked the recognition. It throbbed in response.

"Slide your hand down your breast and keep going. Tell me what you feel."

"Soft skin over, um, gentle hills and valleys. A dip into my navel."

She might be carrying too much weight, but her body did feel good to the touch. Soft, yes, but not flabby. Completely unlike Giancarlo's lean, taut body. But then, he was supposed to feel masculine and she was supposed to feel feminine. And she did.

"Feminine," she murmured. She ran a hand over the flare of her hip. "Curvy, soft."

Then, experimentally, she played piano notes over her stomach. The sensation made her giggle. "Me playing the piano on my body doesn't feel nearly as good as when you do it."

"I'm glad. What are you touching now?"

"The outside of my hip. Moving inward, finding curls of hair. When I slide my fingers through them, they envelope me like a little forest."

"Keep traveling through that pretty forest. See what you can find." The huskiness of his voice told her he was turned on too.

She ran her fingers lower, into familiar territory. This was where she usually started when she masturbated. But tonight her mons, her vulva, felt different.

"Tell me," he urged.

"I'm already aroused," she murmured. "My whole body feels glowing, alive, full of sensation. My sex is pulsing, sensitive, swollen."

She brushed her fingers gently over her labia, her clit. Felt her body's eagerness to respond to even the slightest touch.

"I feel supersensitized," she told him. "Like when you and I make love and you spend so much time touching me, playing the piano on my body, before you get to the actual sex." She gave a soft chuckle. "There's a lot to be said for foreplay."

"If it involves caressing, savoring, appreciating."

Appreciating. There was that word again. She'd felt it in the way he touched her. And tonight, maybe for the first time, she'd explored her own body with a sense of wonder, even admiration, rather than disapproval.

Even a body that wasn't perfect could be cherished. And it should be.

Once she'd had the thought, it seemed so obvious. But now she understood that she'd always denied herself that appreciation.

"Rina? Are you all right? I want to be there with you."

"I'll try. I've never done anything like this before." Her hand was still between her legs. "I'm stroking my, uh, labia. Damn, that sounds so clinical. Spoils the mood."

"Find words that work for you. Be a flower, if you want. A rose."

If she was a rose, her labia would be her . . . "Petals." She tried out the word. "Mmm, like in one of those old romance novels, before they could use the real words. Okay, I'm stroking my petals." She giggled. "No, that's silly."

But God, she didn't want to ruin this magical time. She took a breath, closed her eyes, leaned back against the bath pillow. Felt bubbles lap her chest, warm water soaking away her tension. Her fingers toying with her sex, focusing a different kind of tension. "Okay, my hand's between my legs, fingers stroking lengthwise, feeling warm, swollen flesh." She was back in the zone, her body responding to each caress.

"Yes." His voice was little more than a whisper.

She stroked back and forth, using her fingertips. "I'm gliding, barely touching. Mmm, it's like my body's reaching, stretching. Hungry to catch that touch." A whimper of pleasure escaped. "Just the slightest brush with a fingertip is so arousing."

"Go on."

She'd never tried to describe masturbation, arousal, before. Not even to herself. It was something that just happened. But the need to analyze, describe, added another element. Tantalizing, forbidden. "It's a turn-on," she confessed softly. "You being there. Me telling you this. Okay, now I stroke harder, pressing down firmly. Mmm, yes. Pressing into that . . . oh, mmm . . ." She panted for air. "That growing ache of need." Her voice was uneven.

She stilled her hand. "I don't want to come yet." She fought to catch her breath. "If I wait, build my arousal higher, the orgasm will be stronger."

"Build it up, Rina." His voice was ragged.

She took a deep breath, then let the air out slowly. Her hand rested unmoving between her thighs. "Talking about it slows my reactions. It's hard to describe what I'm doing and feel it at the same time."

"Then it'll take you longer to reach climax. And it'll be better. Don't shut me out."

"I won't," she promised. Then she began to touch herself again. "Okay, more soft strokes. Mmm, yes. A quick touch, then away, and my body's saying, 'Come back.' Getting even more turned on by the wait. Another brush of fingers, God, yes," she panted, her breasts rising and falling. "I have to pull back. Squeeze my legs together."

She squeezed tight. Moaned. "Between them I'm full of that . . . oh yeah, that achy burn of need. Want. Wanting release."

"Keep going," he urged roughly.

God, yes. She opened her legs again. "I'm sliding a couple of fingers inside myself, and . . . Oh, it feels good. My muscles clench and grip them." She was amazed she could talk at all, but somehow the words flowed out of her even as her fingers moved and her vagina responded. "I slide them out. In. Out again." She whimpered as her fingers stroked her sensitive inside walls. "Faster. Everything's building inside me. Focused."

She moaned. "Oh yes. All of me's so . . . focused. Sensations . . . intense."

"Yes, *bella*," he urged.

"Thumb on my clit," she gasped. "Not too hard. Sensitive . . . so sensitive . . ." She moaned as her body twisted. "Fingers faster, thumb . . . Oh God, yes. I want . . . yes . . . I'm . . ." She climaxed with a wrenching shudder and a groan, the phone clenched against her ear.

She pressed her hand between her legs, holding herself through the spasms.

Finally she took it away, her body relaxing against the back of the tub. The water had surged around but thankfully not overflowed.

"Giancarlo?"

"I'm here." He cleared his throat. "It was good?"

"Very good." She was still gasping for air. "How about you? Did you . . ." She swallowed. "Did you come too?" It was so sexy to think that she could have made him climax.

"No, but I'm close."

So she hadn't been sexy enough for him. "I'm sorry," she murmured.

"No! God, no, Rina, you don't know how hard I had to fight to hold back."

"Why would you want . . . Oh!" Enlightenment dawned. "You want to tell me about it, like I did with you?"

He groaned. "God, you're killing me, *cara*. One day, yes. But right now, there's something else I want. Why don't you have a little wine before I tell you."

Mellow from the combination of a great orgasm and a scented bubble bath, Rina leaned over and found her glass. She sipped wine, murmured "Mmm," and put the glass on the edge of the tub. "What else do you want, Giancarlo?"

"Tell me what you see now."

"Hmm? The same as before. What do you mean?"

"Look down. Tell me."

She glanced down. "The bubbles have thinned and scattered. The big puffy ones are mostly gone, but the little ones are still reflecting candlelight."

"And through the bubbles you see . . . ?"

"Glimpses of my body," she said, gazing away and picking up her glass again.

"Tell me exactly."

A long swallow of wine. He knew she was self-conscious about having him see her body. How lame would she sound if she confessed that she didn't even like looking at herself?

She darted a glance down the length of the tub. Well, if she rearranged the bubbles strategically . . . She put down her glass and drifted a hand through the water, chasing the translucent beads. "Okay, I see a froth of little bubbles, the upper curve of one breast, a few glimpses of pale skin through more froth, my right knee sticking up. And now I'm lifting my foot out of the water, and sparkly bubbles are cascading down my shin."

"Pretty." His voice caught.

"Yes, bubbles in candlelight are lovely."

"I meant your foot. Are your toes still painted—what did you call it—claret?"

He remembered the color of her nail polish? "Yes, it's one of my favorite colors. I'm into deep, rich reds."

"I remember that scarf with the bright red flowers, the one you wore to Don Francesco's. One day I'd like to see you in that, red toenails to match, and nothing else."

She chuckled softly. "I'll do it, but only in the dark. You'll have to use your imagination."

"Ah, Rina." He sighed. "What are you doing now?"

"Holding my leg up in the air, enjoying the way the light gleams off my damp skin."

"Mmm, that sounds nice. It's a pretty foot, isn't it? And a pretty leg."

Pretty? And yet, as she studied her leg carefully, there wasn't a lot to object to. Yes, she wore a size 9 shoe, but as he'd pointed out, she was tall for a woman. She'd look ridiculous with feet Jenny's size. She giggled.

"Rina?"

"I'd look silly with doll-size feet."

"God! What man would want doll-size anything?"

Scott, apparently. It sounded like the man was head over heels for Jenny.

But how much did that have to do with her petite body or her glossy black hair? Jen had said, when she met Scott, his type seemed to be tall, curvy blondes. If he loved Jen's body, maybe that was because of the feisty, generous, fun woman who inhabited it.

"Rina?"

"Sorry, my thoughts were drifting." She sipped more wine, glad she'd filled a large glass. Then she put her right leg back in the water and lifted the left one. "I'm changing legs. Watching the bubbles run down."

"Another pretty leg."

"It is. It actually is kind of pretty." Hurriedly she added, "In this light, with the bubbles."

He made an odd sound, like a combination of chuckle and snort. "*Bellissima,* you're driving me crazy."

With a start, she realized he'd been aroused but hadn't come yet. "Giancarlo, what are we doing? Don't you want to come? Do you want me to talk dirty or something?"

"Hmm. Can you do that? You had trouble saying *pussy.*"

"I have no trouble saying *cock,*" she retorted. "Nice cock. Luscious cock. Cock I'd like to wrap my lips around. Giancarlo, I don't want to leave you unsatisfied."

"Believe me, I'm finding this very satisfying. Sharing your bath, long distance. Talking dirty is fun too. But for now . . ." He let his voice trail off.

"What?"

"Put that leg back in the water and sit up a bit, and tell me what you see when you do it."

"You're very strange, has anyone ever told you that?" She slid her leg into the bath. "All right, my leg's back under water and I'm . . . wait a minute, I almost lost the phone . . . okay, I'm pushing myself farther up. Oh."

"Oh, what?"

"My breasts," she whispered. "They're . . ."

"Out of the water?"

"No, but the upper curves are. The water and bubbles are sliding down them."

"Into that beautiful cleavage, then back into the bath?"

"Yes."

"So now there's a frothy line of bubbles, just hiding your areolas."

"Yes."

"Lift yourself a little higher, until your areolas emerge from the bubbles."

As she did, he murmured, "I bet that's a lovely picture. I can't think of anything more beautiful, more feminine, than your breasts peeking out of the bubbles."

Fascinated, she stared down at her chest. Pale olive-toned skin, full breasts separated by a deep cleavage, rosy-brown areolas decorated with a drift of tiny bubbles.

"So beautiful," he said, "it really turns me on." His breathing had quickened.

"Giancarlo?"

"You know what I'd like to do? Slide my dick between those beautiful breasts. Have you squeeze them together to grip me and . . ." His breath hitched. "Pump myself back and forth."

Her nipples were hardening. "Are you touching yourself?"

"Yes," he gasped.

"Holding your cock, pumping up and down?"

"Yes. Imagining it's your cleavage . . . not my hand . . . gripping me." His voice was rough now, his breath rasping. "Seeing those lovely breasts around my hard dick."

"W-wow."

"Yeah. Wow. They're so lovely . . . your breasts. Aren't they?"

She stared down, wondering when she'd last really looked at her breasts.

"Rina?" he asked urgently.

"They look . . . pretty."

"Yes!" he said exultantly, then, seconds later, "God, yes!" on a groan of release that told her he'd climaxed.

11

Monday night, sitting with the Foursome at the Indian Oven on Fourth Avenue, Rina finished her story with, "And he came, just from thinking about my breasts."

"Wow," Suzanne breathed, fanning herself with a hand.

Jenny eyed Rina's chest. "You do have a great rack."

Self-conscious, Rina folded her arms across the front of her loose burgundy-colored blouse. "I'm overdeveloped. I mean, look at the three of you."

Jenny snorted and gestured to her chest, clad in a sequined pink sweatshirt. "Nothing to see here. I'm underdeveloped."

"You think *you* are?" Suzanne said, straightening her chest and thrusting her small, elegant breasts against her blue denim shirt. "I've got your size tits but I'm ten inches taller."

All three of them glanced at Ann, who flushed. The merest hint of lace showed through her ivory silk blouse, softening her business attire into something feminine and mildly sexy. "Okay, I'm happy with my breasts. In fact, these days I'm pretty happy with my whole body." She flashed a grin.

"Adonis definitely likes it. Seems to me, all of us have men who adore our bodies, and that's what counts."

"Giancarlo only adores my body in the dark, or long distance," Rina said, serving herself some chicken jalfrazie from one of the platters. "He's never actually seen it. Remember, I'm the one with the lights-off rule."

"You think the man has no imagination?" Suzanne asked gently. "Rina, he's touched you. Those sensitive fingers of his must have given him a pretty good idea what you look like."

Rina fiddled with her wineglass. "That's a scary thought." She lifted the glass and took a hearty swallow of red wine.

"It shouldn't be," Ann said. "Just thinking about your body makes him climax."

"Hot stuff," Jenny agreed, digging into the lamb vindaloo.

"The thing is," Suzanne said, "every woman has a different body type. Ann's close to perfect, lucky girl."

When Ann snorted, Suzanne waved a dismissive hand in her direction and went on. "Me, I'm tall, slender and mini-breasted. No amount of eating, wishing, or anything short of plastic surgery is going to make me curvier. And Jen eats like a horse and never gains an ounce because it's not in her makeup to gain weight. You, Rina, are meant to be curvy. Like Ann said, we're all lucky we've found men who find our bodies attractive."

"Damn lucky," Jenny said. Then she gazed intently at Rina. "And now that we've got that settled, tell us what happened next. After Giancarlo got his rocks off. Was that it for the night?"

Rina shook her head, smiling. "He said he wanted to go to bed with me. So I dried off and climbed into bed and we kept talking. It must have been a couple of hours."

"Pillow talk," Suzanne said, smiling too.

"Mmm-hmm." They'd talked about everything. Their days, their work, her friends, New York, Vancouver.

"When are you seeing him again?" Ann asked.

"Tomorrow night." Rina sighed in anticipation.

"She's gone," Jenny said to the others, breaking off some naan and dragging it through the mingled sauces on her plate.

"Gone?" Rina asked. "What do you mean?"

"You're starry eyed. You've fallen for the guy. Hook, line and sinker—whatever that means."

Rina frowned. "I like him. A lot. But it would be crazy to fall for Giancarlo." She wouldn't let herself do that.

"Why?" Jenny cocked her head. "That music snob stuff about his work being so crass and commercial?"

"No." Rina wrinkled her nose. "I shouldn't have been so judgmental. He's talked about what he does and I'm getting a much better understanding. I'd pictured pounding music, flashing lights, near-naked girls, and that was pretty much it. But in fact the whole process is complex. And very creative. It takes insight, perception, an appreciation of the audience."

Ann glanced at Jenny. "Yeah, she's a goner. The music snob's respecting a music video director."

Suzanne touched Rina's hand. "Why do you say it would be crazy to fall for him?"

"Our lives aren't compatible. I'm a homebody and he's a jet-setter with an exciting job that takes him all over the world." Rina sighed, her spirits plummeting. "I'm a temporary diversion. He probably has a girl like me in every city he visits." He had to, didn't he? A sexy, good-looking guy like him? Yes, his flirtation and flattery was great, but she shouldn't build it up as being something more than that.

The other three exchanged troubled glances, then Suzanne said, "I hope that's not true. Have you asked him?"

"We haven't talked about our relationship." Rina shook her head. "I'm not even sure it qualifies as a *relationship,* it's so short term."

"Is that how it feels?" Suzanne asked.

Rina closed her eyes and sighed. Reluctantly she admitted, "For me, it feels like it could grow into more. But I won't let it, because it could never work out in the end."

"Because you're tied to your home here, and his work takes him all over the place?" Ann asked. When Rina nodded, she went on. "Do you really expect to find a man whose life matches up perfectly with yours?"

"Uh . . . Well, not perfectly. Though Al came close. If I found one Al, why wouldn't another come along?"

"You rejected Al," Jenny pointed out.

"No excitement, no passion," Ann agreed. "And I'd bet part of that was because he didn't challenge you in any way. Things were too easy; you were too compatible."

"Too compatible? Is there such a thing?" Rina asked.

"I don't know," Ann said, "but look at me and Suzanne and Jenny, and the guys we've got serious about. Suze has all the problems associated with living in two different countries. Jen's got family disapproval on both sides. And Adonis challenged me to re-examine my priorities, change my lifestyle and defy my mother."

"What are you saying?" Rina asked. "That there have to be serious problems for a relationship to work? That doesn't sound right."

They shared a laugh, then Ann said, "No, but maybe if there are problems, it makes both of you really examine your feelings. Do you care enough about each other to work through these things, find compromises?"

"And we all do," Jenny said. "What about you and the piano man? Don't you at least want to know where you stand in the guy's life?"

"Yes and no," Rina said softly. "What if I really am just one of many? Maybe I'd rather not know."

Jenny eyes narrowed. "I want to meet this guy."

"Oh puh-lease," Rina said. "You are *so* not grilling Giancarlo about his intentions."

"Spoilsport," Jenny grumbled. "All the same, it's time everyone met everyone. Next weekend's Thanksgiving." She glanced across the table at Suzanne. "Jaxon's coming to town, right?"

Suze nodded. "He's taking a long weekend, even though it's not Thanksgiving in America. His mom's coming up too. My family's doing a big dinner on Sunday."

"So is Scott's, and I'm invited." Jenny screwed up her face. "Not that anyone'll be giving thanks that he hooked up with me."

"Still, they're including you," Rina said. "That's a good thing."

"Like Scott gives them a choice?" Jenny grinned. "He'll wear both our families down by sheer persistence." She turned to Ann. "And speaking of families, how did it go with your mom?"

Ann reflected, tugging gently on one of her dangly green earrings. Rina had given them to her, to replace the good-luck pair she'd borrowed on Friday. They were earrings that no doubt Ann's mother would disapprove of. A smile slowly formed on Ann's face. "Adonis may be related to Scott."

"Persistence?" Jenny asked. "Water against a stone?"

Ann nodded. "Water's a good way of putting it. He's so . . . serene. He didn't get upset, didn't raise his voice, even when Mother was being obnoxious. Which was a good part of the time."

She ran a hand through her tawny hair. "She cross-examined him about everything, especially his career ambitions. Some of her comments were insulting, but he held his own."

"Good for Adonis," Rina said softly. She broke off a bit of naan, used the soft Indian bread to clean her plate, then popped it in her mouth. Mmm, delicious. She really did miss a lot, avoiding carbs. If a piece of naan meant an extra half hour of yoga, was that such a hardship?

Ann nodded. "The thing is, Adonis has the healthier attitude. And you know, even though my mother's a world-renowned lawyer, he probably helps more people in a day than she does in a week. Or a month."

"Her job has more status and she makes way more money," Suzanne said. "Those are the things she values, right?"

Ann nodded again. "Yeah, and I used to go along. But those things are superficial. Now I think it's more important that Adonis is a good person and a healer. Still, I couldn't say that to her. I didn't want to insult her values and choices."

"She insulted yours and your guy's," Jenny pointed out.

Ann's lips twitched. "Yeah, but she's my mother and it's hard to break my twenty-eight-year habit of saying yes to her. Besides, Adonis chose the higher road. He didn't descend to her level. He answered her questions honestly, not defensively, and he didn't attack back."

"Can't wait to meet this guy," Suzanne said. "I know I'm going to like him."

"Right." Jenny snapped her fingers. "I got sidetracked. What about the Thanksgiving thing? How about all eight of us get together Saturday night? Rina, will Giancarlo be in town?"

"He'll be here through the weekend." Rina paused, thinking about Jenny's idea. Yes, she definitely wanted to meet Jaxon, Scott and Adonis. And why not introduce Giancarlo to her friends? It would be interesting to hear their comments. "Let's do it. Why don't you all come over to my place for dinner?"

"Dinner?" Jenny shot her a dubious look. "No offense, but if the menu's carrot sticks I'm not so keen."

"We'll do potluck," Suzanne broke in quickly. "I'll bring dessert."

"I'll bring something Greek," Ann offered. "Adonis makes great dolmades."

"We can work out the details by e-mail this week," Jenny said. "The important thing is, we're on!"

She raised her glass in a toast. "Here's to the Awesome Foursome and our gorgeous guys."

"Do I look okay?" Rina demanded of her cat as she stared into the bedroom mirror.

Her new cashmere sweater was a deep cherry red. It was more clingy than her other clothes and had a V-neck that showed a hint of cleavage. After all, the man did seem to be crazy about her breasts, so why not show them off a little?

She wore the soft sweater with black pants and accented the outfit with sparkly earrings that cascaded to her shoulders.

Studying her reflection, she was tempted to add a fringed scarf to cover her exposed chest. Yet her skin was smooth and creamy, a nice contrast to the rich red of the sweater. She'd forego the scarf.

As she remembered Giancarlo's sex fantasy about climaxing between her breasts, her whole upper chest flushed pink.

Sabine gave a disgusted "Mrrp" and headed for the kitchen.

Rina followed, and opened a can of cat food. Then she whipped cream and stirred in some Grand Marnier, tasting to make sure she had enough. And that was all she needed to do to get ready for Giancarlo.

When she'd told him she'd invite him for dinner but wasn't much of a cook, he'd offered to pick something up on the way. Something rich and fattening, no doubt. Probably from the fancy restaurant at his hotel.

Going into the music room, she picked up her A clarinet but couldn't concentrate on practice. Her gaze kept drifting over to the window. She'd missed him so much, yet was nervous. It was still hard to believe the man actually found her attractive and wanted to spend time with her, when he had all those singers, dancers and actresses to choose from.

When an unfamiliar van pulled up, she watched as Giancarlo got out. Dressed in jeans and a long-sleeved black shirt, he looked even more sexy than she remembered. She flew to open the door.

He came up the steps, carrying a couple of grocery bags.

"What on earth?" she said. She'd thought he was bringing takeout.

"Rina." He stopped on the doorstep and stared at her, his gaze full of a warmth that heated her from head to toe. Then he stepped past her and put the bags down inside the door. "It's so good to see you." He swept her into his arms and she went eagerly.

His kiss was hot and hungry and for the first few seconds caught her off-guard. Then his hunger and her excitement came together, and she was kissing him back just as greedily. Her body went from anticipation to arousal in a flash.

Vaguely she was aware of Sabine twining around their ankles, but she was way more aware of Giancarlo's tongue in her mouth, his hands gripping her butt and pulling her closer. The ripple of his back muscles under her own hands and the rigid length of his cock pressing against her belly. She wanted more. Everything he had to give her.

His mouth broke from hers and he gasped, "I want you, need you. God, I missed you."

"Me too." She grabbed his hand and tugged him toward the bedroom, where she'd already thought to pull the curtains.

By the time they found the bed, he was kissing her again and his hands were under her sweater, fumbling to release the clasp on her bra. She'd undone his pants before they tumbled onto the bed.

With four hands at work, they freed themselves of their clothes in an instant.

"Shit, condom," he gasped, and groped in the dark for his pants.

"I have—" She scooted up the bed, going for the stash in the drawer of her bedside table.

"Got it," he said triumphantly, then he was beside her, his hands finding her hips then drifting up to her breasts. "There you are."

And then she was spreading for him and he was on top of her, then in her, and she was hot and wet and so ready that she let out a moan of pleasure at that first thrust.

She'd hungered for this man for days and now here he was. Strong and hot, filling her, thrusting into her as if he couldn't get enough.

Nor could she. She gripped him with everything she had. Hands and arms, vaginal muscles, thighs, even her feet. She held Giancarlo as tight as she could and her body rose to meet his.

Oh God, she was going to come.

Her body arched and she moaned as the sensations spiraled through her.

Deep, he was so deep inside her, unerringly hitting all her supersensitive spots. She cried out as the first waves of orgasm built, then began to crest. "Yes, Giancarlo!"

"God yes, Rina!" he called in return as he thrust compulsively, his climax ripping through him as her own poured in waves through her body.

Her head went back, her eyes closed; she gasped for breath as he collapsed on top of her.

He began to lift himself, taking weight on his elbows. She locked her arms around him and pulled hard, and he collapsed again.

Both their bodies heaved as they gasped for breath.

Her man, in her arms. She gloried in the feeling of him blanketing her entirely.

After a few minutes he lifted his head. "Did I ever say hello?"

She opened her eyes, laughed softly. "Maybe not in words."

"Jesus. That was amazing. I really did miss you." The light was dim but she could see the glint in his brown eyes.

"I could tell." Tenderly she threaded her fingers through his soft, curly hair.

He smiled, and she froze.

Oh God, she could see him. Not clearly, but enough to make out his sparkling eyes, his white smile. Damn, she'd been so eager to make love, she'd forgotten to close the bedroom door against the light from the hallway.

If she could see him, he could see her. Or, he would, as soon as their bodies separated.

Shoving at his shoulders, she blurted, "We got so carried away, I'm not sure I remembered to lock the front door."

"I'll get it. And retrieve the groceries before your cat gets into them." He dropped a kiss on her nose, then eased off her.

As he did, she dragged the bedspread over herself. "Thanks, Giancarlo. I'll tidy up and meet you in the kitchen."

He climbed into his boxer briefs—wow, fantastic butt, and the briefs showed it off beautifully—and jeans, then picked up his shirt and walked out of the room.

Rina flung the covers off, grabbed up her discarded clothes and scurried into the bathroom. She did a quick wash with a facecloth, got dressed and tidied her hair. Then she studied her reflection. But for the flush on her cheeks and chest, she looked just as she had before Giancarlo had arrived. Yet her whole body was tingling. Who would have known a quickie could be so satisfying?

He hadn't seen anything, she reassured herself. In the beginning, his eyes wouldn't have adjusted to the darkness. Then their bodies were locked together. And afterward, she'd lost no time wrapping herself in the bedspread. She was still safe.

She found Giancarlo in the kitchen, barefoot, shirt partially buttoned and worn loose over his jeans. Casual, comfortable, looking like he belonged. Sabine sat at his feet, gazing upward hopefully.

What didn't belong in her kitchen were the Italian bread and spinach fettuccine he was taking from a grocery bag. When he added a parcel wrapped in butcher paper, a lemon and capers, she said, "I thought you were picking something up."

He turned and grinned at her. "Something to cook. Quick and easy. Chicken al limone, pasta, spinach with pine nuts and raisins. You don't happen to have Marsala, do you?"

"As in veal Marsala? That sweet Italian wine? No, I don't."

"No problem. We'll soak the raisins in wine and a touch of honey."

He pulled out a few more packages, then a bottle of olive oil.

"Now *that*, I do own," she said.

"No, you don't. You have a pale imitation."

She picked up the bottle and read the label. Nowhere did it say "Lite." Clearly Giancarlo was a man who'd never had to worry about his weight.

"*Bella*, you already worked off the calories." He winked and gestured toward the bedroom. "Relax and enjoy."

She remembered the first night they'd gone out for dinner, how he'd complained about the anorexic women he worked with. He'd said he hated eating with them, because food was meant to be savored. Okay, tonight she'd savor. In small quantities, though.

First, she went to put on some music, choosing Sabine Meyer playing the clarinet, turning it up loud enough to be heard in the kitchen. Then she fed her own Sabine and said, "Now stay out of our way."

Giancarlo laughed. "Does that work?"

"Don't feed her anything and she'll eventually give up and leave us alone. Now, what can I do to help? Open wine and slice some bread?"

"An excellent start. Then mix up some olive oil and balsamic vinegar and we can nibble while we cook. It's been a long time since I ate on the plane."

As she took white wine from the fridge, she asked, "Are you jet-lagged? What time zone's your body in?"

He chuckled as he opened the drawer under the stove and rummaged around in the pots and pans while Sabine got in his way. "I don't acknowledge jet lag. When I arrive somewhere, that's the time zone I'm in. Period. So, right now, it's dinner time." He pulled out a large pot and a couple of frying pans.

"That really works?" She poured wine into two glasses and held one out to him.

"Like a charm." He took the glass and clicked it to hers. "Here's to being together again, *cara.*"

"I'll drink to that." She took a sip, then put the glass down and turned to slice bread.

His glass went down beside hers, then his arms were around her from behind. He rested his cheek against the top of her head. "This is good. Yes?"

"Very good." In fact, she could easily get used to it. And that wouldn't be smart. "Hey," she said casually, "aren't you supposed to be cooking or something?"

He released her and went to fill the pot with water.

Rina took a deep breath. This was a time to enjoy the moment, not obsess over the future.

She blended olive oil—the rich oil he'd brought—with vinegar, dipped some bread in and took it over to where he was crushing garlic with the flat edge of a large knife. When she held the bread to his mouth, he smiled and opened, and she slipped it in.

Then she went and prepared a small slice for herself. "What did you say about soaking the raisins?"

Following his instructions she blended white wine with a little honey and poured in a few raisins. Then he had her toast pine nuts in her toaster oven.

While she was working, he took chicken breasts from the butcher paper. They'd already been pounded thin. After he dredged them in flour, he dropped them into heated olive oil and butter in a large frying pan. The spinach fettuccine went into boiling water, and in a second frying pan he sautéed the crushed garlic in olive oil.

Her kitchen had never smelled so good, and Rina's mouth watered.

He put the cooked breasts on a plate and into the oven to stay warm, and poured chicken broth into the pan in which they'd cooked. Chopped spinach went into the garlic and oil mixture, then he tossed lemon juice, chopped parsley and capers into the chicken broth.

Rina stared in amazement at the way he deftly juggled everything. Then she did her small part by lighting the candles on the already-set table.

"Would you drain the pasta?" he asked as he slid the chicken back into the pan with the lemon-caper sauce. She noted he'd tipped the pine nuts and raisins into the garlicky spinach.

A few minutes later, she dished out fettuccine—just a small serving for herself—and he slid chicken onto each plate and drizzled both it and the pasta with sauce. He added the spinach mixture and she said, "Don Francesco's couldn't have created a nicer-looking meal."

Giancarlo went over to turn off the kitchen light and paused for a moment, taking in the scene in front of him. A cozy kitchen, his beautiful woman at the table. Tonight had felt like a homecoming. He'd greeted Rina with raging passion—and she'd responded in kind. Then he'd taken pleasure in working together in the kitchen, creating a meal from simple ingredients. And now they'd dine, drink wine and later make love again. Could anything be more perfect?

"Giancarlo? Are you coming?"

"Just pausing to admire." He took his seat.

She lifted her glass in a toast. "To the chef."

"And the hostess. *Salute.*" He clicked his glass to hers.

"*Salute?*"

"Cheers, good health." Then he fumbled in his pocket. "Wait a minute, I forgot. Happy one-week anniversary." He pulled out a small box and handed it to her.

She looked a little stunned. "Happy anniversary to you, too, but Giancarlo, you didn't have to buy me a gift."

"I wanted to. And I had a spare hour in London, so I went shopping."

She opened the box and gasped. "They're beautiful."

"I noticed you like earrings. They're really okay?"

Slowly, almost reverently, she drew them out, one at a time. Most of the time it seemed she wore shades of wine-red, so he'd chosen earrings that had small rubies and garnets interspersed with diamond chips. Nothing extravagant, but they were sparkly and fun—and dangly, like the earrings he'd always seen her wear.

"They're perfect. And all the way from London!" The glow on her face validated his choice. "I'm going to put them on now." She dashed off.

When she came back, she tossed her head, making the earrings dance. "Thank you." She bent down and gave him a firm kiss, then took her seat again.

"You're welcome. Now, eat, before it gets cold."

Smiling, Rina swirled a strand of fettuccine around her fork, paired it up with a bite of chicken and chewed slowly. Her face lit up, and again he knew he'd pleased her. Then she tried the spinach and moaned with pleasure. "How did you get to be such a good cook?"

He took a bite himself before answering her question. "I helped my mamma and my nonna in the kitchen when I was a kid."

"I don't remember you telling me that before."

He smiled. "Probably because it wasn't a very *guy* thing to do. But I loved everything about it. The colors, textures, scents.

Nibbling the ingredients. Then the anticipation, as it cooked. Like, tomato sauce. Waiting hours for the flavors to blend and mellow." Patience and anticipation. The same way he was handling his relationship with Rina, he realized. Lessons he'd learned early but forgotten for a while. Until Rina.

He touched her hand. "I learned that wonderful things don't come too quickly or too easily. They're worth working on and waiting for."

"Like music." She nodded, apparently not realizing he'd been talking about their relationship. "I practice and practice, and there's a point where I know it's starting to come together, it's going to be good. Then I just have to keep working on it to get there."

"*Precisamente.* That's exactly so." He swirled bread in olive oil and vinegar, then paused. Yes, that's how it was with her and her clarinet, but . . . "I didn't see that—feel it—with the piano. I was too impatient. When it didn't sound right, I was ready to quit."

"But it *did* sound right, Giancarlo." Rina leaned toward him. "You were an amazing pianist."

He sat back and studied her. Beautiful Rina, black hair tumbling around her face, her earnest expression telling him she meant every word.

"I might have been," he said slowly, admitting it for the first time. "I didn't realize it then. But maybe, just maybe, I was as good at that age as you were. If I'd applied myself the way you did, gone to Juilliard . . . Maybe." An opportunity lost, because he hadn't wanted to put in the hard work. No wonder his parents had been so furious.

He felt a moment's regret, then shoved it away. Maybe he'd had the talent, but he definitely hadn't had the personality to be a concert pianist. To him, practice was boring, not creative. "I love what I do now."

"I see that." She nodded. "And I'm sure you're great at it."

His lips curved. "You're sure? How can you be sure?"

"Because of how you talk about it. The thought you put into it, the creativity you bring to it. Your passion for it."

Wow. Warmth filled his heart. "I thought you disapproved," he said softly.

She wrinkled her nose. "Was it that obvious? Okay, it was stupid. You know classical musicians can be snobs."

"Really?" he teased. "I never noticed."

"Ha-ha." She took another bite of chicken. "Do you ever play the piano now?"

"Only on your beautiful body."

She made a face. "You know that's not what I meant. Why don't you play?"

He shrugged. "Who has the time?"

Her fork went down and she gazed steadily at him. "There's more to it than that."

She'd caught him. It was always easier for Giancarlo to avoid the tough issues, but clearly Rina wasn't going to let him get away with it. "I play sometimes," he admitted. "But I always feel conflicted. Old feelings surface."

"Bad feelings?"

That tinge of regret was back. An instrument he'd loved as a child had become a burden, a restriction on his freedom. "I want to fool around, enjoy the instrument. But there's always a voice in my head saying I'm wasting my talent."

"Whose voice?"

He closed his eyes. "More of a chorus. My mamma, my papa, my grandparents."

"Ouch," she said softly. "And you can't get past it? I hear my mom's voice too. Criticizing, telling me what to do. But I'm a grown-up now. I have to make my own decisions, find my own way." She took a sip of wine. "How long has it been since you played?"

"Over a year."

She sipped again, then studied him over the rim of her glass. "You chose a different career. That doesn't mean you failed. Or that you betrayed anyone. Especially not the piano. You once made beautiful music together. I hate to think that's lost forever." She stroked the back of his hand. "These hands were designed to make music."

"And are happy to do so on your lovely body." With his free hand, he refilled their glasses, not meeting her gaze. The truth was, he did miss the good times when he'd managed to shove away all the negative feelings and just enjoy playing. Creating. Composing.

"Giancarlo? Don't you miss it?"

Reluctantly, he looked at her. Rina, his special woman. He had to be honest with her. Her hand still rested on top of one of his, so he turned his around and linked his fingers through hers. "Yes, sometimes I miss it."

Her expression softened and she squeezed his fingers lightly. "Then you'll find your way back, when the time's right."

"Perhaps. But for now, let's enjoy dinner."

She nodded, freeing her hand so she could pick up her knife and fork. "On the subject of dinner, I have an invitation for you."

Her words reminded him of something. "And I have one for you. But you go first."

"I told you about my girlfriends, the Awesome Foursome."

"The ones you get together with each Monday? Yes, of course."

"We want to have a dinner this Saturday, at my place. The four of us and our . . ." She paused. "Our, uh, the men in our lives."

The thought that he was her man made him beam. "That sounds like fun. Perhaps I can cook something Italian?"

"That would be wonderful. We're planning a potluck meal. You know, it would be fun if everyone brought something that reflected their background. You're Italian, Jenny's Chinese, Scott's German, Jaxon's Jamaican, Adonis is Greek, I'm Jewish. Suzanne's English and Irish, I think, and I don't know about Ann."

"Sounds like an interesting mix. Vancouver's really a cosmopolitan city, isn't it?"

"It is," she said quietly. "That's one of the things I love about living here. But that's not enough for you, is it, Giancarlo? You really love the world out there. And travel."

He nodded. "There's nothing like it. Different sights and sounds, tastes and smells. Lighting, color, art, music. I need all those stimuli for the work I do." He shook his head and laughed. "Who am I kidding? It's not just about work. There's been a bit of the gypsy in me since the first time I saw Venice. I learned that I need to roam. Explore."

"That's what I thought," she said, studying her nearly empty plate. When she lifted her head, her smile looked forced. "It's good to find out what we each need to make us happy."

"It is." And she was what he needed.

In silence she ate the last couple of bites, leaving only a puddle of lemon sauce.

He tore a slice of bread in half and used it to mop her plate, then held it to her lips. "You're missing the best part."

Her smile seemed more natural this time. She opened her mouth and took a bite of bread. "That's delicious."

Her breath against his fingers, the sensual enjoyment on her face, everything about the woman aroused him.

"But I disagree," she said. "I don't think this is the best part."

"Really? What, then?"

Her brown eyes twinkled in the candlelight. "Last time, you were complaining that I didn't have whipped cream."

"You have some?" His dick swelled at the thought of last week's sex play, but this time with rich cream.

She nodded. "It's in the fridge. Already whipped. With Grand Marnier in it."

Eaten off her sweet body. "Now there's a dessert to tempt a man."

"Why don't you find us some music?"

He went out to her living room to select a CD. Staying with the theme of female clarinetists, he chose Emma Johnson, and the strains of a Mozart concerto filled the room.

If Rina hadn't mentioned whipped cream, he'd have been content to spend an hour sitting by the fire with her, chatting and listening to music. Now, though, he was restless and hungry for her. Hard to believe they'd made love only a couple of hours ago.

He realized she'd turned out the kitchen light, and the sound of running water came from the bathroom.

Gathering up the candles and matches, he took them into the bedroom. Maybe if he put the candles on the dresser, across the room from the bed, she'd be okay with it. He lit them, then turned off all the other lights in her house.

She came in, wearing a knee-length kimono-style robe. The dark fabric had a white and gold flying crane pattern on it. "Oh. Candles."

"I got lost in the dark."

"Hmm."

"My turn in the bathroom. How about you go find that cream?"

The toothbrush she'd given him last time was still out, sitting in a rose-colored glass beside hers. The sight made him smile.

When he went back into the bedroom, she was standing uncertainly by the bed holding a pretty bowl filled with whipped cream.

Guessing he had all of about two seconds before she blew out the candles, he went over and scooped out some cream with a finger. "Taste test." He popped it into his mouth. "Mmm, that's good. Try it." This time the scoop went between her lips.

"God," she said, "that could become addictive."

He dipped out some more and painted his lips with it. "Try this."

She smiled. "Sit down on the bed."

He lowered himself and she leaned over to lick him daintily, each stroke of her tongue an arousing caress. Capturing her tongue, he sucked it into his mouth, tasting cream, orange and Rina's own sweetness. Then he released her. "Anywhere else you'd like to lick?" He unbuttoned his shirt and pulled it off.

Her eyes gleamed as she gazed at his torso. "Lie back."

When he obeyed, she sat on the bed beside him and daubed cream on his nipples. Then she took her time licking and sucking them clean. By the time she'd finished, his dick was trying to bust out of his jeans.

He caught her hand and put it on his fly. "Anywhere else?"

"Hold this." She handed him the bowl, then undid the button at his waist and lowered the zipper.

When he raised his hips, she skimmed his jeans down his legs, leaving his boxer briefs in place. She stroked her hand over the front, starting at one hip, drifting across his hard-on, ending at the other hip. "Mmm, those are so soft. What's the fabric?"

"Uh, some kind of silk knit." Was she really more interested in his underwear than what lay beneath? "They could come off," he suggested.

"Silk? You wear silk shorts?" Her eyes twinkled and the corners of her lips twitched.

"Why? Is that too girlie?" Damn it, the things felt good, and comfort was important.

"No, not at all." She chuckled. "It's just a Foursome thing. The other girls have all given their guys silk boxers. They said they feel so good. But you already wear them." Her hand stroked his shaft through the fabric. "And they do feel really nice. Almost as good as your skin."

"I vote for skin." Though her warm palm through the silk felt pretty damn fine too. And as she leaned over him, the neckline of her robe gaped, giving him a great view of her cleavage, decorated with black lace.

"Before we get to skin," she said, peeling his briefs off, "there's the whipped cream."

But she didn't reach for the bowl, she just stared down at his erection. Her breasts rose and fell faster, telling him the sight turned her on.

If she'd always had sex in the dark, she probably hadn't seen many naked penises. He waited patiently while she looked her fill.

Then she took a deep breath and dipped her finger in the cream. When she began to paint his dick, the sensation was strange. She barely touched him, just dabbed cool, wet cream all over. The flick of her warm finger under the cream, the thought of what was to come, was damned sexy.

She bent her head and he held his breath, waiting for the first touch of her tongue.

Her hair fell forward, then she raised her head, laughing. A few curls on each side were frosted in cream.

He reached out and used his thumb and forefinger to lift some off, then tasted it. "Want me to hold your hair back?"

"Thanks."

As she bent again, he used both hands to gather the unruly curls behind her head.

Then she began to lick, starting at the base of his shaft and working her way up. Small, delicate strokes first, her tongue hot through the cool cream. Sensation shivered up his dick and through his body.

Then, when she'd skimmed off most of the cream, her

tongue strokes became longer and firmer. Unbearably erotic. His dick couldn't get any harder without bursting, and he was having trouble lying still rather than thrusting.

She was licking around the head now. God, women were lucky, being able to have multiple orgasms. He really, really wanted to come. Now.

Groaning, he said, "Enough."

Her head came up and she said, "But there's still a little cream here." Daintily she dipped her tongue, gathering what he was sure were drops of pre-come rather than whipped cream.

"Rina, I mean it." He released her hair and it tumbled down around her face.

She straightened, smiling and licking her lips. "Oh yeah, I could definitely get addicted to this stuff."

"I could get addicted to you," he said roughly. "Now lie down, it's my turn."

12

Rina lay across the bed and Giancarlo spread the edges of her kimono open across her chest, down to her waist, then paused to admire. She was wearing a camisole, black silk trimmed with lace. Her skin glowed warmly in the candlelight and her hard nipples poked against the silk.

"Pretty." He traced the lace edge with his finger, down into her cleavage and back up across her other full breast.

Before she could worry that the candles were still burning, he dipped into the whipped cream and painted it along the same path his finger had taken. He followed it with his tongue, in slow, short, teasing licks. Then he eased the lace down a little, painted another band of cream and licked it off too.

He slid the straps down her shoulders under her robe so he could peel the silk and lace lower, and applied more cream.

Her body quivered and her full breasts rose and fell more quickly.

Again he licked her, then slid the fabric down, revealing the top of her areolas. Glancing up, he saw she'd closed her eyes and was smiling.

Oh hell, he couldn't resist. He tugged the silk below her breasts and daubed cream over both nipples and areolas.

"Giancarlo!" Her body jerked and she raised up on her elbows. "What are you doing?"

"Putting the whipped cream on top of the prettiest dessert imaginable." He admired his artwork. "You have the most beautiful breasts."

He remembered how, on Saturday night, he'd fantasized about pumping his dick between them. His hips gave an involuntary thrust, which brought his erection up against her thigh.

She didn't seem to notice. She was too busy staring at her chest.

He dipped his head and licked. The rosy skin of her areola emerged from the white cream.

She wasn't stopping him, wasn't telling him to blow out the candles. Instead, she stared as if mesmerized, eyes wide and cheeks flushed.

He licked the rest of her areola clean, circling the nipple and leaving it for last. Then he sucked it into his mouth and, holding it gently between his lips, swirled his tongue around it.

Her breath caught, her body tensed. Then she breathed again, jerkily, and moaned, "Oh, that feels good."

Giancarlo went to work on her other breast. When he finished, both he and Rina were gasping for breath. He cupped her breasts in both hands and buried his face in her cleavage, where the orange scent of Grand Marnier mingled with the rose scent of Rina.

"You really like my breasts?" she asked hesitantly.

He lifted his head and studied them. "They're gorgeous," he said reverently. "Perfect. The sexiest breasts I've ever seen." He nudged his erection against her thigh again. "Can't you feel how much you turn me on?" Gently he stroked the underside of one breast, then the other.

She reached up and threaded her fingers through his hair.

"When we were on the phone and I was in the bath, did you really come, imagining you were between my breasts?"

His dick jerked at the thought. "God, yeah, didn't you hear me?"

"It really turned you on, thinking about doing that?"

"It's turning me on right now, you talking about it." His breath rasped through his throat.

"Do you want to? Come that way now?"

"Jesus." Startled, he stared into her face, saw that her flush had deepened. "Yes. But Rina, it's not fair. What about you?"

"It would turn me on too," she said softly, then her lips curved. "Besides, I'm betting you could take care of me afterward."

"Damn right." He gazed down at those tantalizing, voluptuous breasts, and again his dick surged.

"Do it," she whispered. "I want you to." Then she reached into the bowl of whipped cream, scooped a little out and slowly spread it along her cleavage.

Hell, it was selfish but he couldn't resist.

He straddled her body and slid his aching dick between her lush breasts. Taking her hands in his, he guided them until they pressed her breasts from the sides, trapping him securely.

Slowly he slid back and forth, staring down at her chest, at the sight of his rigid maleness and her soft female flesh. Gently he squeezed her nipples between thumbs and index fingers and she gasped.

He glanced at her face, saw she'd lifted herself up and was watching, wide eyed, as he pumped back and forth.

The sensation was so incredible he could hardly stand it. Her warm, soft skin gripping him, the cream letting him glide smoothly. Faster he thrust, so turned on he could hardly breathe. He arched back, his balls tightened, he felt everything inside him drawing up, tensing, tightening, readying.

He was going to come. Come between her beautiful breasts. While she watched.

"God, Rina," he cried as the climax tore through him. His dick thrust, pumped, shot his essence in jets across her soft skin.

And again, more slowly, weakly.

And again, until he was empty.

"My God," she whispered.

He raised his gaze from her chest to her face and saw she was still staring down. Then she reached out a hand, fingers trembling, and touched the creamy foam of his come. Slowly, sensually, she smoothed it into her skin.

"That was beyond amazing," he said. And one of the best parts had been the fact that he'd seen her, his lovely woman, in candlelight, and she'd watched too. She was getting over her self-consciousness, coming to believe in the beauty of her own body.

A sense of tenderness and love flowed through him. He released her breasts and shifted position so he could kiss her.

He'd intended a gentle kiss but her lips met his in a hungry demand.

He darted his tongue into her mouth, then pulled away. "And now it's your turn, *cara.*"

The bowl still had a little cream in it. He slid down the bed, wondering if she'd let him take her robe off. Nope. One hand was holding the knotted sash in place.

Not wanting to push her, he slid the hem of the robe up her thighs and slipped his hand under it, exploring. Her inner thighs were damp, the crotch of her panties soaking. He stroked her through the silk and she whimpered and writhed. Oh yeah, she was close.

Reaching up under the robe, he found the waistband of her panties and pulled them off. Then he used a couple of fingers to gather a big dollop of cream from the bowl and ducked under her robe.

Her knees came up and her legs spread to give him access.

He was in a world of near darkness, but a hint of light penetrated her cotton kimono. Mostly, he found his way by touch. Gently he dabbed cream to cover her pussy, and her body trembled in response.

When he began to lick, she squirmed and pressed against him. God, she tasted amazing, her own juices mingling with Grand Marnier cream.

He slid a couple of fingers inside her. She clenched down on him, pelvis thrusting against his lapping tongue.

A fresh coat of cream, and now he was licking harder as she moved even more frantically.

"Yes," she muttered. "Like that. More, give me more."

He slid his fingers in and out of her slick channel, heard her groan.

Then he painted her engorged clit with cream and fastened his lips around it. Gently he sucked it into his mouth like a cherry and she cried out.

He teased her with his tongue, sucked again, then her body was pulsing and shuddering against him in orgasm.

He stayed there, holding her until her body relaxed and she let out a sigh of pleasure. Then he eased out from under her robe.

"Let's get under the covers," she said, giving him a big, satisfied smile.

When they did, she slipped out of her clothes and he gathered her against him so her head was on his chest. "You are one sexy woman."

"I love sex with you." She giggled softly. "As if you couldn't tell."

"Sex, eating together, talking. I love everything with you."

"Me too," she said, then hesitated before going on. "Giancarlo, this probably isn't the time to ask, but we've never talked about, uh, what we're doing. With this relationship, I mean."

Wasn't it as obvious to her as it was to him? "Getting to know each other. Growing closer." He was about to add, "Falling in love," when she interrupted.

"Are you—" She cleared her throat. "I mean, I guess you're seeing other women too?"

"No! God, no. There's only you." Then he frowned down at the top of her head. Maybe he was wrong, and she didn't feel the way he did. "How about you?"

Her head shook, curls brushing his chest. "I was until recently, but I broke it off."

Crap. He hoped he wasn't just a rebound relationship to her. Tentatively he said, "What went wrong, if you don't mind my asking?"

"I guess . . . there wasn't enough passion. He was comfortable to be with, but there was no excitement in our relationship."

Well, he could definitely give her passion. Not to mention whipped cream and candlelight. "Passion's important. Along with comfort." He pulled her closer, thinking how very comfortable he felt right now.

All the same, maybe he shouldn't rush her by confessing the depth of his feelings. Not when she'd just broken off with another guy. But damn, he was tired of all this patience.

Searching for a safe topic of conversation, he said, "Oh, I didn't tell you about that invitation I mentioned earlier. It's next week. A movie and dinner."

"That sounds like fun. What's the movie?"

He'd bet her previous man hadn't offered her an evening like this. "A psychological thriller, with Harrison Ford and Julianne Moore. It was shot in Vancouver and they're having the world premiere here. There'll be lots of celebrities."

She'd stiffened in his arms and now pulled away so she

could turn and look at him. With both hands, she held the covers up to her neck. "Did you just invite me to the world premiere of a movie?"

"And there's a big reception, dinner kind of thing after."

Rina frowned. "How are you involved in this?"

"I'm not. They invited the entertainment and media people who're in town. What do you say? It'll be fun."

"I'm, uh . . ." She shook her head. "That's your world, Giancarlo. Not mine. All those 'beautiful people.' I'd be out of place."

Did the idea of movie stars intimidate her? "They're just people, Rina. Besides"—he jiggled her shoulder—"I want you to be part of my world."

"I don't have anything to wear to an event like that."

"I'll buy you something. Besides, if you get on with the VSO, you'll be at lots of galas."

"The world of symphony is different. You have to be a good musician, and yes you have to dress decently, but it's not about glamour."

She could be as glamorous as any movie star. But he realized she didn't believe that. Rather than get into an argument, he squeezed her shoulder gently. "Think about it. Okay?"

She drew in a breath and let it out slowly. "Okay."

They lay quietly together then, and Giancarlo wondered how he was going to persuade her. Not just to attend the premiere, but to share his life. Seeing her tonight had confirmed everything he'd been feeling. Rina Goldberg was the one woman for him.

To hell with fucking *pazienza*.

Her breathing slowed and he held her tenderly as she drifted into sleep.

Rina woke to darkness and an empty bed. She sat up. Where had he gone?

Then she heard the toilet flush and water run in the bathroom. She lay back, smiling as she anticipated welcoming him back into bed.

But he didn't come.

He moved around in the bedroom—was he picking up his clothes?—then left the room.

She sat up again, prepared to call his name, then closed her mouth. If he wanted to sneak out in the middle of the night, she wasn't going to beg him to stay. But what had gone wrong? Was he mad that she hadn't leaped at the opportunity to attend that movie premiere?

No doubt every other girl he'd known would have been panting to go. But then, they were slim, sleek, looked fabulous in an evening gown and had the self-confidence to mix and mingle with movie stars.

She'd known from the beginning that she and Giancarlo were different people with very different lives, she reminded herself. Maybe he was only just figuring it out.

Earlier, he'd said he didn't want to see other women. He'd talked about the two of them growing closer. Had she completely blown it?

Battling tears, she hugged his pillow against her body. They'd had a good time; he'd made her feel special. She'd always known their time together would be brief, so it was silly to mourn the end rather than remember how much fun they'd had.

When she'd been seventeen, she'd managed pretty well. A great summer romance, then back to real life. She could do the same thing again. It wasn't like she had let herself fall for the man.

Soft sounds rippled through the night air.

What was that? The piano? Giancarlo was playing her piano.

He hadn't gone after all!

And he was playing. For the first time in a long time. They'd talked about the piano at dinner, and now he was playing.

A smile drove away the tears as she listened to slow, gentle scales. Then he drifted into a piece she didn't recognize. He must be rusty, because he stumbled from time to time. Went back and replayed bits in a slightly different way.

And then it came to her. He wasn't just playing, he was composing. Creating new music.

The piece was complex. No wonder he had to work so hard on it. It was warm and harmonious, yet there were subtle notes, minor keys, phrases that wove around the harmony and challenged the ear.

As he became more confident of each section, he played it with increasing meaning. Emotion, even passion.

When he'd worked on it longer and finished it, she knew it would be beautiful.

She hugged the pillow closer as she realized something. She'd been wrong. He hadn't been born to be a concert pianist. To perform other people's work. No wonder he'd been frustrated with repetitious practice. He was a creator, even more than a performer.

The music called to her. She slid out of bed and wrapped her kimono tightly around her. Then she crept silently to the music room and stood just outside the door.

Cautiously she peeked in.

He hadn't turned on a light, but the blinds were only partially closed, letting in enough light from outside that she could make out his form.

He sat on the piano bench, clad only in those silky black boxer briefs. His eyes were closed, an expression of intense concentration on his face as his fingers sounded out the music he heard in his head.

Sabine was curled in a chair, her purring accompanying him.

Rina stepped into the doorway, a floorboard creaked and the cat meowed.

Giancarlo broke off. "Rina." He turned to her.

"Don't stop. That's lovely. What is it?"

"Rina."

"Yes?"

"No, I mean, that's what I'm playing. You. Who you are, the way I feel about you."

Her mouth dropped open and she gaped at him, but he only smiled and turned back to the piano. The music started again.

Rina's heart was beating so fast, she pressed a hand against her chest to calm it. He was composing music about her? Music this complex and beautiful? Music that he played with such intensity and passion?

She crept into the room, picked Sabine up and settled into the chair with the cat on her lap. For half an hour or more, she didn't say a word, just listened.

And as she did, she realized it was too late to rationalize about this being a short-term relationship. She'd fallen head over heels for Giancarlo. When he left, as she knew he was bound to, it would break her heart.

But the music he was playing spoke more of joy than sorrow. That's how he saw her. As a woman who took pleasure from life. Well, so she would.

If there was sorrow in her future, then she'd damned well keep it there. She wouldn't let it spoil her time with Giancarlo.

Finally his hands dropped from the keyboard and he turned to her. "That's it. The best I can do for now. I'll work on it more another time."

She rose, shifting the sleeping cat from her lap back to the chair, and went over to him. "It's beautiful."

He smiled. "Yes. You *are* beautiful." His hand reached out for hers as he slid the bench away from the piano. "Frustrating sometimes, definitely a challenge, but always beautiful."

She stood between his legs, her back against the keyboard. He buried his face against her chest, kissed her skin gently. And then less gently.

Then he was standing, pulling her body flush against his, letting her feel his erection. "You got me wanting to compose again. I didn't know how much I'd missed it, how much a part of me it really is."

His head bent toward hers. "Thank you." Then he kissed her, as passionately as he'd played the piano.

She could still feel the music resonating through her body, keeping pace with his kisses, with her own growing need. Greedily she took his mouth, pouring all her feelings—both lust and love—into him.

He groaned and yanked down his briefs so his cock swung free, a rigid column pressing against her. "I have to be in you. Here. Now."

"Yes!" She wanted, needed that too. So badly.

He sat down on the piano bench. "Sit on my lap."

Arms around his shoulders, she eased down, pulling the bottom of her kimono apart. Straddling him, she slid her legs over the far side of the bench, feeling the urgent press of his cock against her aching sex.

Then he was in her, in one quick thrust that made her gasp with pleasure.

His hands tightened on her waist. "Crap, I forgot. No condom. Rina, I'm clean, I swear I've always used condoms."

"I'm clean too. And on the pill."

But she'd never had sex without a condom. Protection.

Damn, she didn't want to protect herself from Giancarlo. She knew he wouldn't lie about being clean, and she wanted all of him. No barriers. She wanted to feel him pour his essence deep inside her.

"Make love to me," she breathed in his ear. "Now. Like this."

"God, yes." He captured her mouth again and kissed her fiercely as their bodies began to move together.

He felt different inside her, flesh against flesh. More friction, more heat, more sensation. Everything better, more intense. Her muscles tightened around him, then released as he slid back out, stroking every nerve ending as he moved.

Her body was on fire. Gasping for breath, she tore her mouth from his. "This feels so good. I love your naked cock."

"Yeah, it feels great. You are the sexiest woman, Rina. I love being inside you."

He quickened the pace and she felt the achy pressure building. She shifted the angle so his cock would stroke her clit. Her body arched and she leaned back in the cradle of his arms, then back farther. Groping behind her for support, her hands crashed down on piano keys.

Startled, they stared at each other for a moment, then both chuckled. "Beautiful music, in its own way," he said through gasps for air.

She was totally open to him, spread wide between the bench and the piano. He gripped her waist and thrust harder, breath rasping.

Using the keyboard for leverage, only vaguely noticing the discordant sounds, she ground herself against him and the orgasm built inside her and then exploded in waves.

Giancarlo cried out exultantly, thrust harder, then he was coming too.

And, oh God, she felt him. Felt his come, spurting into her, again and again.

Without warning she climaxed once more, calling his name.

* * *

Early Wednesday morning, Rina woke with a start. She'd forgotten to set her alarm, but if she rushed she'd still be in time to meet Levi. She dropped a wake-up kiss on Giancarlo's lips, then grabbed her walking clothes and hurried into the bathroom.

When she emerged fully clothed, he was up and dressing. "I know you need to meet your neighbor," he said with a smile, "so I'll skip the shower."

"Thanks."

He finished buttoning his shirt and pulled her into a hug. Arms looped around her, head resting on the top of her head, he asked, "How's your day shaping up? Want to get together later?"

"I have a few lessons, but aside from that it's practice." She sighed against his chest, torn. "I'd love to see you, but the truth is, I'm obsessed about the audition. I can't handle any distractions."

He pulled away and dropped a kiss on her nose. "I understand. I'll put in some extra time on postproduction."

"What is that, anyhow?" she asked as, arms around each other, they walked toward her front door.

"I work with the editor, putting the video together. Making my vision come to life."

"How's it going?"

"We're getting there. I think Tattooed Elf and their label will be happy."

"That's great. I can't wait to see it." She grinned up at him. "It'll be my very first music video."

He stopped just inside her front door and turned to face her. "Tomorrow, I'd like to take you out to celebrate when your audition's over." His mouth quirked at the corners, like he was planning something special but wasn't ready to tell her.

Hating to be a spoilsport, she said, "Celebrate? Giancarlo, don't get your hopes up. I'm up against tough competition. Besides, I'm afraid it's tempting fate to plan a celebration before I even audition."

"What we're celebrating is your finaling. You deserve a treat after all the work you've been putting in."

She grinned. "Well, when you put it that way . . ."

"I'll work out the details and call you." He pulled her into his arms for a long, steamy kiss.

When they were both breathing hard, she pulled away and shoved him out the door, laughing. "Enough. You're making me late."

All the same, she couldn't resist watching as he walked to the van. His easy, long-limbed stride, his carriage. Even from the back the man was sexy.

And that man had composed music for her.

Shaking her head in wonder, she hurried to put on her jacket and walking shoes, then scurried over to Levi Fischman's house.

The door opened as she went up the walk, and he came to meet her. "So, you kicked your young man out to go walking with the old guy, eh girlie?"

She flushed. "You saw Giancarlo leave?"

He fell into step beside her. "Yeah, I was checking the weather. This one looks better than the dentist. That guy was a *nebekh*. This the one who bought you champagne?"

"Yes." Hmm, so Levi saw Al as a bland nobody. She stifled a quick grin. Okay, his comment was unfair, but Giancarlo certainly did have more vitality.

"Money and good taste, and he treats you right. You could do worse."

"I could. But don't build it into something it isn't. He lives in New York and he's always traveling."

"Oh yeah?" He waved at a neighbor who was out walking

her dog, then turned to Rina, frowning. "Can't do that forever. A person has to settle down sometime."

"I don't think his time has come. If it ever will. He likes travel, his job requires it and he loves his work."

"That's a good thing," he admitted grudgingly. "Too many people get stuck in a job they hate. Really sucks it outta you."

"Yes. I wouldn't want that to happen to Giancarlo." She sighed. She loved him, so would never try to tie him down.

"Makes it tough, huh, girlie?" Levi said sympathetically.

"A little." She straightened her shoulders, tossed back her hair, quickened the pace. "But he and I are having a good time. That's what I'm focusing on."

"You have *sechel*, Rina. Trust in it."

Good common sense? Did she really?

"So, what kinda job's this Giancarlo got?" Levi asked, mangling his name in the process.

"He directs music videos." She explained the things Giancarlo had told her.

When she was done, she was surprised to find they were on the home stretch of their walk. "I talk too much," she said.

"Nah. You like the guy; it's not a sin." He waved a hand as he headed up the walk to his front door.

Rina went in her back door, fed Sabine, grabbed a yogurt and went to her computer.

"Common sense?" she said to Sabine. "I have more faith in the combined wisdom of the Foursome."

Her fingers hovered over the keyboard. No, nothing warranted an emergency lunch. Plus she really did need the time to practice. Instead, she typed:

He composed music for me. About me. Isn't that the most romantic thing you've ever heard? And this from a guy who hasn't even played the piano in a year. It's like, I inspired him or something. Me. Rina Goldberg. And he brought me the BEST earrings as a first-week anniversary present—and he bought them in LONDON.

She paused. Should she tell them the rest?
Yes, she had to tell someone, and she trusted these women.

Okay, here's the thing. I've fallen for him. I think I'm in love. And I know it's crazy, but I'm just going to enjoy it while he's around. You can help me pick up the pieces after he leaves.
Oh, he wants to cook something Italian for Saturday. I thought it might be fun if we each did ethnic.

Of course pretty much everything Jewish was horribly fattening. Knishes, blintzes, challah, bagels. Oh well, it's not like she had to eat much of it herself.

I'll get challah. It's really yummy bread.

She checked her watch. Best put on some coffee. Tara would be here in a few minutes. Periodically throughout the morning, between lessons and practice sessions, Rina checked e-mail.
Suzanne responded first.

Oh, Rina, I'm so happy and so sad for you. I know you wouldn't give your heart if the man wasn't special—and that composing thing is just amazing!—but I hate to think of you being hurt. You know we're all here for you, anytime you need to talk.
Hugs, really big hugs.
Suzanne
P.S. Ethnic's a fun idea. I'll make good old-fashioned

apple pie and ice cream, and Jaxon and I have his mom's recipe for Jamaican jerk chicken.

Jenny didn't e-mail until early afternoon.

Man, Rina, you sure leaped with both feet. You've only known the guy . . . what? Like, a week? But ya know, I always figured if one of us would do the love at first sight thing, it'd be you.

Okay, okay, I know it's not first sight, but you know what I mean.

God, girl, you've actually rendered me speechless. Or maybe that was the firefighters at the calendar shoot this morning <g>.

Sorry. Thinking here . . . Not too swiftly . . .

Okay, look, you're the one who always told us to follow our hearts. And for us, it worked out. So maybe you actually do know what you're doing. Maybe your heart's telling you something about Giancarlo that your brain isn't hearing yet. Does that make sense?

I SO CAN'T WAIT TO MEET THIS GUY.

Jen

Oh yeah, egg rolls and German poppy seed cake. Can you believe I'm with a man who bakes cake? It's his mom's recipe and he says it's a big fave down at the fire-hall.

Rina chuckled as she finished reading Jenny's e-mail. Then she sobered. Had she really told her friends to follow their hearts?

Maybe so. She'd certainly asked them to examine their hearts. And she'd supported them, even when it looked like the odds were against their relationships.

Just as the odds were against hers with Giancarlo.

Her computer pinged to announce incoming e-mail. It was Ann.

> Oh, Rina, I do feel for you. But—I kind of hate to say this but I'm going to anyhow—you know what a romantic you are. Are you sure you're not just getting carried away by the things he's doing? You've never gone out with a man who bought champagne, had you serenaded, bought you a gift in London, wrote music for you.
>
> Anyhow, as Suzanne said, you know we're here for you, whatever happens.
>
> Oh, and Adonis and I will bring dolmades. As for food traditions in my family, that would mean microwave dinners so I think I'll skip that and double up on Greek. How about a big Greek salad?
>
> Can't wait to meet this man!
>
> Hugs too.
>
> Ann.

Follow your heart? Versus being too much of a romantic? Seemed like she was right back where she'd started. She'd enjoy this time with Giancarlo but not get her hopes up that it'd last.

Sighing, she went back to practice. There was one thing to be said for the audition. It did take her mind off her confusing love life. By now she knew the music so well she didn't have to think about the mechanics, she could let herself sink into the emotion, concentrate on giving the most effective interpretation.

Later that night, Giancarlo phoned. "Hello, *cara.* How are you feeling? Ready? Nervous?"

She glanced at the music on the stand in front of her, the clarinet at her feet. "I'm not sure I'll ever feel ready, but it's coming along well. And yes"—she gave a shaky laugh—"I'm terrified." Though it helped to hear his voice and know he'd cared enough to phone and wish her well.

"Anything I can do to help?"

"Just cross your fingers for me."

"I will. And you remember what's important. It's about the music, right? Don't let your nerves make you forget the music."

He was right. She gave a soft chuckle. "As in, slow down, feel the music?"

"Do you still have that Post-It note?"

"No. Today my student remembered to take her music with her."

"Then write yourself another one, and stick it on your audition pieces."

She grinned "Good idea. I will."

"Now, about our celebration tomorrow. Can you get away in the early afternoon?"

"I thought you were talking about dinner."

"That too. But I have more in mind." There was a note of suppressed excitement in his voice.

"Okay, sure. The audition should be over by noon, then I'll want to relax and pamper myself for an hour or so. However things go," she added grimly. It was really hard to believe she could beat out the woman from L.A.

"Sounds like a great idea. Now, do you think you could also skip your morning walk on Friday?"

Did he want to linger in bed with her? That idea was very tempting. Lips curving, she said, "I guess I could manage that. For once." Levi would definitely understand.

"Good. Then pack an overnight bag."

"Oh! Really? Giancarlo, what are you planning?"

"I don't want to spoil the surprise. Can you get away for the night?"

"Uh, sure." Sabine would be fine, and Rina had no other responsibilities. Anticipation fizzed through her, displacing her anxiety over the audition. "Give me a clue what to pack. And what to wear."

"Wear jeans and bring something for dinner. Nothing too fancy. That red sweater would be perfect."

"Okay." She grinned widely. "This is fun. I'm really looking forward to it."

"Me too." His tone was more serious now.

They were both quiet for a moment, then she said, "How was your day?"

"Very satisfying. Everything fell right into place."

"That's great." She paused. "I hate to say this, but I'd like to get in another hour or so of practice."

"Of course. We'll have lots of time tomorrow. Practice well, *carissima,* and sleep well. I'll be thinking of you tomorrow."

"Thanks."

After hanging up, she went to the desk for a Post-It note. After a moment's reflection, she wrote, "It's about the music."

As she stuck the note on her music folder, she knew that, reading it, she'd hear Giancarlo's voice in her head.

Was she getting superstitious, Rina wondered as she waited her turn to audition. Ann's lucky green earrings in her ears, a good-luck e-mail from her aunt in her pocket and the Post-It note sticking up from her music.

No, it wasn't superstitious to carry tokens that reminded her of the people who cared about her and supported her. They made her feel less alone and vulnerable.

Today she was playing last. As she walked out on stage—today with no screen separating her from the audition committee—she found herself thinking about the music Giancarlo had written for her, and the way he'd played it. Music was so much more than combinations of notes, it was about emotion.

And, as he'd said, that was what was important. Not the

symphony, not the audition committee, but the music. It deserved her best, and that's what she would give it.

She straightened her shoulders and breathed deeply, feeling the air flow in and out of her diaphragm.

Randall Chang had been there to greet her. "Don't be nervous," he'd said. "All three finalists have the skill to play principal with the VSO. Now it's a matter of which style of expression the committee prefers."

She had nodded and said softly, "It's about the music."

He had given her a quick, approving smile. "Yes, it certainly is. Honoring the music, and bringing it to an appreciative audience."

Now she felt almost relaxed as she glanced at Giancarlo's note, gripped her B flat clarinet comfortably and nodded to Randall Chang to signal she was ready.

The minutes flew by and when she put her instrument down, she was flushed with happiness and a sense of accomplishment.

Randall took her to wait with the other two finalists. Knowing the committee would be discussing the three of them, she glanced at the other two—a slight Asian who looked barely more than a boy, and the seasoned principal from L.A. The young man fidgeted nervously, staring at the floor. The woman met her gaze, smiled and shrugged. Rina smiled back and resisted looking at her watch.

To distract herself, she turned her mind again to the music Giancarlo had composed.

Her breath hitched when Randall walked back into the room, and she straightened in her chair.

"Thanks to all three of you," he said. "You have made the decision very difficult." He took a breath and Rina held her own. It would be the woman from L.A., she just knew it.

Randall went on. "The Vancouver Symphony Orchestra wishes to engage Ms. Goldberg."

Shit! Had he actually said her name, or had she imagined it?

But he must have, because the L.A. woman was on her feet, smiling graciously and coming toward Rina with her hand outstretched. "Congratulations."

"I . . . I . . . Oh my God, is it really me?"

Randall laughed, abandoning his formality. "Yes, Rina, you're the one." As soon as she'd finished shaking the woman's hand, he held out his. Then the young Asian did the same, his palm cool and sweaty.

Her competitors left and Randall said, "Do you want to discuss the details now?"

Slowly she shook her head. "I won't take anything in." Her voice wavered.

"I understand. How about we get together on Monday?"

"Perfect."

Somehow she made it to her car and then she just sat, her whole body weak and shaking with exhaustion, relief and triumph. She'd done it. Achieved another of her dreams.

Next month she'd be on stage as principal clarinet with the VSO. Holy shit!

Gradually the trembling died down and she was able to drive home.

When she walked up the back steps and opened the kitchen door, she felt as if it was a different, older and wiser Rina who bent down to tickle Sabine behind the ear. She'd gone through a huge, life-altering experience.

She sprang to her feet, tossed back her hair and spun in a circle, laughing. "I did it," she told the cat. "Oh my God, I actually did it."

A weight was off her shoulders and she felt light as air. No more practice, no more stress. Well, not until she met Randall on Monday and got the music for the first VSO performances.

She was free to enjoy the rest of the day and anticipate whatever Giancarlo had in store for her.

First she phoned or e-mailed everyone who was waiting to

hear the results of the audition and collected congratulations. She didn't get in touch with Giancarlo, though. Much more fun to deliver her news in person.

Having been too nervous to eat breakfast, she was now starving. She opened the fridge and stared inside. Normally she didn't eat pasta, but there was some spinach fettuccine, neatly coiled in a plastic bag. Giancarlo hadn't cooked all of it. And what was in that container? She peeled the lid off and sniffed. Mmm. That wonderful lemony sauce he'd made for the chicken.

Humming along to some mellow Louis Armstrong, she took out a pot and put water on to boil.

She cooked the pasta, heated the sauce, and tossed in the pasta and poured herself a glass of white wine. Then she stared at the loaf of Italian bread. The cut end was dry, so she sliced off a couple of inches. Now it was soft, almost fresh; it would be perfect to sop up the extra sauce.

Giancarlo was a bad influence. Normally she'd never consider eating either pasta or bread, much less both.

Maybe this was the time to be extra-diligent with her diet. If she dropped twenty pounds she'd be so much more attractive. Perhaps then she'd be able to compete with the women he worked with every day.

On the other hand, he'd called those women anorexic. And he certainly did seem to enjoy making love to her body, plump though it might be.

"Oh, damn," she told Sabine. "This is my time to celebrate and enjoy. Tomorrow I can diet and stress out over my weight."

She cut a medium-sized slice of bread and took her lunch into the living room, settling in her favorite chair.

Too hyped up to read, she relived every moment of the audition as she enjoyed her meal. After, she washed the dishes, then, rather to her surprise, she felt like doing yoga. She changed into her exercise clothes, unrolled her mat and slid the DVD into the player.

From yoga she went to a luxurious bubble bath, and when she climbed out of the tub she was feeling on top of the world. She put on jeans, a loose black blouse, the scarf with bright poppies and of course the earrings Giancarlo had given her. After tossing a few things in an overnight bag, she made sure Sabine had food, water and a clean litter box, and was just glancing at her watch when the doorbell rang.

She opened the door to Giancarlo, who held one perfect long-stemmed red rose, the stem embedded in a vial of water.

Wow. This handsome, sexy man, the man she loved, was here to make her day even more special. How did she get to be so lucky?

He handed her the rose. "*Cara,* how did it go?"

She inhaled the rich scent of the bloom, then turned a beaming face to him. "I got it."

"Ah-ha!" He caught her up in his arms, actually lifting her off the ground and whirling her around. "You're brilliant, amazing, *splendida.*"

She grinned. "Yeah, I guess I am."

He dropped a kiss on her lips. "I'm buying the first ticket to your first performance."

"It's a deal." How she'd love to know he was out there in the audience that very first time.

"We need to get going," he said, "but I want to hear every detail while we drive."

"Are you finally going to tell me where we're headed?"

"We'll start with the harbor." His brows creased in sudden alarm. "I hope you don't get airsick."

13

"Airsick? No, I don't, but... We're flying?" Rina stared at him. "In a seaplane?"

"Good guess." Giancarlo beamed at her, excited about everything he'd planned. Anxious to get started, he stepped past her into the house. "This your bag?" He nodded to the small case in the hall.

"Yes."

"Don't forget a jacket. The weather's changeable." He was wearing a lightweight black leather jacket over his navy tee and jeans, whereas she just had jeans and a light top, with that poppy scarf. Along with the earrings he'd given her.

She chuckled as she took a three-quarter-length jacket of black wool from the closet. "That's Vancouver. On any given day, you're likely to get clouds, rain and sun."

"Keeps things interesting." He held the jacket so she could slide into it, juggling the rose from hand to hand. Then he bent to give Sabine a quick stroke and picked up Rina's bag. "Ready?"

"I guess. Though I've never been in a seaplane." She laughed a little nervously. "Make that any small plane. Where are we flying to?"

"You'll see when we get there. And I really hope you like it," he said, suffering from a bout of nerves himself. Crap, he could plan and direct an entire music video with absolute confidence, but no video had ever been this important to him.

"I'm sure I will," she hurried to reassure him.

"Then let's go." He stepped through the door and she grabbed her purse and followed, clutching the rose.

In the car, he said, "All right, tell me every single moment of the audition."

He smiled as she rushed on, as eager to share all the details as he was to hear them. It was especially heartwarming when she said she'd heard his voice in her head, helping her stay on track.

"You deserve this, Rina," he told her as he pulled into the parking lot at the Harbor Air terminal in Coal Harbor. "You're so talented, and you've worked hard for it."

He collected their bags from the trunk and they went into the small building, where a few people sat in the waiting area. Giancarlo walked to the desk and said to the pretty Korean woman, "Charter under the name of Mancini."

"Charter?" Rina exclaimed, as the woman flashed a bright smile and said, "Oh yes, Mr. Mancini, we've been expecting you. All the paperwork's done and your plane is ready." She pointed out the window toward the docks and planes below. "It's the little one at the end. White with yellow trim."

"It's cute," Rina said.

"And a classic," the Harbor Air woman responded. "A real DeHavilland Beaver. One of the finest seaplanes ever made. And that's your pilot," she added as a young man in jeans and a brown bomber jacket stepped out of the plane, then down onto one of the pontoons.

Giancarlo led the way outside and down a skid-stripped ramp.

"Okay, I'm impressed," Rina muttered.

He looked over his shoulder, laughing. "I'm not trying to impress you, just give you something to remember. Don't go thinking I'm rich," he teased. "Most video directors don't make that much." He did well enough, though, and worked so hard he had little time to spend his earnings. Indulging Rina was a treat for him as well as for her.

And, if things went the way he hoped, today would be a memorable day for both of them.

The pilot greeted them, and Giancarlo introduced Rina as "the brand new principal clarinet with the Vancouver Symphony Orchestra." The man offered his congratulations, then helped Rina up into the plane. Giancarlo followed and stowed their bags securely.

He'd been in seaplanes before, so the bare-bones interior wasn't a surprise. There was seating for five or six passengers, and Rina had settled by the window on the right side of the plane, in the row behind the pilot.

Giancarlo slid in beside her and took her hand. "What do you think?"

Her eyes were wide. "It's very, uh, immediate. We can see the pilot's controls, watch everything he's doing." She leaned her right shoulder against the side of the plane, then away again. "It seems pretty fragile."

"Beavers are actually really sturdy." The voice was the pilot's, as he climbed into his seat up front and swung sideways to talk to her. "They're built for bush travel."

"That's reassuring." She smiled at the man.

"I'll go over a few things before we get under way," the pilot said. He went on to talk about the noise level, earplugs and—something Giancarlo hoped they wouldn't need—airsick bags. He ended up saying, "The trip should be about forty-five minutes."

"Where are we going?" Rina asked.

He made a zipping-his-lips gesture. "Sorry. Sworn to se-crecy." Then he turned his attention to his preflight routine.

"Forty-five minutes," Rina mused to Giancarlo. "The Sun-shine Coast, Victoria or Seattle, the Gulf Islands . . ."

He put on an innocent expression.

She giggled, then whispered, "This is exciting," in his ear.

"Seat belts," the pilot said over his shoulder.

They both buckled up, then Giancarlo took her hand and squeezed it.

Outside, a man untied their plane from the dock. The engine started up with a rattly growl, and the plane motored away.

The pontoons cut through the water with only minimal bumping. "It's louder than I expected." Rina leaned toward him, raising her voice to be heard. "Have you been on a sea-plane before?"

"A few times. They're fun."

The pilot motored the plane away from shore and Giancarlo and Rina looked back, watching Vancouver become smaller. The engine raced, the plane sped up and then the pontoons were free of the water.

"We're flying," she said, looking almost as thrilled as a kid. "This is so cool. You're right, it's more fun than a big jet."

The expression on her face warmed his heart. "I'm glad you like it." God, but he wanted to make Rina happy.

She turned to peer out the side window. He put an arm around her shoulder and leaned close. "Tell me what I'm look-ing at."

"The North Shore. Look at all the boats down there. What a pretty sail on that big boat." She was quiet a few moments, then, "Oh, wow, we're going to fly over the Lions Gate Bridge!"

So engrossed in the view was she that she didn't seem to no-tice when he unbuckled his seat belt and moved away to get the bag he'd stowed earlier. But she definitely paid attention when he handed her two champagne flutes.

Hurriedly she put the rose on her lap so she could take the glasses. "What are you doing?"

He brandished the bottle of Dom Pérignon he'd had chilling among ice packs. "A celebration calls for champagne."

"You bought me champagne? And"—she gestured around the plane—"and this? This mysterious trip? This is all to celebrate the audition? When you didn't even know if I'd win?"

He fought to hold back an I've-got-a-secret smile. "And because you're an amazing woman, and I'm so happy to be here with you." His fingers were cold and wet from the bottle, but he let the back of his hand drift softly down her cheek.

Her lips curved in a grin that was part wonder and part smugness. "Well, just, wow. That's all I can say."

Chuckling, he eased the cork gently from the bottle and poured into both glasses, then slipped the bottle back into the ice. He took one glass from her and raised it in a toast. "To Rina, the new VSO first chair, and a truly gifted clarinetist."

"Thank you," she said softly. She clicked her glass to his and drank. "This is so good."

"Look, you're missing the view." He pointed past her, out the window.

Her gaze lingered on his face a moment longer, then she gathered his right hand into her left and turned to the window. "Look at the lighthouse. This must be Lighthouse Park." Pointing, she said, "And there are a couple of kayakers."

They'd been talking loudly because of the engine noise, and perhaps the pilot had overheard, because he took the plane down lower, affording a better view. Giancarlo moved closer to her, his chin resting on her shoulder as she peered out the window. Each time she moved, her springy curls brushed his cheek like a caress.

The plane traveled up the coast, with the pilot pointing out Horseshoe Bay, Bowen Island, Gibsons, Sechelt and so on. The trip was all he'd hoped, Giancarlo thought. The sun had obliged and the ocean sparkled, the coastal views were fascinating and the champagne tasted great. Best of all, Rina was as happy as a kid at Disneyland.

Partway through the trip, Giancarlo refilled their glasses and, when they clicked them together, her eyes were warm with affection. "This is perfect. Thank you."

He shook his head. "Thank *you*."

Her lips curved. "For what?"

"For being here with me. For being you." He wondered if his own eyes revealed the depth of his feelings.

Rina held his gaze until the pilot called back, "Half a dozen seals. On the rocks to your right."

She turned back to the window. "Oh yes! Look, Giancarlo."

He put an arm around her shoulders and leaned close, looking for the seals even as he breathed in the rose scent of her skin. When the seals were behind them, he eased her scarf down so he could kiss her neck, and she murmured, "Nice."

Giancarlo wanted to do more. To slide his hand under that loose, tantalizing top and caress her breasts. To settle his hand on her thigh and slide it between her legs. But this wasn't the place or time. Not with the pilot there and Rina enraptured by the ever-changing view.

At Powell River, the pilot said, "We're heading west now. It'll just be ocean and the occasional boat until we get to Quadra Island."

Rina settled back in her seat and turned to Giancarlo. "Quadra? Is that where we're going? That's the island off Campbell River, isn't it?"

"What do I know about BC geography?" he said with a smirk, then refilled her champagne glass.

She smiled at him over the rim. "This is wonderful. A seaplane flight with champagne."

"I think so too. See, I'm selfish about my gifts. I like giving ones I can share." He tucked a curl behind her ear and tugged gently on her earring.

She captured his hand and pressed it against her cheek. "Your kind of selfish I can handle." Then she twined her fingers through his and held his hand on her lap.

It wasn't long before the pilot took the plane lower. "Stow the glasses and buckle up," he called back. "We're going down."

Giancarlo had borrowed a champagne stopper from his hotel, so he quickly sealed up the champagne and carefully packed it and the glasses back in his bag. Soon the plane was skimming just above the ocean. It gave a couple of hops as the pontoons hit the water, then, with a whoosh, it settled.

He peered out the window, anxious to see their destination, April Point Resort.

When he'd told the concierge at the Opus Hotel that he wanted someplace special for a romantic getaway, on only a day's notice, she'd checked several places then recommended this one. He'd studied the website, laughing when he saw the exact description "romantic getaway," but a little troubled by the fact that salmon fishermen also loved the place.

Might it be too rustic and wildernessy for Rina? She was a city girl. Yet he'd learned that she walked, loved to garden and enjoyed eating outside on nice days, so she clearly had an outdoors side too.

As he stared past the docks and bobbing boats to the sprawling wooden buildings nestled among tall trees, he held his breath. Would she like it?

"It's so picturesque," she breathed.

He smiled with relief. "We have a cabin with an ocean view. I hope it's okay."

"It looks wonderful." She turned to him, her lovely brown eyes huge with amazement and pleasure. "I can't believe you did this."

"It was actually the concierge—" he started, then broke off laughing as she punched him on the shoulder. "I want you to be happy," he told her simply and honestly.

"I'm thrilled."

The tension eased from his body. They gazed into each other's eyes for a long moment. Giancarlo wanted to do everything with this woman. Make love to her slowly and lovingly, and fast and furiously. Hold her through the night, keep her safe, celebrate her joys and comfort her through her sorrows.

Her eyes widened and he wondered if she could read his thoughts. Slowly they leaned closer together. Their lips had just touched when the plane bumped against the dock.

"Sorry," the pilot called back.

They broke apart, laughing. "That's all right," Giancarlo said. "We have the rest of the day to kiss." In an undertone, so only Rina could hear, he added, "And do everything else that strikes our fancy."

The pilot climbed out of the plane and secured it, then opened the door and assisted Rina down the few steps to the dock. Giancarlo followed.

She stood holding her rose, head lifted, smiling. "The air smells so fresh and clean."

They thanked the pilot, who said, "I'd better head back before it gets dark. See you folks in the morning." As they watched, he pushed the plane away from the dock, hopped in, then motored toward open water.

Giancarlo and Rina walked along the dock, feeling it sway gently under their feet.

Above them was a higher level of wooden docking set on piles. Back from the water were the resort buildings.

When they'd climbed to the main level, Giancarlo slung his bag over his shoulder and took Rina's hand.

"Look," she whispered, and he saw two giant black-and-white squared boards set out on the wood-planked deck. A couple of men played chess and a man and a woman played checkers, using supersized pieces.

As Giancarlo and Rina walked toward the office, he noticed that a few people stared at them and smiled.

Rina nestled closer and murmured, "I've never been the girl with the rose before. It's kind of fun."

He hugged her tight. If he had his way, she'd always be his girl with the rose.

Inside, he gave his name and filled out a registration form, then they listened to a description of the resort's amenities. Taking the key, they went to find their cabin.

It was simply furnished with lots of glossy maple. As soon as he'd closed the door and put down the bags, Rina came up to him and, putting a hand on either side of his head, pulled his head down to hers.

"Thank you," she said, planting a kiss on his forehead. "Thank you so much." She rained kisses across his forehead, down his nose, onto his cheeks and he began to laugh.

He stopped when she reached his mouth and this time lingered. Hungrily he caught her by the waist and pulled her close, then began to kiss her back, devouring her mouth.

Too much waiting, and wanting. Arousal surged through him and their kisses grew more intense and passionate. His dick hardened and her lower body rubbed against him in tantalizing circles.

She tugged his T-shirt out from his jeans and ran her hands up under it, stroking his back.

He pulled away from her so he could strip off the shirt, then stopped. Taking her by the shoulders, he turned her around. "Remember what I said about that ocean view?"

It definitely was nice—looking over landscaped grounds to sparkling water under a dramatic sky of setting sun and clouds—but any passerby could glance in at them.

"Oh!" She reached out to pull the curtains. "It's a shame to shut it out."

"The view in here's better anyhow."

But Rina was frowning.

"What's wrong?" he asked.

"It's too light in here," she said softly.

"The lights are off. Isn't that your rule?"

"It has to be dark." She sounded embarrassed but stubborn.

He sighed. When would she trust him? Trust in her own body? When she had let him see her breasts in candlelight, he'd hoped she was getting over her doubts.

His groin ached, his dick pressed against his jeans and now she was saying they couldn't have sex until the sun set. Damn.

"Are you mad?" Her voice was barely a whisper and she was staring at the floor.

How could he be angry that she was insecure? "Just disappointed." With one finger he tilted up her chin. "It's okay, we'll make love later."

Then inspiration—or perhaps it was sexual frustration—struck. "No, I have a better idea."

He yanked off his T-shirt, then unknotted the poppy scarf around her neck, pulled it off and handed it to her. "Blindfold me."

"Blindfold you?" Her lips began to curve. "Oh, that's a brilliant idea." A sparkle lit her eyes. "You'll be at my mercy."

"Now there's a scary thought," he drawled, enjoying her pleasure.

"Sit down on the edge of the bed," she told him.

He obeyed and she sat behind him, folding the scarf until it was a long strip. She put the center to his eyes and said, "Hold this in place so I can tie the ends."

Again he followed her instructions. With his eyes open he could see a haze of light coming through the red patches in the fabric, but that was all. Blinking against the silk felt strange, so he closed his eyes. The scarf tightened around his head, but not enough to bother him. He felt streamers tickle his back as she tied a knot.

"Okay," she said. "You can let go now. How does that feel?"

"Fine." He wanted to turn and face her, but the shifting bed told him she was moving. "This is strange. You can see me but I can't see you. When we're both in the dark, it's different."

"I warned you, you'd be at my mercy." Her voice was moving across the room.

He hadn't realized how odd it would feel, though.

"Shoes off, please." A hand touched his shoulder lightly, then was gone. "And socks."

Bending, he felt slightly dizzy and off balance.

"Stand up."

When he did, her hands attacked his belt. "Okay, this I can get into," he told her. His belt whipped through the loops and he heard it hit the floor. Then a hand cupped his dick through his pants, and he thrust eagerly.

"I think it's time you got naked," she said, unzipping his fly. She slid down his pants and underwear and then . . . Nothing.

No touch.

"Where are you? What are you doing?" There he stood, naked and blindfolded, not having a clue what she was up to. Was she watching him? Eyeing his dick? Might she reach out and touch him at any moment?

The idea was disconcerting, but it was highly erotic. His dick was straining upward, literally begging to be touched. "Rina? Where are you?"

"Right beside you. Just looking."

Rina stood back, a hand splayed over the thudding pulse at her throat. God but he was gorgeous. Dark curly hair, lean golden-brown body with lovely musculature. Proud cock jutting up his taut belly. Dark nest of pubic hair, softly hanging balls.

Hers, all hers, to do with as she pleased.

The aching pulse between her legs urged her to impale herself. But that would be too quick, too easy. She'd never before had a blindfolded man to play with. She wanted to make the most of this and build the sexual tension for both of them.

She pulled down the covers on the bed, then came to take Giancarlo's hand.

It jerked when she first touched it, as if she'd startled him. And of course she had. This took some getting used to, the idea that he couldn't see anything while she could. His fingers twined with hers, and she tugged him to the side of the bed. "Lie down."

He let go her hand and groped behind himself, locating the bed, then lowered himself. "What position?"

"On your back."

When he was settled, she admired the picture he presented. One hand behind his head, on the pillow, the other resting at his side. His legs spread slightly with one knee raised, showcasing his package. Full of masculine confidence.

Now, what did she want to do with him? Lick that luscious body from head to toe, with a long, lingering emphasis on the special places in between?

"Rina? What now?"

Next to him, she felt overdressed. There was no reason to keep her clothes on, except her own self-consciousness. But then, she didn't have to look at her body, just enjoy the sensations as it touched his. She could even blindfold herself, if she wanted to.

No, she wanted to see Giancarlo. This was the first time, since they'd both been teenagers, that she could stare openly, for as long as she wanted, at a naked man.

And this one was a prime specimen. Giancarlo had an amazing body. Not to mention, he was extra well endowed. She'd seen the term *Italian stallion* bandied about, with the boast that Italian men were better hung than most.

Here was the proof, right in front of her eyes.

"Rina? Are you still there? I'm getting lonely."

"Just admiring," she said softly. "And now, I need to get ready, so give me a minute."

"Get ready?"

"You'll see." She giggled, feeling as fizzy as the Dom Pérignon. "Oops. I guess you won't, will you?"

She slipped out of her shoes, socks, and jeans. Her loose top hung down to her hips, and below it were black silk tap pants, then her bare legs.

Curvy legs, definitely not slim. But not ugly either. In the bath, when she'd raised them and seen the soapy bubbles slide down, they'd looked pretty. She let her fingers drift down the tops of her thighs, then back up the insides, darting a quick touch over the silk that covered her damp, swollen sex.

She continued up, molding her blouse to her body until she reached her breasts and cupped them. In the bath, they'd looked nice too. And then, with Giancarlo's hard cock captured between them . . .

Slowly she eased her blouse over her head. Now she was clad in a black bra and tap pants. Her nipples were hard buds poking against her bra, and they tingled when she squeezed them.

"*Cara?*" he called from the bed. "I hope that rustling sound is you taking your clothes off."

"You'll just have to wait and find out," she teased.

She went to the bed and leaned over, letting her hair tumble down to tickle his chest. Then she moved down the bed, dangling her hair over his rib cage and his stomach, flirting it around his cock. She bent farther and took one long, firm swipe with her tongue, from the base of his shaft to the tip, and he groaned.

She retrieved the Dom Pérignon bottle and eased the silver champagne stopper out, muffling the soft pop against a shirt. She poured some into a glass and took a mouthful, holding it without swallowing, chilling the inside of her mouth. Then, a bit at a time, she let it trickle down her throat as she moved back to the bed.

She bent to kiss Giancarlo on the lips. His mouth opened to hers and his fingers wove through her hair. After a long, wet kiss, she pulled away.

"You've been drinking champagne," he said, licking his lips.

"I'm willing to share." Instead of holding the glass to his mouth, she let some liquid run onto his chest. Droplets caught in the dark curls of hair and some trickled down between his pecs. "Oops, can't let the sheets get wet." She chased the drops with her tongue, licking up every one.

She felt like champagne bubbled through her veins. Every drop she licked sent a zing of desire straight to her sex.

Dom Pérignon champagne, a naked Giancarlo, the seaplane flight, this wonderful resort—and suddenly she had to laugh with joy. "I'm so happy!"

Before he could respond, she'd dripped champagne into his navel, making him gasp with surprise. She licked it up too, her tongue so close to the head of his penis that she was tempted to lick it as well. But first, a little more of the bubbly.

Carefully she poured a trail along his rigid shaft, enough that the liquid dripped down to his stomach. Then she cleaned him up with tiny, firm strokes of her tongue, delicately lifting his cock so she could get underneath.

She squeezed her thighs together against the insistent pulse in her damp pussy that said, "Inside me! Now!"

Instead, she gave her mouth the treat, sucking him in and taking him deep. He gasped and she saw that both hands were at his sides, clenched into fists, as she sucked and released, sucked and released, sliding her lips up and down his shaft as she did.

"God, Rina," he gasped. Then, "I want to eat you too."

Her pussy clenched at the thought, juices dampening her thighs.

She eased off the bed to find her legs were trembling. Darting a glance at Giancarlo to make sure he was still blindfolded, she stripped off her tap pants and bra.

Naked, she closed her eyes and ran her hands down her front. Soft full curves, hard nipples, smooth stomach, springy curls, wet swollen lips. Every part of her ready and aching for him. Taking a deep breath, she climbed back on the bed. "Slide down."

When he did, she straddled him, facing the bottom of the bed, one knee on either side of his shoulders. Carefully, she lowered herself until her body crouched over his, then took his cock in her mouth again.

His hands came up, found her hips, guided her down to his face.

Thank God for the yoga; she'd never been this flexible before.

And then—oh yes!—he swiped his tongue across her pussy. Her whole body shuddered with a combination of relief and hunger.

She rewarded him by swirling her tongue around his shaft, and he licked her again, and again, pressing his mouth into her.

It was hard to concentrate on his cock when he was creating such delicious sensations in her own body, when need was building so fast she could barely breathe.

His tongue penetrated her, darted in and out, then he was licking her again, tongue bold and confident as it stroked forward. His lips closed on her clit and she moaned, releasing his cock, gasping for air.

He lapped and sucked her as if he couldn't get enough, and she whimpered, grinding herself against his face. "Yes, God, yes." A high whimpering escaped her throat as her body reached flashpoint, and then she was coming, pulsing against his mouth.

Before she'd finished, his strong hands grasped her hips and raised her. "I have to be in you, *cara*. Now!" As he shifted position, so did she, until she was spread-eagled below him. Her hips raised to meet him, his cock found her soaking wet entrance and with one powerful thrust he buried himself in her.

Above her, his chest heaved as he held still for one achingly long moment. He slid out, almost all the way, then rushed back in. He didn't pause this time; he slid back out again immediately, then in, pumping fast, faster.

His mouth came down on hers and she tasted her own juices and his hunger. She kissed him back, wet and wild, as her arousal spiraled again.

Every stroke rubbed her swollen clit. "Give me more," she whimpered. "Faster."

She freed a hand, reached down, circled the base of his cock with her fingers, not squeezing but letting her fingers slide up and down on his hot, wet flesh. Releasing him when he stroked into her, circling him again as he slid out.

His body tensed and he held still for a second, then he plunged into her so fiercely that she began to climax even before she felt him pouring himself deep inside her.

Bodies locked together, they clung tight for long minutes, then finally he raised himself up and rolled over to lie beside her. "Wow." He found a pillow and stuffed it under his head, his actions a little awkward because he still couldn't see. Then he pulled her up so her head rested on the same pillow. "You are so damn hot, Rina."

Curled on her side, she ran a hand gently down the side of

his face, skimming over the blindfold, then dropped a kiss on his lips. "You inspire me."

He caught her hand and held it on the bed between them. "The feeling's mutual."

They lay peacefully for a few minutes, then he said, "What time is it? Do you feel like a walk before dinner, or is it too dark?"

She slid off the bed and went over to twitch the curtain aside. "It's too dark for a walk in the woods, but it'd be nice to go out by the ocean. There are enough outside lights that we'll be able to see."

Pulling her crane kimono and bathroom bag out of her luggage, she said, "I'm going to take a quick shower." She headed for the bathroom and, just before closing the door, said, "You can take the blindfold off now."

A moment later, from behind the closed door, she heard him laugh and say, "Fine, be like that. But I've got the champagne."

She secured her hair under a shower cap and stepped under the warm spray, luxuriating in the feel of water cascading over her shoulders. Gently she soaped her body. Once more it had done a damned fine job of bringing pleasure—both to herself and Giancarlo.

After toweling off, she put on her robe and tended to her hair and face, then brushed her teeth. When she left the bathroom, her lover was sprawled naked on the bed, a couple of pillows behind his back, drinking champagne.

"Your turn," she said, taking clothes from her bag as he went into the bathroom. While the shower was running, she dressed quickly in a black skirt and her cherry-red sweater. Then she rescued the rose from its vial of water and put it in a glass for a real drink. She was sitting on the couch when Giancarlo came from the bathroom, a towel wrapped around his waist.

She held up the bottle of water she was drinking. "There's still champagne left. It's wonderful, but I don't want to get hammered. Maybe we could take it for dinner?"

He dropped the towel and her mouth went dry, despite the water she'd been slugging back. "Let's save it for morning," he said. "We'll keep it chilled, get some orange juice, have mimosas." As he spoke, he pulled clothes from his bag.

"Mimosas," she echoed, barely aware of what she was saying as she watched him dress. More of that silky underwear he favored, smartly tailored black pants, a stylish shirt in a brown-gold color that complimented his chocolate eyes. The man had excellent taste, and a fabulous body to display it.

He picked up his jacket and hers. "Ready to go explore?"

She pushed herself off the couch. "I need a scarf." Hers lay across the bottom of the bed, and she picked it up, then dropped it, flushing. "Maybe not." It was damp. From her pussy juices, when she'd ground herself into his face.

"The gift shop's probably open. I'll buy you another one."

Out into the evening they went, and Rina gazed around with pleasure as she twined her fingers with his. The sky was black and starry, the ocean murmured gently, and subtle lights beckoned them forward. The air was unbelievably fresh, and there was a hint of a breeze.

They moved together toward the sound of the ocean, walking past lit but curtained windows, gigantic evergreens and borders of fading flowers. A boardwalk led beside a rocky pool that looked natural rather than man-made. Then they were standing by the ocean.

"It's so calm," Giancarlo said. "I always thought the West Coast would have breakers."

"It probably does, but this isn't the true West Coast." Pointing across the water toward the lights of Campbell River, she said, "You need to cross Vancouver Island and get out to Long Beach. Here, we're sheltered."

"Have you been to Long Beach?" he asked. "Sounds like it could be spectacular."

She shook her head. "Since I moved to Vancouver, I've tended to stay put."

He draped his arm around her shoulder as they watched boat lights on the water. "You haven't felt like exploring?"

"You know how I feel about travel." Her life, to her joy, had become very home based. She'd left only for an occasional clarinet lesson or conference.

"You're okay with being here on Quadra Island, though?"

"Oh God, yes!" she hurried to assure him. "This is wonderful."

In fact, as they stood quietly together, Rina felt a deep sense of peace. She gazed up at the stars and wished she could freeze this moment to keep forever.

But of course, in her mind, she could. She'd hold on to all of today, and every other time she'd been with Giancarlo, the man she loved. To draw out and enjoy over and over when he was no longer with her.

No! She wouldn't think about him going. Not tonight. Nothing was going to spoil this perfect day.

"Hungry?" he asked her.

It had been a long time since lunch. Sex and fresh air had whetted her appetite. "I could eat," she said with a smile.

With a final gaze and a sigh, she turned her back on the ocean and walked with her lover toward the main building of the resort. They went past the gift shop and he said, "I owe you a scarf."

"No, you don't. It'll wash."

But he steered her inside anyhow and they spent a few minutes browsing. They chose a batik-printed silk scarf in shades of red, then Giancarlo insisted on also buying matching baseball caps with the April Point logo. Because, he said, "Souvenirs are a good thing."

Then they went into the restaurant, where the oceanside wall was floor to ceiling windows. During the summer the place would be packed. Tonight, a Thursday in early October, it was only half full.

When Giancarlo gave his name to the hostess, she led them to a window table with a Reserved sign on it. The man really had thought of everything.

Rina sank into her seat, stunned by the view. "Ocean and stars." She gazed across the table. "And you. The best view of all."

As if by magic, a wine bucket on a stand appeared beside the table. "Did you order something?" she asked Giancarlo. "While I was staring at the view?"

"Earlier," he said. "I thought we'd stay with the Dom, if it's all right with you."

She stared at him. Two bottles of Dom Pérignon in one day? They hadn't even finished the first one. This was pure extravagance.

Delight bubbled through her, as intoxicating as the champagne. She tossed back her hair and laughed. "Yes, that's quite all right with me." Bless the man if he didn't actually make her feel entitled to such luxury.

He gestured toward their waitress, who deftly eased out the cork, poured for them then said, "I'll leave you to look at the menu."

Giancarlo lifted his glass. "To you, Rina. And to us." His tone, which a moment ago had been light, had turned solemn.

She met his glass with hers. "To us." And, as she gazed at him across the table, she silently added the words, *To you, my love, for giving me the most romantic experience of a lifetime.*

He held her gaze for a long moment, as if he was sending a silent message of his own, then raised his glass to his lips.

She did the same, and together they drank.

When they put their glasses down, his light tone had returned. "What do you feel like? They have a sushi bar. Would you like that as an appetizer?"

"Sashimi, I think." Out of habit, she avoided rice.

"Sashimi it is. Let's get an assortment to share."

They nibbled on a delicious array of fresh seafood while they perused the menu. Both decided on wild salmon for their main course. "It seems wrong to order anything else at a fishing lodge," he said.

She agreed, though added, "The prawns are tempting too."

"Maybe next time."

During dinner their conversation drifted easily. They touched hands across the table, watched the lights of boats going by, gossiped about the other diners, speculated about what music she'd play for the VSO. When their plates had been cleared away and he excused himself, she gazed out the window, thinking how lucky she was.

Giancarlo returned and reached for her hand. She felt the usual warm buzz of connection. "When I'm with you," she told him, "I always feel a strange combination of excitement and contentment. Sometimes one's on top, sometimes the other, but they're both always there. I guess the contentment's from having known you when we were both young."

He shook his head. "I feel it too, but it's not due to the past. It's because we belong together."

What a romantic thing to say. Even as she felt a tug at her heartstrings, she reminded herself that it wasn't really true. Their lives and goals were so different. And yet, when they were together, it did feel so wonderfully right.

"You feel it too," he said. It wasn't a question.

She answered anyhow, giving him the truth from her heart. "Yes, I do."

He nodded, then cleared his throat, suddenly seeming a little nervous. "Let's order dessert."

Laughing, she put a hand across her stomach. "I don't have room. I'll just have coffee."

He frowned. "No, we need a special dessert, to cap off a special meal." When she opened her mouth to protest, he said, "We'll share. A taste or two won't hurt."

She smiled with tolerant affection. "If you really want to."

He glanced across the room and lifted his hand. She followed his gaze and saw their waitress beam and nod. But instead of coming over to their table, she disappeared into the kitchen.

Giancarlo reached for the champagne bottle and refilled their glasses. He held his out to her, and it almost seemed his hand was shaking. "Rina, I love you."

"Oh my God!" Had he really said that? Shocked, she stared at him.

His anxious expression confirmed it.

He loved her. Giancarlo Mancini loved her. She forgot their differences, her worries. Forgot everything but her feelings for him, feelings that grew stronger each time they were together.

Her heart expanded in her chest and moisture flooded her eyes. She lifted her own glass, her hand trembling so badly the champagne almost spilled, and confessed how she felt. "I love you, too, Giancarlo."

A huge smile split his face as he clicked his glass to hers. They both drank, then he put his glass down and came around the table to give her a long, passionate kiss.

He loved her. Could it really be true? His kiss felt like . . . like he was pouring out everything that was in his heart. Eagerly she kissed him back, tears of joy overflowing.

"Your dessert," a female voice, bubbling with excitement, interrupted.

Giancarlo broke the kiss, smiling. "Look at the dessert," he told Rina.

What on earth? She glanced at the plate, with a pretty concoction of meringue, fruit and whipped cream, then back to her lover. They'd just confessed their love. Didn't he realize that was much more important than dessert?

"Look again," he insisted.

Puzzled, a little annoyed, she returned her gaze to the plate. Strawberries glinted up, shiny and red and— "OH MY GOD!" Nestled in the whipped cream was a ring. Antique looking, it was rather like a flower. A large garnet surrounded by gold petal-shaped loops filled with diamonds. It was utterly lovely.

With trembling fingers she freed it from the cream and stared at Giancarlo.

14

_____

Giancarlo went down on one knee in front of her, face bright with love and hope, and took her hand in his. "I'm crazy about you, Rina. Will you marry me?"

Her heart leaped with joy, her eyes flooded again and her mouth fell open.

All right, there was only one explanation. This must be a dream. The romantic dream she'd had all her life.

In her dream, when the man she loved proposed to her, there was only one possible answer. "Yes!" she cried. "Yes, Giancarlo, I'll marry you."

He sprang to his feet and pulled her into his arms, crushing her to him and kissing her with joy and promise.

Dimly she became aware that everyone in the restaurant was clapping.

If this was real life she'd be embarrassed, but it was a dream and she was the heroine of a truly romantic moment. When Giancarlo released her, she flicked tears off her cheeks, then waved and smiled to everyone as if she were a princess.

Then he took the ring from her, cleaned the whipped cream

off with a napkin and slipped it onto her finger. "Do you like it, *cara?*" he asked anxiously. "I wanted something different for you. I thought red, because it's warm and passionate like you, and a color you wear so often."

She studied it on her hand. "It's perfect. I love it." It suited her. Feminine but not too delicate. A touch old-fashioned. No generic ring this one; it was unique. Exactly what she would have chosen for herself. Giancarlo knew her well.

But then, she reminded herself, this was a dream. Of course the fairy-tale hero would choose the perfect ring. It even matched the earrings he'd brought her from London, that tickled her neck each time she moved her head.

How long had she been dreaming, she wondered? Just tonight, or had everything been a dream since she'd sent that first e-mail? Maybe she'd gone to sleep that night and fantasized this entire wonderful affair.

"Then don't let it ever end," she murmured.

"No, *cara,* this is forever." He lifted her hand and kissed the ring, then went back to take his seat. "Now, when shall we get married? Let's make it soon."

Practicalities. If she stopped to think about things like that, she'd come back to reality and start worrying. The dream bubble would burst. And, for tonight, she desperately wanted to hold on to her dream.

So she reached across and touched his hand. "Let's enjoy the moment. We can think about the details later."

"You're right." He chuckled. "Sorry, I'm being impatient again. Now, how about that dessert?"

She picked up her fork and twirled a strawberry in the whipped cream, then offered it to him across the table.

"That reminds me of your nipple, coated in whipped cream," he murmured, eyes sparkling. Then he opened his lips around the fork and eased the strawberry into his mouth.

Her nipples tightened, imagining his lips on them.

When he'd swallowed, he said, "My turn," and reached for the dessert plate.

They fed each other bites, in an erotic prelude to sex.

"Maybe we should save some cream, to take back to the room," she said.

He considered, then shook his head. "This time, I just want you. No fancy stuff."

After he'd paid the bill and their waitress had congratulated them a final time, they went outside. The night was chilly but clear and beautiful, so they walked toward the ocean, arms around each other.

"Too bad there are no falling stars," Rina said. "We could make a wish."

"I have everything I could wish for." He turned her to face him.

"Now there's a good point." She kissed him—her dream fiancé—then they made their way back to their room.

Minutes later they were in bed. The room was dark, so there was no need for the blindfold. Rina let Giancarlo peel off her clothes one by one, then she lay back on the bed and listened to the snap, zip, rustle of his clothing coming off.

He sat beside her on the bed and touched her face. "You're beautiful, *cara.*"

She chuckled. "Nice words, but you can't see me."

"Yes, I can."

Anxiously Rina peered into the darkness, to confirm that he really couldn't. "What do you mean?"

He ran his hands down the sides of her face to her neck and then out to her shoulders, where he circled, squeezed, molded the flesh. "Broad, strong shoulders." His hands drifted in again, across her collarbones. "The slightest press of collarbones against your skin, the delicate, kissable hollow between them." He dropped a kiss there.

Everywhere he touched, he lit a flame that made her quiver. He was making her feel desirable. Even beautiful.

His fingers continued their exploration. "Full, ripe, lush breasts with rosy tips. Breasts designed to drive a man mad with longing. Silky skin. Such a soft, womanly body." A finger dipped into her navel, then continued on. "Hips built to cradle a man. When I watch you walk, see the sway of your hips and your fine bottom, it's enough to make me hard."

It was her dream, Rina told herself. It was all right to feel beautiful and sexy. To enjoy all the feelings he was arousing as he cherished and praised her body.

"Springy curls of hair, mischievous, flirtatious," he went on, running his fingers through her pubic hair. She lifted, pressing against him, wanting him to move lower.

Instead he traced down the top of her thighs, spreading his hands to encompass them. "Shapely strong legs, bold legs to carry you forward in the world, wherever you want to go." He carried on down her legs until he gripped her feet. "And these lovely feet with the sexy painted toenails."

His fingers drifted back up the inside of her leg. "I see you, Rina, even if you try to hide from me. I know how beautiful you are."

And then one hand was exactly where she wanted—needed—it, holding her between the legs. Palm on her mons, fingers firm against her labia. She squirmed against him, wanting stimulation, and he began to stroke her.

But suddenly that wasn't what she wanted at all. "I need you," she said urgently. "Plain, old-fashioned sex. You, inside me. Now."

"I can do that." His voice was husky, and in a moment he was between her legs.

The hard press of his cock told her he too was ready. Then he parted her damp folds and surged inside.

She reached up as he leaned forward to kiss her. Slow, soft kisses, bodies locked together. This time, rather than pumping into her, he barely moved his hips.

Tiny, focused, unbearably erotic movements that made her whimper. She accepted the challenge and kept her own movements minimal too. Tilting her hips the tiniest fraction, then shifting the other way. Squeezing her internal muscles against his rigid length. Loosening, squeezing again.

"I love you," she told him.

"Ah, *cara*, I love you too. *Ti amo, mi amore*."

"*Ti amo*," she breathed against his mouth.

She felt as if he was part of her, their bodies were joined so deeply and fully, moving harmoniously together to sustain arousal without letting it peak. Kissing gently, murmuring words of love, letting the movements of their bodies echo those words.

When they finally came, it was together, and she couldn't separate his climax from hers. Both were part of the same soul-deep experience.

Rina woke in the dark, with a headache. Too much alcohol. Suppressing a groan, she crawled out of bed and went into the bathroom to take aspirin and drink as much water as her body would hold.

She poured a couple of pills into her left hand and raised her hand to her mouth. In the mirror, the ring on her finger sparkled. She froze.

An engagement ring.

And a hangover.

The ring belonged in her dream. The hangover didn't.

Which meant . . .

This was real life, and not only had she won the position with the VSO but she was engaged to Giancarlo?

Her heart leaped with joy. The next moment, nausea surged through her. What had she been doing, pretending this was all some rosy, romantic dream? She couldn't marry him.

Damn it, she was principal clarinet for the VSO. No way

was she giving up her comfortable home, her music, and travel-ing all over the world with him while he made videos. It was no more likely he'd give up the work he loved. Besides, he wasn't home oriented. He almost never saw his own family. For him, career had always come first.

What had he been thinking, asking her to marry him?

What had she been thinking, accepting?

Hurriedly she swallowed the aspirin, then dug in her purse for her cell phone. She texted the Foursome.

Help! Desperately need emerg lunch. Anywhere, any-time.

Slowly she drank a glass of cold water, then rested her fore-head against the bathroom mirror. Everything would be okay. Her friends would help her though this.

But first, there was the morning, and Giancarlo, to face.

Giancarlo slept in, a rare thing for him to do. When he woke, his first feeling was joy. Yesterday had gone perfectly, just the way he'd hoped. No, even better. Always, Rina sur-prised him. She was more—more fun, more sexy, more lov-ing—than he'd ever dared dream.

And they were getting married. His heart was so full it could burst.

But where was she?

Here he was, all set for a little morning-after-engagement sex, and his new fiancée was missing from the bed. In fact, when he got up and searched, she was missing from the whole cabin.

Beginning to worry, he slid back the curtain and peered out-side. Ah, there she was, sitting on a bench down by the ocean. Relieved, he realized she must have decided to get some fresh air and let him sleep. But damn, didn't she know he'd rather be awake and with her? Besides, now it was too late for breakfast and the mimosas he'd promised.

In less than ten minutes, he showered and shaved and threw on some casual clothes, then sprinted down the path toward her. The sky was gray this morning, but he barely noticed. Any day that started with Rina was a bright one, so far as he was concerned. "Good morning, *amore*."

She smiled and turned her lips to his for a kiss, but her eyes were troubled.

Oh-oh. Had he been wrong to give into his impatience and propose so early in their relationship? But damn it, they loved each other. She had to feel how right this was. "Tell me you're not having second thoughts," he said, sitting beside her and gathering her hand in his.

She sighed. "I don't know. I do love you, but it all seems so complicated."

Complicated? He didn't like the sound of that. Didn't she realize there was nothing they couldn't work out? "Love always finds a way." He winced, knowing he sounded like lyrics from a corny song.

"Not always," she said softly. "My mother loved my father, but she wasn't happy."

Ah, so that was the issue. In some way—a negative way—he reminded her of her father. "I'm sorry. Uh, wasn't the big issue with them that she wanted to practice her faith and had trouble doing it on Forces bases?"

"The big issue was, they had different priorities."

"Isn't the most important thing to love each other and want to be together?"

"Y-yes. Which they did. Plus, they both loved me and wanted the best for me. But other things matter too. Her faith was such a big thing for her, and the Air Force was huge for him. The two were pretty much incompatible."

He studied her, trying to figure out where this was going.

"Are you saying you want to get closer in touch with your faith? Rina, that's fine with me; I wouldn't stand in your way. Or, do you want me to convert?"

She shook her head quickly. "No, it's not that."

"Then—" He broke off as engine noise made it impossible to hear. A white seaplane with yellow stripes was buzzing them. Half-heartedly he waved, then the pilot flew back out over the ocean and dropped altitude. "Damn, I slept so late. I'd meant to take you for breakfast, but there's our ride."

"I'm not hungry anyhow." She stood heavily, like the weight of the world was on her shoulders. Not like a madly-in-love, newly engaged woman.

He just wished he could figure out what was troubling her.

Back inside the cottage, they hurriedly threw things into their bags. She transferred the rose back into the water vial, then held up the bottle of champagne. "There's still a bit left. I guess it's not worth saving."

"No."

She ducked her head. "Mind if I keep the bottle?"

"Please do," he said with relief. Things couldn't be too bad if she wanted a souvenir.

On that note, he put one of the baseball caps on his head and the other atop her springy curls, where she let it stay. When he opened the door of the cabin and she stepped out, he said, "I really do love you."

"You're sure? It's all so quick. So unbelievable. All these years, the other women you've known..." She shook her head. "It doesn't make sense to me."

"I don't know about making sense, but it's how I feel. All those women..." He shrugged. "I guess that's something I needed to do. But it's done. Past. Not what I want anymore. When I saw you again, I think I knew inside, that very moment. And then, whenever I was with you—even when I was away and missing you—the feeling got stronger."

"But this is so sudden."

"What's the point of waiting?"

"To figure things out. To know for sure," she said strongly.

"Don't we?" He stared into her eyes. "We know each other, Rina. That's why there's the feeling of contentment you talked about last night. It's because we were made for each other."

"I want to believe you." Her brown eyes were huge, melting, troubled.

"Then do. And believe your own heart." He kissed her tenderly and she responded the same way, giving him hope.

Then they went to find their pilot.

The weather was overcast for the whole trip, and Rina sat quietly, nestled into the curve of Giancarlo's arm. He wished he knew what thoughts were running through her mind but didn't want to ask with the pilot there.

When they were in his car, driving across the Lions Gate Bridge to her North Vancouver home, he said, "Tell me what's worrying you."

She turned to him. "Everything. Your work, my work. Your travel, my home. Your values and lifestyle compared to mine."

He shrugged dismissively. "Things will work out. You're fussing over details, when the important thing is, we love each other."

"Details?" Her voice rose. "I'm talking about *life!* It's not all sex and champagne."

"You have to admit, sex and champagne are pretty nice, though," he said, trying to wheedle her back into a good mood.

She snorted. "How can we stand a chance if you won't even talk about these things?"

It dawned on him, they were on the verge of having their first fight. He'd given her a wonderful night away, two bottles of champagne, a heartfelt proposal that she'd accepted, and they'd shared mind-blowing sex. For the life of him, he couldn't figure out what the hell he'd done wrong. He was hurt, pissed, and on the verge of losing it.

The one thing he did realize was, he could blow the whole thing, right here. The problem was, he didn't have a clue what the woman meant when she said *life.*

She'd said she wanted to talk. No big surprise; she was female. The thing was, it wasn't his way to analyze and argue things to death. His habit was to move on. If necessary, to move away. As he'd done with his family.

But damn, he missed his family. And he'd miss Rina even more if he screwed this up.

His mamma was right. He'd met his *donna speciale,* and it was time to stop being a spoiled child and grow up. He reached for Rina's hand and squeezed it. "Okay, we'll talk about everything that's bothering you." They were nearing her house. "I'm supposed to meet with the video editor but I can call and put him off."

She shook her head wearily. "You need to work and I have plans too. How about tonight? It'll give us both a chance to think."

Think? What was he supposed to be thinking about? And what the hell was she going to be thinking about? Was she going to argue herself out of marrying him? "If it's so important to you, maybe we should put off our other plans and have that talk right now."

"No. There's something I have to do first." She twisted the ring on her finger as he parked the car in front of her house.

He held his breath, afraid she'd pull the ring off and hand it back to him, but she let it stay.

Together they walked to her front door. He caught both her hands and, tamping down his misgivings, said, "Then we'll talk tonight. We'll work everything out, Rina. I love you."

Eyes troubled, she said, "I love you too."

She gave him a gentle kiss, then disappeared inside.

* * *

Thank heavens the girls had been able to meet for lunch, Rina thought as she drove back into town an hour or so later, still wearing the jeans and sweater she'd put on this morning at April Point. Crossing the Lions Gate Bridge, she shook her head in wonder. Less than twenty-four hours ago, she'd flown in a seaplane over that bridge.

A single girl.

And now she was engaged. She studied the gorgeous ring, turning it this way and that so it caught the light and sparked, then hurriedly turned her eyes back to the road.

Engaged. Everything was so right, and yet so damned wrong. And Giancarlo—stupid man!—didn't have a clue.

Lunch was at Las Margaritas, so she turned off Georgia onto Burrard, went over the Burrard Bridge, and headed up to Fourth. She was the first to arrive. Turning down the waitress's suggestion of a margarita, she stuck with club soda. After yesterday's excesses with the champagne, she needed a clear head.

Then she sat quietly, trying not to think. When she saw Jenny come through the front door, she stuck her left hand under the table.

Jen wore jeans too, and her lovely long hair was clamped up with a jaws-of-death holder, calling even more attention to her slender neck and the pink butterfly earrings that fluttered there.

"Rina, the symphony thing didn't fall through, did it?"

Rina gave a wan smile and shook her head. "I'll tell you when the others get here."

Jen reached out to touch Rina's new earrings. "These are the gift? I love them. The guy really knows you."

Suzanne, in student garb, and Ann, in a business suit, were only minutes behind. They all congratulated Rina on the audition, complimented her on the earrings, then stared at her, waiting.

Rina closed her eyes for a moment, then opened them again. "Giancarlo asked me to marry him."

They squealed, "Oh my God!" "He what?" "Holy shit!" "Two proposals in two weeks?" "What did you say?"

Rina raised her left hand and flashed the ring.

Three pairs of eyes inspected it, then turned to her face. "You accepted," Suzanne breathed.

"In a dream."

"Since when did a dream yield a stunning ring like that?" Jenny asked.

"I thought it was a dream. I mean, I kind of convinced myself at the time. Everything was so, you know, dreamlike. Perfect."

"Start at the beginning," Ann said calmly, but her eyes sparkled with excitement.

And so Rina did, beginning with the floatplane. At some point nachos and drinks got ordered, then served, but mostly she talked and the others listened with wondering expressions.

When she told them about the ring, and Giancarlo down on one knee, Suzanne said, "That's the most romantic thing I ever heard. I can see why you said yes." Her eyes were damp.

"I wasn't thinking. I was overwhelmed. Pretending it was a dream."

"You let your heart answer," Suzanne said. "You know what you said last week? That when a guy was *The One*, you'd know?"

Jenny nodded and reached for a chip. "He's your *bashert*."

"You do love him," Ann said. "You told us that in e-mail."

"I can't believe he loves me too."

Jen paused with a laden chip halfway to her mouth. "Why the hell not?" she demanded.

"Because I'm me and he's him," Rina said simply. "He's amazing and I'm . . ." She shrugged. "Average." Absentmindedly she followed Jen's lead, dragged a chip through guacamole and sour cream before topping it with salsa, then popping it between her lips.

Flavor burst in her mouth, momentarily sidetracking her. "My God, those are the best nachos I've ever eaten."

"Rina finally discovers real food," Jen said with an eyeroll.

Ann tapped the table. "Back to the point? We're all average. It's how one special person sees us that counts. And just because Giancarlo has a different life than you do, that doesn't mean he's any more amazing. That's just how you see him—and he sees you the same way or he wouldn't have proposed."

"Even if I could believe that," Rina said tiredly, "I don't think it could work. Our lives could never mesh."

"Did you talk to him about that?" Suzanne asked.

Rina groaned and took another chip. "The proposal came out of the blue, and last night I was in this whole dream state. This morning, when I raised the issues, he brushed the whole thing off. Said I was fussing over details, everything would work out. Like, somehow magic happens."

"Typical man," Ann said. "They can be so impractical." She frowned. "You realize, he's done just what Al did, except even quicker. He's trying to rush you into something."

"Except, this time you said yes," Suzanne said. "That has to mean something."

"It means he's her *bashert*," Jenny asserted.

"Rina," Ann said, "you have to make him talk about all the things that are worrying you."

"I know that!" Rina snapped. Then she buried her head in her hands and groaned. "Sorry. Sorry, sorry, I don't know what's got into me."

"I remember you saying something about your parents once," Jenny said. "About how they didn't talk about the important stuff before they got married, then your mom ended up being unhappy."

Rina nodded. "Exactly. I can see history repeating itself, if Giancarlo has his way. We get swept away by the romance, then suddenly we're married and everything starts to go wrong."

"History's not going to repeat itself," Suzanne reassured her, "because you won't let it."

"This is going to be so hard," Rina moaned. "I don't know what to say to him."

"Well," Ann said, "what are the issues?" She made a face. "At least you don't have parents who'll be disappointed in you, like Jenny and I."

"N-no. Though my mom would have hated my marrying outside the faith, and my aunt won't be pleased." In fact, she could hear her mom's voice in her head now. But, as she'd told Ann, a woman had to grow up and make her own decisions, even if they didn't always make her mother happy.

"Can you make your aunt understand?" Jenny asked. "After all, you've been dating—what do you call us non-Jews? Goys?—for a long time."

"I don't tell her much about the men I date. I imagine she guesses." She smiled a little. "Aunt Rivka's not as rigid as my mom was. She'll kvetch, but mostly she wants me to be happy. If I tell her Giancarlo's my *bashert*, she'll understand." All the same, she wasn't about to tell her aunt until—unless—the engagement was truly on. The same with Levi Fischman. Rina didn't want him ranting on about busting Giancarlo's balls if he didn't treat her right.

Despite how stressed she felt, that thought almost made her grin.

"And what about Giancarlo's family?" Suzanne asked, bringing Rina back to the table.

"He's not religious but his family's Catholic." Rina groaned. "Here's another thing. He disappointed his family when he gave up the piano, and he hardly ever sees them. I don't know if he'll even tell them he's getting married. If he does, I'm sure they'll be furious I'm not Catholic."

She gripped her head with both hands. "This is all too complicated. I don't want him to be estranged from his folks."

"Then don't let it happen," Suzanne said. "Make him talk to them, explain things. Do that water-on-stone thing like Adonis and Scott, just wearing them down over time. Besides," she smiled warmly, "once they meet you they'll love you. You'll win them over, the way Jenny's winning Scott's family. And once you give them a grandchild—" She broke off. "He does want children, doesn't he?"

"You think I know?" Rina wailed. "You think we've actually talked about that?"

The others exchanged concerned glances.

"How could he want kids," Rina went on, "when he travels all the time? For him, work comes first. He'd never be home for them, or for me. That's no good. And if I get married, I do want children." Her shoulders drooped. "So maybe that's the end of it right there."

"Don't assume," Jenny said, tapping a pink fingernail against Rina's arm. "Ask. Maybe he's thinking of changing his lifestyle."

"But wouldn't he have said so when he proposed?" Ann asked.

"Yeah, wouldn't you think?" Rina said gloomily. "I don't see that he is. He's trying to get this project in London, and he invited me to a movie premiere and—"

"Wow!" Jenny interrupted. "That's so cool!"

"No, it's not. I can't go to something like that. I'd be completely out of place."

"You're saying you'd feel out of place in his life?" Ann said slowly. "That doesn't sound good."

Rina shook her head. "His life's glamorous and fast paced. And he lives it all over the world. My life's homey and quiet. And I'm sure not giving up my home, my friends, the VSO, to travel all over the place with him."

"No, of course not," Suzanne said. "But everyone makes some changes when they're in a relationship that matters. You'll never meet a person whose life matches perfectly with yours."

"I remember you girls saying that before," Rina said. "And how it's about compromise."

"Well, kind of," Suzanne said. "But it's not so much compromise as learning about what's important to each other. Reaching beyond your own life to share his."

Ann nodded. "I wonder why Giancarlo's always on the go? Maybe he'd enjoy slowing down, having a real home. Like, look at how I slowed down my career and learned the value of balance, thanks to Adonis. And he's not chasing the sun this winter as he's always done, he's staying with me. In a sense we both gave something up for each other, but we've gained so much more."

"I don't see how that would work for Giancarlo and me."

"Are you looking for excuses to ditch the guy?" Jenny demanded.

"Of course not. I love him."

Jen's lips curled in a sly grin. "Then find reasons to be with him, not to dump him."

Rina had to smile. "Believe me, there are reasons. Like, he's a great cook, fun to be with, looks terrific, treats me really well, is an amazing lover. And," she said softly, "he makes me feel attractive and sexy."

"Yes!" Jenny pumped a fist into the air. "I like this guy."

"That's wonderful, Rina," Ann said. "Now, you talk to him about the other things, and be open to making some changes yourself. But don't shape yourself around him; he's got to meet you halfway. And don't let him push you the way Al did. He has to understand what an important step this is."

"Yes, Mom," Rina said, feeling a surge of affection for her friend.

"Sorry, was I being bossy?"

"A little. But everything you said was right." She gave them all a nervous smile. "I just wish you could all be there tonight to help me."

"We could do it tomorrow," Jen said with an impish grin. "We'll sit him on a straight-backed chair and grill him."

Rina chuckled. "Okay, okay. I guess I can handle this on my own."

"You know we'll all be with you in spirit," Suzanne said. "But Rina, what about the dinner tomorrow? Is it still a good idea, if things with you and Giancarlo might, um, be up in the air?"

"I don't know. Let's assume it's on, but don't start cooking until tomorrow. If"—she shivered—"something goes seriously wrong, I'll e-mail you later tonight."

"No negative thoughts," Suzanne said. "Be optimistic."

Rina gave her engagement ring a rub for luck, then dug into the nachos again. "All right, I know what I need to do. Let's talk about something else. Jen, tell us about the firefighter thing." Jenny'd managed to get assigned to cover the photo shoot for the firefighter calendar. It was a follow-up to her *Georgia Straight* cover story on the competition.

Jenny leaned forward. "Oh, man, I wish you girls could have been there. It was so incredible. All these hot, hot guys, half-naked bodies oiled and gleaming. And the photographer posing them, moving around them, shooting them from all angles. With me, standing back, taking candids of the whole thing. I clicked so many photos, I got a callous on my finger."

Suzanne chuckled. "But Scott was still the best?"

"No question. A fact I had to prove to him in the women's restroom."

"You had sex in the restroom at the photo shoot?" Suzanne's eyes twinkled. "That's pretty ballsy."

"Says Ms. Nude Sex at Spanish Banks," Jen retorted, referring to one of Suze and Jaxon's more public displays of affection. "Hey, I was horny. He was horny and feeling kind of jealous that I was ogling the other guys. Seemed like there was one easy solution. A quickie in the john."

"I'll remember that," Ann said dryly. "When your guy's acting jealous, shut him up by doing him in the john."

"Jenny's sage advice for the day," Jen said with a wink. "Free to my very best friends."

Trying to be optimistic, Rina did some shopping on the way home. She bought herself a garnet-colored bustier that laced up the front, the kind of show-off garment she'd never in her life worn before. Then she bought a gauzy white peasant shirt, a style she often wore, but this one was see-through.

At home she responded to more congratulatory e-mails and phone calls, then gave herself a pedicure and painted her toe-nails to match the bustier and her ring. She paired the new clothes with a long black skirt and the London earrings, and went barefoot.

In the kitchen, feeding Sabine, she told the cat, "This could feel so right. Friday night, my man coming home from work. Me dressing up a little, him bringing groceries. The two of us cooking together, eating together, going to bed to make love. Yes, I could get used to this."

But could she see the man as Giancarlo, coming home from a regular job every day?

No, that wasn't him.

She sighed. The truth was, she didn't want it to be. He was exciting, dramatic, stimulating. Not the kind of man who be-longed in a nine-to-five job.

And there was another truth, the one she kept trying to avoid. The one that persisted in coming back and whacking her. They really didn't fit together.

Maybe they could work something out, though. She loved him, and if he really did love her, they didn't have to break up completely. Did they?

Rina sighed and twisted the pretty engagement ring around her finger.

Then she did what she always did when she needed to escape her problems. She went into the music room and lifted her B flat clarinet from its stand. It always soothed her to pick up an instrument. To play those first notes and let herself fill up with the music so that nothing else mattered, or even existed.

She'd played Mozart's clarinet concerto and his clarinet quintet and was just deciding what to play next when she heard a knock on the door.

15

"Oh!" Rina rushed to the door to find Giancarlo standing there holding bags of groceries.

Her fiancé.

Nervously she smoothed back her hair, feeling tongue-tied and uncertain. "I didn't hear your car."

"I know. You were playing. The Mozart sounded so lovely, I just stood here for a few minutes to listen." He ran an admiring gaze over her. "And speaking of lovely, you look great. What's that I glimpse under that pretty blouse?"

"If you're nice to me, maybe you'll find out later." She was trying to joke but her voice came out more anxious than teasing.

"*Amore.*" He came inside and closed the door, put the groceries down then hugged her. "Have a little faith. We're two intelligent adults who love each other. There's nothing we can't figure out together."

"Just promise you won't brush off my concerns. I saw how unhappy my mother was in her marriage, even though I know she loved my dad."

"I promise. If you're worried about something, that makes it important to me. Okay?"

She studied his face carefully and saw that he meant it. That was a relief, and she stretched up to kiss him. He kissed her gently, lovingly. She felt him harden under his jeans but he didn't turn the kiss passionate. Did he realize she couldn't enjoy sex until they'd talked things through?

Breaking the embrace, she leaned down to pick up one of the grocery bags. "Let's cook first, then we'll talk while we eat."

"I brought simple things. Prawns to sauté in garlic and lemon, a little lemon pepper linguine and the ingredients for a tomato bocconcini salad. Sound all right?"

"You remembered that last night I said the prawns looked good."

"Whatever the lady wants, she should get. Speaking of which, shall I put some music on? What do you want?"

"You pick."

As she unpacked groceries, she waited to see what he'd choose. Hmm. Bix Beiderbecke, a musician from the 1920s. One of the rare white men who played jazz. "Interesting choice," she said when he came into the kitchen.

"I think it's neat how his jazz shows the influences of composers like Debussy and Ravel." He pulled out a pot, a frying pan. "Puts me in mind of Karina Bright, the English performer. How she brings classical touches into her very contemporary music."

They discussed music as he moved around her kitchen with easy familiarity, getting dinner going. She did whatever task he handed off to her. Put water on to boil for pasta, rinsed the prawns, sliced tomatoes and soft bocconcini cheese.

In less than a quarter hour, she was tossing the sautéed prawns on top of the linguine and he was drizzling olive oil and balsamic vinegar over the salad, then shredding fresh basil leaves on top.

They sat down to candlelight and chilled white wine.

She tasted everything. "I can't believe how good this is, and it was so quick and easy to prepare. I've never been much of a cook but you're getting me interested."

"I like to, and get so little opportunity."

Now, there was an opening if she'd ever heard one. Nervously she took a sip of wine, then said, "Giancarlo, I feel like I belong here, in this house, this city. With my friends. Tonight, it feels like you belong too. But that's just an illusion, isn't it?"

He looked up from twirling linguine around his fork, his expression puzzled. "An illusion? No, I love it here. I feel at home. With you, in your house."

"But you love all the travel too. Even if it means hotel rooms and not being able to cook."

"Yes, I love exploring the world, it's true."

"And you love your work."

"Very much." He looked a little puzzled.

"So, if I belong here, where do you belong? In foreign cities, in airports, on planes, on video sets and in meeting rooms?"

"Well, sometimes, I guess." He closed his eyes as if he was thinking about it. "And in my head, often. The place where cello music and figure skaters and a half-Indian English performer get tumbled together in my imagination. Where creativity lives, and the ideas come in flashes and jumbles of light and sound and image." A smile lit his face as he spoke, and she had to smile too, seeing his pleasure.

Then he opened his eyes and reached for her hand. "And here, with the beautiful woman I love, a nice meal on the table, music playing in the background, a cat at my feet begging me to slip her a prawn."

"Sabine!" she scolded.

"Ah, let her be. I'll give her one prawn later, if she behaves herself." He touched her engagement ring. "I belong in all those places, *cara*. And I think you have many places too. Walking and celebrating Shabbos with your neighbor, having Monday night dinners with your Awesome Foursome, performing for an audience. And being in that special world you were in when I drove up, where it's just you and the music."

"True," she said softly. "But all those places are here. They don't take me away from Vancouver."

"You never want to travel again? You got that turned off it as a child?"

"Um . . ." Her mind turned over his words "never want to travel again." Were they true?

"I'll take you anywhere in the world for our honeymoon." He gave her an engaging smile.

Honeymoon. He still believed they could make it work.

"What about Italy?" she asked, testing.

"Italy?" One word, three syllables. But, on his tongue, it sounded complex and full of contradictory emotions.

"Giancarlo, you talk about having a home with me. But you had a home, once. And you almost never go back there."

He jerked his head. "I told you. They make me feel like a failure."

"My mom drove me nuts sometimes, and still does from beyond the grave. Of course I disappointed her, and she pissed me off. That's how it goes with parents and kids. It doesn't mean you walk away."

"But your mother scarred you; she made you doubt yourself."

Until recently, Rina hadn't realized quite how much. Still, she knew one thing for a fact. "She loved me, and tried her best." It would be nice to think that, if her mom were still alive, they'd be able to talk as adult women and work things out.

She touched his hand. "Have you ever tried to explain your

career? How you feel about it? The way you have with me? Perhaps if they saw how much you loved it, how creative and demanding it is . . ."

His hand sat unmoving for a long minute. Then he sighed and twined his fingers with hers. "No, not really. When they didn't accept what I wanted to do, the easiest course was to just avoid them."

Her heart clutched. She remembered, that first night at Don Francesco's, how he'd said he was Peter Pan and he didn't intend to grow up. "Is that really so easy? Is that what you intend to do with me? Whenever we have a problem, an issue, a disagreement, you'll just run away and avoid it." If that was the case, she'd give him his ring back. No way did she deserve to be treated like that.

His lips twisted. A touch of anger, bitterness, resignation, and finally humor. His eyes warmed as he gazed at her. "I'm here, aren't I? Not running."

Her heart lifted. "Yes, you are. And that's why I think there's hope for us. But how about your family? Do they deserve less from you? They supported and loved you all those years; I'm sure they still care about you. And you—you cook meals for me that you learned in your mother and grandmother's kitchens. Your family is a part of you."

"Rina . . ." He shook his head slowly. "I'll think about it. Okay? Don't rush me."

She bit her lip, then nodded, hoping she'd planted seeds that would take root and flourish. How could she marry a man who wouldn't give his parents a second chance?

The delicious dinner, most of it uneaten, had grown cold. Half-heartedly they ate a few more mouthfuls.

"Can I ask you about something else?" she said nervously. After all, if their relationship really was doomed, better to find out now.

"I suppose." He sounded tired and wary.

"Children," she blurted. "How do you feel about children?"

"I want them," he said promptly. "I'm Italian, the idea of family is in my blood." Then his eyes narrowed. "Your dream hasn't changed, has it? You still want kids?"

"Yes." She laughed softly. "Yes, I do. Well, at least that's one issue that's easy."

"Have a little faith, *amore*. Trust in our love. We'll work out the rest. The important thing is, we love each other."

He'd said that several times now. Had her father said the same words to her mother before they were married?

But then, Giancarlo had already taken a huge step. He wasn't running; he was talking to her. The conversation might take place over days, maybe even weeks, but tonight had been a good start.

No, she wouldn't push him. So she smiled into his eyes. "You're right. That's the most important thing."

He laughed softly, rose to his feet, and the next thing she knew, he'd hoisted her into his arms, blown out the candles and was carrying her out of the kitchen.

"Giancarlo, wait!"

His body tensed and he stopped. "More? We need to talk more now?"

She smothered a giggle against his shoulder. "No, not now. It's just that we hadn't finished eating, and Sabine will get the prawns."

He threw back his head and his laugh rang out. "Let her enjoy the treat. Now it's time for me to enjoy mine. I want to make love with my future wife."

"I won't argue with that," she said softly, filled with a confusing mix of hope and fear.

When he set her down beside the bed, she gazed up at him and tried to focus on the hope. "I love you, Giancarlo."

"I love you, Rina. I feel as if this was always meant to be."

Gently he lifted the see-through blouse over her head, then stared at her in the garnet bustier and black skirt. "God, I hope our daughter doesn't look like you."

Her arms crossed automatically over her chest. Hurt, she said, "Why not?"

"I'll have to beat the boys off with a stick." Gently he peeled her arms away. "You're utterly lovely."

She relaxed again, basking in his obvious appreciation.

"Someone should paint you like that," he said. "An Italian painter."

"Italian?"

"Only an Italian man can do true justice to a beautiful woman."

Her mouth curved. "Are you going to do true justice to me, Signor Mancini?"

"For the rest of our lives."

She wanted so much to believe him. And for tonight, she'd let herself do it.

He touched his mouth to hers and she melted into his arms. He sucked her upper lip gently, darted his tongue into the crease between her lips, sucked and nibbled her bottom lip. She stood, hardly breathing, savoring every touch.

Through his jeans, his erection pressed against her and she reached between them to undo his zipper and slide his pants down his hips. Her hands cupped his firm butt through his silky boxer briefs but she didn't squeeze, didn't pull him harder against her, just let her stomach rest against his rigid length.

If they got married, she'd never again make love with another man. Not that she could imagine wanting to.

But . . .

She eased her mouth from his. "We didn't talk about, uh, fidelity. Do you believe in it?"

He gripped her shoulders and stared at her, eyes fierce. "God, yes! Don't you?"

She grinned up at him and echoed his words deliberately. "God, yes. But I was just thinking, this is it. No one else, for the rest of my life."

"Good," he said possessively. Then, more gently, "*Cara, bella, amore.* Lovely, warm, wonderful Rina, you're the only woman I'll ever want."

"And you're the only one for me."

"We'll say the vows and mean them, and we'll keep them," he said firmly.

"Yes, we will," she said, desperately wanting to believe it. "Now, kiss me some more."

His lips came back to hers, this time more firmly, as if he was branding her. There was no teasing now, his tongue thrust boldly into her mouth to mate with hers.

She answered back hungrily, and now she did pull him tighter and thrust her pelvis against him, feeling the needy ache in her sex that only he could satisfy.

Easing her upper body away from his, she reached up and began to unbutton his shirt, enjoying the brush of her fingertips against his firm body. This body could be hers, to enjoy for the rest of her life. The thought was so huge, she couldn't take it in.

So she'd concentrate on the moment. The warmth radiating from him, the soft curls of dark hair, the way he sucked in his breath when she ran a fingertip down his stomach.

The fire in his kisses, the thrust of his cock against her belly.

His fingers found the waistband of her skirt and undid the button.

"Giancarlo, the lights."

He dropped his hands and she grabbed at her skirt, holding the waist together.

"Rina, do you really still want the lights off?"

Did she? She'd accused him of running away rather than facing things. Wasn't her lights-off rule the same thing?

This was the man she loved and hoped to marry. She took a shaky breath. "Candles? Can we compromise on candles? For now?"

He cupped her face between his hands. "Candlelight sounds lovely, *cara*."

Holding her skirt together, she hurried to the kitchen to get the candles. She put the tapers down on the dresser and lit them. Then, as he clicked the light switch, she took a deep breath and let her skirt drop to the floor.

Catching her reflection in the mirror, she moved closer, fascinated.

He came up behind her. "An Italian painting," he said softly.

Her skin glowed golden in the candlelight, her black curls were tousled and sexy. Her shoulders and chest looked firm and strong, her breasts in the bustier were wanton and voluptuous, even the curve of her hips in black tap pants looked sexy.

"Lush and lovely," he murmured. "Made to be loved."

Her breathing quickened. Yes, she wanted him to love her, her body cried out for it. And yet, she also wanted to keep looking in the mirror, at this new vision of herself.

She watched their reflections as his hands cupped her shoulders and moved down. Saw his own tousled black hair, the heat in his eyes, his rapt concentration. Now he was untying the bow at the neckline of her bustier.

Those deft, shapely fingers unlaced the garment, one eyelet at a time, and the sides began to pull apart though the weight of her breasts kept them from separating completely. Finally she was standing there with the bustier completely undone and parted down the center.

Her whole body felt hot and swollen and aching. And beautiful.

For the first time in her life, she honestly believed she was beautiful.

Giancarlo stepped closer, so the front of his body pressed against the back of hers, and she realized he'd taken off his briefs and was naked. His erection was hard against her bottom, telling her how much he wanted to be inside her.

But there was reverence, not impatience, in his touch when he used both hands to slowly pull the edges of the bustier apart, revealing her full breasts. Her areolas were rosy and puckered, her nipples beaded.

Giancarlo eased the garment off her arms, then gently grasped her nipples and squeezed until she moaned and pressed back against him.

He moved away and she gave a groan of disappointment, but then his hands were at the waistband of her tap pants, and before she knew it they were gone. She stood in front of the mirror completely nude.

She couldn't remember ever studying her own naked reflection, and certainly not with approval. But now she saw how harmonious her body was. The dark curls on her head matched the ones on her pubis. Her lush breasts balanced her full hips. Her swollen, rosy lips were the same shade as her nipples. Slowly she raised her left hand and cupped her own breast, seeing how the color of the garnet complimented the deep rose of her areola.

In the mirror, a dark, long-fingered hand came to rest atop hers. "Beautiful," he sighed. "You take my breath away."

She'd never have seen herself this way if Giancarlo hadn't come back into her life. Maybe never have eaten pasta and bread and whipped cream without guilt.

Never made love with her entire body and heart and soul.

His hands gripped her waist, pulled her back toward him. "Lean forward," he murmured. "Brace yourself with your hands on the dresser."

She obeyed, watching in the mirror until her torso was stretched forward, her bottom pressed back against Giancarlo.

Gently he reached between her legs, probed her damp labia and opened her. Then, in one smooth stroke, he entered and filled her.

She moaned and thrust back against him. In the mirror, her eyes glittered, her cheeks burned, the London earrings swung and so did her full breasts as he stroked in and out of her, faster and faster.

His eyes glittered too as he stood behind her, gripping her hips and thrusting into her as he stared at their reflections.

It was so erotic watching him make love to her. The handsome man in the mirror moved, the pretty woman responded—and at the same time Rina felt all the building sensations in her body. The hard heat of his cock pressed so deep into her, igniting every inch of flesh along the way. His balls slapped against her with each thrust.

Giancarlo glanced down. "God, you have a gorgeous ass."

She gave a sexy chuckle. If it turned him on, yes, obviously it was gorgeous. She wriggled her booty against him and he groaned.

One of his hands reached between her legs and found her clit, and now everything was speeding up, centering. She moaned as he thumbed her pleasure button, as his cock plunged into her core, as the sexual hunger climbed higher and higher, demanding release.

"Giancarlo, now. Come now!"

"God, yes!" He thrust once, again even harder, and her body began to come apart as he cried out and she felt him spilling his essence inside her.

* * *

Over a breakfast of yogurt and toast in her kitchen, Gian-carlo said, "I was thinking about that movie premiere."

Rina closed her eyes. Yet another unresolved issue. "Yes?" she said warily.

"I said I'd buy you a dress."

"I didn't say I was coming."

He sighed. "Okay. You raised the 'nothing to wear' objec-tion, and I've answered that. Then you said it was my world, and you'd feel out of place. But Rina, we're getting married. My world is going to be yours too."

She stirred her raspberry yogurt diligently. He did have a point, but all the same . . . Softly, she admitted, "I'd feel out of place with those people. They're slim, exciting, glamorous."

He let out a quick laugh. "God, Rina. They're scrawny and neurotic, and glamour's about the trappings. Put you in the right dress, with the right jewelry, your wild gypsy hair, and you'd be as glamorous as any of them."

She put down her spoon and stared at him. "Honestly?"

"Absolutely." He spoke with utter conviction.

Wow.

They ate in silence for a few minutes and she reflected. She was asking Giancarlo to screw up his courage and confront some of his demons—like, with his family issues. And her girl-friends had talked about compromises, or, as Suzanne had put it, reaching past your own life to share what was important to the other person.

"Okay," she said. "But tell me what kind of dress to buy."

"Nope. We're going shopping. And I'm buying it for you."

"Giancarlo! I can't let you do that."

"Please? It'd be fun," he coaxed, eyes gleaming. "I could play sugar daddy. Make you try things on, come out and show them to me."

Her eyes widened. "Like in *Pretty Woman?*"

"Can you imagine what a turn-on that would be for me?"

She laughed. "You really are incorrigible. Well, I guess in the interests of turning you on . . ."

"Do you need something for tonight too?"

"Maybe. But that one I'm buying myself. It's my party, and I'll buy my dress."

"So long as I get a vote."

16

_____

Later that morning, Rina and Giancarlo walked arm in arm into an upscale store in Sinclair Centre. One that the ever-helpful concierge at his hotel had recommended, just after he'd packed his luggage and checked out to move to Rina's.

Only his firm grip kept her from turning tail and running when a rail-thin salesclerk with stylish hair, dressed in elegant black, swept toward them.

"How can I help you this morning?" The woman glanced first at Rina, then at Giancarlo.

Rina's throat was so dry she had to swallow before responding. "I need two dresses. One for an at-home party and one for a m-movie premiere." Her voice squeaked at the end.

To her surprise, the woman didn't look stunned. She simply studied Rina closely.

"What do you recommend?" Giancarlo asked.

The clerk glanced at him and flashed a smile, then turned back to scrutinize Rina again. "For you, it has to be the classics. From the days of movie stars like Elizabeth Taylor and Marilyn

Monroe. The kind of dress women like Catherine Zeta-Jones wear. Yes?"

"I, uh—"

"Yes," Giancarlo said. "Absolutely."

"Speaking of Marilyn," the woman said, "we have her dress, and in the perfect color to match your ring. That might suit perfectly for the at-home. Give me one minute."

Marilyn Monroe's dress? Rina was pondering what that meant, as well as how quickly the clerk had noticed her engagement ring, when the woman returned with a dress on a padded hanger.

"Oh my!" Rina breathed.

It was the dress Marilyn had worn in her most famous photograph. The one where the air from a sidewalk vent had flared the skirt up around her. But this dress, rather than being in innocent white, was in a rich, sultry shade of wine red.

"I can't wear that," she said softly.

"Oh yes," Giancarlo said, at the same moment the clerk said, "Of course you can." Then the woman went on, "Did you think to wear a strapless bra?"

Rina shook her head. She didn't even own one.

"For the moment, tuck your straps in." She studied Rina's shoes—the highest heels she owned—and said, "The shoes will do for now, but of course you'll need strappy sandals."

"Of course," Rina murmured. And next thing she knew, she was in a luxurious fitting room.

She stripped down to her underwear. If she'd been Jenny or Suzanne she'd have gone braless, but that definitely wasn't a look that would work for her. So she slipped her bra straps off her shoulders and, as the clerk had suggested, tucked them into her bra.

Then, reverently, she slipped the dress from its hanger. Taking a deep breath and pressing her lips together so no lip gloss would smear, she let the fabric slide over her head. With her eyes closed, she tugged the dress into place and did up the back zipper.

Another deep breath, then she opened her eyes and looked in the mirror.

The softly draped halter top split deeply in front, revealing lots and lots of cleavage. At the back it plunged halfway to her waist. The knee-length skirt was full, flaring out over her hips in dozens of soft pleats. She took a step forward, noting how the skirt flirted sexily around her legs. The she pirouetted, and it flared out.

Never had she worn, or even contemplated wearing, a dress like this. Was she crazy to think it actually flattered her?

Dare she step outside the fitting room?

Heart pounding, she eased the door open and glanced out. Giancarlo and the saleswoman were over by a rack of evening gowns, in an animated discussion.

Rina walked toward them. As her heels clacked on the tile floor, both turned toward her.

Okay, this dress required attitude, and she wasn't going to let it down. She tossed back her hair, straightened her shoulders and thrust out her breasts. Then she sauntered, hips swaying, toward Giancarlo.

He let out a whistle. "Spin for me. Make the skirt twirl out."

She obliged, realizing she'd never before in her life preened for a man.

"We have to go dancing," he said. "That dress demands it."

"I'd like that." She imagined him holding her close, swirling her across the floor.

The salesclerk walked around her, twitching fabric, then said, "It's a perfect fit. As if it were made for you. You're just the right height, too. But you must promise me, you'll get the right shoes?"

"I promise," Rina said, laughing.

"And maybe a necklace?" Giancarlo said.

"No." The clerk shook her head firmly. "Marilyn didn't wear a necklace. The earrings, yes, and the ring. Anything else would detract from the lady and the dress."

He nodded. "Yes, I think you're right."

The woman raised her eyebrow. "Of course I am. Now, let me bring a selection of evening gowns."

When she'd gone, Rina stepped closer to Giancarlo. "You really like it on me?"

"It's great. Perfect."

All the same, his reaction wasn't quite as dramatic as she'd hoped for. Quietly she said, "You don't seem blown away by it."

"I love it. It suits you beautifully."

"But . . ." She'd expected him to be stunned, dumbfounded by how glamorous she looked. "I've never had a dress like this before."

"Really?" He frowned. "You haven't? Why on earth not?"

And then she realized, of course he wasn't dumbfounded because he'd always found her beautiful. Now she was dressed up and beautiful, but he found her just as attractive when she wore jeans. She didn't bother explaining, just beamed at him. "Because I hadn't met you."

A smile grew on his face. "Then I guess it's a very good thing you met me."

Yes, in many ways it was. If only she could forget all the issues that still remained between them—like how on earth they could possibly blend their two lifestyles.

Did he remember his promise that they'd talk things through? Or did he think he'd managed to distract her with the great lovemaking last night and this wonderful shopping trip?

Well, if that was the case, she'd let him know she wasn't so easily won over. She wouldn't repeat her mom's mistake. A wedding date would never be set until Rina was truly satisfied she and Giancarlo could be happy together.

She forced a smile as the salesclerk returned with half a

dozen dresses. But then, as she examined the woman's choices, the smile became genuine and Rina gave herself up to enjoying the moment. After all, how often did an ordinary woman get to feel like a princess?

The dress she ended up with was the color of a ripe bing cherry. The bodice was tight and strapless, pushing her breasts up the way her bustier did, and the skirt was similar to that of the Marilyn Monroe dress except that it fell all the way to the floor.

The saleswoman studied her, then said, "Your hair should be high, casual and a little messy, tendrils hanging down to emphasize your neck." As she spoke, she scooped Rina's hair up and formed a loose knot atop her head. Another narrow-eyed stare into the mirror, then the woman was smiling approval. "You look lovely."

For a moment, the stick-thin young woman morphed into an image of Rina's slender mother. And, in the mirror, her mom nodded slowly too. "Yes, dear, you really do. You've grown into a beautiful woman."

Rina's eyes misted.

"Add lipstick to match the dress," a voice said. Rina blinked and saw the clerk again. "And eye makeup to play up those big brown eyes."

"I will," she promised. "Thank you so much for your help."

"Just promise me you'll get the right shoes," the woman said with a quick grin.

With the two dresses in a ritzy garment bag, Rina and Giancarlo moved on to find the perfect shoes and a bra that worked with both dresses.

On the way home, they stopped to buy groceries. "This feels so mundane," Rina said as she tossed spinach into a plastic bag, "after all the glamour shopping."

"You wait until you taste my seafood lasagne," he boasted. "It's sublime, not mundane."

It also, she discovered once they were back home and both in their jeans, took lots and lots of preparation. Everything— the tomato sauce, the béchamel, the seafood mixture, even the spinach and garlic layer—was made from scratch. The romano and mozzarella cheeses had to be grated. Giancarlo's only compromise was to use spinach lasagne noodles from a pasta shop rather than make them from scratch.

She chopped, stirred and grated on demand, enjoying the coziness of spending an afternoon together in her kitchen.

How often would this happen, if they were married? Would Giancarlo be the type of husband who flitted into town once a month or so to take her to a movie premiere, buy her fancy clothes, share a couple of homey dinners?

It wasn't enough.

No, she didn't want to push him, but she hated this sense of uncertainty.

When the lasagne was assembled and ready to cook, and the dishwasher humming, she made a pot of Earl Grey tea and she and Giancarlo went into the living room to relax. Just the way she and Al used to do—and oh, how much had changed in two weeks.

"You're a natural when it comes to cooking," she told him as they sat side by side on the couch, feet up on the coffee table.

"My mamma and nonna trained me well." He sighed. "Yes, I've been thinking about what you said about my family. You're right. I've let this . . . breach go on too long."

"I'm so glad." Then she gnawed on her lip. "But they'll disapprove of you marrying a Jew, won't they? I don't want to come between you and them."

Slowly he shook his head. "Of course they'd prefer I married a Catholic. But once I tell my mother you're *mi donna speciale*, she'll understand."

"I'm what?"

"My one special woman. She told me I'd meet that woman. Now she'll be happy to say 'I told you so.' "

"My *bashert*," Rina said softly. "The man I'm destined to be with."

He grinned. "You see, the two of you will get along." Then he added ruefully, "Besides, I'll be giving them what they've always wanted. They'll have a classical musician in the family."

It all sounded so complicated. Giancarlo's family issues, the religious differences. But yet, Jenny and Scott were tackling problems no less difficult. "So," she repeated last night's question, "what if I want that honeymoon to be in Italy?"

"If you're willing to break your no-travel rule, I'll take you to Domodossola. And yes," he nodded, "I'll try my best to explain my work to my family, and reconcile with them."

"Thank you," she said softly, touching his arm.

"Maybe once you've been to Italy," he mused, "you'll be more open to traveling other places? Were there no places you liked living, or visiting?"

She sipped tea and reflected. "Vancouver, obviously. But yes, other places too. What I really hated was not having a home. Knowing there was no point getting fond of a place or making a friend, because we wouldn't be staying."

He nodded understandingly. "Yes, that's like me. My life is in constant flux. I have an apartment in Manhattan but it doesn't feel like home. I'm never anywhere long enough to make friends. Temporary colleagues, yes, but that's it."

"I couldn't live that way. I wasn't truly happy until I moved here."

"But now you could travel and enjoy foreign places and know there's a home to come back to. Friends to send postcards to, and share your pictures with when you get back."

That did have a certain appeal. In fact, she could almost get excited about it. "What are you suggesting, Giancarlo?"

320 / *Susan Lyons*

"If I'm directing a video in a place that interests you, and if your commitments allow it, you come with me. You can explore when I work, and we'd have time together most evenings. Or, if you wanted, you could sit in, watch what I do."

"I admit, you've got me curious about music videos." But then she frowned. "So you're saying, once in a while, when I could fit it into my schedule, I'd travel with you. And you'd make your home base here rather than in Manhattan?"

He nodded.

"But you're almost never there. Which means you'd rarely be here. What kind of marriage is that?"

"Not the kind I'd want," he said promptly. "God, Rina, I want to be with you."

She sighed and circled her cup with both hands. "Okay, we want to be together, yet you have this job where you're always on the road. And I have my career here, which is going to be even more time-consuming now that I'm with the VSO." Despite her anxiety over the relationship, she still felt a glow of pride when she said those words. "Okay, I guess I could come with you occasionally, but not regularly. I'll have lessons, rehearsals, performances."

"Yes, I see what you mean. I hadn't really thought this out."

"No, you hadn't," she said. She knew her voice sounded grim, but damn it, how could he propose without having thought it through?

"There's a lot of music video work in Vancouver," he said slowly. "I could cut down on the travel."

"You could. But do you want to?" When he opened his mouth she said, "No, really think about it."

The wrinkle in his forehead told her he was obeying. She wasn't sure if he was aware of it, but he was stroking Sabine, who was curled on his lap, purring.

Then he lifted his hand and gestured around. "I like this.

You're peaceful to be with, Rina. That's what a home should be."

He glanced at her, eyes twinkling. "And you're sexy and exciting too, and I definitely want that to be part of my home. So, yes, if I had you and a home like this, I wouldn't want to travel as much."

Reaching for her hand, he said, "I do a lot of work in hotel rooms rather than fly back to Manhattan and that tiny apartment. But I could do much of that work here. And, as I said, take more jobs that are based in Vancouver."

He gripped her hand tightly. "The question is, would that be enough for you? Do you want someone here 24/7? Is that your vision of marriage?"

Her first impulse was to answer yes, but was that right? She sipped her tea and thought about it.

Performances would take up a number of evenings. Also, she treasured her quiet nights alone with Sabine, playing music, reading, sewing, even doing yoga, luxuriating in a long bath. Her dinners with the Foursome. The snacks after rehearsals with her colleagues, the drinks after performances. Visits with her neighbors.

Besides, as she and Giancarlo had proved last Saturday, phone sex was fun too.

"No, it's not," she realized. "I value time to myself, and with my friends." Her heart lifted. Could this really work?

"It'd be unconventional," he said. "But we could have the best of both worlds." He laughed softly. "Of all worlds. Home and travel. Time alone and wonderful time together."

"And phone sex." The corner of her mouth tilted.

He laughed. "And homecoming 'I missed you' sex. And sex in Italy, London, New York."

Then his face sobered. "Rina, I love you. I believe we can make this work. What else can I do to convince you?"

She thought about it. Together they'd begun to plan a life that sounded both homey and exciting, like the best of both of them put together. Besides, he'd proven himself willing to confront problems rather than run away, and that was the most important thing.

Wow. They were really going to do this.

A rush of exhilaration surged through her. She and Giancarlo really were getting married, and spending their lives happily ever after!

Fighting to keep the excitement out of her voice, she said, "Well, I guess there is one more thing."

He sucked in a breath and let it out slowly. "Okay, I'm ready. Tell me, and we'll figure it out."

"It's going to take some hard work and juggling and lots of commitment . . ."

"I'll do my best. What is it?"

"Well, there're still a dozen things to do before dinner, not to mention we both have to change, and I guess shower too, because the thing is . . ."

"Yes?"

"I really, really need to make love to you before my friends get here."

He burst out laughing. "*Cara,* you're brilliant. That's exactly what we need to do." And then he was on his feet, pulling her close, and both their bodies caught fire.

They hurried into the bedroom where they tumbled onto the bed in a jumble of arms and legs, soft sighs and moans, wet kisses and searching fingers.

Somehow, all their clothes disappeared, and Rina didn't care one bit that the pale light of an October afternoon filtered through the window.

Her man, her lover, her love. Now and forever. She was so full of love, she felt like it was spilling out of every pore.

Giancarlo seemed determined to play piano music and trail

moist kisses over her entire body. Every time she tried to move, to reach for his cock, to play her part in the mating game, he stopped her. "I want to make love to you. Every wonderful inch of you."

His fingers tapped gently over her inner thighs.

"What are you playing?" she gasped. "I don't recognize the music."

He laughed softly. "I don't even know. A new variation on Rina's song, I guess. If I can remember it when I'm next sitting at the piano. I may need your naked thigh beside me, for inspiration."

Each bar of music, each kiss, each lick, was a tiny ignition of nerve cells, another charge of arousal to her overheated pussy. So that, by the time his fingers played between her legs and his tongue followed, she almost fell off the bed.

Her hands fisted in the sheet below her, her hips twisted, and she pressed herself against him and whimpered.

As always, Giancarlo gave her what she needed. His lips closed gently on her clit and he teased it with his tongue as he sucked.

Orgasm crashed through her and she cried out, then realized she was actually crying for joy, tears cascading down her cheeks. "Come here," she sobbed. "Hold me. Come inside me." She panted for air. "I love you."

She opened her arms as he came into them, and then into her with one powerful surge that locked their bodies together. "I love you too, Rina. *Mi amore.*"

Male and female, lover and lover, soon to be husband and wife.

He brushed moisture from her cheeks. "Good tears?"

"Very good. All my dreams are coming true."

Then he began to move. Slowly, so she could feel every tiny motion, the beautiful friction of her vagina hugging his penis as it slipped back and forth, in and out.

She rested her hands on his back, then began to play music.

He paused, smiled, said, "Ode to Joy," then began moving again.

As his pace speeded up, she couldn't concentrate on the music any longer. Everything inside her, everything sexual and emotional, melted and melded together. She gave herself up to the bliss of his body joining with hers until finally, voices blending together, they cried out in climax.

Half an hour later, Rina was dressed in the Marilyn Monroe dress with her hair piled in a casual tumble atop her head. Giancarlo wore slimly tailored black pants and a crisp white shirt that set off his dark skin. The house was all ready and they still had a few minutes to spare.

She caught his hand and pulled him toward the living room. "Are you nervous?"

"A little. I want your friends to like me. How about you?"

She shook her head. "They'll approve. No question."

"Why?" He took her most comfortable chair, then pulled her down onto his lap.

"Let's see." She ran her fingers through his long curls. "Because you're gorgeous. Smart, interesting. A wonderful cook. But mostly, because you love me. They'll see it."

Leaning back against him, she gathered his arms around her. "It's been an incredible few months. First Suzanne, then Jenny, then Ann, and finally me. We all met special men." She chuckled. "I never thought I'd be the first to get engaged."

"Ah, but you got the man who ran out of patience because he's so crazy about you."

Rina heard the sound of voices outside, Jenny's high-pitched with excitement. She paused to share one long kiss with Giancarlo, then went to open the door.

Jenny surged past, tugging a man behind her. "God, Rina, you look fabulous. Where's Giancarlo? I have to meet him."

The man—Scott—shrugged and said, "Sorry, I know we're early, but she couldn't wait." Then he held out his hand to Rina. "Hi, I'm Scott."

"I know." She took his hand and studied him. Sun-streaked brown hair, strong features, bright blue eyes, and a muscular body clad in tan pants and a pale blue shirt. "Wow, you even look good with your clothes on."

"I'm hoping you're the firefighter," Giancarlo said, reaching a hand past her. "Or you're in serious trouble."

The two men shook firmly, and Giancarlo held out his hand to Jenny.

She stood back a moment, studying him through slitted eyes, looking rather like a cat. A sexy cat, in a brief black mini and a figure-hugging black top, with dangly pink butterfly earrings and a bright pink scarf tied around her neck like a collar. Then she held out her hand. "Yeah, Rina's got good taste."

He chuckled. "Thanks."

"We brought food and wine," Scott said. "Where do you want them?"

"Come on out to the kitchen," Giancarlo said. "We'll open some wine."

Just like he belonged here, Rina thought smugly, turning to Jenny.

Now Jen had turned the slit-eyed stare on her. "Holy crap, girl, I always knew you had a figure."

"Gee, thanks. Guess I was saving it for someone special."

Jen reached for Rina's left hand and examined the ring again. "How's it going with you guys? Are you working things out?"

"We are." Rina felt like she was glowing. "Kids, a home, me doing some traveling. I'll tell you all about it on Monday."

Her friend narrowed her eyes again. "And sex. Methinks there's even been sex recently."

Rina couldn't help grinning.

Jenny grinned back. "Yeah, well, you're not the only one."

She turned toward the kitchen, then swung around and snapped her fingers. "Hey, I forgot. I just got the go-ahead from the *Georgia Straight*. I'm doing a feature on you and the VSO. Local girl beats out international competition. You're going to look great in the photos too."

Rina's mouth fell open in shock. Grinning, Jen strode off to the kitchen.

The doorbell sounded. Rina closed her mouth and opened the door. It was Ann, hand in hand with a man who truly did look like a Greek god.

Slightly dazzled by his utter gorgeousness, Rina reached for his hand. "You're obviously Adonis."

"I've really looked forward to meeting you, Rina. Congratulations on your engagement." He held up a couple of bags. "Where do you want the food?"

"In the kitchen. Just follow the male voices."

Ann gave Rina a hug, then peeled off her coat to reveal a pretty green dress that was cut low enough to show off a couple of inches of lacy lingerie. She was wearing the dangly green earrings. "That's one amazing dress," she told Rina. "It looks fantastic on you."

"Yours is pretty too." Rina smiled. "We've both changed our style in clothes, haven't we?"

"For the better." Ann grinned back. "Everything okay with Giancarlo?"

"More than okay. The wedding's definitely on."

"I'm so thrilled for you. Now, introduce me to this wonderful guy."

"Come on—" But the doorbell interrupted. "He's in the kitchen," she told Ann. "Go on and say hi."

Rina opened the door to Suzanne and another gorgeous man. Jaxon was dressed in stylish black from head to toe, which was particularly striking with his dark chocolate skin. Suzanne pulled off her coat to reveal an emerald-green silk blouse and an ivory skirt. Her fiery red-blond hair cascaded in waves, her shoulders and bare arms looked like cream and she, too, wore dangly earrings. She and Jaxon were both tall and lean, they were absolute opposites in coloring, and they complemented each other perfectly.

"Rina?" Suzanne said quizzically, and Rina realized she'd been staring at them with her mouth open.

"Sorry, but you two are stunning together," she said.

"You're looking especially stunning tonight too." Suzanne studied her with appreciation and a hint of puzzlement. "That dress reminds me of—" She snapped her fingers. "It's Marilyn Monroe's."

Rina nodded. Then she said, "I really am forgetting my manners. Jaxon, I'm Rina."

He shook hands, his grip firm and warm. His smile was white against his dark skin. "I've been wanting to meet you for a long time. Suzanne talks so much about you and the rest of the Awesome Foursome." He hooked an arm around Suzanne's waist and she leaned into him like she belonged there. "Congratulations on winning the appointment to the symphony. That's a huge accomplishment."

Rina murmured thanks as Suzanne said, "Well, she's a fabulous musician. By the way," she said to Rina, "Jen and Ann and I've already talked about it. We're coming to your first performance."

Rina beamed, touched beyond words. "You can sit with Giancarlo."

"Speaking of whom . . ." Suze shot her a meaningful look.

"Everyone's out in the kitchen. Let's go and get acquainted."

When they reached the kitchen door, she let them go through and hung back a moment, taking pleasure in the scene. The room was full of beautiful young women and men—her closest friends and the guys they loved. And her own man, dealing deftly with the food and wine everyone had brought.

This felt so right.

In fact, she could imagine parties to come. Other engagements, Thanksgivings and Christmases . . .

She realized Giancarlo had opened a bag and was holding up a bottle. "Rina, see what we've got."

"Dom Pérignon! Who brought that?"

Suzanne came over and took her right hand. "We all chipped in on it."

Ann walked over too, picked up Rina's left hand and held it up so the ring caught the light. "Because we wanted to toast your engagement with the very best."

"Yeah." Jen came to join them. "And prove that we love you as much as your new fiancé does."

Everyone laughed, but Rina's eyes were tearing up again. "I know you do," she said softly.

"Group hug," Jenny demanded, opening her arms to Ann, Suzanne and Rina.

Everyone squeezed everyone, and now four pairs of eyes were damp.

"Jesus," Scott grumbled. "Tears. I hate it when they cry."

"I never know what to do," Jaxon admitted.

"Just let them cry," Adonis advised. "They actually enjoy it."

"We'll give them champagne," Giancarlo said. "First we'll toast Rina's and my upcoming marriage, then we'll drink another toast to the Awesome Foursome."

"Now you know why I love the man." Rina smiled through her tears as she went to hug Giancarlo.

Here's a sneak peek
at "Coming in First,"
the first story from HANDYMAN,
by Jodi Lynn Copeland!

On sale now!

1

Now, he was the kind of guy she needed to meet.

Parallel parked across the street from the Almost Family youth services building, Lissa Malone stopped examining her reflection in the vanity mirror of her Dodge Charger to watch the guy. He stood in front of the youth building, which was constructed of the same old-fashioned red brick as every other building in downtown Crichton, laughing with a lanky, long-haired blond kid in his early teens. The kid wouldn't be a relative, but a boy from the local community who was going through a rough patch and in need of an adult role model in the form of a foster friend.

Kind, caring, and considerate enough to be that friend, by donating his free time to the betterment of the kid's life, the guy was the antithesis of every man she'd dated.

Make that every *straight* man. And then again, he wasn't the complete opposite.

The way his faded blue Levi's hugged his tight ass and his biceps bulged from beneath the short sleeves of a slate-gray T-shirt as he scruffed the kid's hair, the guy had as fine of a body as her recent lovers. What he wasn't likely to have was their badass hang-ups.

He was one of the good ones. A nice guy. The kind of guy Lissa had never gone for and never had any desire to.

There was something about those bad boys that called to her. Not just their bedside manner. Though she wasn't about to knock the red-hot thrill of being welcomed home from work by having her panties torn away and a stiff cock thrust inside her before she had a chance to say hello.

She shuddered with the memory of Haden, the brainless beefcake she ended up with following her latest dip in the bad-boy pool, greeting her precisely that way three weeks ago. What Haden lacked in mentality, he more than made up for in ability. The guy could make her come with the sound of his voice alone.

Show me that sweet pussy, Liss.

Haden's deep baritone slid through her mind, spiking her pulse and settling dampness between her thighs. She caught her reflection in the vanity mirror as she shifted in the driver's seat. Her cheeks had pinkened—an unmanageable tell to her arousal—calling out her too-many freckles.

Yeah, there was definitely something about those bad boys. Something she wouldn't be experiencing ever again.

Lissa wasn't the only woman Haden could bring to climax in seconds. As it turned out, she also wasn't the only woman he'd been bringing to climax the almost two months they dated. Really, it shouldn't have surprised her. With bad boys, something always ended up coming before her. Another woman. A massive ego. Or worst of all, the bad boy himself coming before her, then not bothering to stick around to see if she got off.

She was sick to hell of coming in second.

In the name of coming in first and being the center of a man's attention if only for a little while, she was ready to give nice guys a try. Her housemate and ex-lover, Sam, claimed she wouldn't regret it, since what people were always saying about nice guys was true: they finished last, and it was because they wanted their leading ladies to come in first.

A nice guy like the well-built Good Samaritan across the street, Lissa thought eagerly. Only, a glance back across the street revealed he wasn't there any longer. Neither was the kid.

"Well, shit." *So much for opportunity knocking.*

Not that she had time to do a meet and greet. She had an appointment with the owner of the Sugar Shack candy store for a potential interior redesign job. Besides, Mr. Nice Guy was likely one among a hundred like him who donated his time to Almost Family and similar nonprofit services.

How many of those others had an ass and arms like his?

A dynamite ass and a killer set of arms, and probably a gorgeous wife or girlfriend to go with them.

Her eagerness flame fanned out, Lissa put her nice guy hunt on hold. She returned her attention to the mirror for a quick teeth and facial inspection. Finding everything acceptable and her freckles had returned to barely noticeable, she grabbed her black leather satchel from the passenger's seat and climbed out of the car.

The closest she'd been able to get a parking spot to the candy store was three blocks away. She was a stickler for arriving early, so reaching the place on time wouldn't require sprinting in her skirt and open-toe heels. Hooking the satchel's strap over her arm, she took off down the sidewalk.

One block in, footfalls pounded on the sidewalk behind her. Not an uncommon thing, given the number of people milling about the downtown area on a Friday afternoon. What was uncommon was how noisily they fell, like the person was purposefully trying to be loud.

Were they in step with hers?

Sam's thing was paranoia, not Lissa's. Only, it appeared her housemate was rubbing off on her. Her skin suddenly felt crawly.

Her entire body went tense with the sensation of being watched. Followed. Stalked.

Oh jeez! Could she be any more melodramatic?

This wasn't a dark, stormy night scenario. The sun shone down from overhead and, while June in Michigan didn't often equate to blistering temperatures, a warm, gentle breeze toyed with the yellow, green, and white flowered silk overlay of her knee-length skirt. And there was the fact she was surrounded by a few dozen other people.

To prove how ridiculous she was acting, Lissa stopped walking. The footfalls came again, once, and then fell silent.

Her breath dragged in.

What if she *was* being followed? The candy store was still a block and a half away. Sprinting the remainder of the distance might be the safest route. Yeah right it would. She was liable to snag a heel in a sidewalk crack and break her neck. *Then* she would have a reason to be concerned.

Ignoring the hasty beat of her heart, she faced her overactive imagination by spinning around . . . and there he was.

Mr. Nice Guy stood less than twenty feet away. Not following her or even eyeing her up, but standing in front of a coffee shop, peering into its storefront windows.

He moved toward the shop's door, pulling it open with a tinkling of overhead bells and placing his ass in her line of vision. Once more she appreciated the stellar view. This time it was more than appreciation though. This time, just before he turned and disappeared inside, he looked her way.

Lissa's heart skipped a beat with the glimpse of pure masculine perfection.

Stubble the same shade of wheat as his thick, wavy hair dusted an angular jawline and coasted above a full, stubborn upper lip. Eyebrows a shade darker slashed in wicked arcs over vivid cobalt-blue eyes. His cheeks sank in just enough to make him look lean, hungry, and dangerous all at once. Then there was the way he filled out his jeans; his backside had nothing on his front half. Beneath the faded denim, muscles bulged and strained in all the right places. *All* the right places.

If not for catching him joking around with the youth services kid, she would have mistaken him for a bad boy in a heartbeat. He wasn't. But clearly her body approved of him.

Heat raced into her face and her nipples stabbed to life, making her wish she hadn't relied on the built-in shelf bra of her yellow short-sleeve top to hold in her cleavage. Her breasts were way too big to be fully constrained by the flimsy little cotton bras sewn into shirts. For whatever reason, she allowed Sam to talk her into giving one a try. Probably because when she slipped out of her bedroom wearing it, he'd taken one look at her chest and offered to give her a pre-appointment mouth job.

Coming from a gay guy, that was a major compliment.

The bells over the coffee shop door sounded as a gray-haired, sixty-something couple exited. Lissa glanced at her watch. Ten minutes till her appointment. A block and a half to go.

She could spend five minutes determining if Mr. Nice Guy was single and searching, and then huff it to the Sugar Shack. Or forgo the meet and greet, arrive at her appointment on time, and take Sam up on his mouth job offer when she arrived home.

As much as she loved Sam, there was no future for them beyond friendship. There probably wasn't one with the guy in the coffee shop either.

Lissa walked back to the shop anyway.

To the sound of tinkling bells, she pulled open the wood door with white-and-red stained-glass coffee mugs designed into its window slats. Entering the shop, she looked up at the bells . . . and nearly slammed into Mr. Nice Guy.

He stood in front of a customer bulletin board, pinning business cards up with long-fingered hands that bore neither rings nor tan lines. After tacking the last card onto the board, he turned toward her, flashed a smile sexy enough to do a fluttering number on her sex, and moved right on past and out the door.

"Well, shit." *So much for opportunity knocking.* Even worse, she was starting to sound like a broken record.

She should forget about him and get to her appointment. But between his lack of a wedding ring and that sexy smile, her eagerness flame was rekindled.

Lissa grabbed one of the newly posted business cards off the bulletin board. THAD DAVIES, HANDYMAN was written in black, and beneath it, in bold, blue lettering, LOOSE SCREWS CONSTRUCTION. Was the company name meant to be a double entendre, and exactly how handy of a man was Thad?

Handy enough to leave her his number.

Smiling, she tucked the business card into her satchel. Later, maybe she would give him a call. Or maybe she would pick up a box of Sam's favorite sweets while she was at the Sugar Shack and use them to bribe him into making good on his mouth job offer.

"You're a bastard!"

Thad Davies sank back against the black metal rails of his headboard and sighed over the glaring brunette standing on the end of the bed's bare mattress.

Naked and flushed with the aftereffects of orgasm, she looked ready to beat the shit out of him. From what little he knew of her, she was nice enough. Her sweat-glistening tits were definitely nice, as they jostled around with her anger. That didn't mean he was ready to forget she was a client and sleep with her for free. "You play, you pay, sweetheart."

With a huff, she bounded off the end of the bed, flashing an ass that was just as nice and well rounded as her tits. "Don't call me that! And don't you *ever* come near me again."

She reached the tangle of sheets, covers, and clothing, which had found their way to the floor in the midst of their wild screwing, and started kicking them apart.

Damn, he really didn't like upsetting women. It wasn't his fault they hired him for sex and ended up falling for him along the way. Not all of them did, but more than a couple had in the five months since the woman-pleasuring division of Loose Screws started up. "You called me," he reminded her.

The brunette stopped kicking to look at him, hurt evident in her eyes. "I *thought* we had something between us."

"We do. A business deal."

The hurt left her expression as cold fury took over. Soft pink lips, which less than ten minutes ago had been wrapped around his dick and delivering him to nirvana, pushed into a hard line. Giving the chaotic pile a final kick, she uncovered a slim red purse and yanked it up by the strap. "Consider the deal off," she bit out as she shoved her hand inside the purse and yanked out a handful of bills. "Don't expect any referrals to be coming your way."

Fifties and hundreds plastered him in the chest and rained down on the bed around him. Some people might feel cheap in a situation like this. For Thad, it was all in a day's work, and he happened to love his job most of the time . . . well, what man in his right mind wouldn't?

Pushing the bills off his chest, he moved to the edge of the bed and swung his legs over the side. He rolled the condom off his deflating shaft, tucked it into a tissue, and deposited it in the wastebasket between the bed and the short black oak dresser that doubled as a nightstand. "Don't you be forgetting that silence agreement you signed."

Midway through diving down to retrieve her bra and panties, the brunette's breath dragged in on a gasp. She glared at him. "Like I would tell anyone I had the poor taste to pay to fuck you."

"You got your money's worth. All six times." Today, she'd chosen to suck him off while he fulfilled her order of oral sex.

The five times she employed his services before this, she'd been after her pleasure alone. The ecstatic cries centering each of those sessions said she'd enjoyed herself plenty.

With a final huff, she jerked the bra and panties off the floor and, not bothering to go back for her skintight white minidress, stormed out the bedroom door. Less than twenty seconds later, the front door slammed. The short lapse of time told him she'd left his rental duplex buck naked.

The neighbors would have a coronary over that exit.

But to hell with what his neighbors thought. Thad had never been a saint a day in his life and he never intended to pretend otherwise, even if the ultraconservative city of Crichton and the surrounding county preferred him to do so.

He scrubbed a hand over his face, aware that line of thinking was a lie.

He didn't want to give a damn what his neighbors thought of him if they discovered he worked part time as a gigolo, but he didn't have any choice in the matter. Thanks to the economy being blown to shit and taking his job with the local automotive plant along with it, staying in the area meant making his money by whatever means possible.

Loose Screws, the construction company he ran with two of his former plant coworkers, was taking off slowly. And business would continue to be slow until the economy bounced back. The cold hard truth was most people didn't have the money to spend on building or remodeling.

Women did have money for sex. Or whatever else might tickle their fancy, or any other part of their mind and body.

Last week Benny pulled in a grand just for spending the afternoon alone with an eighty-year-old widow. Alone and naked, but still that was a helluva lot of dough for a few hours of small talk while being ogled by an old lady.

Speaking of his business partner, Thad thought he should give Benny a call and see if he and Nash needed help at the current construction site. The job was a relatively small one. It was also nearly finished, and the sooner it got done, the sooner they would get paid. Nash could avoid needing the cash by sucking up his loathing for the wealthy and asking his affluent father for a handout the man was eager to give. Benny was doing whatever it took to keep his Alzheimer's-stricken foster mother in an upscale nursing home. Thad just liked to be able to afford to eat and make rent.

After going into the half bath adjoining his second-floor bedroom and getting washed up, Thad pulled on a pair of boxers and jeans, then headed downstairs to the kitchen. He lifted the cordless phone from the counter, planning to punch in Benny's cell number while he discovered what, if any, food waited in the refrigerator.

The phone rang before he could punch the first number. Pulling open the fridge door, he hit the phone's TALK button. "Loose Screws. This is Thad."

"I need you," a low, husky feminine voice implored through the phone line.

One of the reasons he was able to charge as much as he did for his gigolo services was the shitload of testosterone the good Lord saw fit to gift him with. The carnal invitation that seemed to fill the woman's words had his blood pumping hot. His cock joined in, already hungry for more loving. Remembering this was the construction phone line didn't do a thing to calm his body. The woman-pleasing division of Loose Screws originated because of someone calling the company, guessing it to be a hustler service by its name, and hoping one of their employees might be interested in working as a stripper for a bachelorette party.

"Then you called the right place." Letting the refrigerator door shut, Thad focused on determining if she was after business or pleasure. "How might I be of service?"

"The way the ceiling's leaking, I think my roof's about ready to fall through. I need to get it fixed before the next rainstorm."

Serious words spoken in a sultry tone. Didn't tell him a damned thing. "This need business related?"

"It's personal."

If the sigh following her words was authentic, and not just a chirp in the phone line, it would suggest she was after pleasure. Loose Screws couldn't afford for him to be wrong. "So long as your place isn't too big, I might be able to squeeze you in. Lemme check the calendar."

Thad glanced at the hot rods and hotter babes calendar hanging on the refrigerator door. His next pleasure appointment wasn't until the following Thursday, with a woman old enough to be his mother. Tammy might be as old as his mother, but with her all-over tan, shoulder-length bleached blond hair, and silicone-enhanced double Ds, she didn't look a thing like his mother. Unlike Benny's client widow, she wouldn't spend their time together staring at his naked body but would have her hands and mouth all over him.

What about the woman on the phone? Did her sexy voice go with a sexy mouth she had plans to put all over him? "Are you local?"

"According to Sam, I am."

"Come again?"

A throaty, sensual laugh most women could only accomplish with a sore throat carried through the phone line. "I thought you said loco. Sam thinks I'm crazy, but then he doesn't have much room to talk." Her voice returned to the low, husky tone. "I live about five miles out of town, in an older ranch-style house."

"Sam live there too?" More specifically, was Sam her man and crazy enough to take after Thad with a gun should he catch him doing his woman?

"Yeah. Though, he's stepping out pretty soon."

A female construction client wasn't bound to let on she would be alone when he arrived. That pretty much guaranteed it was pleasure services she sought. Until he had a better idea of her relationship with Sam, Thad wouldn't be providing those services—a quick drop-by, however, would give him a chance to confirm she was after sex . . . while checking out the goods he would get to work with. "I'm busy later this afternoon, but I should have time to fit in an inspection before then. What's the address?"

Her voice raised a few octaves as she rattled off the address and told him the color of the house and surrounding landmarks. "By the way, my name's Lissa, or Liss. See you in a few."

Another sigh slipped through the phone line before it went dead. His cock gave a happy little jerk in response. Thad looked down at his groin. "Hate to break it to you, buddy, but she was talking to me. Unless you want Sam putting you out of commission permanently, you'd best not get any ideas about bringing Liss bliss."